52 Stories in 52 Weeks

by

Phillip McCollum

COPYRIGHT

Copyright © 2018 by Fantastic Shorts

www.fantasticshorts.com

ISBN (eBook): 978-1-949728-03-3

ISBN (Paperback): 978-1-949728-07-1

DEDICATION

For Mom and Dad

Acknowledgments

I'm pretty sure when it comes to first books and acknowledgments, it's normal to have a list of names long enough to rival Santa's. But I'm assuming you're so excited to read these stories, you don't have the time or patience for that, so I'll just cut it down to the precious few.

Thank you to my son, Angus. You gave me the burning desire to be a person who does what they say. I wasn't really a writer until you came along.

Thank you to my wife, Taryn. Without your unending support, this wouldn't have happened. And without your first readings, these stories would probably *really* suck.

Thank you to my best friend, Wes, who encouraged me seven years ago to give this writing thing a go.

Thank you to Jocko Willink and his 4:30 AM wake-up-time wisdom. These stories only exist because I put away the excuses and "got after it."

And last, but not least, thank you to all of my writerly friends on the Internet who walked alongside me every step of the way: Marie Bailey, Kevin Brennan, Berthold Gambrel, John Howell, Candace Johnson, Colin Mobey, Carrie Rubin, Lauren Sapala, Linda Washington, and Jill Weatherholt.

Contents

Intro

52 short stories in 52 weeks?

It wasn't going to work. I just knew it. It would be a colossal waste of time and I would be stuck in the same damn rut 52 weeks from now—a hard drive filled with innumerable half-starts and unfinished tales.

First of all, this was just going to set me back. I wanted to write novels. Short stories were OK, but they weren't novels. I'd been indoctrinated by countless 'writing experts' that the two styles were as different as house cats and narwhals and if you wanted to do one of them, you should absolutely, without a doubt, completely ignore the other.

Probably the most important thing I've come to realize over this year is that there's no such thing as a writing expert. There are people that are skilled at what they do, but to call someone an expert in the field of writing is like calling someone an expert in the field of living. There are a lot of variations in how people live their lives and there are almost as many variations in how people write or craft art. There is no single path to success. What matters is outcome.

The second most important thing I've learned is just how much we lie to ourselves in order to protect our fragile egos. I'm not talking massive lies. Just the little fibs that add up over time. You know, the ones we repeat to ourselves on a daily basis until we stop realizing it.

You don't have the time.

You don't have the skill.

Or, more often, the opposite: You're already good at that, so you don't need to rehash or practice more.

So, how did I wind up with 52 complete stories despite my bottomless pocket of untruths?

I wish I could tell you there was a magical moment where the heavens opened up, the angels sang, and the Coat of Instant Confidence™ was draped over my shoulders (BRB, patenting).

Nope. Nothing other than to say I'd apparently become fed up enough with my own excuses and lack of output that I was forced to take stock of decisions I'd made in the past. I asked myself: When I had achieved something great and satisfying, what was the cause?

It turns out there was a common theme: I ignored my impulses.

I ignored the well-worn habit of immediately dismissing ideas out of hand and decided to embrace them instead.

So, I began to take to heart the lessons of prolific writers like Dean Wesley Smith and his wife, Kristin Kathryn Rusch, who constantly preach the importance of practice and why perfection is a dirty word. I listened with an attentive mind to Ray Bradbury as he spoke to an audience of college students, telling them how he spent ten years writing short stories before he could produce a decent one, then writing short stories for eight more years before he wrote his first novel, Fahrenheit 451.

People talk about learning something the hard way. In my experience, I'd say the hard way is often the only way. Those are the lessons that stick. The easy way is often an illusion. Maybe I needed to struggle over the past six years to come to the realization that I ought to be more open to new experiences and ways of doing things.

Here I am a year later, happy as a clam because I have learned so much in writing those stories. I've gotten better at finishing what I start. I have been able to share a part of myself with my friends and family. And last, but not least, I have 52 short stories to revisit when I'm face-to-face with resistance.

Because she doesn't go away.

Motive and Audience

This experiment was almost as much for my fellow struggling writers as it was for me.

Guys, stop being scared.

Honestly.

Whatever reasons you've concocted (and I've concocted plenty), they're not real. You won't die if you give this a shot and fail. More likely you *will* die, in a sense, if you don't try. You'll continue to struggle until you give up or find a way to overcome your fear.

The best way to get better at writing is to write.

You have to be prepared to accept what your brain considers failure. The irony is it's sometimes the stuff you thought you did pretty well on while the stuff you hate garners praise. Funny, right? That's the nature of the beast. So much of art in general, but stories in particular, comes down to taste. One person's failure is another's definition of success.

You are the worst possible judge of your work.

Write that down and post it on your office wall. Make it your writing computer wallpaper. Get a tattoo if that floats your boat.

But take it to heart.

To me, this has been the most freeing concept I've come across in my writing journey (all due credit to the author Dean Wesley Smith whom I learned it from).

Why is this the case?

Think about it. You have these perfectly crisp images in your head, these vivid emotions running through your body, and you're trying to transfer them on to paper so readers can form their own images and feelings which represent yours as closely as possible. It's a skill that writers toil over decades to improve (notice I said *improve*, not *master*), and not only that, every reader is pulling those words through their eyes or ears with their individual set of filters.

You already have your story! This is about giving it to someone else.

Do you see why that one sentence is so liberating now?

You have permission to write what you want, how you want, because in the end, what truly matters is you put it out for the world to read and appreciate—not you.

Now, this doesn't mean you should be lazy. You should always, always come at writing with the best of your current abilities. But once you've done that, once you've got those words on the page, send it out however you like and start sharing the next story. Let those who would love to find it, find it. The others can be ignored because, for that particular story, they just don't matter.

Have a little faith in yourself! Have faith that there are others who can't wait to be entranced by the story you wish to tell them.

Lessons

"Okay," you say, "write to the best of my abilities. But how do I increase those abilities? How do I get better?"

Writing is both a craft and an art and there is always a baseline set of skills for the craft that can improve the art.

We already established that writing a lot is essential, but it has its corollary:

Read a lot.

'A lot' includes reading with depth and breadth. It includes doing a little bit of each with the eye of a student and a lot of each as a reader would—someone just looking for something fun read.

Shortly after kicking off my experiment, I took the advice of Ray Bradbury and read one poem, one essay/article, and one short story each day. During my experiment, I read everything from Edgar Allan Poe's macabre tales to resplendent poems by William Blake to pedestrian magazine articles on bathroom makeovers. Each of them contributed to a story or two. I also spent a considerable amount of time reading Stephen King's fiction and Paul Theroux's travelogues for joy, because I love their way with words and the stories they weave.

So, be curious, man!

By reading everything you can get your hands on, you'll evolve your intuition for all sorts of valuable writing skills—idea development, character traits, story structure, and genre tropes to name a few. As you approach the writing, you'll find the stuff starts to become second nature if you shut up your critical voice and allow your creative side to have his or her say.

You can see this in my process summaries. As I practiced more and read more, I became more comfortable getting by without outlines and mind maps and other pre-writing tools that, in hindsight, were training wheels which, while they helped me build my initial confidence, ended up being hindrances.

Through the reading, you'll also start to improve what I call micro-skills: things like better description of setting and character, how to use metaphors effectively, and using techniques such as cliffhangers to manipulate the reading experience (in truth, all of what I've said manipulates the reader experience).

Take it from someone who *thought* they read a lot—if you're not turning pages at *least* thirty minutes a day, you need to make time for that. Obviously, life happens and you'll miss a day or two. That's okay. It's the spirit of the law and building of the habit that matters.

All of this sort of circles back to another lesson:

Try everything.

It will always be a credit on your career ledger. If the technique doesn't work out, you've learned a method that doesn't jibe with your personality or way of getting the story down. In the end, that's just as valuable as finding what does work.

It's important to ignore and unlearn the advice from all of those 'writing experts' whenever you find it hampering your game, including me. If it doesn't work, it's no good for you.

This idea of trying everything also extends to the medium itself. Play around with voice, point of view, genders, formats, and so on. You'll find an illustrated children's story in this book for goodness' sake!

You have a lot to do at this point. You may be feeling overwhelmed and are now asking, "How do I find the time for all of this reading and writing and experimenting?"

Make the time.

For the past two years, I've woken up nearly every morning at 4:30 AM because I knew I would have at least an hour to spend on writing and at least thirty minutes to read that day. No matter what else may come from work or family later on, I could avoid the self-flagellation that came at the end of a day with absolutely no forward movement in my work.

I removed time-wasting apps from my phone. I used social-media and website blockers for a while. I cut down television consumption. I 'economized' my sleep.

The two things I did not carve time away from were family and exercise. For me, family and health above all else. That doesn't mean I spent inordinate amounts of time on either, but the quality had to be there or else I would find myself a year later hampered by diabetes and without a wife and kid to look after me.

To iterate, it's the building of the habit and the spirit of the idea that's important. The writing and reading didn't happen every day. I got sick. The day job had its emergencies. My house got flooded.

None of this stopped me for an extended period of time. At the next available opportunity, I hopped back on that writing horse.

Speaking of time:

Deadlines work.

More than a few times, I found myself running out of time to finish the story in the week I'd given myself. Towards the end of the challenge, I even found that I was several stories behind and had to cram more than one into a week. And you know what? I did it. I could have thrown in the towel. I was even thinking I could change the title to something like *44 Stories in 52 Weeks.*

That would have been ridiculous.

So instead I told myself that I just didn't have a choice. I had to figure out how to wrap up a story or get past a roadblock that had been in my way. The only way I found to do that was to, once again, kill that critical voice that had a knack for popping up at inconvenient times. Sometimes I tossed away thousands of words which are always precious to us writers. But it had to be done in order to get the story out.

And that, my friends, is the whole point of being a published writer.

* * *

I'll stop here. Too many lessons are easily ignored. Hopefully you can take the few listed above and focus on those. Try them out. If they don't work for you, so be it. I can only tell you what works for me and hope some of your wiring is the same.

But be honest with yourself. Did you stop because something simply didn't work or did you stop because it seemed too hard? All too often, I've mistaken the former for the latter.

Go. Write.

And when that annoying little critic freezes up your fingers and has you second-guessing yourself? Take out your proverbial irons and pistol. You know what you need to do.

Then get back to the joy of writing.

Seven Hundred and Seventy-Six

Statistics

Synopsis: Floyd Usher, a timid bank clerk working in a small town on the Arizona frontier, encounters a strange man and an even stranger gun.

Word Count: 6,000

Genre: Weird Western

Completed Week: July 31st – August 6th

Seven Hundred and Seventy-Six

The handle of the revolver was the nicest part. That wasn't saying much. It hung down like the long, bulbous nose of a drunkard. It may have been a smooth chestnut brown at one time, but now it was chipped and cracked, covered in scratches like a rattlesnake that had been on the losing end of a badger fight. Running along the side, between the trigger and the hammer, was what may have once been fine silver plating. Now it was tarnished to match the rusted barrels and cylinder.

Floyd Usher wondered about the last time it had been fired, if ever.

He lifted his eyes from his desk where the pistol lie and blinked at the man seated across from him. "You say you want $776? Nothing more. Nothing less."

The man shifted uncomfortably in his seat. "Well, yessir, I... It's just...I need a coach to Tombstone and a train ticket out of there."

Floyd wasn't sure what to say. Was this some sort of practical joke on the part of the security guards? He noticed Carl standing against the wall near the front door with his arms crossed, one boot pressed against the floor, the other against the wall. His face was expressionless and it was hard to tell what he was looking at under the lowered brim of his hat. He was always funning Floyd, and if this *was* one of his jokes, Mr. Howard would hear about it once again. If it wasn't, well, Floyd was glad it was Thursday and Carl was on shift.

The man took a kerchief from his pocket and wiped his dirty, sweat-streaked forehead. It was a warm June day for sure, but the inside of the bank was cool enough.

Floyd knew a little about guns. It was nearly impossible not to when living in a land where the law was thin and enforcement was thinner. But he was still a bank clerk and his weapons were pen and script.

Eyeing the gun again, he realized it wasn't a modern revolver, like a Colt or anything like that. It was an older flintlock. Something of a relic.

"You don't need $776 for a ticket," Floyd said, thinking in the back of his mind that if this gun was all the man had to offer, he wouldn't get seven cents.

Floyd was half-listening to the man's stammering reply and, for some reason, decided to pick up the weapon. It felt unusually heavy and uncomfortable in his hands and he put it back down immediately. He lifted his head to see traces of a hopeful smile disappear from the man's face.

"I'm sorry, Mr..."

A momentary pause.

The man said, "McKay." He let out a deep breath as if he had been holding it since walking in. "And save it." He pushed his leather chair back, stood up, and leaned in to Floyd. "Just tell me if you're gonna give me the $776 or not. I ain't got time for chewin' the fat."

McKay's breath was putrid, a result of yellowed teeth and dark gums hanging inches from Floyd's face. Steam piled up on the banker's circular lenses. He leaned back and removed his glasses. He pulled his own kerchief from a shirt pocket and wiped them vigorously, as if they had contracted a disease.

"Look," Floyd said, feeling slightly unnerved but still observing a habit of politeness. "I don't know that this is worth enough for what you need. It appears to be pretty old and has clearly seen better days." He was being generous. "The manager isn't going to authorize any loan based on this.

You may want to check with Dade down at the general. He could be will-ing—"

McKay interrupted, "Already did. Why do you think I'm here?" His eyes darted almost aimlessly, like a man caught between decisions. Beneath the wiry, unkempt beard, his flesh wobbled and shook like a bowl of gelatin pudding.

"Everything okay?"

Floyd felt his skin cool. Carl had approached quietly from behind and stood stiff and imposing behind Mr. McKay.

Well played, Carl, Floyd thought. Well played.

Floyd decided he could play along too and said, "Mr. McKay is look-ing for assistance, but we can't provide him any."

"I guess that means his business is done here then?" Though phrased as a question, no answer was expected.

It was in that moment that McKay's cheeks shook even more and his eyes started welling up. Floyd felt a sudden sense of shame. Maybe the man was serious? He looked toward Carl for a hint of a smile. Something to indicate the jig was up.

If this was a joke, Carl gave no sign.

Floyd's good Christian sense tugged at his heart, but it was quickly put back in its place as Mr. McKay spread his hands and shoved all of Floyd's pencils and account books off his desk and onto the floor.

Carl took another step toward Mr. McKay, but the man grabbed his worthless pistol and ran out the door before a hand could be laid upon him.

"Some folks ain't got a lick of sense, huh?" Carl asked no one in particular as he walked away.

Floyd stared after him, dumbfounded. The idle sounds of the bank seeped into his ears once more, beckoning him back to work. He bent down and picked up his papers.

* * *

Darkness greeted Floyd as he locked the door behind him and began the quarter-mile journey toward home. Mr. Howard, the manager, had headed left early to catch a coach to Tucson and entrusted Floyd to wait for Tony, the night guard, before locking up. The problem was the oaf was late, again, and Floyd had waited him out until his stomach started growling. Tony had his own set of keys anyway. Floyd would have yet another conversation with Mr. Howard tomorrow.

Not that J. Howard Bank & Trust saw much action anyway. It was a small fish. It had a tiny safe, miniscule compared to the larger vaults out of the Tucson or Flagstaff banks, and it never held a large reserve of precious metals or cash. For those lucky few who prospected the surrounding desert mountains and actually found something, it was mainly a temporary holding spot, a safer place than loose pockets.

Floyd debated whether or not to go straight home. His nerves were shot after his encounter with the strange man and he didn't feel like dealing with Jinnie. Something had gotten into her over the past few months. Floyd couldn't entirely place its cause. He'd tried to dig into it occasionally, but she would button up and tell him he's imagining things, relentless in her secrecy. She seemed resentful, of leaving Boston and moving to Cordson, this tiny frontier town in Arizona. But some days she would have a smile on her face and would move with such grace, as if her feet were being carted around on tiny rickshaws. Those were the good days. On most of the days, though, Floyd had only come home from the bank because the bed was more comfortable than sleeping on a stiff chair.

We should never have come here, she'd often say. *It's so damn boring.*

Floyd cringed whenever she cursed.

He would offer to take her out, but she'd refuse, saying that if she had to step one more time into the Coyote Saloon, she'd seize up and die right on the spot. Several times, he'd gotten so frustrated with her inexplicable mood swings to the point that he began thinking really hard about throwing her out. It was he who owned the deed to the house, after all. But he knew he was too much of a coward to do such a thing. Though they hadn't touched each other in months, he'd convinced himself that there was still hope.

All of this ran through his mind as he realized he had turned around and was headed toward the Coyote for a sarsaparilla and a meal. Jinnie probably wouldn't have made him any supper tonight. Besides, it was always entertaining to watch braver men gamble on hands of faro.

* * *

If not for the light wind carrying across the main street, Floyd would have lingered in his thoughts, undisturbed by what sounded like deep, heaving sobs.

He halted to determine the source. The cries stopped just as abruptly, but turned into frenzied, whispered shouts.

"I tried!" the voice hissed. "I tried! I just can't."

Then the sobbing returned.

Floyd squinted and picked up his hat as if it would help him hear better. It was hard to place the source, but it sounded like it was coming from fifty or so yards across the street, under the moonlit shadows of the stoop outside the livery.

The harsh whispers came again. "Shut up! I won't do it!"

The violence in the voice made Floyd's neck hairs come to a salute.

A final, painful cry.

And then a loud bang.

Instinctively, Floyd ducked down behind the picketed, wooden railing on the edge of the boardwalk and held on to the top of his hat.

A puff of white smoke drifted out from the side of the livery. Now he could see a lightly drawn silhouette of a man pressed against the wooden slats of the livery. Shock and a general unsurety of what to do kept Floyd in place.

For just a moment, there was no discernable motion from either Floyd or whoever was across the street. Curious, he started to straighten up.

Another shot and another puff of smoke.

The vibration and splintered piece of boardwalk inches from his right shoe indicated that he was the intended target.

"Nooo," the voice cried. The silhouette became flesh as it emerged from the shadows and barrelled toward Floyd.

The frightened banker's legs decided that someone ought to step up, so they took on a life of their own and Floyd was immediately running back towards home. He felt he was moving quickly, but he turned and it seemed the man was moving more quickly. Floyd realized he wouldn't make it to the house before being overtaken. A quick decision was made to hole up inside the bank. What safer place?

He scrambled breathlessly, his feet pounding the boardwalk, until he reached the bank door and yanked at the handle. It barely budged.

Idiot, he thought.

He fumbled for the keys in his pocket. Mr. Howard had insisted on two separate locks when he had the door installed and now Floyd cursed him for it. A part of him told him to look back, to be aware, but his focus was on stilling his shaky hands, retrieving the keys and getting inside.

"Mr. Usher."

The familiar voice was directly behind him now and as he lifted the ring of keys to the bottom lock, they slipped from his fingers onto the wooden boardwalk. Floyd's stomach dropped.

Am I the only one awake in this town, he asked himself. But of course he knew from experience that if there was trouble, the few residents would rather ignore the situation than get involved.

"Please. Turn around, Mr. Usher. I don't want to shoot a man in the back."

McKay's voice was shaky.

He's trying to rob me, was Floyd's first thought. His second thought was that he'd be very disappointed as it was the beginning of the week and most of the bank's reserves were off with Mr. Howard to those vaults in Tucson.

Finally, after enough thinking, Floyd conjured up the bravery to turn around. The barrel of the rusted flintlock was pointed in his face. From any other viewpoint, it would be a humorous thing to see. A part of him could hardly believe the antique worked at all, but his memory quickly reminded him that he had been shot at once, maybe twice.

Floyd raised his shaking hands. "Please, Mr. McKay—".

"Shhh…" McKay interrupted. "Do you hear it?"

Floyd nodded his head like a woodpecker.

"Yes, I heard the shots, I—"

"No!" McKay said. Floyd noticed that his voice was choked with emotion and under the half-moon, he could see tear-carved streaks running down the man's dirty face. He inclined his nose towards the flintlock. "The whispers. The goddamn whispers." Mr. McKay emphasized *goddamn* as if he were literally cursing something.

Floyd began to realize that he was dealing with a madman. In the seven months that he and Jinnie had been in this tiny town, they'd heard tales of men found dead in the surrounding granite hills, driven insane by their lust for gold and silver and their lack of results. Now here was another one, only this time, he didn't have the decency to die outside of town and he was going to take out Floyd instead.

"Don't kill me," Floyd pleaded, "please Mr. McKay. If it's money you want, I know the combination to the safe." Floyd would have to hope that whatever was in there would satisfy him.

There was no reason to believe he wouldn't be killed afterwards, but it was a play for time. Time to think. The only time available right now.

"I told you. I want you to buy this gun for seven hundred-and-seventy-six dollars."

Floyd stared at him. His lips parted slightly. He was unsure of what to say, so he said nothing.

"Please," McKay said quietly as if to no one in particular. "Open the doors, get the money, and buy this gun." Pain was evident in his words.

Floyd mustered a reply, trying to sound braver than he felt, but his voice cracked as well. "Mr. McKay, I'll open these doors, open the safe, turn the whole place upside down for you. But I'm telling you right now, we don't have even a quarter of that amount of money right now."

The madman released a huge laugh mixed with a howl. It echoed across the street and through the tiny alleyways. He shook his head and looked at the ground. "I know, I know," he said. To Floyd, it looked like he was talking more to the revolver than to him. "Time's run out," he finished.

So this was it, Floyd thought. He closed his eyes and clenched his teeth. God, I hope it doesn't hurt.

"You ain't gonna tell me what to do no more!" McKay yelled. Floyd was trying to process just what he meant by that when the shot went off and his ears rang to the high heavens. Floyd screamed, or thought he did, and collapsed onto the ground.

He wondered, where had it hit? The chest? His head? He couldn't feel anything. Only the stiff slats on which he fell upon. He'd never been shot before so he could only guess.

After what felt like an eternity, Floyd peeked through squinted eyes and breathed in deeply. He shot up and ran his hands over his face, his skull, his body. Looking for any indication of slippery blood or something out of place.

Nothing.

Nothing but Mr. McKay lying on the dirt, in the very spot where he had just been standing. His head was lolled to the side like a rag doll, his eyes staring lifelessly at the wall of the bank. Fresh blood covered his matted beard and mangled jaw.

Floyd looked around, bewildered, but something caught his eye. It glinted in the dirt next to McKay's open hand.

A revolver.

A flintlock revolver.

Clearly it was not the rusted junk that had been in McKay's hand previously, though it in fact looked like the very same model. Yet this one's silver was gleaming in the moonlight, looking as if it had just been polished. There were no signs of wear on the varnished, deep brown handle. Floyd crawled over to the dead man, his legs still unable to hold him upright. His eyes remained focused on the gun. It seemed to be pulling Floyd into its ethereal orbit.

He questioned, had this been the one he really shot at me with? It didn't make sense. Floyd clearly saw McKay holding a worthless relic in his hand before he closed his eyes.

If Floyd Usher ever did anything boldly, it was as a result of his relentless curiosity. He reached out and felt the gun. As his fingers touched the handle, his head darted around and he searched the darkness. He could have swore he heard something, somebody, breathing a deep sigh of relief.

* * *

"You killed a man?" she asked. Jinnie's voice betrayed her incredulity.

Breathless, Floyd attempted to explain. "No, I didn't. He tried to kill me. McKay. He was...earlier...in the bank...I...I think he killed himself."

She stood there in thick cotton pajamas, her long red hair tied into a tail running down her back. Heat radiated from the wood stove and filled the room. There were a couple of tin plates on the table, though both were dirty.

A twinge of shame pulsed through Floyd. She had made supper after all.

"I don't have the time nor patience for a wild story. I have dishes to take care of." She began to pick up the tableware. "You know, most men would be grateful for a hot meal."

That hurt Floyd. He was still sensitive to one of the reasons they had left Boston. Jinnie had readily admitted her 'indiscretion,' even started attending church with Floyd on a regular basis. But phantom pains remained even after their move. He pushed the feeling down.

"Didn't you hear the shots?" he said, almost pleading. His frustration overtook anything else he was feeling then. "It was down by the bank!"

She said nothing, only moving to wash the dishes in the basin, treating him as if he were a boy again making up wild tales to explain to his mother why he hadn't slopped the hogs.

Floyd paced back and forth. "I gotta go back," he said. "McKay's body is still down there. Maybe I was mistaken. Maybe he's really okay." He headed towards the door, not getting very far before Jinnie was grabbing at his arm.

"You need to sit down and think about this," she said.

A general sense of panic seemed to have overtaken Floyd that wasn't there before, and he didn't know why. Tonight had been a culmination of one confusing thing after another. He decided that listening to Jinnie right now might make good sense, so he took a seat.

There was a clunk on the floor.

They both looked down at the same time and saw the pistol.

"What's that?"

"The gun," Floyd replied almost as a question. "The one McKay was going to kill me with. I think." He didn't remember picking it up, but there it was.

Jinnie squinted at the gun and then looked into Floyd's eyes, a half-smile on her lips. "You sure he was going to shoot you? I think he'd have a better chance killing you by hitting you over the head with that thing."

"Huh?" Floyd looked down. "Well, yeah, it's an older model, but I'm telling you the thing still works."

Jinnie bent down to pick it up, but quickly dropped it back on the floor. "Damn, it's heavy."

Floyd flinched at her swearing.

She said, "Well, assuming it wouldn't blow up in your hands, I don't know how anyone could shoot that thing. It doesn't even have a trigger."

Now a panic swept back through Floyd's body again. "What are you talking about? It's right there." He leaned over, picked up the gun, and cradled it in his hands. It felt oddly warm. His index finger massaged the trigger and there was something unsettlingly comfortable about it's curve. He was reluctant to let it go.

A garbled whisper entered his ears.

"What did you say?" Floyd asked his wife.

Jinnie's eyes were blank, but had a lightness in them. "If I didn't know you better, I'd say you've been drinking firewater down at the Coyote."

Floyd shot up to his feet with an intensity that surprised him. "Of course not!"

She shook her head slowly. "Floyd, I don't want to hear any more about this. I'm going to bed. If you want to go down and see the sheriff, you may as well ask if you can stay the night."

If there was a door on the entrance to the bedroom, it would have slammed shut. Instead, Jinnie just disappeared into the darkness.

* * *

Floyd felt a pang in his conscience. He knew he couldn't leave the man lying there. Someone would find the body and there would be a lot of questions from the sheriff; questions that might best be answered now. Knowing he'd have to deal with Jinnie later, he ran to the bank and froze as he came down the main street. He saw the back of Sheriff Bohannon. He was on one knee, leaning over Mr. McKay's lifeless body.

Floyd's stomach gurgled and then he looked down at himself in horror.

He was holding the gun in his hand. He wondered again how it wound up at his side.

Instinct told Floyd to turn around. He was certain now that coming back was a bad idea. He had no way of proving what happened. It was only his word against a dead man's and though he was on the sheriff's good side on the general account that he'd never stirred up any trouble, being possibly accused of murdering a man didn't sit well with Floyd.

He obeyed his body's wishes and was several steps toward home before the call came.

"Hey!"

Floyd stopped cold. He slowly slipped the gun into his right pocket, trying to be smooth about it, before he turned around.

The sheriff was standing now, looking at Floyd. His hands were on his hips.

"Gimme a hand here. I *could* carry this fella over to Dade's myself, but I don't necessarily wanna."

Floyd approached like a wary animal and confirmed the fella was indeed Mr. McKay. His head was still a butchered mess, laying in a pool of blood that still hadn't dried.

"Well?" Bohannon asked. He had ahold of McKay's wrists and was nodding toward his feet.

Floyd snapped out of his reverie and shuffled towards McKay's boots. He was glad the sheriff chose the parts closest to dead man's head. Bile rose up to his throat and it was all he could do to keep from gagging.

"What…what happened?" Floyd asked. I sound like stuttering fool, he thought.

"A good question. Ready?"

Floyd grabbed the dead man's ankles and nodded lightly.

They moved down the street, Floyd facing Bohannon as the sheriff walked backwards at a steady pace. Dade's General Store was about a hundred yards away. In a town as small as Cordson, there wasn't a specialized undertaker. That job fell on the man who could nail a box together better than others.

They crossed the front of the store and wound up in the rear.

"He always keeps an open casket out back. No sense in bothering him about it tonight, though." Bohannon lifted a shoulder to his cheek to wipe off the sweat. "We'll just lay the lid on it for now. Keep the coyotes from gettin' to him til' Dade can dip him in arsenic."

By the time they got McKay into the box, Floyd was panting and had to sit down. He collapsed on an upside-down crate.

As he did so, the gun fell out of his pocket and thumped onto the dirt.

The sheriff looked down.

Floyd decided then and there that if he ever got out of prison, he'd have Jinnie make him pants with bigger pockets.

Bohannon squatted down and picked up the gun.

"This yours?" he asked.

Dread left Floyd with a lump in his throat.

Bohannon turned the gun over in his hand and examined it closely.

Floyd noticed his legs were nervously bouncing up and down. He concentrated on keeping them still.

The sheriff said, "Wow, a Collier. I ain't seen one of these since my grandpappy's, back in Virginia. Wished I had it. It was in much better shape, but I imagine it looks a lot like this one now." He looked up at Floyd. "Where'd you get it?"

Floyd hesitated.

"Don't remember it being this damn heavy," Bohannon said, "but that was a long time ago." He extended it toward Floyd who opened his palms. It fell like a stone but landed like a feather in Floyd's hands.

The sheriff was looking at him quietly now. It unnerved Floyd. He couldn't resist the urge to confess.

"He killed himself!" Floyd blurted out. "I swear it!"

Bohannon scrunched his eyebrows and looked back at corpse. He took a deep breath.

"Well, unless he was deliberately poisoned, which I don't see why anyone would do that to poor Mr. McKay, there's no doubt about that." The sheriff winked and flashed a joker's smile.

Floyd was taken aback. "What do you mean?" There were hundreds of subtleties to that question.

"The man came down here only last week, a smile on his face, buying people drinks down at the Coyote as sure as any newcomer that he'd pull enough out of the Santa Ritas to leave with pockets full of silver. Like many of the dreamers who come out here and keep our little town alive, he didn't find what he was lookin' for and he came back in a few days ago appearing worse for it."

Bohannon shook his head.

"Anyway, I'd guess heat exhaustion. Ticker couldn't take it. Or he had himself a little too much tornado juice, though they're usually lying in a pile of their own puke when that's the case."

Floyd rose slowly and looked into the open casket. As plain as day, the bottom half of McKay's face looked like chopped beef. Red pools of blood had already seeped into the oak.

"But what about...his face?"

"I shut his eyes for him. Looks like a sleepin' baby don't he?"

How could Bohannon not see what Floyd was seeing? A haphazard pile of bone, blood, and skin.

"You looked rested enough," the sheriff said, "Help me get this lid on."

* * *

"Rrrrraaaahhh!"

The shout came suddenly and shook Floyd from a deep sleep. His head was pressed into the pillow. The surrounding darkness and chirping crickets seemed uninterrupted.

Maybe it was a dream. He had been tossing and turning all night. At some point, his mind finally shut down, tired of attempting to process the day's events.

Floyd pushed himself up onto his elbows and looked over at Jinnie. Her back was to him. He could hear the ups and downs of light snoring. Floyd remembered crawling into bed after helping Sheriff Bohannon, not wanting to sleep on a hard chair. Just wanting something warm and comforting, no matter how cold and uncomforting the person next to him was.

"Hey!"

The voice of a man came unmistakably from the front room. It was a whisper, but loud. Floyd wished desperately that he had kept his only means of defense in the bedroom. Not that it would have mattered. The Winchester rifle his father-in-law had gifted him before moving out was useless without bullets. Floyd foolishly thought he'd never need them.

He wanted to cry. Why was all this happening to him?

"Don't be scared," the voice rasped. "We need to discuss things. Come out."

Floyd looked over at his wife again. He considered shaking her, waking her up to the potential danger.

"Don't bother."

Floyd knew the voice was right. He was losing his mind. No sense in trying to convince a woman already set on her thoughts. He rose quietly from the bed and tiptoed toward the front room. He debated lighting a lamp, but quickly decided it wasn't worth the effort. His eyes were already adjusted to the dark.

"Are...Are you the ghost of McKay?" It sounded foolish as soon as it left his lips, but what was foolish at this point?

"Ain't no such thing as ghosts." The reply was swift and emanated from the table. He looked but saw only empty chairs. "Have a seat. I'll fill you in."

Floyd saw no reason not to comply, so he pulled up a chair.

"Here's the deal. You has to kill someone."

The whispers. The goddamn whispers.

He was certain now about what McKay had said. The voice, the whisper, was coming from the Collier. Floyd remembered now, leaving it there before tottering into the bedroom earlier. He leaned in as if he were trying to read it like a small-print book.

"Boo!"

He bounced back and the chair fell backwards from under him. There was a creaking noise from the bedroom.

"Floyd! Keep it quiet out there!"

He waited, hoping Jinnie would fall back to sleep. After thirty seconds of silence, Floyd picked up the chair and sat down once again.

"Sorry," the gun said with a chuckle. "Couldn't resist."

Floyd decided he was so far over the edge of sanity, there was no point in *not* talking to the gun.

"What...what do you...what are…" He wanted to converse with the thing, but he didn't know what to ask.

"Lookie here," he said, "I'm gonna' sum it up for you. I'm a curse."

A curse? Floyd scratched his head and reached for his glasses. He put them on as if they would help him think.

"What do you mean?"

"My name is—was—Cincinnatus Jones. Bought and sold for seven hundred-and-seventy-six dollars. Things was ok for what they were, til' the man who bought me said I stole somethin'. I know I hadn't. I know it! Anyway, he killed me with this here gun, and as I lay bleeding, I curse it. I didn't mean to. But you know how's it is, when you dyin'. Right?" It breathed sonorously. "I s'pose note. Well, you don't got time to think things through. So I said some words my grandmammy taught me when I was a youngin'. Of course, she would say them if she stubbed her big toe. Don't think they had much juice to them then, but let me tell you, they mean somethin' when you's dyin'."

Floyd sat and stared at the gun.

"You remember how's I told you that you had to kill somebody?" the voice asked. "Well, you don't have to. You don't have to. But you need to sell me for the going price. You saw how hard that was though. Might well just shoot somebody and save yo'self the trouble."

Stunned, Floyd tentatively picked up the gun and examined its fine condition. "But if you look like this, I won't have any trouble selling—"

"Part of the curse. I only look like this to *you*. Every time I help someone kill a man, I inch a little bit closer to my end. Sometimes it's a scratch, sometimes I lose somethin' more."

It would explain why Jinnie didn't see a trigger. Floyd nodded his head as if he understood. The truth was that he was going mad, just like McKay. But maybe it wasn't madness, Floyd thought. Maybe this *was* the truth.

"But I ain't dead yet," the voice continued. "And that means you got some killin' to do, one way or another. Three days, Floyd. Three days."

"Three days?" Floyd asked, unable to hide the shock in his voice. His mind raced through possible victims, everyone he knew, strangers he didn't yet know. How could he just kill someone?

"Can't I just shoot a rabbit? Or a ground squirrel?" Floyd pretended that he even had the capability to do those things.

"Nope. Gotta be human flesh and bone. Look, take yo'self some solace in the fact that no one will know it. You may see 'em as bein' shot, but to everyone else, they look like they just fell asleep."

Floyd found no solace in that, but it solved another mystery.

The gun continued, "Now it ain't that I can make a man do the killin'. He gotta figure that out on his own. But if you don't, well…" Floyd swore he saw a tiny puff of smoke emerged from the barrel of the pistol.

"Well, what?"

"I don't mean to be the way I'm bein', but I *am* a curse. I need blood, Floyd. If you can't give it to me in three days, I'll take it."

Floyd knew exactly what that meant. McKay's lifeless eyes were fresh in his mind.

* * *

The next two days at the bank, at home, and everywhere in between were filled with frantic thoughts. He got no sleep and stopped eating. In the beginning, he debated telling Jinnie, but he had already stepped all over her last nerve and he knew that all hope of her believing him was lost.

How was he going to get out of this one? He didn't want to die. He was only twenty-four, for Christ's sake. But he couldn't imagine intentionally taking a person's life.

More than once, Floyd found himself following strangers down alleys, his hand in his pocket, his finger wrapped gently around the trigger, only to lose his nerve and turn around.

At the bank, he tried to put on his normal demeanor. Still, people would ask him if he was alright, to which he would reply "of course" or sometimes just continue staring off into space, always with one hand in his pocket.

At one point, he thought he could get away with burying the gun about a mile away, among the scrub and prickly pears, but somehow, it found its way back into his desk drawer.

He could swear it laughed at him.

* * *

"Day three, Floyd. The clock's a'tickin'. You got a choice to make."

"Floyd!"

He snapped to attention. Mr. Howard was standing before him, a scowl on his face, his bald head scrunched up with wrinkles.

"Do you have them or not?"

"Have them?"

The bank manager shook his head. "The promissory notes I need to take to Tucson." He scrutinized Floyd carefully. "You haven't been lookin' yourself the past few days. I want you to go home and rest up."

"Yes," Floyd said absently. "I think...I think that's a good idea."

Floyd left the bank early and ambled toward home. He would say goodbye to Jinnie. He would apologize. Try to make amends before walking out to the hills and let the gun do its dirty work.

As he approached the house, he heard what sounded like howling.

It was Jinnie.

Fearful that somehow the curse had affected her, Floyd dashed into the house. The front room was empty. More screams from the bedroom. He rushed in and his stomach dropped at what he saw.

A flurried tangle of flesh wrapped in flesh, moving back and forth, up and down like the rods and wheels of a locomotive. The screaming stopped and two pairs of eyes were focused on Floyd.

Carl rolled over onto his back, naked and without an ounce of shame in his face. The grin on his face made Floyd nauseous.

Jinnie came right out with it.

"You're no man," she said. There was almost a fury on her face as she rose from the bed. Her bare breasts bounced as she poked a finger in Floyd's chest. "You brought me out here and you work all day, socializing, burying with your nose in those bankroll books while I sit here bored to death."

Though Jinnie was in his face, Floyd couldn't take his eyes off Carl.

"This is *your* fault," she continued on.

Carl butted in, "She ain't wrong, Floyd." He leaned over to his side and pulled out a roll of smoking papers from his pants that lay next to the bed. "Why don't you get back to work, so we can get back to work." He winked at Floyd.

Later, when he would occasionally run through the scene over and over in his mind, he was never able to remember the bits of time between pulling the Collier from his pocket, Carl grabbing at the fresh hole in his chest, and Jinnie falling back onto the bed, blood streaming from her forehead.

* * *

"I'm sorry you had to find them this way." Bohannon put his hand on Floyd's shoulder. "Must've really been somethin'. To die in the heat of the moment like that."

Floyd looked at the Sheriff who quickly cleared his throat.

"Don't forget that," he indicated towards the ground. "Probably won't get much, but you may be able to sell it to Dade. Help pay for any funeral expenses."

On the floor besides the bed lay a rusted flintlock revolver, broken in two.

"I don't want anything to do with it," Floyd said, almost trancelike.

Bohannon bent down. "Well if you don't mind, it's a nice memento. Reminds me of my grandpappy." He reached out and Floyd thought he heard a sigh in the air.

Process Summary

Seven Hundred and Seventy-Six is my first story in the #52ShortStories challenge and also the first one, that I can recall, in which I started and finished within one week. This was a big milestone for me. The great part about this challenge is that it's going to continually push my capabilities. No resting on my laurels (do they sell laurels at Ikea?).

My initial idea was to block out at least one hour a day, from Monday to Sunday, in a very orderly fashion:

- Monday – Brainstorm/Plot
- Tuesday – Write First Act
- Wednesday – Write Second Act
- Thursday – Write Third Act
- Friday – Read and Revise
- Saturday – Read and Revise
- Sunday – Publish

While blocking out the time was useful, I ended up writing all over the place. I would get stuck and instead of wasting time banging my head on the same problem, I decided it might be wiser to write something else. That something could be in Act 3, it could be back in Act 1, it could be a Q&A session with myself. I just wanted something that kept me moving forward in one way or another.

Come Sunday morning, I was as done as I could be. I printed the story out and enlisted my wife to provide her usually brilliant feedback. It really helps to be married to another creative.

So let's look at how the story came to fruition, shall we?

When I first sat down to write, I had no idea what I would write about. When that's the case, I usually turn to an idea I've recently read about, or word or image association. I'm looking for a seed to plant; something on which I can build off.

It started here:

> **Pink Noise and Brown Noise variations**
>
> Although all frequencies are produced in equal intensity, white noise sounds much brighter than what we would expect from a spectrally flat noise. This is due to the nature of our hearing, which doesn't sense all frequencies equally. Therefore, people often prefer to listen to Pink Noise, a noise that boosts the lower frequency range to compensate for the unnatural brightness of white noise, or Brown Noise, a noise that puts even more emphasis on the lower frequencies. When one exactly compensates for the particular sensitive curve of the human hearing, white noise turns Grey.

This bit of text comes from a noise generator I use when I want to get some serious focus going. I put on the noise-cancelling headphones so I can crank up the brown noise (ironic) and drown out everything else. For some reason, that highlighted bit of text (my highlighting) said, "Pick me!" And so I did.

Then came the mind map:

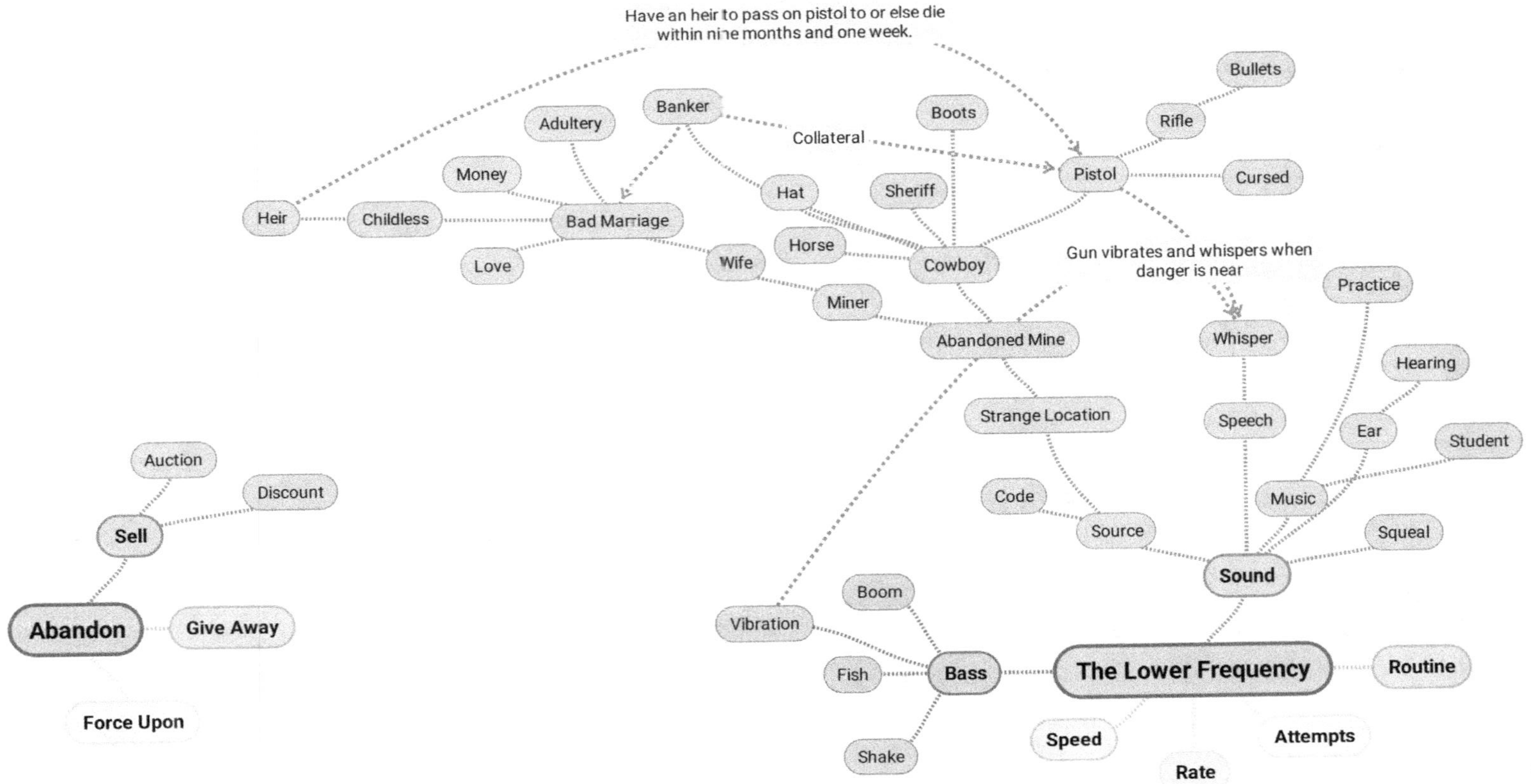
Have an heir to pass on pistol to or else die within nine months and one week.
Banker
Adultery
Boots
Bullets
Rifle
Money
Collateral
Hat
Sheriff
Pistol
Cursed
Heir
Childless
Bad Marriage
Horse
Cowboy
Love
Wife
Gun vibrates and whispers when danger is near
Miner
Whisper
Practice
Abandoned Mine
Hearing
Strange Location
Speech
Ear
Student
Auction
Code
Music
Discount
Source
Squeal
Sell
Sound
Abandon
Give Away
Boom
Vibration
Fish
Bass
The Lower Frequency
Routine
Force Upon
Shake
Speed
Attempts
Rate

The mind map is something I've only started doing regularly, and let me tell you, I love it. There's a lot in there that never made sense or applied, but it generated the ideas that stuck. I used this again for the story I've started this week and it's already gotten me excited about the new idea.

But you can see there are some obvious things seeping into my creative brain (notice the Western theme which was inevitable given all of my recent Western reading).

If you're interested, I built that using SimpleMind. I find it works very well for me, especially given my horrid handwriting.

Right after that, I started a general 'scratch file' that contains the following:

- A very basic outline
- Any prose that bubbled up into my head during random times of the day
- Research needs
- Questions
- Thoughts and Ideas
- Revision Notes

I maintained this scratch file throughout the process, jumping in and out of the actual manuscript occasionally.

Now, if that's not enough of the process for you and you want to read the scratchings of a neurotic writer, feeling much better about yourself in the process, I also maintained a daily journal.

Some of my favorite entries:

- Already feeling so much resistance — this is going to suck, people will hate it.

- Had some moments of fear, but not too bad today. I doubt all of the days henceforth will be so fearless, so it's nice to catch the breaks when they come.

- Only 500 or so words in 50 minutes. Wow…. 10 words a minute? really!?

Overall, this has already turned into a fruitful experiment. Even if I were to throw in the towel right now, which I won't, I would have a finished story that I could start submitting.

I hope those of you that are filled with fear and dread when it comes to writing can learn from the Fear Master™ himself. Don't wait for the courage. Don't wait for the time. Make them both and give us all a piece of yourself we can enjoy.

THE BITTER BUFFOON

Statistics

Synopsis: Tamsin Lamb, chief and CEO of the Blood Tasters, an ancient line of people gifted with the ability to taste a person's morality in their blood, is confronted with the news that her services are no longer needed.

Word Count: 1,500

Genre: Science Fiction / Fantasy

Completed Week: August 7th – August 13th

The Bitter Buffoon

Among many societies, there used to be a deeply-held belief that drinking someone's blood gave you their power. Not only did it turn out to be a ridiculous thought, but in the end, one which nearly proved fatal and came close to ending the line of the Blood Tasters.

In these days, the modern days, the more sophisticated days, Tamsin only sipped, swished, and spit. As chief of the Blood Tasters tribe, and chairwoman of their corporation, she rarely tasted blood anymore. Her 35,000 employees, each holding the pedigree that had made them so important to society, carried out the task of judging the blood of the people against the ancient Scriptures.

She was in mid-spit when Logan rapped on the French doors.

"Sorry to disturb, Ms. Lamb. A lady, Ritesh Guan, is at the gates. She is the new head of the Agency."

Bits of blood and saliva swirled down the drain of the pearl clamshell sink, leaving only a trail to prove from where it had come. She watched and waited.

"A facial identity search has confirmed her claim," Logan finished.

Tamsin grabbed a clean towel from the rack beside the sink, leaving another trace of the blood as she wiped her lips.

"Please see her to the sitting room."

"Yes, Ms. Lamb."

She returned to her dimly lit bedroom. The rising sun peaked through gray satin curtains as Tamsin picked up the tablet from the nightstand. After keying in her discoveries, she threw it on the bed and proceeded downstairs

* * *

When Tamsin entered the room, Ms. Guan was standing with her back towards her. The woman's hands were clasped together as she peered up at the collection of ancient tapestries, framed awards, and antiquities adorning the white walls.

Tamsin said, "That is the first spit bowl recovered from the initial settlement just outside of North Veza. By the grace of the Prophets, there has been little damage done to it over sixteen centuries."

Ms. Guan turned around. A smile was already on her face. "Fascinating," she said, sounding anything but fascinated.

She smelled of cigarette smoke. It was in her dark, ear-length hair. It was on the lapels of her wool suit coat. Tamsin would have Logan order a cleaning service. On any other day, under any other circumstances, she would have the woman thrown off the estate simply on the grounds for polluting a sacred environment.

Logan came through the doors like a ghost, carrying a tray of barely jingling china. There were two cups: one of hot tea accompanied by a small pitcher of cream and a bowl of sugar cubes. The other held room-temperature water. They were placed on the small table in between Tamsin and Ms. Guan. Logan disappeared as if he had never been in the room.

Ms. Guan eyed the cups.

"Please," Tamsin said.

"Thank you," Ms. Guan said, "but I'm not thirsty. I'm afraid I drank too much as it is during the long journey." She laughed a nervous laugh. "Your butler is quite attentive. He barely left my side after being kind enough to show me to the washroom."

Tamsin said nothing. She made a mental note to review the recorded video feeds later. Her security systems confirmed a lack of transmission and reception devices on Ms. Guan, otherwise Logan would have informed her. Still, the Agency's *raison d'être* was based on the concept of coming up with new tricks and it was hard to believe that they wouldn't try to capture this moment, if not for tactical and strategic means, for posterity's sake. And maybe, Tamsin pondered, for private viewing sessions where many of them believed they would lounge on long couches while holding glasses full of champagne, all of them laughing at the downfall of the most powerful tribe and enterprise in the country.

Ms. Guan cleared her throat. "In respect of your time and authority, Ms. Lamb, I'll come right out with it. Your services are no longer required."

Tamsin took a moment to appreciate the words and let Ms. Guan savor them as well.

"Of course," she continued, "you and your people will be compensated for the centuries of exemplary service." Ms. Guan's smile appeared almost painful. She couldn't even refer to the Blood Tasters by name.

"Compensated?"

"In many ways. The Agency has granted a stipend to be paid in perpetuity to all of your living employees. Education and retraining will also be a large piece of the package. Oh! And how could I forget. Discussions are underway regarding a glorious museum." Ms. Guan nodded towards the spitting bowl on the wall. "We've already picked the perfect spot; right on the cliffs of North Veza. Let me tell you, Ms. Lamb, the views are stunning. Whenever you would like, I will personally give you a tour at your convenience."

Tamsin could tell the woman was not accustomed to displays of false enthusiasm. Her demeanor came off bitter and she wondered how Ms. Guan climbed to one of the country's most powerful positions without the ability to opaquely kiss ass.

Tamsin sat down on a loveseat and took a sip of water. "So tell me how we have become obsolete." She was pleased to catch subtle signs of discomfiture in Ms. Guan's reaction, but the agent recomposed herself quickly.

"There was a breakthrough."

"When?"

"Several months ago."

A deliberate pause.

Ms. Guan continued, "We've known for some time now the location of genetic sequences which drive and direct moral behavior."

"Yes, that is nothing new."

The woman nodded her head. "Indeed. What*is*new, is that our scientists have discovered a way to manipulate those genes. To edit them." Ms. Guan decided to take a seat on the sofa opposite Tamsin, only to lean forward and almost whisper, "To remove what we know to be immoral, or just as bad, amoral."

Tamsin thought she could see blood dancing behind the agent's eyes. She leaned back into her own loveseat, stretching her arms across its crest.

"I see."

"It's true. We have successfully replaced the sequences of hundreds of subjects. In fact, your people have confirmed it for us."

Tamsin raised an eyebrow.

Ms. Guan said, "I apologize for the seemingly underhandedness of it all, but it was required, you see. We certainly did not want to spoil the test results by having your people aware of the situation." Again, the smile on the agent's face screamed that it was merely surface-level.

Tamsin only stared as Ms. Guan picked up the cup of tea and swirled its dark waters, looking into it as if reading omens. "It's a simple procedure now," Ms. Guan continued. "The Agency has ordered kits be shipped to doctors across the country over the next week. A device will be attached to the neck of the patient and then they are sent home. It runs an analysis, immoral sequences are replaced with moral sequences, and three days later the person is, for a more poetic turn, born again."

She seemed absurdly proud of herself.

"They will of course be installed in pre-natal centers as well, ensuring that future generations will no longer require the technology. The idea is to begin passing down the traits naturally."

There was only silence.

Ms. Guan met her eyes. "Tamsin."

Tamsin bristled at the casual use of her first name.

"A great burden has been lifted from your shoulders," Ms. Guan said. "Whereas your people have been confined by destiny to one path, to one way of life for so long, just imagine the freedom in this news."

"All things must come to an end, is that it?"

Ms. Guan shrugged, leaned into the sofa, finally deciding to take a drink of her tea.

"It's the way of things."

Seconds ticked down.

Tamsin broke the silence.

"There seems to be a great assumption in the world, Ms. Guan. That this is all the Tasters do. That we taste the blood of the people and sense their moral compass based on the Scriptures of the Prophets. In these days of 'modern man,' we're rendered obsolete. Because it's a service we've performed since before the Agency was even an inkling of thought, there is a tendency towards complacency."

Tamsin leaned forward, supporting her elbows on her knees.

"You are a trained scientist. Surely you recall the one who once stated something to the effect of, 'those things that are in motion tend to stay in motion.'" A smile formed on her lips. "We knew that there had been an unnatural change to things. An immoral change."

The color drained from Ms. Guan's face.

"I tasted your blood this morning, Ritesh. It's bitter."

Ms. Guan placed her cup on the table and jumped to her feet. "I would think twice before attempting—"

"You're free to leave any time," Tamsin said. "I'm afraid you won't have anywhere to go, though. The Agency is being dissolved as we speak and its research facilities are undergoing…renovations."

Later, Tamsin would want to replay this footage. Perhaps at the next holiday party, the Tasters would be the ones savoring champagne and celebrating the demise of one more vain attempt to bring down an adaptable group of people who had built an empire.

The woman was visibly shaking. Tamsin walked over and placed a hand on her shoulder. "Dear, *this* is the way of things. Take comfort in knowing that while the world moves at a breakneck pace, its foundation will remain the same."

Process Summary

The Bitter Buffoon is story number two in the #52ShortStories challenge.

Challenge is certainly the right word. I took a week off from work for "vacation," and this threw off the routine (in the most wonderful way, of course – fun times with friends and family, plus Angus's 3rd birthday).

The inspiration for this story seemed to unconsciously come from a National Geographic article based on the idea of humans driving their own evolutionary advancement. It mentioned the CRISPR project which essentially is a method in which specific genes can be targeted and permanently modified.

I had read the article earlier in the week, but as you'll see in my mind map, the influence wasn't direct. It even hopped off from the title of a Dostoyevsky book. I love stuff like this!

Obviously, the impact of something like CRISPR on society is huge. I went about my usual process to pull out a story. I'll acknowledge that with my modified schedule, I simply didn't put in the required time to really dig into this. I feel like I could have made this story so much more, but I was worried that if I let it get away from me, I wouldn't be able to wrap it up within a week. I suppose that's one of the challenges of writing short stories: it forces us to be concise.

Anyway, I hope some of you enjoyed it. It was good for me to write this for two main reasons:

- As a way of building the habit of buckling down when time is short. Come Sunday morning, I knew I had to wrap it up no matter what.

- There was a point where I hit a major roadblock which I had to fight through. I had no idea what to write, so I had to really explore why that was. You can see this in my daily journals linked below in this post. I finally realized that my protagonist lacked an immediate goal. This was an "a-ha" moment that hit me while I was folding laundry. Once I knew what was wrong, I simply brainstormed a little more and was able to get past the block.

Here's the mind map:

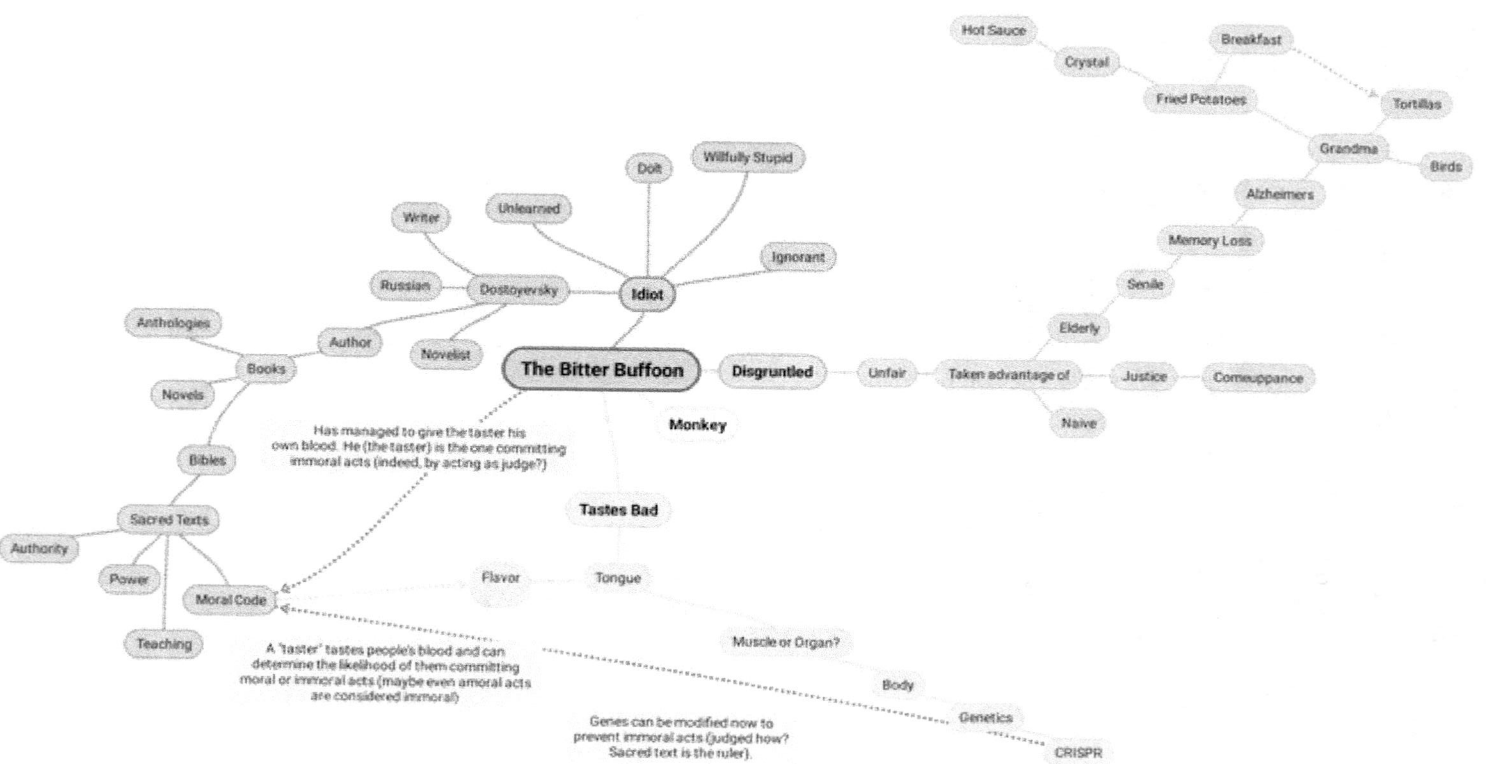
Hot Sauce
Crystal
Breakfast
Fried Potatoes
Tortillas
Grandma
Birds
Alzheimers
Memory Loss
Senile
Elderly
Justice
Comeuppance
Naive
Dolt
Willfully Stupid
Unlearned
Writer
Ignorant
Russian
Dostoyevsky
Idiot
Anthologies
Author
Novelist
Books
The Bitter Buffoon
Disgruntled
Unfair
Taken advantage of
Novels
Monkey
Has managed to give the taster his own blood. He (the taster) is the one committing immoral acts (indeed, by acting as judge?)
Bibles
Tastes Bad
Sacred Texts
Authority
Power
Flavor
Tongue
Moral Code
Teaching
A 'taster' tastes people's blood and can determine the likelihood of them committing moral or immoral acts (maybe even amoral acts are considered immoral)
Muscle or Organ?
Body
Genetics
Genes can be modified now to prevent immoral acts (judged how? Sacred text is the ruler).
CRISPR

A Pinnacle to Heaven

Statistics

Synopsis: Tony Stratta was a mob enforcer who finally confessed his sins.
Now that he's arrived in Heaven, he's itching to bust out.

Word Count: 3,500

Genre: Fantasy / Gangster

Completed Week: August 14th – August 20th

NOTE: This story won an Honorable Mention in Quarter 4 of 2017 in the
Writers of the Future contest.

A Pinnacle to Heaven

And my flame made a pinnacle to heaven

As I walked once round it in possession.

—Robert Frost, *The Bonfire*

"I'm bustin' out, Sol."

Tony Pistratta shrugged his shoulders and cracked his neck like a boxer getting ready to go another round. The temperature was a nice 78 degrees. Low humidity. A slight breeze. It reminded him of the time he took a trip to San Diego, assisting his employer with a troublesome client. Back then, he thought it was the most perfect place on Earth.

Now he walked home with his only friend and a stomach full of pastrami on rye, but still feeling unsatisfied.

"You're full of it," Sol said. "Forget why you're doing it. Where you gonna go?" There was little humor in his voice.

Tony hadn't thought too hard about that. Why should he? He always was of a one-track mind. He hated overthinking things. In a former life, more former than his recently clean life, he was a dog player at the tracks. Went with his gut and felt his way out of things. Those familiar feelings returned.

"It don't matter, but I'm done. No more harps, no more people smiling for no goddamn reason, and no more of this thing following me around everywhere." Tony reached up and knocked on the glowing golden ring hovering over his head like a big brother.

"I think you need to get your noggin checked, kid."

Kid. Sol reminded Tony of his grandfather, even kind of looked like him, only he wasn't. His grandfather was somewhere else. A place that got a bad rap, but that Tony was certain was a hell of a lot more fun than where he was at. Since Tony arrived, Sol had taken on the wise old man role. Almost like how a buddy is assigned to you during your first day of school, but this buddy had a silver widow's peak sharp enough to impale a goon and puffy red bags beneath each eye that made it look like he was smuggling poker chips.

He was a good guy.

"You know what your problem is?"

Tony stood with his hands in his pockets, staring at the old man with raised eyebrows that said *educate me.*

The old man flicked the side of his head with hard finger. "You left whatever lick of sense you may have had, down there." He pointed toward the ground that supposedly lay far below the thick layer of clouds on which they stood.

"Yeah, you forget already?" Sol said. "You finally did the right thing. You confessed your sins. And I don't mean you just said what you did wrong and went on with the rest of your life. You *confessed* them, Tony. We all heard you up here."

Sol shook his head so long that Tony thought it was stuck in motion, like one of them clacking ball and magnet paperweights that sits on the desks of CEOs. "You turned your whole life around just to get on the VIP list and now you say you wanna leave?"

Shit, Tony thought. Was he being rash? His hand motioned towards the coat pocket he didn't have, searching for the pack of smokes that didn't exist.

"I didn't know it would be like this," he said. "I don't think I've been here two months and I feel like I'm gonna lose it."

"132 years."

"Huh?"

"132 years, but it probably feels like two months. Time's a little different here."

They walked among skyscrapers. All of them shined. Smooth white marble adorned with gold trim, they reached into a set of clouds even higher than those on which they stood. Like Manhattan, only without the street noise and stench. Why they gleamed, Tony never understood. There was no sun in sight. Just a radiant light bleeding out of every available space.

People of all types populated the streets, some walking just like Tony and Sol, others riding in carriages pulled along by some sort of quiet, invisible machinery. Every face was plastered with a smile, but to Tony, their eyes seemed to be hiding something.

Sol said, "Let's say you find a way to break out. You think those cherubs are just gonna let you walk…float…jump…whatever, right out of here?"

"What's going to happen if I try?"

Sol stopped walking and grabbed Tony's arm. His grip was strong for an old man.

"Look, Tony, just think long and hard about this. You ain't a goomba eatin' clams down at Don Peppe's anymore. Don't throw this away."

The expression on Sol's face reminded Tony of a pleading bloodhound.

"You sound like you know somethin'," he said. "Level with me. What's gonna happen if I try?"

"I don't know anything. Can't say it's ever been done before, so long as I've been here."

"How long's that? You never told me."

Sol sighed. "A long time, Tony."

They continued walking in silence until they reached Sol's apartment. The two of them parted ways and Tony didn't look back.

He never looked back.

* * *

Night arrived, though it never got truly dark here. Instead, there was almost a permanent dusk, purple and orange. There were no streetlights to be found. Only a glow that surrounded the Heavens. When he left his apartment, there were still people milling about, a few sitting on stoops and outside of cafes that smelled of weak coffee. Most people were sleeping. Tony didn't understand the purpose of sleep anymore. He never felt tired. Still, many people carried it on as if it were a habit they weren't interested in breaking.

He'd been walking for a while now, and though he hadn't found the edge yet, Tony wasn't going to turn back. There *had* to be one. He remembered how clouds looked when he was on Earth and they always ended.

Hills of white fluff beckoned him and on he went until he finally reached a point of exhaustion. To be in Heaven and still be out of breath. It was a funny thought. He fell to his ass on an undistinguished cloud, kicked off his shiny black leather shoes, and rubbed his feet. If not for the random changes in elevation, Tony may have felt like he was walking in circles. There was a small fear of getting lost, but the shining beacon of the city remained at his back. Not that he considered it an option.

"Are you lost, Tony?"

A voice emerged from above him. It was garbled. Almost like when you talk to someone on the phone and the signal is weak. He looked around.

"Huh?"

"I said, are you lost?" The voice sounded clean now, somewhat hoarse, and it was obvious where it came from.

He looked up and saw the ring above his head. It glowed orange and red as if it had just been pulled from a fire.

"You found me," it said. The ring vibrated like it was giggling.

A corner of Tony's mouth turned up.

"Sol, you fuckin' with me?"

"No one's fuckin' with you," the voice replied. Its tone sounded so odd, Tony had to laugh.

"And this isn't, Sol," it said.

Tony's heart skipped a beat.

"What are you looking for way out here, Tony?" it asked.

Tony stood up and stared as much as he could at the ring. It was difficult because it was always on the edge of his vision. It aligned with the top of his skull and if he moved, it moved.

"I don't answer questions unless I know who I'm talkin' to," he said.

"No matter. I know why you're here."

"Then why you askin'?"

"This happens every once in a while." The voice sounded so impersonal. As if it could have been talking to anyone. "You should know that. You're not the first person, and you won't be the last, to think there's something better out here. Even if you could see what you're missing, you don't want to, Tony. Trust me. Go home."

His head began to hurt. He was suddenly thirsty and he couldn't remember the last time he drank anything. One of the downsides to his impulsiveness was a lack of planning. He brought no water with him. No food. Did it matter anymore? Maybe not, but the feelings in his stomach and throat told him it did.

"The cafes are always open, as you know. You like, what, cannolis? Pasta with a thick red sauce? Have you been to Salmucci's yet? They make a good martini."

Tony chuffed. "Yeah, if you like them fruity virgin drinks. Not a drop of liquor in this place."

"Alcohol brings trouble."

Tony ignored the comment. "I assume that by the fact you're talkin' to me through this…contraption…that you have some know-how. You a cherub? Without mouths, maybe, you know, this is how you guys communicate."

Silence was the only reply.

Tony's stomach churned. He swore he smelled stewed tomatoes. He shook his head like he was trying to clear a settled fog. The realization settled in that he wasn't going to get what he wanted. At least not today.

"Yeah, alright," Tony said. "I could use a bite." He knelt down and put on his shoes, suddenly feeling reinvigorated. He asked, "You want to tell me who you are or not?"

"You can call me the Don," he said. The ring vibrated again as Tony sensed another childish giggle.

The Don. The Man of Mystery living in the Grand Palace who supposedly ran the whole shebang.

"Yeah, okay, *the Don*. Thanks for the advice."

* * *

Seeing a waving set of hands, Tony skipped Salmucci's and wandered instead into a cafe named Tiki Piña. Sol was sitting on a shaded patio and waved him towards a seat. If not for the hollowed-out coconut sitting on the table, capped in tiny, colorful umbrellas, Tiki Piña wouldn't have looked much different from the hundreds of other cafes spread throughout the city. Airy piano music filled the room. Something like jazz. Completely unfitting for the name. It was also the most boring jazz Tony had ever heard.

The men exchanged small talk, ordered teriyaki chicken, and Tony told Sol what had happened.

"Just chalk it up to another lesson learned," Sol said. "You don't seem any worse for the wear."

A faceless waiter brought Tony the same decorated drink as Sol. He wondered if he could get to the straw without losing an eye.

"You think I'm going to let that stop me?"

The chicken arrived. It was sickly sweet and after the first bite, Tony pushed it towards the center of the table. Sol seemed to be enjoying his own and stabbed a fork into Tony's pieces.

"I think that your head is just as hard as it was yesterday. I could take a sledgehammer to that thing and I'd probably have to buy a new one."

Out of the corner of his eye, Tony saw two muscle-bound cherubs floating silently down the side of the street, inches off the ground. It always unnerved him, their quiet. He'd never gotten used to their lack of mouths. Instead there was only a patch of flesh. But they seemed to be made for simple purposes. They were soldiers, policemen, guardians of property. A distant memory surfaced of Tony's days working with other enforcers. He could have used some cherubs back then.

Sol seemed oblivious to their presence and he was going on about something regarding the sauce on the chicken when the cherubs stopped abruptly just outside of the cafe and entered the patio.

Tony once had a keen sense for trouble. It was still there, lurking under the surface, but now he kicked himself for letting it grow dull. The cherubs hovered over to the table and looked down at Sol. They ignored Tony. Each grabbed an arm and lifted the old man effortlessly from his seat. A forkful of chicken fell from Sol's hand and somehow clinked on the clouds beneath their feet.

Tony jumped out of his chair.

"Hey, what the—" he said, but his plea was cut off as he was pushed back down into the chair by the free hand of one of the cherubs. It felt like being crushed by a '41 Continental.

"Tony, don't start no trouble." Sol's voice was oddly calm as he hung between the arms of the cherubs like laundry drying on the line. "I'm sure they just got some questions. Routine stuff." He looked like a little old baby in their arms. The people sitting around them watched without expression. The piano man never let up with the faux-jazz.

It took all of his nerve to sit and watch as the cherubs carried Sol out of Tiki Piña and turned into tiny specks moving toward the Don's Palace.

Questions? How the hell were they gonna ask 'em, Tony wondered.

* * *

Sol was right. Time's a little different here. Though he hadn't seen his only friend for what could have been minutes or millennia, Tony made a decision as soon as they laid their hands on the old man. Now, he sat on the perfectly cut green grass of one of the many perfectly landscaped parks, pretending to soak in the sunless light. All the while, he recorded notes in his head. Patrol schedules. Routines. Fixed action patterns.

Tony smirked at the regularity of it all. Though they were big and strong, the cherubs would have never lasted two seconds on Mulberry.

He twisted the thin wire around in hands. It felt familiar. That was good. Tony doubted the piano man at Tiki Piña would notice only a clack coming from the underused high F-key

* * *

Tony pulled until his hands bled. He wondered if the cherub was screaming inside. This guard was number four of four and he put up the hardest fight. Still, getting into the palace was easier than Tony thought it would be. This is what passed for security?

Maybe he should have been more suspicious, but for the moment, he focused with a white heat on finding Sol.

* * *

The palace looked much bigger on the outside. After running through a couple of ivory-tiled hallways and up three sets of stairs carpeted in purple velvet, he found what he was looking for. Through the powers of deduction, not to mention a bright red and white plaque that said *The Don*, Tony kicked open the only door at the pinnacle.

As it flew open, a hint of a thought told Tony he was being a little too carefree. Nothing else mattered now. He came this far and doubted any punishment handed out for the murder of four cherubs would be lenient.

Sitting on a white leather chair, aside a fire roaring in the most flamboyant fireplace, was one of the fattest, ugliest men Tony had ever seen. In one hand was a rocks glass filled with amber liquid. The other rested on the head of an ebony cane carved to look like a winding snake. It's tongue stuck out just beneath the man's palm.

He grinned with yellowed teeth.

"Not bad," he said. His voice was slightly hoarse. Tony recognized it instantly. The fat man took a sip of whatever was in his glass. Ice clinked. "Not bad at all."

Tony didn't have to be asked. He took the open chair opposite The Don. There was an untouched glass holding the same liquid and a couple of ice cubes.

The Don extended an inviting hand. "Salud," he said.

Tony took a sip. The burn was magnificent and he savored every second.

"I thought you said alcohol brings trouble."

"It certainly does." The Don took another drink.

"Alright," Tony said. "I'll admit I'm a little slow on the take these days. Where's Sol?"

The Don shifted in his seat. His movement released a horrible smell, like the decay of undisposed bodies. It was an odor Tony hadn't smelled since…before. He also noticed for the first time that there were two tall cherubs standing motionless in the shadowed corners at the rear of the room.

"Sol's no longer important. He got you here and that's all that matters."

"He matters to me."

The Don rolled his eyes and said, "Don't test my patience."

"Or what?" Tony felt oddly unafraid. He placed his glass on a table next to his chair, reached into his pocket and wound the piano wire around his fingers.

The two of them stared at each other until vertigo overtook Tony and he felt like he was going to fall into oblivion. He shut his eyes and leaned back into the chair.

"I work hard on maintaining a certain type of atmosphere here," the Don said. "We don't have a lot of trouble. I like to keep it that way."

"I wouldn't have thought there'd be any trouble in Heaven."

The Don burst into unrestrained laughter. Tony's body shook and his eyes snapped open in time to see the old man's chins quivering, one on top of the other like a stack of pancakes drenched in a syrupy sweat. Tears streamed down his loose-hanging cheeks. It seemed to be minutes before he recomposed himself. He pulled a red kerchief from a pocket and dabbed at his eyes.

"You're right, Tony. You *are* a little slow on the take today."

Tony felt his face flush. His temper, the one he had worked so hard on pushing against the very day he fell on his knees and confessed his crimes, came roaring back and he jumped from his chair.

"No more games you fat fuck."

He expected the cherubs to move on him, but they stood still. Tony rushed towards the The Don, the piano wire lined up, ready to slide beneath the bottom chin.

He felt a snap and the wire turned limp.

He stopped in place and looked at his hands. A tiny snake started twisting up each arm. Tony danced like a gypsy having a seizure and threw the slimy bastards from his body. They slithered into the fireplace and disappeared into the flames.

The Don adjusted himself again and took another sip of liquor.

"You're to come under my employ."

Tony straightened up. His stomach climbed up toward his throat. There comes a time in everyone's life when the reality of a situation just hits you upside the head, sort of like Sol, and says, "You fuckin' idiot."

"I'm not in Heaven," he whispered.

The Don sighed. "It's a good thing I don't hire on intelligence." He set his glass on the table beside the chair and placed both hands on top of his cane. His eyes bore into Tony's as he lifted himself up from the seat. Tony swore it sounded like all of the air in the world had been released from a vacuum. The fat man grunted and groaned, his face turning redder than a tomato until he was finally wheezing on his feet. The top of his combed-over head came up to Tony's chest.

"But I confessed my sins," Tony said. "I did what I was supposed to do." There was a crack of pain in his voice now. "I turned my whole god-damned life around."

The Don grabbed Tony's chin, as gently as examining a flower, and directed his face down.

"There's always a scale. After decades of, if I might offer some praise, *beautiful* brutality, becoming Mother Teresa wouldn't have earned you a place in Heaven."

It took only a moment for Tony to compose himself. He had always been quick to accept a change in situation.

"Was this some sort of test? Killing your guards?" Tony asked. He shook his head. "What's the point? You're the damned Devil."

"I like a little drama." He giggled that little schoolgirl giggle. "In all seriousness, because I'm a serious man at heart, I occasionally run into a fella like you. Most folks, they come here, they're practically in a trance and they're satisfied. Yeah, it's boring as shit, but Tony…" He paused and leaned in as if revealing a great secret. "Most people *are* boring as shit."

Tony couldn't remember the last time he felt so helpless. His legs felt weak, shaky. He knew he was standing, but barely. He would have lost his bowels if he had eaten anything for lunch.

"It's been fun, but my appointment book is overflowing today. We'll talk soon." He laughed again. "Well, at least one of us will." He snapped his fingers and Tony watched him zoom by, chin by chin, until his eyes were at his feet, until he was falling into a darkness

* * *

The player was at it again, playing the same damn riff. Tony wanted to tell him to learn a different song or else he would rip his fingers off. But he knew he couldn't—neither tell him nor rip his fingers off.

Instead, all he could do was float and watch Sol chat with a goon over sticky chicken and a coconut shell topped with too many tiny umbrellas.

Process Summary

A Pinnacle to Heaven is story number three in the #52ShortStories challenge.

As the epigraph of the story implies, the springboard for this story came from a Robert Frost poem. I'm thinking pulling potential titles from poetry is going to be a regular thing as the imagery just comes so naturally. But…

…that is where the inspiration seemed to end. I really struggled on the first day of planning and brainstorming. It quickly became obvious I was trying to write a story that my subconscious had absolutely no interest in composing.

Here's the initial mind map:

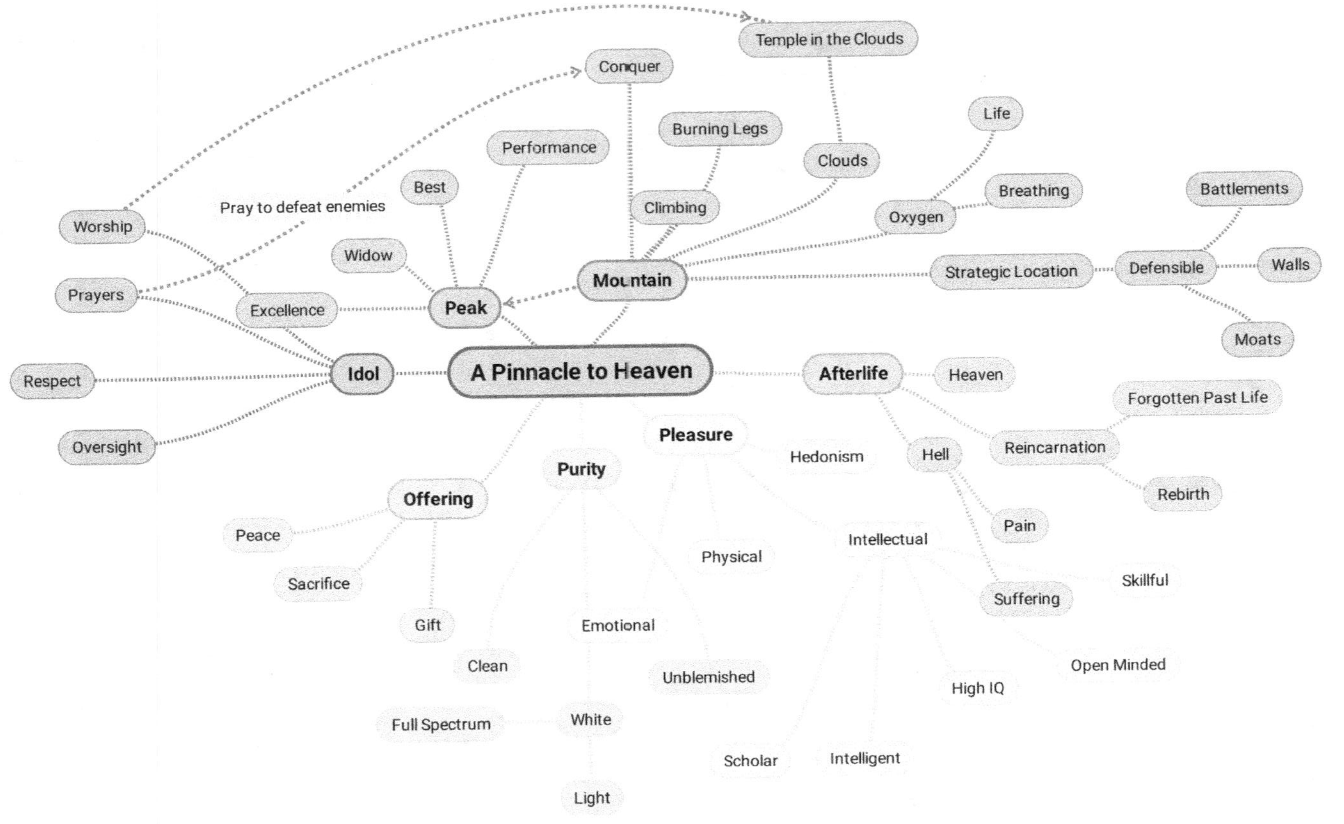
A Pinnacle to Heaven
Mountain
Peak
Idol
Afterlife
Pleasure
Purity
Offering
Temple in the Clouds
Conquer
Performance
Burning Legs
Clouds
Life
Climbing
Breathing
Battlements
Best
Oxygen
Pray to defeat enemies
Worship
Strategic Location
Defensible
Walls
Widow
Moats
Prayers
Excellence
Respect
Heaven
Forgotten Past Life
Oversight
Hedonism
Hell
Reincarnation
Rebirth
Pain
Intellectual
Peace
Physical
Sacrifice
Suffering
Skillful
Gift
Emotional
Clean
Unblemished
Open Minded
High IQ
Full Spectrum
White
Scholar
Intelligent
Light

As you can see, there are only a few items which wound up in the finished story.

After the first day, I was pretty frustrated. The next day, I decided to Write in the Dark and see what happened. I suppose that's just what I needed because I began to write something that my brain latched on to.

Almost every day, I try to copy a page of prose from a well-respected author. Lately, it's been Raymond Chandler. I think you can see where the no-nonsense protagonist came from. The language definitely influenced the build of the characters.

I began to weave in and out of different angles in approaching the story. The main thrust of the reformed mobster was always there, but initially, I had an alternate-Earth setting in mind with alternate cultures and religions (a more Buddhist-like religion where the mobster achieved spiritual enlightenment).

I was looking at Sumerian mythology as a model. Just didn't jibe. Then there was a romance angle I was intent on taking, of which you'll see on some of the random prose in the scratch file.

In the end, I let go of the reins and stopped fighting the challenge of writing in an uncomfortable voice and setting. Since my first reader (my wife) really liked it, that was enough proof for me that this was another fine example of the invisible magic happening inside our heads.

I'm reminded of a recent dentist visit when the hygienist was trying to scrape clean my back teeth. If I opened my mouth too widely, the jaw muscles tightened and she couldn't reach them. I had to relax a little and provide some give.

As artists, we can grow too controlling of our work. We're better off remembering that we're our minds' collaborators.

A Hundred Eyes

Statistics

Synopsis: As a young boy in a remote 16th-century Polish village, Casimir Pitsudski must give up his life to the hundred-eyed monster in order to save the world.

Word Count: 3,400

Genre: Horror / Historical Fantasy

Completed Week: August 21st – August 27th

A Hundred Eyes

Casimir Pitsudski would not stop working.

He refused to look back at the one-eyed creature until he was done.

With each mark of charcoal, he felt the monster's rhythm of inhale, exhale, inhale, exhale on the back of his neck. Sweat poured down his face as if a thousand steaming kettles were going off at once. It took every ounce of will to remain conscious.

With each mark, it became clearer why the beast hadn't snatched him. Why it was called the monster with a hundred eyes. Why it hadn't done to him what it did to Sylwia.

His canvas, a tiny portion of gray stone among vast cavern walls, came together slowly. A nearly empty lamp of oil provided the only illumination. Casimir fought to maintain focus and forget the fate of his recently-met companion, yet at the same time, hold it in his mind.

Lines and shadows emerged from his shaking hands.

With each mark, it helped to remember everything that happened.

* * *

They woke the priest.

"You cannot send my son," his mother started.

Casimir was nervous. He knew coming to the church under the cover of darkness was a bad idea, but his parents were afraid to rouse suspicions among the other villagers.

Father Bogdan shook his head, wiped at his eyes and tried to look at the three of them. Curly salt-and-pepper hair bounced off his forehead.

His gaunt cheeks brought to mind more a monk than a priest. "Are you so special?"

"It's not fair," she replied. "He's only a boy."

"This is the way it's always been. Your son's name was drawn from among the others. There is no better way."

"Let's petition the magnate." It was his father now. "Maybe he will send knights." He was a short but stout man with a long, brown beard and thick arms. They reminded Casimir of the trunks of dark beech trees surrounding their remote village. Casimir was ashamed to think that his father lacked a deep-thinking mind, yet the man could never be accused of not caring for his family.

"You have a short memory, Piotr," the priest said, not completely unsympathetic. "Do you remember the last time we did such a thing? Go, wake Irena. Ask about her daughters if you've already forgotten. One taken away like chattel, the other scarred from eye to chin by the whip of one of his soldiers."

His mother started now. "But if we can show him—"

Father Bogdan raised a hand. "Show him what? When is the last time you saw his face? He never leaves his castle except to fight a war and win more land. His men would never dare to waste his or their time with the folk tales of peasants."

His father seemed to withdraw a little.

The priest took an exasperated breath. "The magnate cares not about excuses. It's grain he wants. We all wish things could be different, but this is a contract that was made long ago. We invite death if we violate it."

"To hell with the contract!" Casimir's mother yelled, oblivious to her initial desire to keep things quiet. "My son. Does he not die?"

"He is but one. Would you rather we all be killed?" Father Bogdan looked directly at Casimir as if the decision lay in his hands.

"We'll discuss this no further," the Father continued, holding his hands up before them to brook any protest.

He turned to Casimir and spoke as if they were the only two standing in the tiny room at the back of the church. "Gather the things you'll want to take. You're to meet the other one at the crossroads in the morning."

"What will happen?" Casimir asked.

Father Bogdan began to bless the boy who had barely turned fourteen last month. "I don't know," he said.

Casimir knew it was mostly a lie. He wasn't sure why he had asked.

* * *

What does one want to see, or hold on to, before one dies?

It was a question Casimir pondered on a sleepless night, the arm of his snoring mother wrapped around his waist. She refused to let him lay down alone that night.

Pale moonlight slipped through a crack in the stone wall of their cottage and as soon as he had decided what to take with him, he gently removed her arm, careful not to wake her. Quietly, he gathered a few items in a woven sack and left without saying goodbye.

He supposed it was a mistake, but he knew that any long farewell would only frighten him more.

* * *

Casimir traveled lightly.

But for a small bag of black charcoal, blank drawing papers as well as some of his favorite sketches, he brought only a water flask, a few pieces of hard bread, and a lamp filled with oil as well as flint for lighting it. The journey to the crossroads was half-a-day's travel. He followed the rising autumn sun which barely crested the tops of the beech trees as he left the outer reaches of his village. Dry, fallen burrs crunched beneath his feet every step of the way. Along the occasional half-leafed branch hung crude hand-carved imitations of the hundred-eyed beast. Dziady, the feast of remembrance, would arrive tomorrow and it would be the first time Casimir celebrated without seeing the tears and recounting the memories of his friends and family.

He wanted to stop and draw the scene as a testament to those who would travel the same path next year, and the year after that, but he knew it would be in vain. It was something he should have thought of earlier.

Instead, he continued walking, his head down and his eyes focused on the forest floor. Casimir remembered that last year it was the Halina, the tanner's plump wife. The year before that…it bothered him that he couldn't recall.

* * *

The stranger stood cloaked and motionless at a corner of the crossroads. One hand peeked through an oversized sleeve, hanging by the person's side. The other hand grasped a walking stick.

Their eyes met as Casimir approached, or so he thought. The stranger's face was shadowed by a hooded cloak. What little features Casimir could make out were pale yet wrinkled and rough like aged leather. There was something generally odd about it, but he couldn't place why.

"So young," she said.

A woman with a gravel voice.

There was an awkward silence. Casimir felt her examining him like a blacksmith examines a freshly wrought horseshoe.

She stretched out her free hand.

"I am Sylwia."

Casimir took it. It felt cold to the touch.

"Hello. I'm Casimir."

A lump caught in his throat. "You are from the east village?" he eeked out.

She nodded once and said, "We should continue on. We have another half-day's journey to go and we don't want to be wandering at dark. The wolves are hungry most nights."

What did it matter, Casimir thought. But then he felt suddenly ashamed. He remembered it mattered a lot.

* * *

They walked in silence, following a small stream winding south towards its source deep in the Carpathian Mountains. After some time, they came to a large pile of rocks surrounded by sharp sticks dug into the ground, pointing skyward. They were grouped sloppily alongside the foot of an overgrown trail which veered southwest. The rocks were marked with faded skulls and words such as *groźba!* (*Danger!*) and *pokraka* (*Monster*). One fallen log rested on the forest floor in front of them all. It was covered with a hundred crudely drawn eyes.

Sylwia looked up at Casimir. Was she seeking confirmation? Proof that he was willing to come along? He froze. Before he could answer, she shrugged her shoulders and walked on.

Casimir felt resistance in his body. As if he was stuck in a pit of tar. His flask was half empty and he suddenly found himself more thirsty than he had ever been before. He refilled it from the stream and caught up to the surprisingly fast older woman. She seemed to be in such a hurry to die, Casimir thought.

The uphill march may have been half-a-mile, perhaps a full one. They were both breathless by the time they found the dark entrance. A damp heat emanated from the cave, amplifying the sweat covering every inch of Casimir's body. Even though he smelled the ripe scent of Sylwia beside him, he suddenly felt alone.

"Do we go in now?" he asked. For some reason, it seemed natural to him to allow Sylwia to make the decisions.

She shook her head. Her gaze never left the cave. "No, we camp tonight and come back tomorrow. It is not yet the day of Dziady."

Of course, he thought.

* * *

Dusk snuck up on Casimir and they circled back to make camp only a hundred yards from the entrance. Even from there, they could feel its uncomfortable warmth.

Casimir lit a fire only for the comfort of the light. His strength had left him and he felt more tired than he ever had on those long days of scything wheat.

Night's arrival brought an eerie silence. Casimir realized the quiet had been with them since they neared the cave. Neither crickets nor birds could be heard. Only the sounds of the fire crackling from sappy wood.

Casimir studied Sylwia sitting quietly on a stone across the flames. Just as quiet as everything else. Shadows danced over her hooded face. Her arms rested on her lap as she leaned forward, her legs slightly crossed, flicking a sandaled foot back and forth. The walking stick lay on the rock to her left. Her head moved only to follow the occasional spark floating towards the heavens.

She wasn't saying a word and Casimir felt he would go out of his mind if he didn't occupy himself, so he reached into his sack and pulled out the tiny bag of charcoal and a piece of paper.

With the paper resting on his lap, he tried to conjure an image. This would be his last work. What would he sketch? A scene in the village? A memory of his parents? Nothing seemed to satisfy. He looked across the fire and saw Sylwia looking back at him.

"You are an artist?"

Casimir wasn't sure how to respond. He had never become an apprentice to a true artist. It was a hobby he took upon himself after sneaking into the church one day and looking through Father Bogdan's bible. Within were fascinating illustrations of The Garden of Eden and the Tower of Babel. They brought the stories he heard every Sunday to life. He wanted that power. To do the same for the stories that surrounded him, waiting to be captured.

No, Casimir thought, he wasn't a real artist. Real artists had their work in grand cathedrals or put in books. He sketched only to unwind from long days in the fields and never showed them to anyone.

"Before I got sick, I worked in Kraków," Sylwia said. "I was an attendant to Bona Jagiełło."

Casimir's jaw dropped. The old woman said it so nonchalantly, seeming to pay him no mind. Her eyes refocused on the fire as if she were seeing her life play back within the yellow and orange hues.

"The Queen had many pieces of art brought into the palace from the Italian masters." She mused, "Let me tell you. The colors. The lines." Her eyes lit up nearly imperceptibly. "A thousand thoughts and voices on a single piece of canvas."

Casimir felt himself flush. Could she be telling the truth? Maybe it was a joke. He would probe her further.

"How were you sick?"

Sylwia sighed, picked up the walking stick at her side and stirred the dirt beneath her feet. "Many of us working for the queen began to grow ill at the same time. Our hair turned suddenly gray and then began to fall out. I can't tell you why. I don't know. They said we were possessed, cursed with leprosy, and the Queen had us all sent away with nothing. I had to return to the village I left as a young girl." She looked at Casimir. "Back to this."

He tried to swallow but his mouth was dry. He reached over and took a swig of water from his flask. His stomach rumbled. He set his materials aside and began to chew on his ration of hard bread.

Sylwia stood, reached inside her cloak, and walked to Casimir. She pulled out a lump of her own bread and handed it to him.

"Aren't you hungry?" he asked.

"A little," she said, as if that was the only answer needed and that she would refuse him if he tried to give it back to her.

She walked back to her stone and sat again. Casimir ate in silence and Sylwia watched.

"Why were you chosen?" she asked. "Did you commit a crime? Steal something? Hurt someone?"

Casimir stopped chewing and shook his head.

"It was by lottery," he said. "That's what we've always done."

Sylwia lifted her head in assent, as if the final piece of a puzzle had fallen into place.

"Do you mind if I remove my cowl?" she asked. "It's rather warm here."

A strange question, Casimir thought. "Of course."

She pulled back the hood, never dropping her eyes from Casimir's. His breath caught in his throat.

"Go ahead," she said. "Stare. It's okay."

She sounded as if she really didn't mind.

Casimir realized now what was so strange about her face when he first saw her. She had no eyebrows. And just as she said, but for a tiny, wild tuft on her left temple, there was not a single hair on her head.

Sylwia said, "I suppose, in a sense, you are lucky to have a lottery. It seems more fair. In our village, they simply choose the person with the least to offer." She laughed. "Let me tell you, everyone was quite relieved when I showed up again."

Casimir sensed a sadness in her voice, but she quickly straightened up.

"What do you know of the monster?" she asked.

His face lit up with memories of his youth. "When we're children, we are first told about the pact. About the need for our two villages to send someone every year or it will destroy the world. The priest does not hide it from us." For some reason, talking about their fate made him feel a little better.

"Do you believe it?"

He thought for a moment. "I don't know. I suppose. How can I not?" Casimir was afraid to even imagine burning in the torments of Hell, knowing that if he refused the call, he would be held responsible for the deaths of so many.

"It's supposed to leave two behind after the destruction," Sylwia said. She smiled but it was not a happy smile. "A man and a woman to continue the race and provide offspring. Sustenance. Though obviously no one has tested this theory. Maybe we should run off to Lithuania? Be the first?"

Casimir's eyes widened.

She laughed. "I jest. Not that they would let us get away with it if we tried. They would find us, tie us up and deliver us to the foot of the cave themselves."

"Why does it want us?" Casimir asked.

Sylwia took a moment to reply. "I believe it's lonely."

Lonely. Then why would it devour them, Casimir wondered, but did not say aloud. Instead he asked another question.

"Are you afraid?"

Her answer was swift. "Only of the pain."

They left it at that.

Casimir knew now what he had to do, so he dropped his bread, picked back up his charcoal and paper and began to draw.

***

Bones.

Femurs and lower jaws.

Hands, feet, and skulls.

In a large chamber, deep inside the sweltering cave, what was left of past villagers stood piled high towards the cavern's ceiling. All of them white, yet dirt-stained memories scored with scratches and punctures. Casimir looked at Sylwia under the light of their oil lamps. His legs shook and he would have urinated had he not relieved himself that morning. The older woman grabbed hold of his hand and squeezed. Her steadfastness encouraged him and together, they stood and waited.

***

It was difficult to tell how much time had passed. At some point, they sat down and continued waiting.

"Where is it?" Casimir asked. He estimated that the oil in their lamps was nearly half gone. "Maybe it's not true? Maybe there is no monster," he followed through. As soon as the words left his mouth, his eyes focused on the proof piled before them.

"Can I see your drawing?" Sylwia asked. Her voice was as calm.

Casimir hesitated, but only for a moment. Why not, he thought. What's the point in being shy now? He grabbed the paper from his sack and handed it to her. She held it up to the lamp's light. Casimir watched her. Part of him wanted to turn away. He girded himself and held steady.

A tear fell down her cheek that she wiped away quickly. Sylwia looked at him. Her eyes bore into him and now he couldn't help but avert his gaze.

She stood and stretched her arms, bending down to place the paper before him.

"Thank you," she said.

A sudden joy rose in Casimir's spirit. He felt the urge to show her more of his drawings. He turned and reached into his bag for the finished ones he had brought along.

"I have—"

A whip of air crashed against Casimir and he fell over trying to scramble to his feet. He looked around desperately at the surrounding darkness. His chest tightened, cutting short his breath.

Sylwia was gone, leaving behind only her walking stick laying in the dirt. Casimir's sack had fallen open. His charcoal and drawings also lay scattered on the floor. His skin crawled as he not only heard, but felt something approaching from the black. He wanted to run, but his feet refused to unglue themselves from the floor. Casimir could only stand there in abject terror as he saw the creature emerge.

But for a single feature, it was as horrid as his worst imaginings. Blood caked its thin, hairy body. Despite it being twice as tall as Casimir, long, lanky arms reached almost to the floor. Sticky drool dripped from the two sharp teeth that peeked out from each side of its wide, pink mouth. But the most horrifying thing of all was the large, solitary eye in the middle of its face. It had no eyelid. No way to blink.

Casimir didn't want to see it happen. He wanted to close his own eyes, but was powerless to do so. He whimpered and this time, evacuated his bowels.

The monster's face was inches from his now. He could smell bile on its breath. And then it did something strange. It turned its head down and looked at the floor. Casimir was still frozen and could do nothing as the beast picked up one of the drawings and examined it. Through the thin paper, Casimir could see the marks he had made.

He had captured her pain. Her humor. Everything that he saw of her in the single day they had spent together.

The creature held the picture in its clawed hand and returned its gaze toward Casimir.

A single thought entered the young man's mind.

More.

* * *

When he was done, Casimir stepped away from the wall.

His patron's single eye appraised the work. It was of the beast itself, sinking its teeth into a young girl, her parents mourning.

It turned to Casimir and a rush of thoughts entered the boy's mind.

The truth about the creature came in an instant. Sylwia had been correct. It was lonely. It didn't want to eat people, but that had seemed the only way to truly know their lives, their experiences. Fear and intimidation was the only way it knew how to feed its appetite. But if man could offer something like this, it had no reason to devour them at all.

It could see everything.

Process Summary

A Hundred Eyes is story number four in the #52ShortStories challenge.

The title for this one changed on the last day. Again, I started with different phrases from a Robert Frost poem (The Line-Gang) and picked the one that lit up my ear the most. In this case, "An Oath of Towns" was the winner.

I had another image in my head that I wanted to incorporate: A giant squid monster. This thought makes a regular appearance since I read a National Geographic article late last year. The funny thing is I wanted to provide a link to that article, only to discover it's about…wait for it…octopuses. I guess they're both cephalopods, but still…

Goes to show that even a faulty memory can work in one's favor.

From that point, I launched into my usual mindmap:

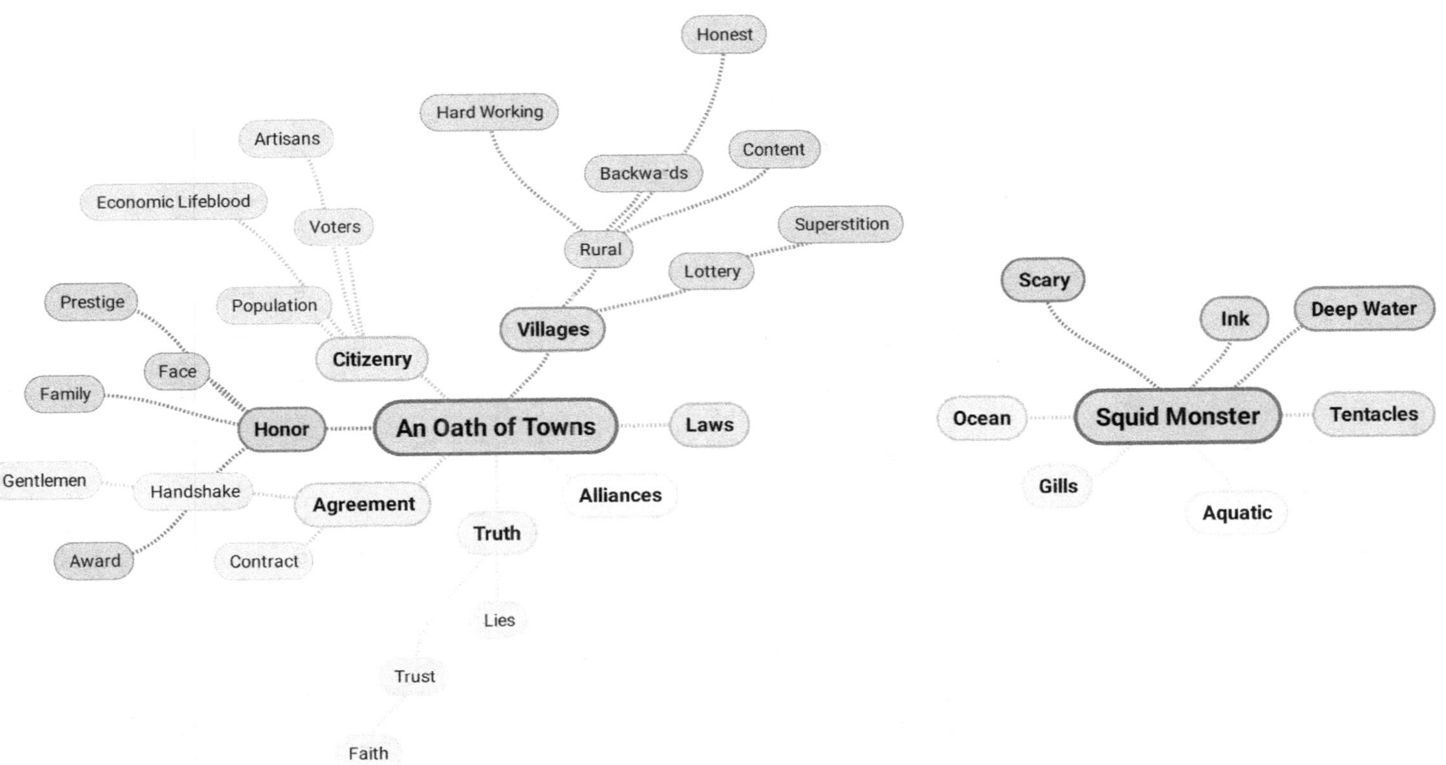
Honest
Artisans
Hard Working
Backwards
Content
Economic Lifeblood
Rural
Superstition
Voters
Prestige
Population
Villages
Lottery
Scary
Face
Citizenry
Ink
Deep Water
Family
Honor
An Oath of Towns
Laws
Ocean
Squid Monster
Tentacles
Gentlemen
Handshake
Agreement
Alliances
Gills
Aquatic
Award
Contract
Truth
Lies
Trust
Faith

My initial instinct was to create a story based on a group of towns that made a pact to go out and fight this squid monster.

How did I end up setting this in 16th-century Poland and with a monster that had nothing to do with squids?

Before I get into that, I want to mention that I've always had this impression that an artist's influences had to operate on a subconscious level. That actively stealing was considered ill form. But I'm quickly learning that belief makes little sense. Stealing is stealing and all great artists do it — it's all about execution. How you get the ideas shouldn't really matter.

The latest issue of Military History Quarterly had a couple of essays on Polish soldiers: One about a man named Casimir Pulaski (now you know where my protagonist's first name from), father of the U.S. Calvary. The other about Józef Piłsudski (…and there's the last name), a soldier who fought back the Red Army. As you can see, neither of these men were around before the 19th century. I thought an earlier period worked better for the story because it was a time during which, especially in remote regions, superstitions and local mythologies could still be so real.

What about the squid monster? I somehow came up with the idea of the beast eating people because it craved their experiences and that's how it absorbed them. If it could be done another way, like through perceiving human expression through art (also influenced by a NatGeo article), it would. I couldn't figure out an easy way to have the villagers make art underwater, but maybe that could be for another story at another time.

You may notice a pattern with my scratch files. I'll start one, fill in some information, come back to it occasionally, but it's rarely ever a fully fleshed out document. I primarily use it as a sounding board and when I get what I need, I set it aside and dive into the prose itself.

It's interesting for me to look back on this and my journal entries because I had so many ideas that never came to fruition or it was the opposite — seeds that bloomed into full-blown, fruit-bearing trees.

WAKE

Statistics

Synopsis: Okomi, chief of the pre-Columbian Nuwa tribe, abandons his wealth and status in order to visit a notorious witch doctor who he hopes will save his son.

Word Count: 3,000

Genre: Historical Fiction

Completed Week: August 28th – September 3rd

Wake

The boy's eyelids had somehow popped opened again. He stared up into the star-filled heavens.

Okomi, his father, shooed away the buzzing flies and swept his hand down over his son's face. He then turned and made another attempt at fire. The tinder wouldn't take. The fallen logs were soaked through from a recent rain and rubbing the stick back and forth, grinding it into the flat piece of wood, felt futile.

Yet he did not stop.

It took his mind off things. The cold desert night. The journey from home. The journey to see the witch doctor.

After some time, his hands nearly rubbed raw, smoke finally rose and the tinder glowed until flames spread onto smaller pieces of brush. He nursed the fire carefully until it was roaring at last. Seeming to sense Okomi's victory over the elements, coyotes howled in the distant hills. He hoped it was a sign of things to come.

He didn't want to rest, but he had been around long enough to know that if he kept on, he risked death. If that happened, all was hopeless. There was still much ground to cover before the doctor could wake his son, but his legs refused to carry him any further. Deep pain radiated across his chest and shoulders. Pulling the sled through gravel-filled washes and over uneven outcrops of granite taxed Okomi greatly.

He would soon cross into Vanyume territory. Every ounce of wit and strength he could muster might be enough to see him and his son through safely.

He pulled his son's sled next to the fire and drew a blanket from his supplies. Upon finding a suitably curved stone on which to rest his head, Okomi cleared the ground of rocks and made his bed. Some of the stars moved tonight, each one zipping off until its light went out in a brief but brilliant flash.

He thought about yesterday. Okomi had been a wealthy man. Chief of all the Nuwa people because of it. Now he carried only a fraction of his riches, forced to abandon the rest to the tribe. He turned to his son, reaching out to stroke the black hair caked to his forehead. The boy's face was pale and starting to swell. His head cold to the touch.

Let the fools fight over trinkets and chiefdom, he thought.

* * *

He dreamed of the boy's mother standing in the village, all of the Nuwa lined up at her side. She cursed Okomi for refusing funeral rites. She said that if he left the village with their child, then Pokoh, the god known as The Old Man, would punish them both for wandering from their homeland. Behind her stood the god, his feet thicker than twenty men clustered together. Taking the form of a snake, the god's great head touched the clouds and grounded back and forth with a terrible noise.

Okomi ignored their warnings. He declared he would go south and fight the Sun and the Moon to find the witch doctor. Pokoh lifted his great foot. It blotted out the night as it came rushing down on top of Okomi.

His eyes shot open. The stars were still there. The crickets were singing. He got up and added more wood to the fire until it roared once again. While he swept a scorpion and several vinegaroons from the blankets wrapped around his son's body, his eyes appraised the boy.

Let Pokoh and his people bluster, he thought. If Okomi buried his son, it would be an act of murder.

* * *

Before the Sun showed itself in the east, gusts carried dust across the land. Knoton, god of the wind, was angry. He always seemed to be angry in the vast desert lands south of the Nuwa border. Knoton's breath carried an odor and Okomi quickly realized it was coming from his son. Time was running short and though he knew deep down that it was the right decision, he cursed himself for not having traveled through the night.

He quickly packed camp, latched the sled's connected rope to his shoulders, and trekked south. After many more painstaking miles, Okomi came upon the great river that would eventually lead to his destination: a cave tunneled into a mountain beside a creek and spring of hot water. It was home to the secluded witch doctor, notorious throughout the land for her power, called upon during times of ceremony and distress. The Nuwa had a medicine man, but all he cared about was the rain.

Okomi walked along the river for a little while until he grew thirsty. He stopped and leaned down to drink from the river. A rock splashed inches from his face. He drew himself up quickly, nerves on end, looking for the perpetrator. Not twenty yards away, three dark men in loincloths stood watching him from a weed-covered slope. The two young ones were armed. One had a bow at his side. Another, a sling in his hand. They both appeared to be about fifteen winters in age. An older man stood between them. Okomi recognized the Vanyume chief by his long, crooked nose.

"You are foolish to come here, Nuwa-man."

Over the years, the two tribes had alternated trading and fighting. This was an age of war.

Okomi lifted his hands and spoke, "I am in your care, Huukp. I seek only to pass through to see the witch in the mountain." He nodded his head towards the sled carrying his son and belongings. "I bring you many gifts to pay a toll."

One of the boys, the one with the sling, walked cautiously towards the sled. He approached Okomi's son and within several feet, pinched his nose. He looked at Okomi with disgust.

"Why do you bring him with you?" he asked.

He answered Huukp as if he had asked the question. "As I said, I wish to see the witch. So that she will wake my son."

The boy looked back at the chief. Okomi could tell Huukp was mulling things over. Running into the Vanyume was a risk Okomi had been willing to take when he decided to follow the river. It was the quickest route to his destination.

After several moments of silence, the Vanyume chief spoke.

"Come with us."

Okomi looked at him with caution. His hands were still raised in supplication.

"You will be our guest for only today," Huukp said.

Not wanting to stop, but more not wanting to risk his goal having come this far, Okomi reluctantly reattached the ropes to his shoulders and followed the three of them.

* * *

"He must stay outside of the village."

Okomi didn't budge. They stood outside a tiny grouping of huts lining the outer banks of the river. The boy with the sling narrowed his eyes. His fists were curled.

"It's okay, Cairook."

The boy looked at his chief.

"But—"

Huukp held his hand up as if he were going to strike the boy. Cairook fell silent.

"You can leave your son beside the hut," Huukp said to Okomi. "Downwind."

The chief led him toward the indicated hut. Okomi pulled his son's sled to a spot where he could see him through the door while the boys went through the last of Okomi's material wealth: necklaces made of shells and several large geodes filled with purple amethyst.

"Your sons?" Okomi asked as they entered the tiny, rectangular dwelling made of yucca and willow brush. A small fire burned in the middle. Smoke flowed out of a hole in the roof.

"One of them has my temper, but my wisdom has yet to make itself known," Huukp replied.

Okomi tried not to appear anxious.

"Please sit," Huukp said. He sat on the dirt floor and indicated toward a spot beside him.

A woman entered the hut carrying a large bowl of steaming porridge and a baby at her breast. Huukp's wife, no doubt. The chief took the bowl from her hands and the woman left as silently as she had entered. He offered the bowl to Okomi.

Though his arms and shoulders screamed as he lifted the bowl to his mouth, Okomi found the acorn stew both sweet and nourishing. Huukp smiled slightly and nodded.

Okomi handed the bowl back to the chief and wiped his lips with the back of his arm. "I thank you for your hospitality and safe passage," he said.

Huukp slurped at the bowl. His mouth was full of porridge as he said, "If I suspected foul play, I would have killed you at your camp last night." He swallowed and handed the bowl back to Okomi.

Okomi looked at him, his eyebrows raised slightly.

"We have many eyes," the chief said.

They finished the bowl in silence. Okomi suspected the serving woman was watching because as soon as the porridge was gone, she reentered the hut carrying a long pipe and a handful of jimsonweed. Huukp packed the pipe, lit the weed with a burning stick from the fire, and puffed until the smoke entered his lungs. He coughed a little and handed it to Okomi.

Okomi took a hit from the pipe. It had been many moons since he had last smoked and it took only a few minutes for the lightheadedness to come.

"You are foolish to seek her aid," the chief said. His voice wheezed. "Though the doctor knows many things and her medicine is big, what you ask is…" His voice trailed off until he arrived at another question. "You do this for one son? Do you have no others?"

"Pokoh never blessed me with another," Okomi said.

Huukp stared at him and nodded towards the pipe. Okomi reluctantly took another puff. His head swam and he was growing tired. He tried to focus on his son's face through the bright entry. The wind kicked up the edges of blanket that covered him. An edge slapped lightly against the boy's cheek.

"How did he end up in this condition?"

Answers were not coming easily, but he was in the Vanyume's hands. He couldn't risk alienating the only thing standing between him and the witch.

"His first hunt," Okomi said reluctantly. "Five moons ago. He was to return to the village with a kill."

Okomi smoked the jimsonweed, taking it into his lungs, succumbing to its power now. His eyes never left his son's face, still pale, but now fat with bloated lips. He closed his eyes, trying to remember how his son looked before he [departed for the hunt].

"The Moon rose and he did not return. My wife begged me to go and find him." Okomi shook his head as if he were looking at her. "I told her that he was becoming a man. He must learn."

Pain choked his voice. "He must learn," he said again.

Okomi absent-mindedly handed the pipe back to Huukp, laid down on the blankets pulled over the packed dirt and closed his eyes. The initial swimming of vision calmed down. He heard the dull throb of his heart beating rhythmically in his ears.

"When I found him in the morning, he had already fallen asleep beneath a ridge. I could not wake him. His body was cool and stiff." He shook his head. "It must have been a very cold night." Okomi closed his eyes even tighter as if in physical pain. "The trail of the snake was carved in the dirt beside his body." An image of two bite marks on his son's left ankle filled his mind.

"I should have…"

The thought remained unfinished as he covered the boy's wound with one hand, looked up, and saw the great foot of Pokoh blotting out the Sun.

* * *

Something woke Okomi, eyes full of sleep. He was in the hut. It was night. The fire's embers were glowing and he turned his head to see Huukp snoring. There were faint whispers and the sounds of shuffling feet. He looked through the hut's opening and saw his son being dragged away by the legs.

"Let go of him!" he said, leaping to his feet. He ran outside and saw the outline of Huukp's sons.

"He should not be here," said the one who earlier had the sling. "You bring us all bad luck."

"Then we will leave," Okomi said. A fury stirred within him.

The young boys looked at each other and dropped the child's legs. They fell with a thump onto the dirt. Okomi looked inside the hut. The chief was still asleep. There was no sense in waking him. Okomi would travel now. He looked at the stars and determined the Sun would rise by the time he reached the creek.

* * *

The chief must have previously gotten word out to all of his scouts for Okomi and his son arrived at the creek, unmolested. The night had been another cold one. Steam rose from one the springs next to the cave. The Sun had shown itself just as Okomi expected, revealing that his son had not fared well on the journey. Bloody foam was running from his nose and mouth. Okomi stopped and cleaned his face.

As if expecting them, the witch stood in front of her dark home. Her hair was matted with mud and her pendulous breasts were wrinkled. They nearly touched her belly. She was tall for a woman, and like Huukp, she also had a crooked nose.

"Bring him inside," she said, smiling a toothless smile.

He followed her in. There was no fire lit and it took a moment for his eyes to adjust to the black. The witch seemed to have no problem finding her way around. She shuffled various bowls of clay and wood on a flat piece of stone, emptying their contents into a shallow mortar. She ground the ingredients with her pestle. Okomi collapsed on the ground beside his son, allowing himself to feel the lingering drowsiness of the jimsonweed. He had made it.

Unhurried, the witch continued her work. Okomi grew impatient.

"Can you wake him?"

She ignored Okomi. Now she took a blunt rock and hammered a large root into powder, finally mixing it with the rest of the ingredients. Watching her and listening to her work felt like a dream. After what seemed a hundred moons, the commotion stopped. She scooped the mixture into a small wooden cup carved out of an acorn and walked outside. Okomi wanted to follow her but his legs refused to cooperate. He had pushed himself to his limits to arrive here. His train of thought mattered little as she strode back in through the bright entrance.

"Drink," she said. She handed him the wooden cup, now full of warm liquid. Okomi felt steam rise and spread onto his face.

Is she blind, he wondered?

"I am not the one that is sick."

"Drink."

The scent was noxious. There was nothing else to do now. No other choices. Okomi had to put his faith in the witch. At first he sipped, but the taste was so bad it made him retch. He looked at the witch. She nodded and he gulped it down, ignoring the heat.

Now she took a seat on the ground beside him. Her knees cracked as she collapsed. The creek's running water echoed in the cave.

"Now what?"

"We wait."

The red foam began to accumulate again on his son's face. Okomi reached out to clean it but the witch grabbed his arm and forced it back into his lap.

"What are we waiting for?"

"The spirits."

He fought to stay awake. The jimsonweed, the hard travel, maybe even whatever he just drank, seemed to conspire together to distract him from his task. With the patience of an ancient tree, Okomi watched the shadows at the entrance of the cave change slowly from the movement of the Sun.

At some point, he stood forcefully. He placed a hand on the cave wall. It took every ounce of remaining strength to remain upright. The witch stared up at him and he stared back.

"I have traveled far, faced my enemies, and you tell me to wait for the spirits. Make them come!"

He demanded an answer and he would beat it out of the crone if she refused.

"You bring me your son. You want me to wake him."

"Yes," Okomi said, exasperated. She was finally understanding. Living alone for so long and communing with ghosts had confused her mind.

"But, Nuwa-man, he is not the one sleeping," she said.

The once powerful chief sunk to his knees beside his son, unable to fight the dizziness any longer. Crimson lather caked the boy's bloated face. From the corners of his mouth, a trail of tiny maggots marched out onto his cheek. The smell that had been there all along seemed to increase in strength. Okomi laid down on the ground and put his hand on his son's chest. He felt his own heartbeat pulsing through his body, radiating outward into his fingertips. Time slowed. The old woman became a blur in the corner of his vision.

* * *

He dreamed again. They climbed the mountain east of the village. He felt the arrows shake lightly across his back. With the bow hanging over his left shoulder, his son stepped in front of him and took hold of an outcropping. He was about to pull himself up, but Okomi grabbed ahold of his arm and held him. His son looked back. The chief held a finger to his lips and then used it to point at the ground several feet in front of them.

A trail wound through the dirt, leading toward the dark shadow of a rock.

His son smiled.

It was the first of many days in which they would hunt together. The dream would never end.

They went another way.

Process Summary

Wake is story number five in the #52ShortStories challenge.

I took a different tack with this story. Normally I kick things off with a mind map, but an image of a Native American man sitting in front of a roaring fire in the middle of a cold desert night refused to leave my head. It made sense to me to just jump right into the prose and discover what he was doing there.

One of the things I've learned in my study of writing is that it's hard to keep things interesting when someone is alone with only their thoughts. It may be fascinating to me as the writer, but as a reader, long internalizations need to strike the right chord if I'm to stick with them. So I compromised. Okomi was not alone, but only in the sense that his son's body was there with him.

As soon as I determined that, the questions started coming rapid fire: Why is he sitting around a fire with his dead son? Is he waiting for something or someone? Going somewhere? What happened to his son?

That only got me so far. I hit a bit of writer's block, so I pulled up the mindmap. I took a temporary title of "The Dead Son" and a wonderful phrase from a Ralph Waldo Emerson poem to see what I could devise:

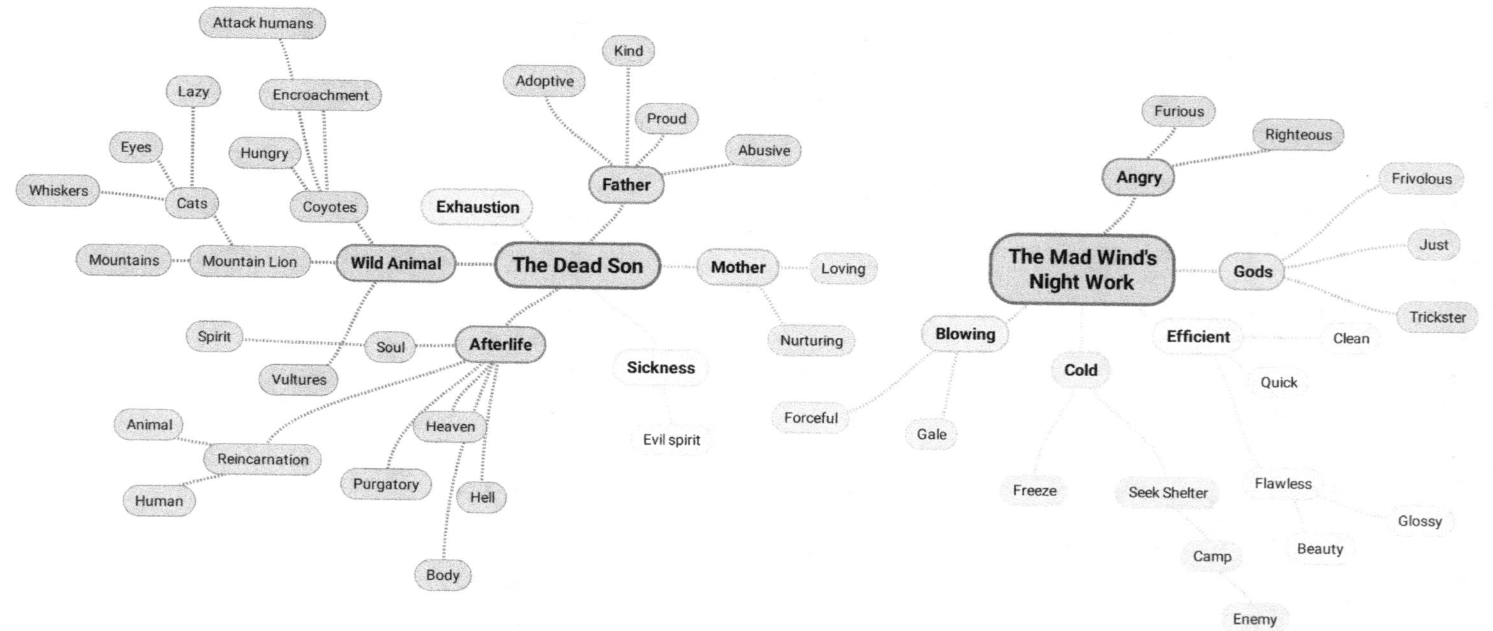
The Mad Wind's Night Work
Angry
Furious
Righteous
Frivolous
Gods
Just
Trickster
Clean
Efficient
Quick
Flawless
Glossy
Beauty
Camp
Enemy
Seek Shelter
Cold
Freeze
Blowing
Gale
Forceful
Mother
Loving
Nurturing
Sickness
Evil spirit
The Dead Son
Father
Kind
Adoptive
Proud
Abusive
Exhaustion
Afterlife
Soul
Heaven
Purgatory
Hell
Body
Reincarnation
Animal
Human
Spirit
Vultures
Wild Animal
Mountain Lion
Mountains
Cats
Whiskers
Eyes
Hungry
Coyotes
Lazy
Encroachment
Attack humans

There were some useful elements to be found here, but nothing really beckoned me forth. I ended up reading some of the Native American reference books I have in my library and that helped.

I set Okomi up as a chief of the real Kawaiisu tribe in the Mojave Desert of Southern California. They referred to themselves as the Nuwa and to their south lived another real tribe, the Vanyume. These interested me because I grew up in the original territory of the Vanyume. There's not much known about them, unfortunately (or fortunately, since it gifts me a lot of poetic license). It's almost certain that they lived a hard-scrabble life in such a harsh environment, though.

There was opportunity for conflict here. Both the Vanyume and Kawaiisu are described as a mostly peaceful people, but there was likely the occasional border dispute and fighting over sparse resources.

From there, I sprinkled in some mythology and I was on my way. You can read my scratch file and journal entries for more detail. You may get a chuckle out of the fact that my temporary names for Okomi and his son were Bob and Alex, respectively... Quite authentic, I know.

THE RUNNER

Statistics

Synopsis: The Tendai monks of Japan are an ascetic Buddhist order where the highest honors go to those who complete a 1,000-day run. With one day left to go, Kenichi-san finds himself running directly into the unexpected.

Word Count: 3,000

Genre: Supernatural

Completed Week: September 4th – September 10th

The Runner

A man is a god in ruins.

- Ralph Waldo Emerson, *Nature*

They call this the land of the rising sun, but as I soaked in the rays of a full moon, I thought it was beautiful enough to have equal claim.

Leaning against an uncomfortable boulder, I rubbed the sleepiness from my eyes and looked east over shimmering Lake Biwa. It loomed large, even when seen from nine hundred meters above sea level. In the humid summers, it's one of the few sources of relief to those living below. But here, atop Mount Hiei, the air was crisp.

Behind me, down the mountain, sat Kyoto. After nearly seven years, I had almost forgotten the misery of day-to-day living on its sweltering blacktop streets and cramped office spaces.

Since then, I've been running.

The *kaihōgyō* is a mission of selfless devotion in search of enlightenment, practiced by the Tendai monks for a millennium. This mountain has felt my trampling feet for nine hundred and ninety-nine of the required thousand days.

Thirty kilometers a day, one hundred days each year, for the first three years. Then it's two hundred days for years four and five.

Those first few years were difficult in many ways. My feet had been abused and molded into something resembling hard oak and whatever exposed skin, into the toughest leather. But that fifth year seemed to be a turning point. For seven-and-a-half days I went without food, water, or rest, forced to sit in a temple and chant. My fellow monks ensured I did not fall asleep and there were many times I felt that I was no longer in my body. I saw things I never wished to see again and I was happy to be running the trails once more.

The distance doubled in year six, though back to one hundred days. And now, in year seven, eighty-four kilometers for one hundred days, returning to thirty for the final hundred.

Each of the billions of steps I've taken up to this point have had the same result: one more step.

It would all end, soon.

The next several thousand will be more significant than any other. My fellow monks are waiting for me at Enryaku-ji.

Number forty-seven! they'll cheer as I climb the carved steps to the central temple.

No one can remember number forty-six, but his name is recorded in a book somewhere deep inside the monastery.

I stood up, adjusted my oblong wooden hat, and stretched my legs before descending down the back of the mountain.

* * *

She was a simple silhouette in the middle of the trail.

Hikers aren't an unusual sight on Mount Hiei, but never in the shade of night, and never one whose aspect matched that of this woman. She was facing the stones and shrubs that smothered the steep hill to my left, such that I could only see the outline of the left side of her body. A perfect gap in the trees filtered moonlight around her form.

Her hair was cropped close to her head. A hump rose over her stooped back. I expected her to have a cane or a walking stick, but her small hands hung low and empty at her sides. The dress she wore was thin and certainly not made for hiking. Except for a white cotton throw draped over her shoulders, she must have been freezing.

I didn't have a watch, so I don't recall the exact time, but I had become adept at reading the stars and knew that dawn would not arrive for some time.

"Hello," I said.

She didn't reply.

"Are you lost?" I asked.

Concerned, I walk toward her, hearing every crunch of my straw sandals on the packed dirt. I stopped maybe a meter from her and she still hadn't moved or responded in any way.

I followed her line of sight and was not completely surprised to see a small, red-furred fox peeking its head out from a bush of geraniums. They tend to hunt this time of night, especially with the lack of foot traffic.

I tried again. "Pardon me, miss, do you need—"

She turned her head and I shrank back, losing my balance, waving my arms wildly to avoid a fall to the ground. My stomach felt as if it would drop out of my body. Her lips were twisted into a snarl on the right side of her mouth, connecting to a blackened cheek. One eye was fleshed over, missing an eyebrow and I saw now that her hair was missing on the right side of her skull—all part of a continuous flow of scarred skin that resembled melted cheese.

I recovered and felt ashamed at my behavior. Still, I kept a respectful distance.

"I'm sorry," I said, stammering out an excuse. "There is usually no one else here at this hour."

She tilted her head as if confused and slowly turned back towards the bottom of the trail which disappeared into a curve lined with cedar trees. Again, I followed her eyes and saw a group of strangers. It was difficult to separate them out as they were huddled together, but I guessed there were about ten or fifteen of them. Skinny and tall. Short and fat. Everything in between.

I admit I grew frightened again. I couldn't tell you why. It seemed the explanation could have been as simple as a tour group left behind.

Yet I ran back up the hill. It's what I did best. I decided I would catch the other trail that came down the side facing Lake Biwa and double back on a side trail to the monastery.

It wasn't until I reached the apex where I had earlier been sitting that I stopped to catch my breath. I was used to keeping a steady pace when running, but the uphill sprint left me breathless and an old familiar pang radiated through my quadriceps. I paced slowly back and forth, my hands above my head so that I could take more air into my lungs, staring back in the direction from which I had come. There appeared to be no one following me.

Feeling the shame return, I thought that maybe I should go back and try to help them. Somehow, though, I convinced myself that it would be wiser to continue down the back trail and wind around the mountain to Enryaku-ji. I could alert the other monks and they would want to help.

* * *

They say that when you're young, you dream of the future, but when you're old, you dream of the past. I hadn't dreamed of anything in a long time, but as I found myself coming around another corner and facing the old woman again, I had to wonder.

This time she faced me directly. The moonlight, again, amplified her frightful condition. She stood in front of a group of people. The same? Maybe.

Nineteen total.

I counted them quickly. I had always been good with numbers.

I noticed they all had a grayish look about them, like they were coated in dust.

This time they were lined up only a few meters behind her, hand in hand, blocking the trail like a human fence. I was taken aback to realize there were children there. Little girls in flowing blue kimonos and young boys with buttoned white shirts, their hands in their pockets. School uniforms.

Movement at the woman's feet caught my eye. It was another fox.

A part of me knew it was futile to run back up the hill. I turned to do so anyway, but my legs lost their strength as the damned old woman was in front of me once again, this time a similar group of people behind her.

Twelve, now. Their flesh also faded and dirty.

"What do you want?!" I shouted. "Help!" came inadvertently after, useless since it was choked off by the lump in my throat. I could only hope another monk was taking a midnight walk, but it was unlikely this far up the mountain.

The fox walked through the old woman's legs, brushing up against them like a cat, and sauntered forward. I was frozen. My mind calculated the possibility of jumping down into the steep ravine on my left, but the drops in between stone bastions were too steep. I'd never make it.

"You lost your hat."

My hand went to my bald pate. I shook my head, first slowly and then quickly. My eyes focused on the fox. I don't know that I could see its jaws moving or that it would have mattered. I was sure I was dreaming now.

I shut my eyes. "Wake up," I said quietly to myself. A cold breeze stirred, chilling the sweat on my skin.

Something tugged at my white robe. I looked down and saw the fox with the bottom of it between her sharp little teeth.

"I said, you lost your hat," the fox spoke again, slightly muffled by the material in her mouth.

After three hundred days of running with the hat under my left arm, like all Tendai monks, I was given the privilege to wear it on my head. Since then, it had rarely left, even at night when I used it to shade my eyes during sleep. It must have fallen off during my frantic run.

A disturbing realization swept over me.

"Am I dead?"

Was that why she mentioned my hat? Inside of it was a coin, a roku-mon-sen, used to pay the toll to cross the Sanzu River should I perish before the end of my seven-year journey.

The fox let go of my robe and tittered, or what I think was a titter. Foxes make the strangest sounds.

"No, Kenichi-san. You don't need your coin today. Unless you so choose."

I looked up at the people again. All emotionless, staring at me with lamented eyes. Memories of childhood flooded my mind: stories of the wood spirits known to populate Mount Hiei. And Inari, that tricky goddess who often appeared in the form of a fox.

It had to be a dream. I convinced myself it couldn't be anything but. So I played along hoping it would usher its end and I would wake on the top of the mountain, sleeping high above the lake, ready to complete my trial.

"You are Inari?" I asked.

In the blink of an eye, the fox was gone and I found myself facing a beautiful, and completely naked, woman, the likes of which I'd never laid eyes on. The moon revealed straight, black hair with a tint of red. Her eyes resembled terracotta, shaded slightly by long, thick eyelashes. And her lips. They were crimson against snow-white skin. I had a wife once who was pretty in her own way, but never like this.

I attempted to direct my eyes away in modesty, but her hand gripped my chin and gently held it in place.

"I am," she replied. Her breath smelled of sweet mint leaf.

With her other hand, she turned my right arm over and pushed its sleeve up to my elbow. Her hold was gentle and every muscle in my body relaxed in her presence. She looked down.

"Pretty. What do these mean?"

I strained to look at my arm. Though I saw my flesh every morning, every time I bathed, every time I changed my robes, it had been almost seven years since I had *looked* at it.

"They are nothing," I said and attempted to pull my arm back. The woman's grip tightened like a snake around a rat.

"They are *not* nothing," she said, this time quite forcefully. "Tell me what they mean."

I really wanted to wake up. I did not want to look at those markings again. If I could have cut them from my body, I would have. I felt strangled by the presence of the others. Though they hadn't come any closer, it seemed as if they were collapsing in on me like mahjong tiles.

I took a deep breath. My eyes traced the faded, but still intricate patterns which coated my arms and ran up into the hidden confines of my robe.

They were my *irezumi*—my inserted ink. My wrist marked the end of a series of vines that twisted together and wrapped around the edge of a samurai's blade. Its honed edge sliced through the middle of a delicate pink lotus.

"They mean that I have lived another life."

"What kind of life?" Her question was swift.

I looked at her light brown eyes and saw that she was already peering back at me.

"I was an accountant."

"Things sure have changed in the world," she said. "A money counter with such beautiful pictures pressed into his skin."

"I don't want to talk about this. Please, Inari, let me go. I need to return to the shrine."

"You have been on a long journey, Kenichi-san. I'm sure you are tired." She let go of my arm and it felt as if a hot iron had been pulled from my flesh. I still felt the sting of her grip.

"I will let you go, of course, but first you must answer some questions."

I would have done almost anything to be free of the goddess and those who surrounded us now.

"Yes, anything," I replied.

"What will you do when you return?"

The question struck me odd. I replied, "I will probably sleep for a very long time," though I doubted I would ever sleep again after tonight.

"And then what?"

I hadn't thought that far ahead. In all honesty, it was a question that had been in the back of my mind, but I was afraid of answering. Over the years, I had put all of my energy and thoughts into only one thing: the next step.

"I suppose that I will pray and tend to duties around the monastery."

"I see," she said. She backed up a little now and her companions seemed to follow in lockstep. It gave me full view of her body and try as I might to look away, I couldn't. The goddess didn't seem to mind.

"I've done my time, goddess."

"Your time? For what? Have you committed a crime?"

Why did I say that? Her questions opened up old wounds. I straightened up and looked her in the eyes.

"I have committed no crime."

Inari stretched her arms in indication of the people surrounding her. "There is some disagreement there."

I stared at all of them. The life had been sucked out of all of their faces and their dead gazes made the hairs on the back of my neck stand up. "You know who I am."

"Tell us."

I ground my teeth until I could finally force the words.

"I worked for the Yakuza," I said, exasperated, "but I only kept their books. And I have not lived that life for many years!" My voice pleaded, "What do you *want* me to say?"

She stepped up to me again and laid her hand on my cheek. Her eyes were expressions of empathy. "I want nothing but for you to understand that which you already know."

Now I grew indignant and crossed my arms. "Understand what?"

"Why you are on this mountain. Why you are responsible."

That was the heart of things, then. A memory buried deep in my subconscious. I wondered when the last time was that I thought about the beginning of my journey. A lost soul arriving at the temple, looking to get away from something.

"I was simply an accountant." It came out as a whisper.

"Simply," she said with little emotion. Inari tutted her tongue as she turned and looked at the old woman. "Simply ensured that your bosses could pay the men who burned Yoshiko to death in her home because her son could not remit his gambling debts." She looked at the small children covered in dust. "Simply ensured that the pockets of thugs were filled with coin so that they willingly buried an entire village alive because their elder had repeatedly refused protection in the marketplace."

My heart constricted and tears streamed down my face, blurring my vision. I bawled like a baby while the goddess still had her hand on my cheek.

"You thought that you could run away," she said. The gleam in her eyes still evoked compassion. "You can, you know."

I looked at her and then at the dreary people behind her who shuffled and spread apart, leaving a gap to the trail.

"Run?"

"Either that or use the tools that were given to you at the beginning."

I looked down at the short, sharp blade and piece of hemp rope that were attached to my belt. All Tendai monks are given these in case they cannot fulfill their thousand-day journey. Disembowelment or hanging—dealer's choice.

"If you return to the monastery, you will die anyway," she finished.

I finally understood. I looked at the people, then to the opening. Their eyes had turned away. Inari stepped aside, providing me an opportunity.

I wiped my tears away and ran through them all until I was out of breath and I finally collapsed onto the ground.

* * *

My back ached and I jumped up, realizing where I was. The moon was hanging over Lake Biwa. My hands went to my head. I felt the thin wooden slats of my hat and sighed.

I ran down the mountain and soon found myself standing timidly behind a grouping of cedars. Enryaku-ji was only twenty meters away. Red and white streamers hung across the gates and a pair of monks were busy standing up a large sign with the number *forty-seven* written across.

I looked down at the rope and knife. They felt heavier than I've ever known them to and I realized that I had already made my decision.

My sandals crunched on the packed trail dirt as I turned back, relaxed my shoulders, and took one step in front of the other.

Process Summary

The Runner is story number six in the #52ShortStories challenge.

This one was unusual for me in several different ways:

I didn't mind map at all.

I don't know why, but I decided to skip the mind mapping and just use freewriting to flesh out the concept. It seemed to work.

I wrote in the first person.

The only reason I thought to do this was to help myself grow beyond my defaults. I always default to the third person because when I first started writing "seriously" six years ago, I had read that it's what agents and publishers wanted.

Really?!

I realized how stupid it was that I've stuck with this idea for so long. It's always challenging to move beyond the defaults, but well worth it in the end. I know there are some tricky tense errors in there, but like all of these stories I've written, it'll go through a copy editing process before being professionally published.

After a painful slog through the last story, writing this one was more enjoyable.

I needed this easy (easier) win. After the last couple of stories, this one seemed to fly off the keyboard in comparison. I don't know if it's a fluke. Is it because I didn't mind map? Is it because I was more comfortable with the subject matter? Is it because of this…because of that? Will the next one be so easy?

How about after that?

So many questions and I'm not sure I can answer them all. Still, I'm trying to keep track in the hopes that all of the data will amount to some insight.

One thing I found funny is how this all started.

There I was, in the middle of sit-ups at the gym, when my brain latched on to a setting that I hadn't read about for some time—the running Tendai monks of Mount Hiei. Funny how the subconscious works. I'm sure the fact that I was abusing my body in the name of good health had something to do with it. I quickly made some notes on my phone (see Monday's journal entry) and after some podcast inspiration from Ryan Holiday on getting over the fear of the blank page, I started writing as soon as I got home.

Again, you'll see in the scratch file an evolution from concept to story. There are quite a few dead ends, but I found my way eventually.

I'll wrap this up here, but thought I'd leave you with a little quote from Tuesday's journal entry: *I'm having fun. I suppose that's the most important thing needed to produce every day.*

Lights Out: An MC Ruff and DJ Tumble Adventure

Statistics

Synopsis: MC Ruff and DJ Tumble are a pair of hip-hop throwbacks, touring the galaxy in support of their new album. Unfortunately, someone is looking to force them into an early, permanent retirement.

Word Count: 11,400

Genre: Sci-Fi / Mystery / Humor

Completed Week: September 11th – September 30th

Lights Out: An MC Ruff and DJ Tumble Adventure

Break it down,

Shake it down,

Ruff and Tumble make your world go 'round.

A small amount of feedback came through the stage monitors. MC Ruff made the universal *turn it the hell down* symbol to the girl running the sound booth.

You,

know,

we ain't gonna stop,

Not 'til we done make your booty pop.

The crowd waved their raised hands from side to side, barely visible through a haze of synthetic smoke and beams of red and green light. Ruff could smell years of accumulated sweat and spilled alcohol. He zeroed in on one young kid and his girlfriend as a mass of fans pressed the two of them against the front of the stage. The girl's hands were wrapped around the boy's left arm. While he bounced around to the beat, she held on, staring listlessly at Ruff as if she were dreaming about planning their nuptials and the resultant seven little brats.

Since it was impossible to see the majority of the audience because of the lights, Ruff liked to focus on people in the front row. They paid the most credits anyway, so why not make them feel special? Besides, they would tell all of their friends about the amazing night ("I swear, Rhonda, he was looking right at me!") Word of mouth sold tickets and tickets sold merchandise and that's where the real money was. No cut to the venue. No cut to Sharky, their manager. No cut to the record label that Ruff and his partner had signed their life away to in youthful ignorance.

Just pure credits deposited directly into his Intergalactic Blockchain account.

From behind the couple, a familiar face emerged, or rather, a familiar hairdo.

Ice Cubicle: Ruff and Tumble's tongue-twisting, rapid fire-spitting rival from Newtonium Records.

His coiffed tower of aqua-blue hair stood a foot tall like a tapered, upside-down salt shaker. Even through the haze, Ruff could swear he saw him wink and smile.

Whatever. Though he was probably here to try and throw off the dynamic duo's game, he was just as free as the rest of the crowd to be entranced by the mad skills of MC Ruff and DJ Tumble .

Ruff looked back at the man behind the turntables. His friend of funkified flow. His compadre of beat concatenation. Long ago, in a galaxy not so far away, they were young punks sneaking into shows just like this. The deft DJ slid his hands smoothly across the reproduced vinyl and scratched out a little ditty. Then he spun around while the corners of his red leather jacket flipped in the air. He picked up the beat without a moment's hesitation. His gold-capped teeth gleamed in reflection of the stage lights. Tumble was too busy to notice Cubicle. All for the better, Ruff thought.

He turned back toward the front of the stage. Cubicle was gone. He was lost in the packed sea of two hundred clubgoers. Not a large crowd by any means, but Chubb's was a tiny venue. Normally, Ruff and Tumble played arenas averaging fifty thousand, but they liked impromptu gigs in tiny clubs every once in awhile, especially with new releases. They would announce the ticket sales on their Twister account the night before. These types of gigs kept them grounded. Closer to the fans.

Tumble's rapidly clicking hi-hats faded out and the crowd applauded wildly.

"Meridia 7, we love you!"

Ruff knew it was cliche, but that never stopped the people from going wild every time they heard their home planet mentioned.

"I just want to say that y'all have been the funkiest, freshest crowd we've played for."

A pair of incoming panties landed on his shoulder. He raised his eyebrows and picked them off. Pink, gigantic, and unadorned, they looked like something his grandma would have worn.

"Aww. Y'all know how to make this MC and DJ feel welcome."

More screams and applause. The auditorium vibrated under pressure.

"Unfortunately, all good things must come to an end."

Now groans reverberated through the crowd.

"But we gonna send you off with somethin' you ain't never gonna forget!"

On cue, Tumble launched into their newest single. Analog crackle permeated the air. The thumping 808 kickdrum seemed to envelop them all like a warm, smothering hug.

Boom.

Boom.

Boom.

Boom.

Hundreds of years after its invention, the famous Roland drum machine sample was still a staple, though highly regulated. Because it was a low frequency sine wave that could cause structural damage if left unchecked, every sample was automatically run against a cryptographic hash function to ensure it didn't exceed Federation parameters on auditory tones (Section XVII, subsection 12, paragraph c, subparagraph iv of Federation Statutes on Audio and Visual Performances).

A dreamy, distant saxophone loop rode on top of the beat.

"Who... wants… to rumble?"

Ruff held the mic out over the audience.

We do! We do!

"I said, who... wants... to rumble?"

We do! We do!

The music stopped. The crowd hushed.

"Ha ha. Yo..."

A brief pause.

"...you know you can't mess with Ruff and Tumble."

A sonic assault of blistering breakbeats was unleashed. Ruff watched as a mad intensity swept through the crowd until they became one pulsating mass. He used the opportunity to bend down behind a speaker cabinet and take a quick swig from his hydration bottle. The next verse was a long one. As he lowered himself, he felt a little twinge in his back and so he slowed himself. He shook his head. This is a young man's game, he thought. He and Tumble had only been halfway through the first track before he began looking forward to getting back on the ship, taking a shower, and picking up where he left off on Grandmaster Bash's thought-provoking *The Rise and Decline and Re-rise of Hip Hop - An Historical Introspection - 1979 to 2133.*

Of course, that wasn't going to happen anytime soon. There would be the impromptu autograph sessions on the way out of the venue. Kids trying to upload their tracks directly to his ID cube in the vain hope of securing their own record deal. And then Tumble would want to invite some of the better looking groupies into the dressing room, partying until who knows how late.

These were only a few of the thoughts racing through his mind when the music halted and the lights went out. The roar of the crowd turned into a few moans of confusion.

Ruff looked back at Tumble, but couldn't see anything but a vague outline standing still with his hands to his giant earphones.

Damn it. Can't this facility keep their act together long enough for us to finish the show?

He had barely peeked his head out over the Mars Shell speaker cabinet to see what was happening when something bright and red flew by his face, tickling the right side of his head. He instantly smelled burnt hair.

"The fuck?" he said.

No sooner had the words emptied from his mouth then he felt a body fall on top of him and press him painfully into the ground. If his back wasn't already going to be sore tomorrow, that about guaranteed it.

"Clear a path! Set up a perimeter!"

The voice was loud and clear even through his earplugs. Ruff didn't know what was happening, but he was relieved that he recognized the voice as belonging to Nizumi, his head of security. Otherwise he would have jammed an elbow into the busta's face and fought his way back onto his feet. He hadn't been back to the neighborhood he grew up in for many years, neither physically nor mentally, but the street-smart instincts were still burned into his nerves.

"What's goin' on?" he asked.

Nizumi ignored him. "Metsk, verify the back entrance. Dado, you got Tumble? And Sanchez, tell this shit venue's so-called security team that they need to get the crowd out of here."

Ruff heard no reply. Nizumi was likely using her nanoset to communicate. He thought it best to wait. Sounds of chaos were still evident in the crowd, though it seemed to grow quieter.

After countless curses and a few "good"'s, Nizumi finished with, "Okay, I'm bringing him through."

The lights were still out but by now, Ruff's eyes had adjusted. "You want to tell me what's up?"

"Other than the fact that someone tried to shoot your face off, I'll let you know as soon as I find out," she said.

The red light. A laser weapon.

"Shoot me? For real?"

"For real."

Ruff took a deep breath. The rap game was getting dangerous these days.

Nizumi picked up Ruff like he was made of paper and rushed him along toward the back of the stage. Phase pistol in hand, she shielded him every step of the way. They wound their way through a narrow hallway and made it to the dressing room. Inside, they paused for moment. Tumble was standing in front of the mirror in which they had meticulously checked their fly outfits only an hour earlier. The DJ seemed shaken up, but that only meant his eyes were a little less glazed over than normal. Dado, Nizumi's unassuming, yet dangerous cousin, stood beside him, his eyes focused on the door through which they just entered.

"You cool?" Ruff asked Tumble.

"Yeah," Tumble said. The disappointment was evident in his voice. No groupies tonight.

Metsk was peaking out the rear door. His enormous back was to them. He was a big man—half Samoan, half German—nearly seven-feet tall with a dark brown ponytail reaching his waist. The constant odor of spam followed him around like a lost puppy.

"We're clear," he said.

"Sanchez," Nizumi said into her nanoset, "we're headed back to The Fly Honey. Stick around and find out what you can. We'll pick you up in a couple of hours."

Ruff and Tumble were ushered outside under Meridia 7's dim green sky and shoved onto their transport. They collapsed onto a pair of dark leather couches lining the inside of the cabin. The propulsion drives kicked in and they were on their way back to their ship.

"Keep an eye out," Nizumi said to Dado. He manned the navigational controls instead of relying on autopilot.

Then she turned to Ruff.

"You're welcome."

Ruff smiled graciously and nodded. She could have this one. He had debated bringing the full security detail with them. It took away some of the intimacy of the small club shows, but Nizumi had managed to convince him otherwise. He insisted she do something fun for the night, maybe even, you know, relax, but she insisted right back that nothing could be more fun than security and there was no way she could relax knowing he and Tumble were playing Chubb's without their own eyes and ears.

At least tonight, he was glad for her stubbornness.

* * *

"It had to be Cubicle!" Ruff said.

"Seems likely," Nizumi replied.

Tumble only nodded and poured himself a Tanqueray and soda from The Fly Honey's well-stocked wet bar.

"Which is why I have my doubts," she finished.

"I don't doubt anything," Ruff said. "That sucka's been bitin' my rhymes for so long, he finally decided there was only enough room for him in the game. You've seen his numbers. He hasn't gone platinum in two albums. Homeboy's jealous." He looked up at Nizumi. She was pacing the titanium floor as she always did. "You got the Meridia authorities involved, right?"

She shook her head.

"What? Why the—"

She held up her hand.

"That's not the only reason I have my doubts." She walked over to the communication console and docked her ID cube. Sanchez's face flashed on the screen and Ruff knocked over a pair of half-empty cocktail glasses on the table besides him.

Next to him was the girl from the front row. Her face was smeared with eye shadow left behind by poorly wiped tears.

"Sanchez, tell him what you told me," Nizumi said.

Sanchez spoke. "She says she saw who fired the shot."

Ruff's jaw was slack. "No shit?"

"No shit," Sanchez said.

"Well let's hear it!" Ruff said. Tumble nodded his head quickly.

"Mr. MC Ruff, I...When...I..."

She swallowed, or tried to, but her tongue was tied. Ruff was anxious to find out what she had to say, but he knew she needed to feel comfortable first.

He tried to put on a congenial smile. "Take a deep breath, girl."

Her chest, graced by a tank-top bearing an image of Ruff and Tumble's first album cover, rose in an exaggerated manner.

"I'm only telling you because—"

"Yo, you don't need to explain. Just tell us who did it."

She sighed.

"It was Derek."

"Derek? Who the hell is Derek?"

"My boyfriend."

"It wasn't Cubicle?"

"What? Was he there?" Her face lit up momentarily. So much for fan loyalty.

"Have you told anyone else?" Nizumi interrupted.

"No," she replied. Her voice was choked. "I thought I should—"

"Good," Nizumi replied. "Did anyone else see him?"

"I...I don't..."

She was growing flustered again. Ruff stepped in. "It's okay. Look, don't fret, girl. Do you know why he tried to shoot me? I mean, I know a lot of peeps didn't like our change of direction on this last cut, but damn..."

She shook her head and her face lit up. "Oh no, Mr. MC Ruff! We both love Broke No Mo'. It's one of your best yet." There was that gleam in her eye that he saw earlier at Chubb's.

"So why'd he do it? Tumble was cuttin' so hard. Ruined his flow, man."

Tumble scrunched his eyebrows and looked indignant.

"Derek's a good dude," the girl said defiantly. "Something...I don't know. It was like he snapped. As soon as the breakbeats kicked in on the last song, he stopped moving and got real stiff. Then all of the sudden..."

"All of the sudden what?" Nizumi asked.

"You're gonna think I'm crazy." She looked at Sanchez.

"Tell 'em what you told me." he said.

She paused for a second and took another deep breath.

"I swear, it was...a laser shot out of his eyes. Or his eye. His left eye." Obviously still in shock, she was searching for the right words and memories. Ruff felt some sympathy for her, but then remembered he had to be on his guard. She could still be lying about this whole thing.

"Where is he now?" Nizumi asked.

"I don't know," she said.

If she was acting, Ruff thought, she was pulling it off.

"I lost him as soon as the crowd panicked. After the shot, he seemed to...wake up. He was still dazed and I backed away from him." She shook her head. "I was so scared, I didn't know what was happening. And then these big security guys pushed through, knocked me over, grabbed him and took off. I could barely stand up, the crowd was just going crazy. Even when I got to my legs, they were so shaky and there was a mad rush to the door."

"Security guys?" Nizumi looked at Sanchez.

He shrugged. "Not us," he said. "Chubb's lead says none of his guys were involved. He shamefully admitted none of them were even on the floor at that time."

"What did they look like?" Nizumi asked.

"They were just...big. It was too dark to see and they had helmets on."

Ruff could practically see the synaptic connections forming in his head of security's mind.

The girl continued. "By the time I got outside, Derek was gone. I asked everyone that was still around but no one knew anything.

"When I saw him asking questions," she indicated toward Sanchez, "I thought you guys would know where he was. I even hoped it was a part of the show."

"I had her call his ID cube," Sanchez said. "It's registering as disconnected."

The tears came bursting through again as the girl broke down.

"Come on now, girl," Ruff said. "We'll find out what's going on. What's your name?"

"Nina." Or something that sounded like that. Hard to tell through the sobs. "I don't know who really tried to hurt you tonight, Mr. MC Ruff, but I know it wasn't Derek. He would never try to hurt you. Or Tumble."

Tumble smiled.

"Sanchez, Metsk is already on his way to pick you up. We'll talk more when you're back on The Fly Honey."

The screen shut off and Nizumi stepped in front of Ruff.

"She telling the truth?"

"We have to assume so." She shook her head in disgust. "Chubb's didn't even have their feeds running, so we have nothing to verify. It probably would have been useless through all of the smoke, anyway."

Ruff sat down again, exasperated. He noticed Tumble was already on his third cocktail.

"I'm glad to have you, Nizumi," he said.

"Don't be. You were almost killed."

"You couldn't have—"

"It's my job."

She was always too hard on herself. A trait that made her sometimes miserable to be around but, Ruff supposed, good at what she did.

"And you know what makes me most nervous?"

It was a question not expecting an answer from anyone but herself.

"You two are playing to a sold-out crowd at Ruebos in two days. After tonight, I'm supposed to keep you safe at one of the galaxy's largest festivals? Between now and then, I need to figure out who's got it in for you."

"*We*," Ruff said. "*We'll* figure it out. Look, I ain't frettin' over it."

Artists were used to lying.

Tumble shook his head in deep contemplation while his knees bounced nervously up and down.

"Man, what happened to the days of dissin' on records and battlin' on the mic?" Dado chimed in. "Now we got fools shootin' lasers out of their eyes? On the last track, too! You guys were tearin' it up."

Nizumi looked at him. "I'm going to sequester myself, turn up my nanobuds, and get to work. Let me know when Sanchez and Metsk are back." She walked off toward her quarters, her bootsteps echoing along the corridor.

Ruff contemplated what he should do next. He was shaken, but didn't want to show it in front of his crew.

A call was coming into his ID cube. He really had no desire to talk to the guy on the other end, but he knew he couldn't avoid it.

"Ruff, what the *fuck* is going on over there? You okay? I heard about it on the feeds. I can't have my prime source of income bleeding out on the floor of some little piss-filled club. You know how I feel about those shows. And what was Nizumi doing? She ought to be fired, Ruff. I'm sorry, but there's no excuse here. Nope. I know you have this thing for her, but if she can't—"

Ruff turned off the audio feed, but didn't hang up. His head hurt and he poured himself a gin and pineapple soda. After a couple of sips, he hit the button again.

"—and if you think that I'm going to let you play at Beat Street Fest without some extra security, you're fuckin' mad. *Fuckin' mad!*"

Ruff noticed his manager wasn't concerned enough to call the whole thing off altogether.

"We'll be fine, Sharky."

"Fine?" Ruff could almost see his manager tearing his hair out in clumps. "Fine!? I've made some calls, Ruff. Got the Meridia 7 police involved. Also filed a report with the Federation. I can't believe Nizumi didn't even—"

"Enough. Nizumi is why Tumble and I are still here. No one expected something like this to go down."

Sharky spoke in a low whisper, as if it made a difference. "Tell me, who do you think did this?"

"I really don't know. I mean, this girl's saying it was her boyfriend, but then I know I saw Cubicle in the audience."

"Cubicle? Well there we go. I'm going to call his manager. This shit has got to stop."

Ruff leaned forward on his elbows over the tiny table. "Look, Sharky, I don't know it was him. It was dark and smoky in there, but it seemed like it."

"Take care of yourself. Get some rest. Stay in orbit for awhile. I don't want you going anywhere, doing anything, until I meet you on Ruebos. That goes for Tumble too."

"Okay, *dad.*"

Tumble snorted. He couldn't hear the conversation, but Ruff was sure he had a good idea at this point who was on the other end of the call.

"This ain't no joke," Sharky said. "You do what I say if you want to keep being relevant."

Ruff pulled away from the ID cube and scrunched his eyebrows at it like it was Sharky himself.

"See you in two days, pops" Ruff said and hung up.

He chugged down his cocktail, bid everyone a good night and headed back to his quarters.

Stripped down to his leopard-print underwear, Ruff spread himself out over his most welcome gold satin sheets.

What came next? They would arrive for rehearsal a day before the festival kicked off. He had a lot of faith in Nizumi, but it had been a long time since he had been shot at, let alone on stage. None of the story made sense, so far. Lasers being shot out of eyes. Some dude that may have been Ice Cubicle stalking them from the club floor.

Ruff fell into a restless sleep, dreaming intermittently about being a young man again. He was playing a block party with Tumble behind the tables. He wore a red Kangol hat, Adidas low-tops whose replicated blacks and whites were even deeper and brighter than the original issue, and a gold chain with links thicker than his wrists. Cardboard was scattered throughout. People clapped their hands while the breakdancers spun in circles and did their thing.

Ruff was about to kick off one of his favorite rhymes when the ground shook and people started to scream. He looked at Tumble who was wobbling around, trying futilely to keep his LPs from flying off the table and smashing into the concrete.

"Get up!"

His eyes stung. He needed more sleep. Nizumi stood at the foot of his bed.

"What?" he said. "What's up?"

"Unscheduled landing. The engine's burning up."

"Overheating?" Why did she need to wake him for that?

"No, it's literally on fire."

* * *

Ruff smelled smoke, but he knew it was just in his head. The engines were compartmentalized and secured from the main cabin, so there was no way for it to leak through. Everyone was on the command deck by the time he had pulled on an old silver sweatsuit and exited his cabin.

"We have to come down on…" Dado squinted his eyes at the console. "…QEN-888."

"QEN-888?" Ruff asked.

Then Sanchez. "Man, is there even a port down there?"

"I don't know," Dado replied. "It doesn't matter. The flames have been put out, but the power's barely piping through. Unless you want to take the chance of drifting through open space and generously gifting every last one of your credits to raiders, we don't have much choice."

Tumble looked dazed, more than usual, but he wrapped his fingers tightly around the gold chain hanging from his neck.

"We gotta do what we gotta do, but be gentle with my baby," Ruff said. Hip-hop was all about status and status was made known through symbols. The Outie Z-7K was Ruff's symbol. He had spent nearly his and Tumble's first advance on the ship. Chromed out from front to back, whenever they came close enough to a star, the heat generated by the reflection was sufficient to refill the energy stores. Tumble had been pissed until he took a nap on one of the hammocks and drinks were somehow delivered automatically every time he grew thirsty.

Sophisticated technology for the sophisticated gentleman.

Metsk and Nizumi entered the navigation deck from the rear. Black and brown oils stained both their clothing and skin. Though Nizumi's hair was caked with sweat and grease, it fell on her forehead in perfect strands.

"You find us a place to land yet?" Nizumi asked.

Dado punched a couple of commands into his terminal. He laughed out loud.

"The good news is that I found us a lot of places. The bad news is that this planet is completely void of life."

QEN-888 grew in size as they approached.

"Better strap in," Dado said.

* * *

Yellow. Flat. Dusty.

Not even a mining camp or polluting industrial complex.

"I just got off the comm with Triple J," Dado said. "They can have someone out here in half a day."

"Half a day?" Ruff asked. He looked up at the sky. The landscape was not only barren but hot as the sun beat down on their heads. *I must be paying for my sins early,* he thought.

His voice squeaked a little. "Man, there's no way we're going to get to Beat Street in time for rehearsal."

All they could do was wait.

Metsk said he was going to take a nap. Sanchez, Tumble, and Dado whittled away the time by throwing dice inside the cool ship. If there was one thing the DJ loved more than spinning records, it was rolling bones. Ruff had quit playing with him after he had caught on to his cheating ways, even though he could never actually seem to catch him in the act.

Ruff couldn't find Nizumi, so he exited the ship to find her sitting fifty yards away atop a waist-high boulder, knees pulled up to her chin and looking out over the endless sea of nothingness.

"You mind?"

She said nothing, but Ruff sat down anyway.

"I guess we have some time to talk. I know you feel bad about everything."

She laughed ruefully. "Feel bad? First I let someone get the drop on you, and you're still breathing only due to their incompetence. Then the engines catch on fire? Something's up, and I don't know what. *That* makes me feel bad."

Ruff tried to empathize. He understood that the professional was a professional by virtue of execution. What else did you have but your rep?

"We'll get to the bottom of it. You think it's an inside job? I mean, the ship was secure, right?"

"It was locked down, supposedly being watched by port security on Meridia 7. The access logs didn't record anyone coming in or out unless they were tampered with, which, who knows." She paused.

"Could it have been done before we arrived? A timer or something?"

Nizumi looked at Ruff. Her deep brown eyes seemed to pull him every time. "I'm beginning to believe anything's possible at this point. If there was any evidence, it's burned to a crisp."

Unsure of what to say next, Ruff simply looked into the distance, watching waves of heat flow into the horizon.

* * *

The dude from Triple J showed up nearly before the sun fell.

He was a fat man, sweating under a stained baseball cap before he even stepped foot onto the ground.

"They call me Monkey," he said as he shook everyone's hand, never bothering to explain why.

Metsk escorted him to the engine room and after several minutes, the two of them returned.

Monkey took off his hat, used it to wipe his moist face, and slapped it back on. Then he shook his head.

"The damned thing's burnt to a crisp, which is weird since engines don't just catch on fire anymore."

Nizumi looked at Ruff.

"That is, unless they're knockoffs," he finished, holding up a circuit board which he proceeded to crack in half with a flick of the wrist.

Now everyone else looked at Ruff. He felt himself shrinking back, wanting to hide. "What? I got a good deal," he said almost in a whisper.

Monkey shrugged. "My grandma used to say, 'the cheap comes out expensive.' You need a new one, top to bottom. The quantum mender has lost any ability to charge its flex coil. Every capacitor is warped. Every inch of wire is now a part of the new soot carpet gracing your engine room."

All of the technical jargon was so much noise to Ruff.

"Okay, okay," he replied. "Fine. Just tell me how many credits it's going to cost and bring us a new one."

The man laughed. He sounded like a braying donkey and his unshaven cheeks jiggled like gelatinous sacks.

"This Outie Z-7K *should* have a two-thousand microcylinder engine. I can't just *bring you a new one*,'" he said, crooking his fingers in air quotes. "And I certainly can't bring you another knockoff. That's against Triple J policy. Nope. I'm going to have to call in a Beryl class tower who can drop it off at an Outie-authorized repair shop."

"Why can't you tow us?" Ruff was desperate not to be stuck QED-whatever.

"I don't have the means to pull you out of the thermosphere with my little dinghy." Monkey snickered.

Great.

"But, I can give someone a ride along the way. I'm not flying a Starhound, so I can't take everyone, but I can drop one of you off so long as it's on the way back to the depot."

"Ruff," Nizumi said. "As much as I don't like having you out of my sight, especially now, maybe you ought to go so you can make rehearsal. It may be safer than here."

Ruff shook his head. Though he was more concerned now about Nizumi, Tumble was his excuse. "An MC is useless without a DJ."

Tumble beamed.

"Anyone else want to go?" Ruff scanned the faces of each of his friends.

Everyone shook their head.

In it together. He loved this crew.

"Look," Ruff said to Monkey, "call in whatever you gotta call in."

Monkey tipped the bill of his hat and hopped back inside his tiny cockpit, closing the hatch behind him. From the other side of the glass, Ruff watched him talk animatedly, laughing several times and throwing his hands around. Ruff was doubly glad to stick around since the guy was already getting on his nerves. He was afraid he might punch Monkey out, hurting any chance of making it to Beat Street. He knocked on the window after a couple of minutes. The dude seemed irritated and put off, but he wrapped up his call and opened the cockpit.

"Okay, I got you a Beryl."

Ruff released a breath he didn't realize he had been holding.

"It ought to be here…" Monkey pulled back the sleeve on his left arm and looked at his wrist chronometer. He tapped it several times, each tap harder than the last until he finally smashed the watch with his fist.

"…in a couple of days."

Ruff felt his bowels shift.

"Whoa. A couple of days?! I can't—"

"Because you're outside of the authorized range, this service call costs an automatic fifty credits. Corporate has already withdrawn it from your account. Thanks for choosing Triple J!"

Before Ruff could get a word in, Monkey slammed the hatch, fired up the engines and left as quickly as he came.

Ruff turned to his companions, breathing heavily.

"Remind me to cancel my Triple J when we get home."

* * *

There was the hope that night would arrive soon, but just as one sun was setting in the east, another's edges peeked up from the west. What a miserable hole, Ruff thought. The only consolation might have been that The Fly Honey wouldn't be short for power to the auxiliary systems, but Nizumi refused to run anything until a thorough sweep of the ship could be completed.

We don't know what the hell else is built with flimsy Chinilium parts, she had said with edge to her voice.

Ruff hesitated at first, but decided to call Sharky to report the situation and see what magic he could work. The bum wasn't picking up, so Ruff decided to take a walk, only to return within a few minutes as every step reminded him that this place was as dead as they were.

"What kind of hellhole doesn't even have bugs?" he wondered aloud.

It was on the sixteenth re-lacing of his Adidas low-tops when a loud hum pulled his attention to the sky.

A ship approached.

Ruff knew what a Beryl-class tower looked like, and if this was one, it was not only smaller than average, but the most tricked out that he had ever seen. It shined just as much as the Fly Honey, but instead of chrome, it was wrapped in plates of gold. Stabilizer jets shot out in various directions. Nizumi emerged from their own ship and joined everyone in a run to get behind a large boulder, avoiding the rocks and dust being kicked up in every direction.

When the ship finally touched down, its engines cut out. Only the sound of metal settling in the heat remained.

How the hell is this going to tow us out of here, Ruff wondered.

There was a loud hiss as an exit hatch opened up and a ramp unraveled in layers until it made contact with the flat earth. For some reason, Ruff felt uneasy.

"You have your gun?" he asked Nizumi.

"Always."

* * *

Boots on metal.

Two pairs of giant feet clambered down the ramp, slowly revealing their owners. Their height would have been enough to disclose the fact that they were Temelians, but their flat snouts, pointed ears, and tattooed arms confirmed it. Temelians were essentially bipedal pigs, only slightly more intelligent. Excepting their arms and faces, the huge beasts were nearly covered in armor. Each one cradled a phase rifle, though, in their hands, they looked more like squirt pistols.

They stopped at the front corners of the ramp and stared.

Someone else began to descend.

If the shoes were the only thing that Ruff would ever see, it would have been enough to confirm his suspicions.

Blue and white Frankish Peasants.

FPs for short.

Ads were plastered throughout the known galaxies, primarily showing the street-cred shoes on the feet of only one man. He came down and stood between the Temelians, his head barely above their waists.

"Woooh-eee, Ruff."

Ice Cubicle held a hand over his sunglass-covered eyes.

"You sure pick shitty vacation spots."

Ruff and his crew slowly came out from behind the large rock.

"Come to finish the job?" he asked.

Everyone reacted cautiously, trying to read the new arrivals' intentions. Ruff noticed that both Nizumi and Metsk had pistols in hand behind their backs.

The tension lasted for several seconds until Cubicle had his guards lower their weapons.

"Sasha, Masha. You girls can head back into the ship. I need to have a chat with Ruff and Tumble."

Without hesitation, the Temelians walked back up the ramp and disappeared.

Cubicle, hands on his hips, looked at Nizumi expectantly.

"It's alright," Ruff whispered to her.

"I don't trust him," she said.

"Neither do I," Ruff replied, "but I trust you."

A glimpse of a smile appeared. She nodded reluctantly and took the crew back into The Fly Honey. Ruff was comfortable knowing she'd find some way to watch them. After everything that's happened over the past twenty-four hours, she wasn't going to let him or Tumble out of her sight.

Cubicle removed his sunglasses, revealing heavy bags under his eyes. It was obvious he hadn't gotten much sleep. He pulled a piece of rolled up electro-parchment out from the inside of his glittering gold jacket and handed it to Ruff, but Tumble grabbed it and unraveled it so he could check it out first.

The DJ's eyes grew wide as he read. He passed it to Tumble.

The Sorse Magazine - News Alerts - Stardate 187272.51620370362

Are Ruff and Tumble Out of the Office?

Last night, terror ensued at a discreet, pop-up show at Chubb's on Meridia 7, put on by hip-hop luminaries MC Ruff and DJ Tumble. The small concert was presumably a test run of their new album, and witnesses say that near the end of their set, an attempt was made on Ruff's life. Someone reported a laser was fired at MC Ruff. Another fan said it was certainly a mini-wormhole grenade.

The entire club broke out into pandemonium.

There have been no reports of the duo's current status. Attempts to contact their manager have been unsuccessful and a representative from Dope Planet Records has refused to comment.

Fans are concerned that Ruff and Tumble won't be reporting in for their headlining act at Beat Street, but fear

*not, hip-hop aficionados. Should the icons continue suffering
from an acute case of stage fright, guess who's set to take over?*

*That's right. The dynamic duo's mortal enemy, Ice
Cubicle.*

*Whispers and rumors implicate him in taking part
in the attack, but authorities say that there is no evidence that
he was involved.*

*Regardless, with the battle for old-school street-cred
heating up to a new level, both groups are topping the charts
as their tracks hit a record number of downloads over the past
24 hours.*

It took an effort not to knock Cubicle into the dirt, but he was sure

Sasha and Masha were watching them all just as keenly as Nizumi.

"Did you just want to rub it in or what?" Ruff asked. "Congratula-

tions. You're headlining Beat Street."

Cubicle grinned. "Come on, Ruff. You're slow on the take, brotha.

Who do you think's gettin' the real scrilla? All these album sales this is going

to generate? You and I know we're barely gonna see three-percent on that."

The notion hit Ruff in the face like a sock full of billiard balls.

"Man, you need to tell me what you know or just shoot us already. I

don't like this beatin' around the bush nonsense."

"You're no fun, you know that Ruff?" Cubicle looked at Tumble.

"Your boy here, he's no fun."

Tumble just stared at him.

"Alright, alright. I don't know nothin', but I have my suspicions that

your team and my team are trying to play us."

"What? Who?" Ruff looked over his shoulder at The Fly Honey, but

failed to keep it discreet.

"Do you trust your peeps?" Cubicle's eyes followed Ruff's.

"With my life." There was no hesitation in the reply.

"You may want to rethink that," Cubicle said. "How about your manager?"

"Sharky?" Ruff had to think for a few seconds. "As much as you trust yours."

"Right."

Ruff scrunched his face. "Wait, wait. You think he was involved? In trying to kill me? That doesn't make any sense."

"I don't think he wanted to kill you. Actually, I'm positive he didn't. He just wanted to create some drama. Drum up more album sales. Thinks he's keepin' us relevant and at the top of the game. You know these new kids coming up, all about the violence. Your Sharky, my Poindexter, they're afraid we're approaching our expiration date. No more free lunch for them."

"Poindexter?"

"My manager."

"Poindexter?"

"Yeah, yeah. Trust me, I give him shit all the time. But I just know this is some nonsense they agreed to behind our backs."

Now Ruff was beginning to question everything.

"So this Dylan guy is working for Sharky? And Poindexter?"

"Dylan? Who's Dylan?"

"Some girl was at the show with her boyfriend. Dylan? Dave? Anyway, she said he tried to shoot me with a laser from his eye. And then some big dudes swept him away." His eyes fell on Cubicle's ship, thinking of a couple of big "dudes" waiting impatiently on the inside.

Cubicle's mouth was a straight line. The sound started low, an almost inaudible rumble from the depths of the rapper's belly, until it couldn't be contained any longer and he nearly fell to the ground, tears in his eyes, overcome with a fit of laughter.

Tumble looked at Ruff. Ruff returned the stare.

Cubicle managed an out-of-breath reply. "Are...you...kidding me?" He wiped the moisture from his cheeks. "Shot a laser...out of his...eye? What kind of...*sci-fi* shit is that? You *believed* her?"

Ruff crossed his arms in a classic B-Boy stance, slightly embarrassed and tried not to show it. He kind of hoped Nizumi would just pop out and shoot him now.

"Why would she lie?"

"Brotha, I was almost seein' things myself in that crowd. I don't think I could find the ceiling through the cloud of SynthaChronic™ smoke."

Tumble snorted and nodded in agreement.

"She probably saw your own light show, saw Sasha and Masha, and jumped to some tripped-out conclusions. I'd bet my last royalty check that this Danny boy ditched his girl and hooked up with some skeezer."

Now that the proposition had been repeated, it was less convincing. Ruff *did* remember the air was thick with the vapor of the mind-altering substance. He had assumed the girl's eyes were red just from crying.

But he still had some questions about Cubicle's presence. "Hold up a minute. Why were you even at the show?"

"You think I'm an idiot?" Cubicle's tone was sharp. "Research. That's what smart MCs do. I wanted to see how you were going to roll with this new album. Besides," he dipped his head in the direction of The Fly Honey, "if I wanted to kill you, I would have just dropped some bombs on your head instead of coming down here and shootin' the shit."

Ruff said, "You also could have flown right by and played tomorrow's show to a sold-out crowd. So why are you really here? You want something."

Cubicle shifted his stance. "Yeah, I want something. I know we got some beef, but it's our beef. I'm tired of bein' played by some leech in a suit."

Tumble hummed an *mmm-hmm*.

Ruff didn't like the feeling either.

"Besides, people are starting to dig too deep into my past. My fans start finding out I went to Old Yale and spent my summers in the Old-Earth Hamptons, I'm afraid my street cred will take a hit."

"Wait, wha—"

Cubicle held up a hand.

"So, I've come to offer a ride and a chance to show these bustas that we can't be messed with."

It became clear to Ruff that he had two choices. Sit here and probably miss the show, likely playing right into Sharky and Poindexter's hands. Or he could take a leap of faith, hitch a ride with his archnemesis, and spin their managers' heads around like one of Tumble's records.

"You can take all of us?" he asked. He wasn't going anywhere without Nizumi and team. He was sure they wouldn't let him go if those were the terms, anyway.

"Of course," Cubicle said.

After a moment's hesitation, Ruff said, "Okay."

Cubicle bleached teeth shined bright under the suns. He held out his hand. Fighting his gut inertia, Ruff took it into his own, wondering in the back of his mind if he was making a deal with the Devilbot.

"So what's the plan?" Ruff asked.

"I'll explain it on the way, but the bottom line is this: We're both gonna be at Beat Street and we're both gonna take control of this whole thing."

Ruff liked the sound of that.

* * *

The look on his face may have been worth the price of a new engine alone.

Sharky stood over the catering table with a mouth full of pretzels. He was a short, thin man, who wore round, wire-frame glasses with green-tinted lenses. His salt-and-peppa hair was slicked back, held down against the forces of gravity by a gallon of Jimmy Oil.

"Ruff! Tumble! What..."

He tried to hide his split-second of surprise by launching into one of his usual verbal onslaughts.

"You made it in one piece! I knew you would! What the hell happened? I've been worried sick about you boys. I have the Feds scouring the galaxy for you. You don't call. You don't message. I got zero sleep last night. My hemorrhoids are really acting up. Guys, guys...things have changed and there's been some rearranging. I don't know if we can get your headline spot now. I've been trying to get them to hold off, but at this point, the sponsors are all expecting Cubicle to take the stage. Can you believe it? It's killin' me. *Killin' me!* The——"

Ruff drowned out the noise and worked through the plan in his head. He and his team had landed the night before. They kept a low profile and stayed at a nearby hotel booked under one of Cubicle's many aliases. The rappers agreed to proceed under the public's assumption that MC Ruff and DJ Tumble would not make Beat Street and that Cubicle would indeed take their place as the headline act. If things went down as expected, in a roundabout way, Sharky and Poindexter would get their wish, only not on their terms.

"—so I find you guys here and see you still have this shit team working for you." Sharky pulled his glasses down over the tip of his nose and gave Ruff and Tumble's posse the stink-eye. "Look, I can't dictate who you hire for security, but you're making my job real hard by putting your life in jeopardy."

Ruff could practically feel the heat emanating from Nizumi's face. Metsk's breathing increased in pace and you could hear his teeth grinding over the pulsating music emanating from behind the backstage walls. He knew he could rely on both of them to play it cool, but Sharky was pushing it. If Dado and Sanchez were here instead of helping Tumble prep his equipment, he might not have been able to hold back the combined forces.

"Sorry for the inconvenience," Ruff said, trying desperately to keep his eyes from rolling out of his head. "We had a little engine trouble. I tried to call you. Why didn't you pick up your cube?"

Let's see you sweat a little, he thought.

Sharky wiped crumbs from his thin lips and the lapels of his checker-green suit. He pulled his ID Cube from his pocket like it was a piece of court evidence.

"It's garbage. Ruff, let me tell you, I've been trying to get it fixed for the past day. It's been doing weird stuff. Clicks, whirs, beeps. First it started out small, waking me up in the middle of the night playing creepy lullabies. I thought the damned thing was haunted. Turns out it was just hacked."

"Man, it's a dangerous world out there," Ruff said. "It's hard knowing who to trust. Do you know who hacked it?" He was having fun now, seeing just how far Sharky would take his story.

"No. Tech support wouldn't say once they found the problem. Said it was a matter of network security and they would handle it. Probably some punk ass kid trying to steal any correspondence between us so he can post it on the fan boards."

"Huh," Ruff said, feigning interest. "Well, I hope it gets sorted out. So you say we're not headlining. No way we can get the sponsors to change their minds?"

Sharky crossed his arms and managed a poor imitation of being really upset. "You think I haven't tried? That I won't keep trying?"

It felt good to play the player.

Sharky continued. "You know how much money the label's put out there promoting this?" He held a fist to the air. "I told them you'd make it. Told them flat out."

Then came the expected excuses. "But these sponsors like to play it safe. Cubicle was here last night for rehearsal and they liked what they saw. As far as I'm concerned, these Beat Street sonsabitches can have him. If they want some real superstars, they're gonna have to pay double next time."

Good show, Ruff thought.

"Look, I'm gonna see what I can do. Try to work some goddamn magic. But the opening acts are nearly done and primetime is in an hour. You might as well enjoy the show until I get back to you." Sharky patted Ruff on the back and as he passed by Nizumi and Metsk, they stared him down, causing him to trip over a loose grouping of power cables and nearly fall to the ground.

Embarrassed, he straightened his coat and picked up the pace.

"Piece of shit venue!" he yelled into the air as he left. "You need to hire professionals!"

Metsk chuckled.

"It would be so easy," Nizumi said. "No one would know, Ruff. I promise."

Ruff furrowed his brow. "Sometimes, I don't know if you're joking or serious. I don't think I want to know."

"No, you don't," Metsk said.

"Look," Ruff continued. "We have our plan. Tumble is getting ready. I need to go over some things myself."

Muffled sounds of the current act continued to echo backstage. He recognized the group as a favorite of his: UFO. Unbelievably Fly Operators.

"We'll be watching," Nizumi said, oddly hesitant. And then Ruff realized why as she reached in to give him a quick, tight hug.

"Thank you," she whispered into his ear, "for everything."

If she had worn perfume, its scent would have left a mark on his memory. But Nizumi always said that smells were traceable, so he was left with only the vague memory of her touch as she and Metsk walked away.

* * *

Blue smoke filled the stage, triggering post-traumatic stress symptoms nailed into Ruff's memory banks courtesy of Sharky and Poindexter. Ruff shook them off though, reminding himself that he and his team were in control this time. There would be no lasers grazing his or anyone else's head tonight.

Sharky had disappeared since their earlier meeting, probably working with Poindexter to figure out what to do now that Ruff and Tumble were actually here.

"You ready?" Cubicle asked.

They were standing at the bottom of the rear steps leading to the stage. Tumble was already in place, standing behind a wall of said smoke and his prized pair of turntables. The stage was surrounded by giant video screens reaching several stories high. Images of breakdancers wearing FPs and track pants flashed in and out as Cubicle's opening track began to play. Half the crowd cheered and Ruff could have sworn the other half was booing. Admittedly, it made him feel a little warm inside. A week ago, a Cubicle sample album would never have been allowed to be within fifty meters of one of Tumble's record players, let alone making contact with a needle. Ruff laughed at how such a big change could happen in such a short period of time.

"Let's do this," he said.

* * *

The music halted.

The screens went blank.

The alternating cheers and boos subsided while the blue smoke hovered silently over the stage.

Suddenly, the larger screens lit up again, only this time displaying a series of video clips synchronized to the 808 kick drum bleeding out of every monitor.

Boom.

Bronze sword slamming into bronze shield, each shattering into thousands of pieces.

Boom.

A glass jar of oil and water being dropped to the ground, exploding on contact.

Boom.

A liquified yin and yang pattern, spinning around until it became an indistinguishable, inseparable whole.

Boom.

Now every monitor showed the same thing: To the left, Cubicle's name built out of blocks of shining gold. To the right, MC Ruff and DJ Tumble's monikers scribbled in graffiti against a brick wall.

The smoke machines cut off, the haze disappeared, and the crowd roared as Ruff and Cubicle ran to the front of the stage, each with a microphone in hand. Tumble spun up the saxophone loop.

There were no adequate words for what Ruff saw in the audience. Ecstasy? Rapture?

It didn't matter.

No more boos. All cheers. Butterflies fluttered in Ruff's stomach to a level he hadn't felt since he and Tumble played their first show back in New-New Queens.

Cubicle took the lead as planned.

"Whoooo wants to rummbble?" he asked, positioning the mic out over the audience.

Weeee doooo! Weee doooo!

Now Ruff: "My boy Cubicle said, 'Whoooo wants to rummmmmble?'"

Weeee doooo! Weee doooo!

Nizumi and Metsk were at alternate sides of the stage, each looking out over the crowd. Ruff smiled at Nizumi, but she was so busy watching for potential trouble and ensuring Beat Street security were doing their job that she didn't see him.

Back in her element. Unrelenting, Ruff thought.

"Yo," he said.

The music cut out along with the lights. You could have heard a termite sneeze. If there was a greater feeling than taking control of a crowd of tens of thousands, Ruff had never experienced it and didn't much care.

"You know you can't mess with the combined, universal, imperial, soopa-doopa, hella-dope, greatest, motha-fuckin' unstoppable forces of Cubicle, Ruff, and Tummmmmmmbbbbllleee!"

The most glorious sight that Ruff's eyes ever beheld took place. The lights kicked on, controlled and synchronized perfectly with the breakbeats flowing out of Tumble's gear. The entire arena went insane.

In.

Sane.

Looking back, Ruff realized the irony of that thought.

That brief moment of glory, that feeling of control, was rudely interrupted by the notion that something very wrong was happening. He seemed to notice it before Cubicle did. His old rival was completely oblivious. Cubicle's gleaming teeth could have lit up whole cities as he smiled on the crowd like a damned fool, then turned to Ruff and kept on smiling. It wasn't until a thin red laser bored a perfectly round hole through his coif that he, too, realized something very wrong was happening.

His smile began to fade.

More red lasers appeared, shot out randomly from the audience. Some didn't travel more than a few meters before finding another body to slam into. Others began punching holes in the stage equipment, generating sparks and small fires. Ruff halfway hoped this was some part of the act which Cubicle neglected to mention. That half wanted to whoop the MC's ass, but caught only the back of his new fairweather homey's smoking blue hair as he went running off the rear of the stage.

Time seemed to crawl. In the audience, people were panicking as they had at Chubb's, only this time, the mass was so large that it looked like waves crashing against each other. Arms and legs flew crazily. Heads snapped back and forth. Screams mixed with shouts mixed with cries.

Ruff's legs were frozen, but he turned and saw Nizumi rushing toward him.

Another laser went right through the framework holding the giant stage monitors over the DJ's head. Metal creaked and twisted. Tumble took his headphones off and looked up in a daze, only to be tackled and swept away by the giant, moving shadow that was Metsk. The DJ folded in like a leaf. A skinny, cracked-out leaf.

Ruff's eyes met Nizumi's, letting her know that though he wouldn't mind her body on top of his again, she didn't need to tackle him to the ground. His legs seemed to have regained full functionality and he followed her toward the back of the stage.

Everyone was there at the bottom of the steps. Cubicle was pressed tightly between Sasha and Masha. His legs and arms were visibly shaking.

"There, there," Sasha said. Or Masha. Ruff felt embarrassed he couldn't tell them apart. Either way, one of them was stroking his blue hair with her hand while the other hummed to him softly.

Ruff hoped there was no press nearby. The "lyrical gangsta'" was not making it easy on himself to keep up his rep.

Sharky was arguing with another man, who but for a bald head and thick glasses, could have been the manager's twin.

Must be Poindexter.

"Alright," Ruff said, trying to catch his breath, "don't you guys think you're taking this a little too far? You almost killed my homeboy out there!"

Tumble scowled at the stage, obviously upset his records and turntables were there and he was here.

Metsk held on tight to Tumble's arms. "Let them go, Tumble. Let them go."

"Almost killed your homeboy? What the hell are you talking about?" Sharky asked.

"We know what you two are up to," Ruff said. "Enough. I knew you were a schemer, but this is ridiculous. I'm pretty sure attempted murder is enough justification for me to tear up our contract."

Sharky looked at Poindexter who shrugged in response. He made a motion toward Ruff.

"Look, Ruff, my man, I—"

Nizumi swung around like a lithe cat and wrapped her arm's around Sharky's neck, putting him in a sleeper hold. His eyes grew big as he gasped for air. Within seconds, they were closed and Nizumi laid him gently on the ground. Now that was something Ruff was not used to seeing—a quiet

Sharky.

Nizumi stood and looked at Poindexter. He scrambled behind Sasha and Masha.

"I don't know what you've been told," he said, "but we had nothing to do with this!" His voice was nasal. Near falsetto.

"Yeah, we'll see about that," Ruff replied. He looked at Cubicle who was audibly whimpering.

Man, still a sucka MC after all, Tumble thought.

Screams, shouts, and the movements of the agitated crowd could still be heard from behind the stage walls. But then there was another sound that caught everyone's ear. Loud. A combination of high hiss and low thunder. The entire ground shook and every piece of the stage rattled.

"What the hell is that?" Cubicle asked. By the expression on his face, Ruff hoped the poser had packed a second pair of pants.

Ruff looked at Nizumi. They ran up the stairs and peeked around the stage walls.

Nizumi spoke into her nanoset, calm and collected. "Sanchez, Dado. Get us a transport back to the hotel. Now."

Ruff tried to remember if he had also packed a second pair of pants.

* * *

Partly, it was the make and model of the ships.

Partly, it was the insignia, a red sword and shield hovering over a golden star, painted on their gunmetal gray sides.

But the strongest indicator that Ruff may have had everything wrong was the tetracarbon-suited troopers dropping down from said ships, descending on the crowd like they were performing a choreographed dance number.

He and Nizumi were transfixed on the action.

Soldiers poured down slick nucleon ropes like spiders on a string of web, hitting the ground and taking cover behind any apparatus they could find: Speaker cabinets, turned-over merchandise tables, even Blue Bowl™ machines filled with energy supplements, though these ended up being shoddy cover because lasers were punching right through the cans within, showering what was left of a panicking crowd with caffeine and guarana extract.

It was a battlefield of chaos as fans were running towards all directions, trying to avoid both soldiers and those who had initiated the shooting.

Ruff focused on a particularly pudgy kid who confirmed that the girl from Chubb's may not have been so high after all. Pudgy was running, or rather, waddling around. His belly bounced up and down until it could no longer be contained by his tie-dyed Rob "Reggae Mon" Charley t-shirt, revealing its pale and hairy glory. It was the only fluid part of a body that appeared as stiff as a board and from the kid's eye (Ruff was certain it was his left eye) came red laser after red laser. They were flying in the direction of the troops, though seemingly without any particular target in mind.

One of the soldiers popped out from behind a canvas-covered pretzel stand and fired in response. A direct hit to the groin and Pudgy collapsed.

"They're killing these kids!" Ruff said.

"Not killing, just stunning."

Ruff turned around and saw four people standing behind him and Nizumi. Three were towering Temelians and Ruff wasn't about to try and guess their gender. The other was an older man, maybe in his fifties, sporting a flattop and wearing a blue-and-gray military uniform with enough bling across his chest to make Ruff twinge with envy. He seemed completely relaxed with his hands in his pockets.

"Nizumi," he said with a smile, "is this what you've been reduced to?" The soldier indicated Ruff with his elbow.

She said nothing, only giving him a glassy stare.

"We need you both to come with us," he said.

Ruff looked at Nizumi for affirmation. Her eyebrows indicated that they had better comply.

* * *

The whole crew was in the large dressing room they shared with Cubicle before the show. They were lined up on a sofa from big to small like those old Russian dolls.

Cubicle was sitting on Sasha's (or Masha's) lap like a child, sucking on a pacifier. He'd obviously been 'medicated' and was trying not to grind his teeth. The man had no shame.

Sandwiched between Metsk and Sanchez, Tumble looked dejected with his head in his hands.

Finally, Dado, Poindexter, and Sharky finished the line-up. Poindexter was holding a wet cloth against Sharky's forehead. He flinched slightly when he saw Nizumi walk in, but Dado and Poindexter tried to soothe him.

The Federation had already taken over the room. Plastic cups littered every counter. Ten, maybe fifteen, soldiers spoke over each other into nano-sets while status reports came in left and right.

"You want to tell us what's happening here?" Nizumi asked the man who led them.

"Have a seat," he said. "Can I get you some coffee?"

"No," Ruff said. "You can't get us some coffee and you can't make us take a seat."

The soldier looked at him and smiled. "Suit yourself." He turned to one of his Temelian adjutants. "The usual."

The Temelian walked away, leaving the other two hovering behind.

"Do you want the short version or the long version?"

"Look, Colonel Flattop, give me whatever version explains why you're ruining what was going to be one of the better performances of my career and why kids are trying to kill me by shooting lasers out of their eye."

The 'Colonel Flattop' quip seemed to annoy him. "It's Captain Desmond, and you damned hip-hoppers have egos the size of Sol. No one's trying to kill you. In fact, that's why the program was discontinued."

"Huh?"

The previously dispatched Temelian returned and handed Desmond his cup of coffee. He took a long, annoying slurp.

"Exploring the galaxy is dangerous work. There's a jerk in every neighborhood. Back in the old days, everything in our solar system was a known quantity. But we've been expanding so quickly, we don't know what we're bound to run into. So, some genius Federation bureaucrat decided a couple of decades ago that we ought to have the means to deal with any hostile forces at any time with the slightest amount of notice.

"The project was dubbed Conscription 2.0. 'The draft without the hassle,' is still burned into my memory banks." Captain Desmond took another sip of coffee as if it would wash away a bad taste.

"Anyway, a random number of babies born between the years 2111 and 2116 had nanochips implanted in their skulls, each one connected to various parts of their anatomy."

"Man," Ruff interrupted, "that cannot have been legal."

The Captain snorted. "*Legal* is as simple as a digital pen stroke. It was all above water. You don't have kids, so you wouldn't know, but there's a mountain of legal documentation that parents are forced to sign before the hospital will release a child into their custody. It was all in the fine print that their child might be randomly selected for beta testing.

"Of course, like any ridiculous idea dreamed up by some fatcat politician with an excess of money but an absence of brain matter, it was a failure from the start. The chip work had been outsourced to Chinilium, and since the marching orders from these types of projects are always 'Ready, Fire, Aim,' these pieces of junk had already been rolled out to a significant portion of the population. By the time it was determined that enough Federation funds had been pissed down the drain and that these new citizen-soldiers wouldn't work out as well as hoped, many of these kids were already enrolled in school and living their lives without a clue of what was in their body."

"It's a familiar story, Desmond," Nizumi said, "But why now? What's causing these kids to ... activate?"

"That's where you all come in. The scientists and sponsors agreed that the best way to trigger the function was to use a combination of tones that were unlikely to be emitted from any source other than the government. If the time came, there was a procedure to send them through ID Cubes and nanosets. Well, apparently they did a piss poor job of choosing the trigger, believing no one would dare think of violating the <u>Federation Statutes on Audio and Visual Performances</u>."

As if through some magnetic force, everyone looked toward Tumble.

His head didn't move, but his eyes shifted around looking for a means of escape.

"Man," Ruff said. "You tweaked the 808 during the breakbeats, didn't you?"

Tumble pursed his lips, gazed at the floor, and shrugged.

"How did you know it was going to happen in Chubb's?" Nizumi asked.

Ruff thought back to the girl's story of her boyfriend—Daniel?—getting carried away by a couple of big guys.

Captain Desmond snorted. "Luckily, one of the scientists working on the project has horrible taste in music. He detected it when he downloaded your latest album and warned us as soon as he saw your Twister message go out."

"So what do we do from here?" Ruff asked the Captain. The room was still humming with activity. Muted sounds of hoverships wavered just outside.

"You don't do anything except sign this pile of electronic forms," he said. One of his Temelians handed Ruff a small tablet. "You and your DJ will consent to having your album pulled from every distribution network and deleted from every traceable Cube. The original cuts, as well as tracks in your possession, will also be destroyed."

Tumble released an audible howl.

Unbelieveable, Ruff thought. A thriving career single-handedly put in jeopardy, not by new trends or shady managers, but by a goddamn combination of tones.

"You're making a lot of noise out there," Ruff said. "How are you going to keep this from getting out?"

"The standard Federation Procedure. We'll blitz the news sources with one of our false narratives. Space terrorists, probably. Mothers Against Hip-Hop. Of course, we'll have to seed some conspiracy theorists to balance things."

"And if I don't sign this?" Ruff said, holding the tablet out as if it was one of his post-show, sweat-drenched undershirts.

"I'm sorry. You seem to be under the impression that we're asking. If we catch word that you have a leaky ship—" Desmond looked around the room "—we'll dispatch someone to patch it."

The rest of the night became a blur to the exhausted MC. He and Cubicle exchanged no words as the chump slinked off quietly at some point with his girls and Poindexter. Sharky was still on edge, keeping a polite distance from Nizumi. The only consolation for Ruff that evening was seeing a fully-functioning Fly Honey waiting for them at a nearby spaceport.

Everyone boarded in silence and, except for Ruff and Nizumi, went their separate ways. The two of them slumped down onto the leather couches.

"You knew that dude?" he asked.

"We've worked together in the past," she said and left it at that.

Ruff took a long, deep breath. "As crazy as this has all been, I'm glad it's over."

"Yeah," Nizumi said, a hint of disappointment in her voice. "Me too."

"Don't worry," he said, putting a comforting hand on her arm. "I'm sure there will be more ridiculously fantastic action for you to come and save me from."

* * *

Tumble fiddled faders and twiddled knobs behind the engineering console. Instead of a Roland 808 bass drum, the DJ plugged in a sharper sample—more along the lines of the 505. Ruff stood in the isolation booth, feeling his warm breath reflect off the hanging microphone. He monitored the track through a pair of black, over-the-ear headphones. Like any good artist, he weaved the truth into his craft.

Yo, take a step back,
while we wind up for the attack.
We'll take control of your brain,
Drive ya'll insane.

Some bustas thought that they could lase us,
but, yo, them fools don't faze us.
Doesn't matter if you're terrorists,
Ruff's spittin' rhymes like fists.

So, set your phasers on stun,
and let's have some fun.
Ruff and Tumble,
will always be Number One.

Process Summary

Lights Out: An MC Ruff and DJ Tumble Adventure is story number seven in the #52ShortStories challenge.

Oh boy…where to start.

Challenges from every direction this time around.

Parts of this story had been tickling the back of my brain for a couple of years, but I'd been afraid to write it. I didn't think I was ready to do it justice, but with six stories in the can, I heeded my own advice of pushing through the fear and went for it. I figured I could introduce the characters and setting within a week — a trial story of sorts.

I dove in without an outline. There was a lot of freewriting as I had only vague generalities in mind.

Nearing Friday of that first week, I panicked. I knew that I was not going to be able to wrap this one up by Sunday, therefore violating the implicit schedule of one story a week I'd been marching toward.

Okay, no biggie. One story behind. I'll find a way to handle it.

Here we come, Friday of week two, aaannnddd no end in sight. In fact, I was completely stuck as to how I was going to resolve everything.

Shit.

The whole premise had humor built in, but I originally wanted to put a serious mystery behind it. Nothing was coming to me, so in desperation, I put aside my ego and consulted with my wife. She thought I needed to continue along the humor route since the whole idea was so far out to begin with.

Of course, she was perfectly correct, and once I acknowledged that, the rest of the story came more easily. I wrote with abandon and my word count really popped up on the third week. I'm happy to say that the ending came together by Saturday and I celebrated by sleeping in on Sunday.

Did it all work out?

Well, all I can do is leave the answer to that in the hands of my audience.

I've got some exciting ideas of where to take these characters and the world they inhabit. While I'll need to really buckle down at some point and make up those two missing stories, I'm glad I took the plunge on this one as I think it can find a niche audience.

The Monster in the Door

Statistics

Synopsis: Paul, a young boy in a tiny desert town, is thrust into a newfound world of responsibility when a monster appears in his bedroom door and asks a favor.

Word Count: 4,500

Genre: Supernatural / Urban Fantasy

Completed Week: October 1st – October 8th

The Monster in the Door

Mom's dark curly hair came first, then her round, large-frame eye-glasses, followed by the rest of her plump face. As she peeked through the doorway adjacent to my bed, I got a whiff of the perm she had gotten earlier that day.

"Is everything alright?"

She sounded slightly concerned.

I hesitated for a moment, but said, "Yeah."

"I thought you called." Her tone changed, and she stepped further into my bedroom, hands on her hips. "Are you playing your little football game? You need to go to bed. You have school tomorrow."

"No!" I shouted. She was always accusing me of playing the football game. I pointed towards the closet. "It's not even near me. It's all the way over there."

"Okay," she said without looking. "Well, go to sleep."

She reached in for the doorknob.

"Mom, wait!"

"What?" she snapped.

"Can you leave it open?"

Slowly, she pulled her hand back.

"You have a nightlight. I don't want the hall lights keeping you up."

"They won't. Please?"

"Yes, fine."

She stepped out into the hallway, and her slippers shuffled against the carpet until the sound faded away.

* * *

I really wanted the door closed, but I knew that if I shut my eyes and opened them, even for half of a second, it wouldn't have mattered.

The door would be open again.

The monster would be peering back at me once more.

I heard the television much more clearly now. An hour ago, I was laying across the living room floor, arms propped on a couch pillow while I watched my two favorite TV shows: *ALF* followed by *The Hogan Family*. Then nine o'clock came around, and once the opening sequence to *DC Follies* started playing, that meant it was time for bed. I was okay with that. For a show with funny looking puppets, it bored me to death.

I had brushed my teeth and put on my pajamas, and now as I lie in bed with the comforter pulled up to my chin, the TV's exaggerated voices and canned laugh track made my bedroom walls vibrate.

I stared at the open door and it stared back. The monster was imprinted onto the wood. Its eyes were dark and hollow. Light, wispy fur covered its face. What looked to be its hands were at its ears, maybe helping it listen to everything around.

For as long as I could remember, the monster had always been there, but it had never talked to me before.

"What do you want?" I whispered.

Even though I could barely hear myself, it seemed to understand me loud and clear.

"I told you, kid, you don't need to be afraid. Believe me, if I had a choice, I would have picked something else. A teddy bear. One of those robot toys you have that turns into a car. But I think I'm stuck with this thing."

His voice sounded scratchy.

"Hell, it doesn't matter. You'd probably crap your little underoos either way."

He laughed, sounding like my dad's cigarette smoke if it could laugh.

My fingers squeezed the bedding into my palms. The pattern of black-and-white kittens playing with red balls of yarn did nothing to comfort me. They felt as useful as a knight's shield made out of construction paper.

"I don't wear underoos! And I'm going to tell Mom and Dad about you," I said.

"Paul, go to bed!" came a shout from down the hall.

"Go ahead, *Paul*" the door replied, "if you like being grounded so much. Your folks can't see or hear me. I'm just a pattern to them. A funny looking grain in the wood." The monster sighed. "Christ almighty, I sure hope I made the right choice. I had to choose quick. For some reason, you came to mind."

I had no clue what he meant.

"I don't think I have a lot of time," he continued, "so I'm going to ask you some questions and I'll need you to answer me straight."

I didn't say anything. I don't think he expected me to.

"You know the house on the hill?"

Honestly, I thought it was a dumb first question. Everybody knew the 'house on the hill,' though our town of 25,000 had several hills covered in several houses. I didn't even need to think about it as the image popped clearly into my mind. It wasn't a huge place, like a mansion or anything, but it was bigger than my house and looked way cooler. At least from the outside.

I'd never been inside, but nearly every weekend, I rode my bike on the dirt trails that wrapped around the boulder-covered knoll on which it sat.

"Batman's house?" I asked.

That's what everyone I knew called it. Whether it was the real Batman or just the chubby guy that *played* Batman, no one seemed to clarify.

"Jesus H. Christ, for the life of me, I don't know where you kid's come up with this BS. But, yeah, sure, Batman's house."

The door was silent for an uncomfortable amount of time. I could hear the television again. It sounded like a boring doctor show.

"Hello?" I whispered.

"Sorry, I get pulled away sometimes. Where were we?"

"Batman's house."

"Yeah, right. Anyway, you're the kid that's always riding his bike around the place, right?"

I was *one* of the kids that rode around there. I'd seen others as well.

But I nodded and was about to say 'yes' before the monster continued.

"Good, good. That's a relief. It's hard to see clearly like this. Everything's thick and run together like mud." He paused. I thought I heard him take a deep breath. "Before we go any further, what does your old man do?"

I didn't take any time to ponder why the monster was asking me such weird questions. Adults, and the monster sounded like an adult monster, were always asking weird questions.

"He's a mechanic. He works on trucks at the mine out in Laverne Valley."

"Good. Very good. A man who works with his hands is probably someone with zero political agenda."

Politics? Part of me wanted to ask him why a monster was concerned about politics, but honestly, I didn't think I cared no matter what the answer would be.

"Not that it matters," he said. "You're not going to say anything about anything, right?"

I didn't respond quickly enough.

"Right?" He entered into a coughing fit from that final word's harshness.

"What if I do?"

"You don't want to mess with monsters, *Paul.*"

The reply came without hesitation and made me believe that he was probably correct.

"I won't say anything," I said, though inside, I thought maybe I had just lied.

The monster was silent for what seemed like a long time, and I think I fell asleep to the sounds of my parent's TV show before he spoke again.

"Okay, then. I need you to do me a favor."

* * *

I never found out what the favor was, or if I did, I didn't remember.

The next morning, I ran out of my room as quickly as I could, my eyes avoiding what I wanted to believe was merely a product of my imagination—a mere nightmare. I made it to the bus stop just as I heard the pneumatic hiss of the bus's opening doors.

I tried to distract myself with tetherball during first recess, but I lost three rounds before the bell rang and we all had to line up for class.

Mrs. Kirk quizzed us on summing coins and then read aloud a chapter of *Bridge to Terabithia*. Before lunch, she finished the first half of a lesson on the Civil Rights movement and talked about how the government was mostly good, but had made some 'mistakes' in the past.

Sitting in the cafeteria, my ears were filled with the echoes of noisy kids and plastic trays clacking against long, polished tables. I smelled nothing but soggy green beans and peanut butter sandwiches. I thought of telling one of my classmates about the monster in the door, but I decided not to say anything, thinking it may have just been a dream after all. I wasn't really close with any of the kids anyway. They would probably call me stupid and tease me about it the rest of the school year. So, instead, I sat and poked at my rectangular slice of cheese pizza, listening to the two boys next to me argue over which was the better *Garbage Pail Kid*: Adam Bomb or Up Chuck.

By the time the bus dropped me off, I felt unexplainably exhausted. I stayed far from my bedroom as long I could until I fell asleep in the middle of *Airwolf* and Dad woke me up to brush my teeth.

Mom had closed the door, but now I was wide awake, waiting. I gathered enough courage to look up toward the door, even shut my eyes several times to see if it would open, but it remained.

* * *

It was Saturday, late morning. I had last seen Dad sunken into his living room chair, watching *Dr. Who*, one hand in a plastic bag of Taco-flavored Doritos. Mom was getting her hair done at Mr. Orlando's beauty shop.

After I had eaten breakfast and watched my third episode of *Scooby*

Doo, I now stood with a pile of paper towels and a bottle of *409* at my side.
I held my breath and scrubbed at the pee-stained rim of the toilet. This was
'my' bathroom, so I knew the grossness was because I was always in a hurry,
but that didn't make it any better. My only consolation was that this was my
only chore of the day.

I thought I heard Dad calling me, so I stepped outside.

Ex-ster-mi-nate! Ex-ster-mi-nate!

Just a *Dr. Who* dalek.

I turned back to the bathroom and grabbed the *409* to apply a couple
more squirts. Again, I swore I heard someone saying my name, but I couldn't
dismiss it as coming from the television.

I approached the bathroom doorway and listened intently.

"Hey, Paul."

A cold chill ran through my body and my stomach dropped. The
plastic bottle fell from my hand, thunking heavily on the linoleum. I looked to
my left and saw my bedroom door. It was closed, but that meant the monster
was now facing me on the outside.

My next thought was to run and tell Dad, but I could only stand
frozen with fear. If I had drunk more water that morning, I'm pretty sure I
would have peed my pants.

"Stop being such a baby. I know this isn't the best look for me, but
like I said last time, beggars can't be choosers."

The monster in the door was speaking again. And as much as I had
hoped I was having a dream, I pretty much knew that this was really happening.

"We have some unfinished business, you and I, and it's gotten more urgent. I wanted to talk to you last night, but I got some things going on over which I have no control."

If a door could shiver, this door shivered.

"I need you to go to the house—Batman's house—and get something. Can you do that?"

"I gotta finish cleaning the bathroom." As soon as the words left my mouth, I felt ridiculous. What did a monster care about that? And was I actually agreeing to his request?

"Fine." He sounded firm but calm. "But after that, I need you to ride over there."

"Why do you want me to go to the house?"

"There's a key inside. Behind the television opposite the master bed. I need you to get that key."

"What for?"

"We'll talk about that later. Right now, I just need you to get it."

I hesitated.

"What if Batman's there?"

The monster sighed.

"Look, I hate to disappoint you kid, but Batman's not there. He doesn't live there. Never has. Never will. No one's home. Trust me."

Sure, trust a monster in my door, I thought. And for some odd reason, a part of me did. Though he looked like a monster, a part of him didn't seem like one. More like my grumpy Uncle Louis.

"Is the door unlocked?"

"No, but there's a fake rock by the row of yucca trees lining the driveway. It's orange, slightly faded, but the roundest rock of the bunch. Pick it up and you'll find a little compartment holding the house key."

I had so many questions.

"How do you know all this? Do you live in a door there too? And what are you going to do with the key behind the TV?" I didn't see how he could use it.

My bedroom door shook a little and I stepped back. "Tarnation kid, you're wasting time in which I'm short supply. This is why I don't have any little brats. Now go clean up your piss and *Get. The. Key.*"

It sounded like the monster ended the sentence with a couple of coughs.

"And what if I don't?" I hated being ordered to do things.

I stared at his unmoving face for several long seconds. Beeps and bloops from *Dr. Who* resonated in the background. The monster seemed to have gone away again.

Every question in my mind seemed to lead to more questions. I began to suspect that this monster wasn't lying. He really wasn't in my door and that was just the form he took.

But in that case, who *was* he? Why did he need a key?

I snapped out of my reverie, realizing that I was going to do what he asked, if only to sate my curiosity and solve a mystery like Scooby and the gang.

* * *

According to my plastic wristwatch, it took me all of seven minutes and sixteen seconds to traverse the two or so miles from my house to the foot of the hill. I had pedaled my Mongoose with every ounce of available energy until my body was drenched from exertion under the August sun.

I viewed the steep pavement which ran along the hill's side and led up to Batman's house. A sudden panic swept over me.

What if someone really *was* there and I got in trouble for trying to get inside? I could picture it already. The cops finding my body behind one of the big boulders on the hill. Or I'd wind up in juvie for breaking and entering.

My parents would be pissed.

I shook my head and leaned forward on my bike, pushing hard on the pedals as I slowly climbed the hill. I'd come this far. If I could talk to a monster in my door, I could do this.

* * *

Winding blacktop gave way to a cement driveway lined with yucca trees that I had never paid much attention to. I was half searching for the round, orange rock and half keeping an eye on the windows of Batman's house. Reflecting sunlight made everything glare so that I couldn't look very long.

I walked my bike up the driveway and into the garage beneath the main level. There were a couple of cars parked inside. On first glance, I almost hopped back on and took off down the hill, but noticed both vehicles were covered in a light coat of dust. One was a red, almost orange, Porsche. It didn't look like one of the newer ones. The other was a silver Lincoln Town-car. I didn't think either had been moved in a long time, though when you live in the desert, the dirt doesn't take long to stick to things.

I calmed myself and turned my bike around, leaning it against a pillar so I could make a fast getaway.

The false rock was ridiculously easy to spot among the other gray and brown stones. Sure enough, there was a tiny compartment inside which held a key. I took a deep breath and walked up the broad, curved staircase to the top floor.

I saw why Batman would want to live here. The tall, distant mountains that walled our town like sentries were visible all around me. Below them, sporadic houses held tight to the desert floor, connected by miles of both dirt and asphalt streets. And with such an unobstructed view of the sky, spotting the bat signal at night would be no problem.

I could have spent hours just looking out and around the property, but I knew that Dad and Mom, mainly Mom, would worry if I wasn't back for lunch.

I found what appeared to be the only door, inserted the key, and turned it.

Three seconds later, I was inside, my chin practically on the floor. The living room was vast, dressed in puke-yellow carpet. Colorful bean bags and two large sofas were clustered around a coffee table. Near the far window sat a long dining room table surrounded by dark wooden chairs. The place seemed clean and tidy.

"Hello?" I said halfheartedly.

No reply. Only the cawing of a distant crow from the open door behind me. Inside, the air felt oddly cold and still. It gave me goosebumps.

I shut the door and walked around the room. As I did so, there were two things that caught my attention.

One was a large boulder poking through the carpet at the corner of the dining room table. Jagged, yet polished, it looked every bit a part of the furniture as the rest of the stuff. I wondered if it came out of the ground or was placed there, but it was the second thing that obliterated any more questions and caused me to rub my eyes like some sort of cartoon character. Behind the far end sofa was a swimming pool.

A swimming pool.

In the house.

I never knew such a thing was possible. I walked towards it and saw that it was actually only *part* of an egg-shaped pool, the larger section running beneath the floor-to-ceiling windows and onto the outdoor balcony.

It would have been the most amazing thing I had ever seen had it been filled with water, but it was empty, stained with age at the bottom, and looking kind of sad.

I explored the rest of the house. There was a kitchen, a couple of tiny guest bedrooms, and a humongous closet filled with pressed pants and cowboy hats.

The master bedroom was almost as awesome as the living room but in a different way. The queen-sized bed was encased in a fancy oak headboard and footboard. Like any kid does to a perfectly-made bed, I jumped on and spread myself out over the cool comforter. To my left were seven rifles leaning against wooden shelving built into the wall. They looked like shotguns, for hunting maybe, and though I wanted to grab one and check it out, I was afraid to touch them. Next to those were rows of framed photos, most of them black-and-white. In each, there was a man who looked kind of familiar, but I couldn't place him. It had to be the guy who owned the house, because he was posing with lots of different people, and he was usually wearing a cowboy hat. I actually recognized some of the people from old movies my grandparents watched.

I pushed myself up against the pillows and looked forward. There was a stone wall housing a fireplace in the middle and a television set to the right, reminding me why I was there.

Reluctantly, I got up and stood in front of the set. I wondered how I was going to pull it out of there until I saw it was sitting on a wooden platform with a lip. I pulled at the lip and it slid right out with the TV on top. It must have been built that way so it would be easy to work on. It came out far enough so that behind it, I could see the shape of a key hiding under an inch of dust bunnies. I grabbed it, wiped my hands, and shoved the television back in.

On any other day and in any other situation, if someone would have asked me what I did the rest of that afternoon, I would have told him that I sped home, inhaled my lunch, and called my friends to meet me right back at Batman's house until the sun fell.

The fact was that after that day, I never wanted to step foot in there again.

* * *

The door was closed and then it was open.

"Paul."

His voice sounded weak.

"Paul, you got the key?"

I sat up in the bed and leaned against the wall. I could hear Mom and Dad watching their medical drama again.

"Yeah," I replied.

"Dynamo!" he shouted, triggering a series of coughs.

I waited for him to finished before asking, "What do you want me to do with it?"

"It'll get you into where you need to go. It's a master key for the city. You know where the Los Ranchitos real estate office is?"

I knew it was near the bank Dad went to and so I nodded.

"That key will unlock the back door. Once you're inside, you'll head right down the hallway and open the last door on your left. It'll say *RE-CORDS* on the nameplate.

"Inside, there's a cabinet marked *Declarations of CC&Rs*. I need you to take a specific folder filled with papers inside, labeled *LEGACY*. Leave everything else. I want you to take that folder with you."

It seemed like a lot to remember.

"Are you with me?" he asked.

"Yeah...down the hall. The records room. In a cabinet with Declarations."

"Declarations of CC&Rs."

"What's that?"

"Doesn't matter to you. Just some paperwork."

"Okay..."

"But don't take it home!" A couple more coughs. "This is very, very important. You need to take it out to an empty field somewhere and burn it."

I wondered if I heard him right.

"Burn it?"

"Yup. Don't forget to grab some matches on your way out the door. You know where your old man keeps 'em."

"I feel like I'm going to get into trouble for this."

The monster was silent for a moment.

"You won't. Paul, you can trust me. You'll be doing me a huge favor. You'll be doing the *whole town* a huge favor."

"What do you mean?"

I thought the monster had left again, but then it spoke.

"You're young, but I'm betting you've already made a few mistakes in your life, right?"

Of course, I thought. I cringed, remembering last month when I stole a kid's Twinkie from his lunchbox when he wasn't looking last month. I never fessed up, even though I felt bad when he popped another boy in the nose over it.

"If you had the chance, wouldn't you try to fix those mistakes?"

"Like a do-over?"

"Like a do-over."

"Yeah, sure," I said.

We were both quiet.

"When do you want me to do this?" I finally asked.

"Tonight. After your folks go to bed."

That would be pretty soon, I knew. Tomorrow was a weekday and Dad would be up at five-in-the-morning getting ready for work.

I had never snuck out of the house at night before. The whole idea was thrilling and made my stomach feel a little funny.

"Deal," I said.

The central air kicked on and I felt a rush of cold air spew from the vent near the ceiling.

"Paul, I don't think we'll be talking after tonight so I want to let you know you're a good kid. I'm sorry I threatened you when we first met. I didn't mean any of it, but everyone needs motivation."

I shrugged my shoulders.

"I also want to thank you."

"For what?" I said. "Burning some papers?"

"For helping a monster with his do-over."

* * *

In the still of night, a place you know so well in the daytime seems like another world entirely. The Los Ranchitos office wasn't far from Batman's house, so I made it there quickly on my bike. Along the way, I had to swerve several times on the streets to avoid crashing into bounding jackrabbits. Luckily the moon was full and provided a decent amount of light by which to navigate.

The key unlocked the door just as promised. An uneasiness settled over me again, and I wondered too late if there might be a security guard on duty or if an alarm would go off.

As I swung the door open and walked inside, it became apparent that I didn't have to worry about either. Maybe that was one of the nice things about living in this small town.

Following the monster's instructions, I found the room he mentioned and flicked on the light. Filing cabinets lined every wall. Some drawers were at a level twice my height and it was on one of these that I spotted the label I was looking for.

I grabbed a stool and dragged it over beside the cabinet. The drawer was stuffed with manila folders and papers. I shuffled through them until I found the folder marked *LEGACY*. I pulled it out and jumped down to the floor.

A decision had to be made. Should I look through the papers and see just what I'd be getting rid of, or was I better off not knowing? I doubted I would have wanted someone to thumb through my mistakes if they were written down. But I also knew that I was only here because even though I had come to more familiar terms with the monster, it had originally threatened me.

There were only about six or seven pages of typewritten text on stiff paper, yellowed with age. It seemed like a bunch of business mumbo-jumbo, but as I scanned, my eyes locked on to something that jogged a recent memory from Mrs. Kirk's class and made a stolen Twinkie seem like child's play.

"No part of said property shall be used or occupied or permitted to be used or occupied in whole or in part by any person of African or Asiatic descent or by any person not of the white or Caucasian race, except that domestic servants, chauffeurs, hostlers, laborers, farm-hands, or gardeners of other than white or Caucasian race may live on or occupy the premises where their employer resides."

* * *

Even at night, summer made the desert hot.

I crouched in the middle of an empty field of creosote bushes, a half-used matchbook in my hands and the folder lying in the dirt.

What sort of mistake was I fixing? What I read seemed like a really bad thing and the monster made it sound like *he* was responsible. I had been taught to help people, sure, but monsters? I found myself having to make more decisions over the past few days than I had in all of my life.

I tore out a stick, stuck it between the folded book and pulled. I always loved the sulfury smell of matches. I had left the folder open to the questionable page and the tiny flame gave the passage an eerie glow.

For helping a monster with his do-over rang repeatedly in my head.

* * *

"Nate Carp passed away this morning. Down at St. Marie's."

Dad handed the paper to my mom and took a quick sip of his Folgers.

She was in her maroon-colored nightgown, no makeup, head tilted up but eyes peering down through her glasses. "I didn't even know he was in the hospital."

"Hell of a way to go," Dad said. "Apparently he'd been ravaged by diabetes. Lost his arms and legs. Began to sink into dementia before giving up the ghost."

"Come to think of it, I haven't seen him for a couple of years," Mom said. "He used to come down to the church during the annual rummage sale and shake our hands. Seemed like a wonderful man."

"He had a great vision for this town. His legacy will definitely live on." Dad smiled, rubbed the top of my head and picked up the sports page.

I didn't really care that much as the maze printed on the back of my *Cookie Crisp* cereal box held my attention, but something caught my eye when Mom laid the paper down. Beneath the headline of *Nate Carp, Town Founder, Passes Away at the Age of 80* was a photograph.

In it stood a man in a cowboy hat, looking proudly into the distance as his hands gripped the railing surrounding Batman's house.

"Mom?"

"Yes?"

"Hold on one second." I ran to my room and looked up at the monster in the door. I searched, trying to discern any hint that he was still there. Instead, I saw only a funny shape of grain in the wood. I bent down beside my bed, and pulled out a dirty envelope from underneath.

As I zoomed past the door, I made a silent apology.

Process Summary

The Monster in the Door is story number eight in the #52ShortStories challenge.

The challenge of this story is that I had so many of the elements firmly in mind from personal experience, I needed to make sure I translated them into something that reader could see just as well. I don't know if I did that, but I gave it a shot (and that's what this challenge is mostly about — giving things shots. Like a doctor. Or a mad scientist. Yeah, definitely the latter.)

The initial inspiration was this:

That's the door to my childhood bedroom and it's still there (though the room has become a home office). You can imagine a kid with a fertile imagination would have some interesting thoughts regarding that grain pattern in the upper-right corner.

And like any small town, there are colorful bits of history and local lore that can be weaved into an intriguing story. There is a "House on the Hill.". And that little bit of text in the CC&R papers? Yup, it's real. Sad, but true.

The writing was fluid for the most part, I think because I was so familiar with many of the elements. I also decided to set this in the 80s, hoping that I could evoke a sense of childhood by using my own experiences as fodder.

I'll probably come back to this setting from time to time. Though I haven't lived in the area for a couple of decades, there's something about the hometown that leaves its mark.

Home for a Fish

Statistics

Synopsis: Larry, a veteran of skid row, stumbles into his friend's pawn shop to give her a gift and say goodbye—he's leaving for outer space.

Word Count: 3,800

Genre: Sci-Fi / Humor

Completed Week: October 9th – October 14th

Home for a Fish

It was small, yellow, and swimming tiny circles inside a discarded tin of SPAM.

"Oh, Larry. You know I'll take most anything from you, no questions asked, but gimme a break here. You're taking this to a whole other level."

Larry hunched over the opposite side of the glass counter. Zora could hear his hands digging around the pockets of his grease-stained raincoat as he pulled out a handkerchief. He blew his nose. It sounded like a tanker coming into port through a thick fog. They both looked down and studied the overactive goldfish.

"He's special," Larry said. "Real good luck. I wanted you to have him before I go. Give him a good home."

Zora ignored the fish for a second and locked eyes on his dirty face.

She had known Larry since before the shop was open. During construction, he would come by and talk about how he was going to be her best customer. He always had something to pawn, he said.

I'm a man of means!

He didn't exactly look like a man of means, what, with the laces fraying on his dirty white tennis shoes and a wrinkled dress shirt half-tucked into his way-too-big pants. Zora used to worry that was code for sticky fingers, but nothing he brought in was ever reported or verified to be stolen. She also never asked what he did with the money. He never paid back his loans and his stuff always sold easily—high-definition televisions, fancy stand mixers, and boxes of retro video games.

"Go where?" she asked. She was surprised at how deeply his words shook her.

"The big time! Outer space!"

It finally happened. Larry was always teetering on the edge, mostly engaged in harmless flights of fancy, but he had never fallen off.

A bald man thumbing through a box of LPs glanced in his direction and snorted, but looked away sheepishly after Zora gave him a hard stare.

She crossed her arms and leaned on the counter. Her slight paunch rested on the lip of the glass and she turned up a corner of her mouth.

"Oh yeah? Outer space? That's great! I've heard it's beautiful at night. Where to? Mars? Venus?"

Larry's eyes looked more rheumy than normal. He had the kind of face that would reject a beard if it crawled up and settled in, but patches of whiskers poked out from the top of his weather-worn cheeks like poorly planted sod.

"This isn't anything to laugh about, Zora. The aliens gave him to me." He raised his eyebrows at the fish. "They're taking me out of this place. Say they'll give me a *home*." His voice choked a little as he emphasized the word and a breeze of mint caressed Zora's face. She didn't know why, but the one thing Larry refused to let follow his appearance was his breath.

"I'm sorry," she said. "I didn't mean to make light. That's great. Really, really great." As the words left her lips, she was figuring out who to call. Most of the nearby shelters were good when it came to food and a bed, but the mental health professionals on staff left something to be desired. Calling the police would be even worse.

Still, Zora was concerned about Larry. She worried that 'outer space' may have been code for something far more darker that he was planning. Had his spirit finally been broken? It didn't seem to be the case, but she'd heard somewhere that those who were on the cusp of suicide often seemed happier right before the event. In the meantime, she would try to keep him in the shop until she could come up with a decent plan.

"So what does this all have to do with the fish?" she asked.

"Ho ho!" His smile came back and made the skin crack around his lips. "It's a wonderful story."

Zora's dimples lit up and she raised her eyebrows, trying to generate some enthusiasm. Though their faces were already inches apart, Larry found a way to lean in closer.

"The Sanderson brothers, who everyone knows aren't really brothers, have been elbowing into my turf for a while, harassing me, taking my stuff, so I decided to find somewhere new to hole up. Now, I'm not one to slum, but I needed to go somewhere while I figured out someplace better. I grabbed my cart and parked out at O'Charley's temporarily. I lit a fire, just stood there and thought." He tapped his finger on his temple. "It's funny, the things you think about when you're forced outside of your comfort zone. You should make it a regular habit, you know."

Zora nodded, imagining such a thing would be doubly difficult for Larry. His comfort zone seemed to stretch for miles on end.

"So there I was, warming my hands over a barrel behind O'Charley's, no one else around and all of a sudden, I feel something brush against my hat."

She'd never seen Larry wear a hat.

He backed up and looked at the worn gray carpet of the shop, spreading his hands as if presenting something. "Then I hear a smacking sound on the asphalt. I bend over and from the light of the flames, I see him. There he is. Kenneth."

"Kenneth?"

"Oh, yeah," he bowed his head towards the fish. "Named him after a brother I had long ago. Still have. I think." He waved his hand. "You know what I mean."

Zora smiled gently.

"Anyway, there he is, poor little guy, flippin' and floppin' around like...like...hah! Like a fish out of water!" Larry stood up straight and beamed around the room as if expecting applause from the two other customers. He seemed to be satisfied with the response even though the bald man was halfway out the door and an older woman was intently examining a collection of old *National Geographic* magazines. "So, I look around and found that empty can of SPAM laying beside the dumpster. It still had some of that jelly inside, so I emptied it, filled it up with water from the faucet and put Kenneth inside. He started to swim like the dickens!"

Zora looked at Kenneth. She didn't know what a happy fish looked like, but he didn't appear to be sad, either. She turned back to Larry. Maybe she should call Daniel, her brother-in-law. Zora's husband had accidentally confessed one night that his brother was seeing a shrink. Compulsive gambling issue. It would open up a whole can of worms, but Larry's life may be on the line here and maybe Daniel could put her in touch with the right person.

"I looked down at Kenneth and told him, 'You're lucky, pal. You might have been my dinner. I can't throw you in the fire now. Wouldn't be right. But if you had landed in there, well, I would have had no choice but to make a meal outta ya. Be happy I don't eat that damned sushi!'"

He talked directly to Kenneth as he repeated that part of the story.

"Anyway, I'm holding the can in my hand, trying to keep it away from the fire so the water don't get too hot. I start to think about how I'm gonna' feed Kenneth. I don't know what fish eat. Never had one. Had a dog once. I'd pet him real hard and then he'd puke all over me. Weirdest thing." Larry's eyes stared off into the air and then he snapped out of it.

"But as I stood there thinkin', I see some shadows cast against the back of O'Charley's. Nearly scared the bejesus outta me, so much that Kenneth's home nearly fell out of my hands. I turned and saw a family—a man with his wife and little girl. I mean, think it was his wife and girl. They were dressed...oh, I don't know...different. It wasn't like they was wearin' space suits or anything. But the clothing looked off. I thought they was European."

"'Larry?' the man asked?'"

Larry leaned further in still until the tips of his eyeballs were almost touching Zora's. "Now, I know lots of the neighborhood regulars and I also know they don't know my real name. In fact, Zora, you're the only one 'round here that does."

Larry pulled back again. "So I'm thinkin', these must be friends of yours.

"'Zora send you?' I asked. The man looked at his wife and daughter, seeming a little confused. 'No,' he said. 'We've lost something.' Then he looked down at his little girl. '*She* lost something.'

"The accents were a little funny, so I kept on thinkin' they were from Europe. Brave as anyone I'd ever known, the girl walked right up to me and reached for Kenneth's new home. At this point, I'd grown protective of my little golden brother, so I pulled him back into myself and looked at the father. 'How you know my name?' I asked. I was also thinkin' of some place to run, but they were blocking the only exit.

"He looks at his wife, who, just like the little girl, is as quiet as a mime in handcuffs. By the way, probably not important, but besides the clothes, these were some of the *ugliest* people I'd ever seen."

Zora tried hard not to giggle at the incongruity of Larry calling other people ugly. Maybe he cleaned up well, though.

"Finally, the dad says, 'Facial recognition technology.' Or something like that. Anyway, the girl, she's a real cutie. Cute as a button and she puts on this sad little face that just about broke my heart. So I took a deep breath, knelt down and placed the SPAM can on the ground. She looks inside and sees Kenneth swimming around and her smile could have brought joy to Lorenzo's face."

"Who?" Zora asked.

Larry paused for a second and tilted his head. "I ever tell you 'bout him? My old traveling buddy a few town's back. That guy always complained about something. Bitched about uncomfortable boxcars. Bitched about the weather. I think he finally bitched about the wrong thing to the wrong person and I woke up one morning to find him gone with half his stuff left behind."

"I see," Zora said. "So, the little girl, she obviously didn't take the fish." Zora was trying to steer the conversation back on track, mainly to divine Larry's real plans.

"Yeah, yeah, gettin' to it. Gettin' to it." By now, the store had emptied out and it was nearing midnight.

"Keep on," Zora said as she walked toward the front door, flipped the OPEN sign to CLOSED, and pulled down the metal security shutters on the surrounding windows. As she came back, she slyly picked up the cordless phone beneath the register and stuck it in her back pocket. She decided she would excuse herself shortly and call Daniel.

"So I said to the dad, 'I can't take a little girl's pet. I done some things in my time, Mister, but I have my limits.' I backed away and the girl scooped the can up with both hands.

"'Thank you,' he said. He put a hand on his daughter's head. 'We're here on vacation and the fish was a souvenir. Unfortunately, we didn't realize the ship's AI would consider it a potential threat and-'

"'Come again?'

"The man squinted his eyes.

"'The A-what?' I said.

"Then his face seemed to clear up.

"'Oh. Our...computer. It sucked him up and dumped him outside the ship. Luckily we were just clearing your planet's mesosphere or else he probably would have been burnt to a crisp. I must say, I'm quite surprised to find him still alive, but Hyacinth insisted we come back.' Then he looked at his little girl with a crooked smile. 'Looks like I'll have to make some tweaks to the defense systems configuration.'"

Larry grunted. "Let me tell you, Zora. At that point, I thought it was all coming together. *Hyacinth*. This poor girl was stuck with some strung out, ex-hippies for parents."

"Oh my," said Zora. Now she was concerned not so much for Larry, but for this potential family. Maybe he'd been telling the truth in his own way. Were these some weirdos trying to take advantage of him? She was second guessing whether or not to phone the police. She would need more information.

"Then what happened?" she asked.

"Then it was like a fog cleared and the mom spoke! 'We want to thank you for your help,' she said. Her voice was—I don't know how to describe it—almost like she was speaking through bubbles. A little gurgly. 'Is there anything you need?' she asked me. I figured I would have a little fun, crack a little joke, so I said, 'Yeah, a home with HBO, a hot tub, and a large pepperoni pizza. Extra pepperoni.'

"The dad and mom looked at each other kinda funny. 'You want a second home?' the man said? Of course, I laughed. 'No, no. Just one. I'm not a greedy man.' They whispered to each other, looking around the alley, checking out my fire. All the while, Hyacinth was looking down at Kenneth like a doting mother and said, 'Can we keep him?'"

Larry ran a hand through his greasy locks and he locked eyes briefly with Zora.

"Something in her voice, I knew right away that she wasn't talkin' about my little golden brother. Alarm bells went off in my head. I was already kicking myself for temporarily hunkering down in a place with only one exit. There's some real freaks out there. Serial killers, and so on. Never heard of no serial killing family, but I didn't want to be the first to find one neither.

"'Look,' I said. 'I'll be on my way now. Glad you got your fish back.'

"'Where are you going?' the dad asked.

"'None of ya' damned business,' I said and looked down at Hyacinth who was now gaping up at me as if I'd just shot BBs into every dream she ever had. 'Pardon my French.'"

Larry shrugged while he drummed his fingers on the glass case. "They didn't stand in my way, really. Just sort of watched as I walked away, which I thought was odd for a family of serial killers. I was almost out of the alley when I just felt this pang hit my conscience. Maybe this Hyacinth's brain had been twisted by these folks. If she was in trouble, I couldn't leave her behind. I had to stall to figure things out."

Zora chuckled at the irony.

"'Look,' I said. 'I'm a little hungry. I could use a couple bucks just to grab a pastrami on rye down at Dale's.' Then they were whispering once again and I had half a mind to grab the girl and run, but you know, my bum knee.

"'Hyacinth, do you think you're ready for a new level of responsibility?' the mom asked."

A smile crept up on the corners of Larry's lips. "Zora, you'd think the girl had just been told she could have anything she wanted for Christmas. She hopped up and down like a frog on uppers.

"'Yes! Yes!' she said, holding her hand over the can of SPAM to keep Kenneth from flying free again.

"The mom and dad looked at each other and nodded.

"'Larry,' the dad said, 'we can give you that home you want.

"'Okay,' I said, "I've had about enough of you people. I don't know what you want, but—'

Larry stared absently at the shelves of baseball cards behind the counter. "And I don't know any other way to put it, Zora, but time just seemed to stand still as I watched the man literally pull his face off. I nearly fainted but for the mom running over to catch me. My senses slowly came back to me and by the light of the flames dancing in the barrel, I saw something...not of this world. A pair of eyes the size and shape of big blueberry muffins. A tiny slit for a mouth and three holes for a nose. The color of his flesh was milky white. I managed to look down at Hyacinth and she was still smiling."

Zora's eyebrows shot up. Larry didn't look like he'd been on anything, but she wondered if whatever he took had nearly worn off at this point.

"Somehow, through that tiny mouth, the dad spoke again, 'I don't mean to frighten you, Larry. But we want you to know we're telling the truth. We're not supposed to reveal ourselves when we travel, but you seem like a nice being and a fellow in need.'

"Maybe any other person would have run out of their screaming, but I've seen all kinds of people with all kinds of afflictions, so maybe his appearance didn't bother me so much. I managed to remain standing on my own two feet again. The mom still looked like the mom, Hyacinth, like Hyacinth.

"'Am I dreaming?' I asked.

"'Lucky for you, no,' the mom said. 'We're bending the rules a little here and we need to have your answer now. We're already running late for our next stop.' She looked at her husband. 'Aunt Geoaokeokmnnhfhfvamim is going to be upset if we miss dinner. *Again.*'

Zora almost questioned if Larry was having a stroke.

"Well," he said, "it was something like that. Ain't exactly a name that rolls off the tongue. Anyway, of course, I thought long and hard about the situation. After three seconds, I said, 'Are you offering me a job?'

"'Not exactly. Have you ever owned a pet, Larry?'

"'Yeah. Had a dog once. Used to pet him real hard until he'd puke all over me.' The mom looked at me kinda funny, but the dad just shrugged.

"'Okay, he said. Well, that would be you. Hopefully without the puking.'

Zora scrunched her face like she'd just bitten into a rotten lemon, rind and all. Larry waved his hand.

"Hey, hey, let me tell you. I was instantly offended at the idea. A *pet?* But then I began to think about most every pet I've ever known. Always got fed. Always slept whenever they wanted to. Played whenever, too. You name it. And so I began thinkin' that this wasn't such a bad idea after all."

Larry sighed.

"'I'm tired of this place, Zora. What have I got here besides trash can fires and an aching back from sleeping on the hard ground?"

Screw it, she thought. She was calling Daniel. Her left hand searched absently for the phone in her pants.

"I understand," she said.

"'So, I asked, 'I'll have a home? Regular meals?'

"'The mom smiled at me and nodded.

"'I thought, what did I have to lose? 'You got yourself a deal!' I said, reaching out to shake hands with them. The little girl squealed and hugged her mom's leg. She looked down at Kenneth and said, 'We're going to be soooooo happy together!'

"And then, poor thing, her dad dropped the other shoe: 'Honey, you know the rules. Only one pet.'

"She looked a little down, but it was obvious she had made up her mind. Cute kid. At least the face I saw. Maybe she's all bug-eyed like her old man, but I could get used to it. But the way she looked at me, I dunno...she reminded me of you, Zora. And I knew that I had to come and say goodbye."

"Oh. I don't know what to say." She searched for the words, knowing that he would probably be angry with her after she called for help. Might never want to speak with her again.

"Instantly, I said 'If you need to unload Kenneth, I know someone who would take real good care of him. If you'll give me twenty minutes, I'll run over and drop him off.'"

"So the girl gives me the fish and here I am." His eyes fell to the content little goldfish bending around the can of SPAM.

"Larry, you're an amazing man and you know I love you." She reached over the counter and hugged him tightly, never realizing how much she'd grown used to his street scent. "I think I have a fish tank in the back that someone brought in a few weeks back. I'm going to get it, clean it up a little." She pulled back and held his shoulders. "We'll give Kenneth a good home and then I want to buy you dinner."

"No, no." He removed Zora's hands and clasped them between his own. "They'll be here any minute. I just wanted to say goodbye and thank you for always being kind. I hope my brother brings you good luck too." His eyes were beyond watery now. A solitary tear crossed the gullies carved across his weathered face and he started toward the door.

"Larry, please, if you can just wait a few more—"

As Zora reached for the phone, the glass case rattled lightly as did the shelves all around the store. The ground vibrated and a pair of tall speaker cabinets slammed flat onto the shop floor. She panicked and her first thought was: *Earthquake.*

But then a blinding light streamed through the front door and cracks in the metal shutters, casting geometric shadows against the vintage neon signs and electric guitars lining the off-white walls.

Zora shielded her eyes with a hand.

Larry smiled. "Told 'em to meet me out front."

Mesmerized, she watched as he opened the door. Only the jingle of the bell hanging on the handle pulled her out of her stupor. She ran after him and despite the blinding glare, she managed to see his outline approaching the source of the light. Whatever it was, it sat in the middle of the street, maybe the size of a semi-trailer but its design was impossible to make out other than appearing 'round.'

The ground outside was still trembling under a low-grade hum. A car alarm went off in the distance. As Larry's silhouette grew smaller, Zora's breath almost got away from her as three other shadows appeared. Two tall-ish, one small.

They merged into a single black blob until they were swallowed up by the light. The world around her settled once again as the giant luminescent ball lifted from the ground and zipped toward the starless city sky.

If anyone had asked Zora what had happened that night, she couldn't have explained it. Of course, she wouldn't have to. No one would come looking for Larry. But a funny thought occurred to her as she entered the front door. She might actually have a fish tank in the back.

Process Summary

Home for a Fish is story number nine in the #52ShortStories challenge. Oh boy.

In a sense, I love boundaries. They force me to make a decision. I think this works for so many people and why an American fast food joint like In 'n' Out does amazingly well. The menu is limited which ends up making lunch an easy proposition. Do you want the burger, or would you rather have the burger? Maybe a burger would be better instead.

So I took my three StoryCube dice and dove in:

Some interesting things I'm discovering at this stage in my journey:

Folk wisdom wins again. You can't please everyone all of

the time. It's been interesting to see the varied opinions depending on the reader's preferred genre and style. So far, this is my first reader's favorite story. She likes my 'lighter' fare. But, I've had much more solid responses among my writer friends on my more 'literary' pieces. One advantage to writing these short stories is that I can truly experiment without a lot of upfront investment and steer future works toward the appropriate audiences.

I'm relying less and less on planning before diving into the writing. I don't foresee that working for something novel length, but what do I know. That's just guessing at this point. But, I've been happy with having an image or an idea in my head and letting it grow naturally from the writing. Things certainly seem to be more fun this way.

The writing is coming more naturally. I've developed a rhythm over the past couple of stories and I feel like I've crossed that threshold where writing nearly every day is built on muscle memory. It's just something I do every morning after I exercise. I fret maybe a little, maybe not at all. But the heartburn isn't there nearly as much as it was 7 stories ago. To me, *this* was my primary goal with this challenge and Icouldn't be any more ecstatic now that I've finally built this habit.

I guess it's true that writing isn't some dark art beyond the standard means of improvement.

Practice, practice, practice.

Discipline, discipline, discipline.

It works. There aren't any shortcuts, and let's be honest: Wouldn't it be a shame if there were?

The Bubble Man

Statistics

Synopsis: A man is on trial for the abduction and murder of four children.

When the truth is revealed, will anyone believe it?

Word Count: 2,800

Genre: Fantasy / Historical Fiction

Completed Week: October 16th – October 21st

The Bubble Man

They call me The Bubble Man.

By 'they,' I don't mean everyone—just the aggrieved citizens. And by 'me,' I don't mean the current me—I have no more bubbles to blow. I've blown nothing but stale air for at least two weeks, seeing as how my barrels of stock were kicked over on their sides and rolled into the river while my cabin was burned to its dirt-packed foundation.

The sheriff told me that though he didn't make it before the vigilantes came, I ought to be satisfied that he arrived when he did. Even with a night as black as tar, I was sure I saw the eyes of his deputy through the holes of a hooded face—one blue, the other green—while someone else tied my hands, and while yet another person drew a rope through the nearest oak tree.

Even with the title no longer accurate, my home in flames and my life's work destroyed, they *still* call me The Bubble Man.

* * *

"You kidnapped them all. And then you killed them. And still, you've not the basic human decency to tell us where you've buried them."

The fat lawyer's face was ruddy, his nose bulbous and crimson red. I knew that face well enough. It was eager to get out of here. Ready to join its friends at the Red Eagle saloon and take its medicine.

"Isn't that true?" he finished.

"I did nothing of the sort, sir."

He looked at me like he was waiting for a signal. A pugilist preparing for a parry. The courtroom was silent except for the sequential tapping of his fingers along the rail of the jury box.

"Four children, Mr. Conklin." He turned to the jury. "Four lives snuffed out like freshly lit candles." He stopped moving his fingers and faced me again. His fist slammed down on the rail like a smith's hammer. "They'll never have a chance to illuminate this world and bring joy to their parents."

Such theatrics. I wondered if he'd been a part of the local Shakespeare company.

An indignant outburst would do me no favors, though.

"I did not kill those children," I said measuredly, "and they brought their parents no joy. If anything, I've given them a chance to live." From the audience behind the bar, there were grumbles and squeaks from people shifting on wooden benches.

I'll save us all the trouble and shoot the sonofabitch myself.

The not-so-subtle whisper came from Charlie's dad. I'd never met him, but from everything that Charlie had told me, I knew exactly who he was. Muffled cries came from the frumpy woman at his side. She buried her face into a lacy handkerchief and laid her head on his shoulder.

I looked at the jury again. By my account, ten were stony men who had made up their minds before they'd even taken their morning coffee. The other two looked timid enough to ride the prevailing winds.

"A chance to live, you say?" The corners of his mouth turned upward and he faced the jury while still addressing me. "Of course. Do you want to recount for us how you've given them this chance?"

The crowd settled again, perversely eager to hear something they didn't want to believe. I knew the truth and if I was going to die today, which I certainly was, there was nothing left to be a coward about.

"I put them in bubbles."

"In bubbles?"

"Yes. That's right. I put each one in a bubble and let them float away." My eyes lost focus as I stared at the ceiling. "Ernest, the freckle-faced boy who likes trains and baseball. Rose, a girl who loves playing in the mud. Emma, who wants to be a button-nosed doll and live in a giant doll's house. And then Charlie, for whom there is no greater joy than holding a picture book in one hand and a penny-sack of licorice in the other."

Charlie's mother released a whelp.

"I let them all float away from their unhappy existences."

The attorney wanted to smile. I could tell. An open-and-shut case and I had just provided him the munitions he needed. But he was too well trained to betray any sense of impending victory, so he kept his mouth taut and put on a show of utter disdain.

"You're of the worst sort, do you know that, Mr. Conklin? Do you *realize* that?" He addressed both the audience and jury. "There are street urchins of every kind in this world, but you can sniff them a mile away. You know better than to invite them into your homes. Even if it isn't obvious, there's always something to give them away—a gleam in their eyes, a scent on their person."

His finger was like an arrowhead aimed at my heart. "But this *monster*? He sits here and tells the most ridiculous lies as if he can get away with them. He recounts these children's lives as if they're still here, pouring salt into our community's fresh wounds." He looked at the judge, then the jury, and shook his head. "He's much too dangerous to be allowed to roam the towns and cities and every farmhouse in between. His is the face of innocence. Of the kindly uncle. Of the old lady giving a lad a handful of sweets for tending the weeds around her home.

"But his soul?" The lawyer shrugged uncaringly as if someone were telling him about the weather in Siam. "Unfixable. Rotten to the core."

He held himself up against the edge of the jury box. Sweat held down strands of auburn hair against his rolls of pasty neck fat. "No, no, gentlemen. Though we've come pitiably late to our discovery, we should be thankful that we've come at all. The sheep's wool has been sheared and the wolf has been revealed."

* * *

I knew judgment would come swiftly, despite the judge's request for a brief recess so that the jury could reconvene. My holding cell was bare. Quiet. It left me time to remember.

I recalled the faces of each of the children, and as I did so, the fear of my impending appointment mellowed. The hardest, most unyielding fist could not have dislodged the smile from my face. The kids were better off because of me. Of this, I had no doubt.

As far back as I can remember, I was an inventor filled with ideas, but I was never able to come up with the one thing that would catch on. Failed invention after failed invention eventually left me hungry, so I gave up for several years and took on more menial work. It would turn out to be just what I needed.

The idea of the bubbles came after another sixteen hours of working a flatboat along the Mississippi. It was one of those days when every muscle fiber felt like tenderized beef. I had spent hours on end picking up and throwing down sacks of grain flour.

I was soaking in the tub on that particular evening, out behind an excuse for a hotel in La Crosse, Wisconsin. Of course, by the time it was my turn, the water wasn't much clearer than the grand river herself. Still, I didn't mind being last. It meant I did not have to rush. It gave me time to think.

I had put in an excess of soap and amused myself with the froth of bubbles floating along the top. They reminded me of my youth when such frivolities were a fascination and I thought that if there was a way for children to take them wherever they went, I could bottle those frivolities and sell them in every town along the river.

So, I got to work and sought out pharmacists at every stop made along the river. In only a month's time, I was able to work out my own formula to build the most stable bubbles, many of them lasting long enough to float tens of feet into the sky before sailing downward and popping on the ground.

I promptly set up shop whenever we were in a town for more than a day. I was correct in my estimations of demand as jars of Mr. Conklin's Bubble Elixir sold almost faster than I could produce new solution. When the costs of storing the liquid grew due to the owners of the flatboats charging me exorbitant prices to use their 'valuable' storage space, I knew something had to change.

Heady with thoughts of fortunes, I immediately quit, filed a patent and settled back in La Crosse. I spent the rest of my small savings on a shack by the river, a dog for companionship, and enough ingredients to see me through the end of the year. I had labels drawn up by a local printer, using an illustration of my new canine friend, Jack, and I sold barrels of wholesale solution to flatboaters.

Finally, nearly a month after moving in, word spread within La Crosse itself as well as neighboring villages. The children came from all over. With each bottle and piece of looped wire I sold, I was paid in coin and flashes of joy at seeing them smile and play.

I began to know many of them well, and they, me. That's also when I began to learn of the dastardly events through which some of them suffered. One would arrive with a black eye, another with a limp in her walk. They trusted The Bubble Man. They confided in me their misbehavior. How they had done something wrong, though they couldn't always figure out what, but that their father or mother had rightly corrected them.

Charlie had said: *My papa, sometimes, he says he wishes I'd never been born. That I'm costing him too much money. Just another mouth to feed. I s'pose he's right. I'm always hungry.*

And Rose: *Mama says I'm too ugly to ever find a husband when I'm older. That's why she makes me work hard, she says, 'cause I'll need to support myself.*

My heart ached for these children. Each was a reminder of demons from my own childhood.

But who was I, a man selling simple amusements, to do anything about it? I truly believe my inventive subconscious listened to that aching heart and between the two of them, came up with an idea.

One day, I returned home with supplies from the local pharmacist. My head was somewhere else, worried for those children, as I mixed a fresh supply of bubbles. It wasn't until I poured the last ingredient that I realized I had gotten the solution all wrong. The mixture was thicker than normal and not bubbling as easy.

In my anger at having wasted money and, I suppose, my impotence in the children's lives, I took the barrel outside and turned it over onto the ground so that its contents spilled towards the river. Fortune had it that Jack was laying in the path and scrambled to get out of its way. As he flicked his paws back and forth in order to dislodge himself from the slippery substance, a large bubble began to form, eventually sealing him in and carrying him up into the air. I immediately ran over, but instead of popping the thing, I stood and watched, fascinated. The poor dog, he was clearly scared, but no matter how much he pawed at the bubble, it did not break and he continued to drift until he was twenty feet over the river.

Then it hung for maybe ten seconds after which it slowly sauntered down, finally meeting the currents of the river. It popped. Jack was free, paddling himself back to the shore.

For me, it was another one of those moments in life when dreams and ideas slammed together like the horns of two rams, rattling me awake.

The following week was a blur. I missed several deliveries and angered several flatboaters, but that was fine. I was doing *real* work, now.

I finally prepared a solution that saw large bubbles floating into the clouds, eventually disappearing from sight. Generating them was easy now. It could be done with a large piece of wound wire whipped through the air and around the subject. I wrote a letter, stuffed it in a bottle, and sent it into the sky.

Three weeks later, I received a reply in the post from a Mr. Bartleby Sloane. He stated that he had found my bottle sitting in the crook of an ash tree and that he hoped the three-foot-deep snow from Buffalo's exceptionally cold winter would not impede his reply.

A throat-clearing cough and the squeak of rusty hinges disturbed my thoughts.

"Mr. Conklin."

I rose slowly, turned to have my wrists bound, and followed the bailiff.

* * *

The deliberation was swift and met all expectations. I was to hang in the middle of town before sunset.

* * *

I thought I would be brave, but thoughts have a way of giving way to the baser instincts. Trying to lift my legs was like trying to haul up a boat anchor using only my pinky finger. The gallows were a short walk from the courthouse, maybe fifty yards, but if not for the two lawmen holding me by my arms, I do not believe I would have made it.

I'd never seen so many people gathered in such a small space. Elbow to elbow, they were nearly falling on top of each other. Surely they weren't all local citizens. By now, the newspapers would have spread word throughout the county. I was escorted through the sea of red faces and by the time I made it to the steps, my collar and cheeks were soaked in other people's spit.

Time warped itself so that it was unrecognizable. I saw the bottom of the stairs. And then the top. Suddenly, fibers of hemp were scratching at my neck and I thought I smelled rain.

A preacher mumbled something as I swayed side to side.

Another voice asked, "Mr. Conklin, do you have any last words?" I turned and saw the sheriff. The blue-and-green-eyed deputy stood at his side.

I tried to say something, but my mouth was too dry. And even if I could, I don't know that I would have been able to hear my own voice over the growing tumult of the crowd.

"May God have mercy on your soul," the preacher said.

I closed my eyes.

And waited.

A pair of hands struggled to tighten the noose around my neck.

Goddamn it, who tied this knot? I heard the deputy say.

There were shouts from the citizenry, but nothing was happening.

What's going on back there? It was the sheriff.

I felt the energy of the crowd change. They quieted and anger turned into confusion.

Get out of here!

Where are your parents?

I opened one eye.

There was a commotion in the back of the crowd and it was spreading to the front.

I opened the other eye and straightened my head, wanting to rub away the blur, but unable to with my hands still bound.

Children.

They came running up the middle of the mob like an army of toy soldiers. There must have been hundreds of them. Some had shotguns and though the look on their faces said they might not be ready to use them, the people parted anyway.

They swarmed until they reached the foot of the gallows. Their little feet clambered up the steps and onto the wooden platform.

"What in God's name are you kids doing?" the sheriff asked. "You get away from here!" The deputy drew his pistol, but the sheriff pushed his hand down on it so that it was lowered reluctantly.

All of them, familiar faces. Margaret had a large piece of wire in her tiny hands. Another pair, Todd and Henry, carried a wooden bucket and placed it in front of me. The kids with the shotguns pointed them at the law while the rest of the children, one by one, walked up with jars in their hands and emptied the contents into the bucket.

Someone untied my wrists. I took a deep breath as I pulled my head free from the noose.

Margaret smiled at me through the gap in her teeth and when the last jar was emptied, dipped the wire into the bucket. She picked it up and drew it around my body. The sound cut out around me and I saw the world through a soapy film.

It was an exceptional feeling, watching them from above as they watched me from below. I wondered what would become of them all.

I wondered if the snow had melted yet in Buffalo.

Process Summary

The Bubble Man is story number ten in the #52ShortStories challenge.
Not gonna lie, the inspiration for this was pretty pedestrian:

Yup, my kid's bubble bath solution. But I guess that's the magic in
writing, huh? Taking the mundane, the everyday, and trying to spin a bit of
immersive magic with it.

This was a situation of waking up on Monday morning, knowing I
had a story to write, but nothing really calling me. So, as I'm turning on the

coffee machine, I saw that pink bottle and said, "Sure."

The boys in the basement got to work and *The Bubble Man* is the result. Again, no real outline. Just a lot of discovery and watching scenes play out in my mind. One thing I noticed is that about halfway through, I wasn't sure how I was going to end this. Or even whether or not the whole premise would collapse under its own weight.

For such a fantastical notion, I was worried about being *too* fantastical. It sounds ridiculous looking back, but things can appear different when you're in the midst of it all. Something told me, "Just go nuts," and I'm glad I did.

It's a healthy reminder that I'm writing fiction here and as much as I want to "say something," entertaining the reader comes first.

Apollo's Revenge

Statistics

Synopsis: Private Hubert Bausman fought the Nazis in a bloody battle at Monte Cassino and now he's ready to come home, but something beyond his control is keeping him there.

Word Count: 4,000

Genre: Fantasy / Historical Fiction

Completed Week: October 23rd – October 29th

NOTE: This story won an Honorable Mention in Quarter 1 of 2018 in the Writers of the Future contest.

Apollo's Revenge

This wasn't the Italy of passionate opera, nor the Italy of Da Vinci and Michelangelo.

Maybe it was the Italy of the Romans.

Not that Private Hubert Bausman had half a clue about those guys. All he remembered were primary school tales of men in togas who turned Christians into lion chow. And not that it was the Romans he had to worry about, anyway. It was their Teutonic brethren from the North, members of that overall not-so-nice-guy organization popularly known as the Nazis.

Only weeks ago, they had been here at Monte Cassino, about eighty miles south of Rome. Axis and Allies faced off against the elements as much as each other. Even though it was well into Spring, Bausman felt New England weather had nothing on this place. Maybe it just seemed that way.

"You're up, Chief."

A puff of steaming air wandered out from Private Munson's mouth, curling beneath the three-quarters moon.

Munson extended his hand and pulled Bausman up onto his feet. Bausman's muscles ached. He cursed himself for not standing and moving around, but he acknowledged that three to four hours of sleep would, without fail, eventually have its way.

In a daze, he popped on his helmet, slung the strap of his Browning A-5 over his shoulder, and marched towards the designated lookout point.

"Where do you think you're goin'?" Munson asked.

Halfway through the question, Bausman realized he'd forgotten something. He reached into his shirt pocket, pulled out a nearly-empty pack of Lucky Strikes, and tossed it into Munson's receptive hands.

"Sarge seems to be agitated," Bausman said. "Command's probably itching to send us to another slaughterhouse. Best hide yourself well."

Munson fell on his ass and flicked the flint wheel of his Zippo as if he hadn't heard a word. The amber glow of his cigarette could probably be seen from a mile away.

* * *

Bausman and Munson were two grunts tasked with keeping watch over a hundred-yard section of winding road leading past a Polish Army operating base and up to a bombed-out monastery. Four months ago, the two of them along with the rest of the US 36th Infantry Division had initiated a trade in flesh for these seven acres.

The price was steep.

The two privates were survivors, though. Two from a regiment of originally one hundred and eighty-four soldiers, all who had been delivered into the earth's snowy maw by chattering *maschinengewehr* and camouflaged Panzers.

Of course, other armies came and made their sacrifices: the Brits, the Aussies, along with more nations than Bausman had ever bothered to learn about, with the Poles finally wrapping things up.

For some undefinable, yet likely bureaucratic reason, Bausman and Munson's commanding officer decided it would be good for morale to bring the surviving Americans back so they could participate in the final assault: to see, Bausman supposed, what all the fuss was about. It had been several weeks since the landmark monastery was captured. War raged further north while their small contingent was left behind.

And that's how Bausman and Munson came to shiver in the middle of the snowmelt, handpicked for the privilege of scanning the night's forest for the ghosts of partisans who were long gone.

* * *

Knowing he would be undisturbed during his six-hour shift, Bausman deviated from his assigned route as he had the past few nights and walked to the ruined abbey.

He hoped that Francesca would be in the cellar.

Last night, he had drunk wine and conversed with the monk, Benedict, instead. God's man was good company, admittedly, but the woman was better looking. Her raven hair and oceanic eyes reminded Bausman of Hedy Lamarr. So what if she berated him over his "barbarian" manners. He liked a woman with a little fire in her veins.

Maneuvering among the crumbling structure was an exercise in extreme caution. Bausman had already sprained his ankle a week ago, and it was finally feeling good again. His flashlight lit the way, only beginning to flicker near the middle of the abbey. He turned it off to preserve the batteries for the walk back. Besides, there was an oil lamp hanging off the wall near the bottom of the basement staircase which gave off enough light by which to navigate to his destination.

As he rounded the corner of the dusty library archives, he couldn't help but smile.

She sat at a thick wooden table, intently reading a book.

"*Buonasera.*" It was one of three Italian phrases Bausman knew.

"What took you so long?" she asked drily. Though her English was heavily accented, Bausman was happy that he didn't *have* to learn more than three phrases. He pulled up a chair opposite Francesca and a poured a cup of wine from a clay pitcher. Being the gentleman that he was, he topped her's off first.

He swirled the cup under his nose and sniffed.

"I got here as quick as I could. It's a real war zone out there." He snorted at his own joke but quickly stopped. Francesca was not amused.

Her nose was still buried in the book. Script was handwritten on one page and there was a drawing on the other which the private couldn't quite make out.

The air in the library was thick with silence. Bausman sat back in his creaking chair and surveyed the crooked shelves lining the walls. By modern standards, the place was tiny, but he pictured the monks reading the same few books over and over again. It must have been utterly mind-numbing, but he guessed that was the point of being a monk. He was just amazed that the room survived the heap of bombs that had been dropped on it.

"Benny sleeping?"

She may have nodded.

Alright. If she wasn't going to be much company, he could sit here in silence too. It didn't bother him much. So long as he could drink and look at her, he'd be fine. Bausman took another sip of the wine. It was nothing like the rotgut he was used to drinking back home—at least when he drank wine, which wasn't often. This vintage wasn't nearly as sweet as what he was used to and he spent time swishing it over his tongue, trying to discover the nuances that rich folk seemed to find all the time.

He swallowed.

And burped.

Francesca looked up.

He smiled.

"Why are you here?" she asked.

"I like good company," he said.

"No. Why are you *here?*"

He threw his hands up. "What, in Italy? On Earth? You gotta help me out, little lady."

She breathed in deeply and closed the book. Dust puffed out into a small cloud as the pages slapped shut.

"I think the *real* question," he said, leaning forward, "is 'Why are *you* here?' Did you lose your home? Husband grow tired of your charm?"

Francesca laughed and it startled Bausman, but he was happy to see some cracks in her facade.

"Yes, *Hyooo-bert*. Yes. I've lost my home. Just like you."

The way she said his name made the hairs on his arm stand straight up, but in a good way. He took another drink, this time slugging the wine straight down his gullet. He poured himself some more.

"I know exactly where my home is." He looked at the bookshelves as if reading a particular binding. "374 Peck Street, Charlestown, New Hampshire."

Her fingers traced the embossed pattern on the cover of her book. "So when do you plan on heading home?"

"As soon as the fuckin' Army—pardon my French—lets me go. My tour's up in a couple of weeks."

"You must really be looking forward to it."

Bausman had to really think about his response. He assumed he'd be shipped back to Texas, and from there, he'd had the vague notion that he'd get a ride back to New Hampshire. But then what? He'd see his parents and they'd be happy to see him. His old man would likely bring him back on as an insurance agent.

So instead of answering, he simply took another drink and changed the subject.

"You know, Franny, if you opened up a little more, these conversations would probably be a lot more pleasant."

Her eyes narrowed, turning their blues into a darker ocean.

"Fine," Francesca said. "Let's discuss all of the *pleasant* things going on around us, okay? Have you been to the cinema lately? Read the papers? I hear there is a bit of drama happening in Russia. Things are heating up further east in Japan. Oh!"

Her voice quickened and her eyes widened again.

"Then every once in a while, I hear a child in the forest crying out for his parents. It's been happening for months. And that wonderful odor? Can you still smell it? I can. Your men may have removed the corpses of German soldiers, but some things tend to linger."

She clapped her hands and it made Bausman flinch.

"So many pleasantries, my soldier, so many. Which would you like to talk about first?"

"Enough," Bausman said. He felt his blood rushing through his veins, heating his face. "For someone hiding out in rubble, you sure know a lot about the world."

She sat back down and stared off into space. "I know enough."

As Bausman imagined the horrors through which she had suffered, which she *continues* to suffer, his demeanor softened. He imagined that feeling of powerlessness, the case of being a mere civilian at the mercy of a deranged government. And as much as he supposed standing around in the middle of the night in a foreign land was next to helpless, at least he was doing *something*.

"Seriously," he said. "Don't you have any family that can take you in? Who brings you food? Benny?"

"I'm not very hungry these days. The wine sustains me."

He reached across the table and grasped her hands. She didn't pull back. For Bausman, to feel her soft skin was like grasping his own little slice of heaven.

"I'm sorry. I know it's really none of my business. I just..."

She shrugged and smiled gently. It may have actually been genuine.

"No matter, she said. I am here. You are here. Let's drink some wine while we can, no?" She lifted her cup. Bausman met it. The clacking echoed lightly in the tiny room and they both took a gulp.

The young private licked his lips and held his cup up to the light, examining it like a tiny idol. "I don't know how this has remained undiscovered, but I'm as happy as a pig in shit. You don't want to know what those Poles out there would do for a sip of this, let alone barrels full of it."

* * *

The previous few hours were a blur. The memory no more than a wine-induced vision. Bausman found Munson sitting in the same position, smoking a cigarette as if he had been frozen in time since the moment they parted company.

"Welcome back," Munson said, nearly expressionless. "You catch any bad guys?"

"Of course," Bausman replied. "Hitler and Mussolini both. Found them holding each other in their arms and smooching down at the inn. In fact, I'm booked on a transport out of here tomorrow and FDR is scheduled to wrap the Medal of Honor around my neck." He winked, though he doubted Munson could see the gesture.

Munson took a long drag of his cigarette. "Careful you don't choke." He snubbed it out just in time for the morning shift to arrive.

The two of them walked back to the base in silence.

* * *

"Before all this," Benny said, waving his hand around, "a temple to Apollo stood here. People made sacrifices, you know. Human sacrifices."

He poured himself what had to have been his fifth cup.

"The altar was smashed. His sculptures were destroyed and a tiny chapel was built in its place."

By Bausman's count, they had been engaged in conversation for barely an hour. He'd always assumed most monks were in it for the drink, but could he blame them? After all he had been through, he was ready to throw away his rifle and sign up himself.

"You really know your history," Bausman said. "Must be all the time you have to read these dusty, old books."

Benny laughed uproariously. It was the kind of gregarious laugh that could carry for miles on a light breeze. "Must be," he said. "Someone has to read them."

In fact, as soon as Bausman stepped into the cellar this evening, he realized that the monk had the same book open as Francesca had the previous night.

"I have a wrinkled copy of *Hamlet* in my footlocker," the private said, "a gift from a long lost friend, but haven't touched it since February." Bausman felt his thoughts beginning to sink, so he took a large drink. "What's that one about?"

"Just what we've been discussing," Benny replied, opening his hands. "History. The present. The future." He paused for a moment. "Time, really."

"Time?"

"Sure." The monk smiled. His teeth were stained a rose red. "You know, we're all prisoners."

Bausman's look demanded an explanation.

"Of time," Benny said. "There's no escaping it."

The conversation was growing a little too philosophical for Bausman's tastes. He had a sudden urge to see Francesca, but he didn't want to be rude. Instead, he did what he usually did in this sort of situation. He made a joke: "Well, I'm pretty sure if you put a bullet through my head, I'll be free of it."

Benny sank back into his chair and just stared at Bausman. The muscles on his face were taut. Clearly, the joke did not sit well.

"You're wrong," he said.

At this point, Bausman had enough wine in his system and was feeling slightly punchy. "Oh, really? How do you know? How are you ever going to prove it?" With only a slight hesitation, he pulled his Colt .45 from its holster and laid it on the table. "Let's make a deal. Why don't you shoot me and I'll come back to haunt you. I'll let you know how things are."

The monk said nothing. His glassy eyes stared at the gun while his head bobbed slightly in every direction. Images of the bookshelves reflected off this corneas through the low light of the oil lamp. Bausman was about to check his pulse when Benny slammed a fist on the table. His cup of wine fell over. Red liquid spilled out onto the wood and the sound of it pouring over the edge seemed much louder than it really was.

"Do you think this is funny?"

Bausman sobered up a little. He raised his hands in surrender. "Look, Benny. Just a joke. Come on." The monk had never been so serious before, especially after a bottle. He expected that sort of indignation from Francesca. "I don't know what's gotten into you and Franny lately, but it seems the wine is making you so serious lately. Maybe we ought to open a different barrel."

Benny leaned across the table. The elbows of his robe dipped into the spilled wine as he took hold of Bausman's hands. The monk's palms were freezing. Bausman shivered at the contact and tried to pull away, but Benny's grip was too tight.

"You. Me. Francesca. We're all prisoners of time, even after death. Why won't you admit it?"

For some reason, Bausman grew furious and he ripped his hands away from Benny's, nearly pulling the monk over the table. The private was on his feet now, his chair tipped to its side on the ground. He felt his breath quicken. There was drunk, and then there was *madness*. He wondered if God's man had finally slipped too far to the other side.

"You don't believe me?" The monk slid back into his chair, picked up the book and launched it at Bausman's chest. Dust puffed into the soldier's face as he quickly caught it.

The book felt as if it weighed fifty pounds. Its binding was thick, the pages within nearly the same. How Benny launched it with such force, Bausman didn't know. Didn't *want* to know.

"Read," Benny said.

Bausman dropped it onto the table and looked at the cover for the first time.

Monte Cassino: A History

Astonishingly, the words were written in English. He imagined these monks would be reading Italian. Bausman flipped it open and looked at Benny. He could humor the guy if it would put him in a better mood. "Any place in particular I should be starting?"

The monk crossed his arms, tossed his head to the side and stared off into space. "It doesn't matter."

For the first time since they'd met, Benny looked utterly exhausted. A rush of cold air came down through the cellar entrance and Bausman shivered.

The first page was titled *The Dedication of Apollo's Temple - 312 B.C.*

An illustration of the mountaintop depicted those toga-endowed Romans that were shades of Bausman's childhood memory. They wrapped around a humongous, stiffly-posed statue of Apollo sitting on a stone. A harp lay on his lap while in his hands was a bow with an arrow drawn, pointing north. Someone was being carried overhead to the altar, their hands and feet bound by golden rope.

Bausman thumbed to the next sheet of paper: *The Destruction of*

Apollo's Temple - 529 A.D.

Smoke reached into the dark sky and over the decapitated and cracked statue of Apollo, hundreds of tiny arrows fell from the clouds onto the monks below.

Private Bausman had never been what one would call a scholar, but he found himself being pulled into the story of this tiny piece of the world. There was a kinship to it that he couldn't describe. The breeze that had come from above ground seemed to kick into a wild howl now and he buttoned his coat as he flipped the pages to a new chapter titled *The Lombard Invasion - 581 A.D.*

Dark-Age soldiers with pointed helmets rushed toward the flaming abbey of Monte Cassino. One of them depicted a warrior holding the decapitated head of a monk who had been dressed just like Benny. Another showed a bearded man with a vicious smile on his face, looking up at a baby propped high on the end of his spear. Bausman skimmed the vivid descriptions of death and destruction.

He turned through the pages again.

The Saracens - 884 A.D.

Turbaned soldiers in chainmail rode horses along the steep roads of the mountain. The monastery sat quietly atop, waiting, while hundreds of bloodied bodies lay behind the riders.

Bausman's breath left him momentarily as the wind kicked up. It was strong enough to rattle the table and spill his wine onto the page. The red libation stained the page, drying instantly.

He looked up at Benny who nodded at the book. The seriousness was gone, but his face was grave nonetheless.

Bausman did not remember turning the page, but he looked down and read:

The Americans - 1944 A.D.

Depictions of giant planes flew over Monte Cassino. An uncountable number of bombs screamed toward its peak.

The wind stopped as quickly as it had started. An eerie stillness remained. Bausman frantically flipped through the rest of the book.

Blank pages.

He backed away from the table and grabbed the nearest bookshelf to keep himself from tipping over. His stomach lurched. He thought he was going to be sick.

"What—"

"Rest, soldier," Benny said gently. "Time is going nowhere."

Private Hubert Bausman caught his breath, though a dull pulse punched his brain at regular intervals, matching the rhythm of his heartbeat.

"I've...been here before," he said as if he already knew the answer.

Benny nodded.

Bausman looked down at the book. Images of murder and rape sprung into his head. Images he didn't remember seeing in the book itself. Images that held back nothing and finally drove Bausman towards a half-filled barrel in the corner of the room where he evacuated the jug of wine he'd just consumed.

When he was sure he could speak again, he talked with his face held down.

"You're saying I'm one of these people? That I'm one of these *monsters?*" His voice grew indignant. "We came here to *save* you!"

"Yes and no."

He flung his head up. A bad idea as the throbbing punches turned into needle-like stabs.

Sitting in the same chair where Benny had been was Francesca. Bausman hadn't heard the monk leave. Hadn't heard Franny arrive.

"At least, you're not an intentional monster," she said. "Not this round. It's complicated. You fought to liberate this place from the monsters this time, but you've still destroyed the abbey. Still killed those inside seeking refuge."

Bausman indignance allowed him to ignore Benny's vanishing act for a moment. "We didn't know. We thought the Germans were here."

Francesca dismissed the notion with a wave of her hand. "It doesn't matter."

"What do you mean it doesn't matter? Of course it—"

Bausman took a deep breath and wiped sweat from his eyes. "Please, Franny..."

"No matter. Things are looking up, no?"

Hubert blinked. Francesca, gone once again. Benedict was back.

"We all come out of darkness and toward the light," he said. "Only, the light always seems just out of reach."

Bausman felt disoriented again. He leaned over the barrel, unsure of what he had left to give.

He stared at the unholy mix of puke and wine. At his reflection. At someone else's reflection. A glint of light reflected from the steel helmet that was not on his head. He reached for the mangy beard and long, matted hair that was not his own. Finally, he saw a whiskered GI who wanted nothing more than to go home.

He pushed himself off the barrel with what little strength he could conjure. "Why?" he asked weakly.

"You're tied to this place," Francesca said. "*We're* tied to this place. A curse of Apollo, maybe. There's something sacred about this ground. Something tied to time and space."

"We'll all be leaving soon, but we'll meet here again," Benny chimed in. "They rebuild, we come back, they destroy. *Ad infinitum.*" He chuckled. "Or in your case, *ad nauseam.*" Bausman heard Francesca laugh as well.

The world was collapsing in on the young private. He had to get out of the stifling cellar. He ran up the stairs, foregoing one last look at the company he had been keeping for nearly a week. His legs carried him over the rubble as he navigated only by a thin strip of moon.

Bausman's irregular breathing made him cramp up, so he stopped and leaned on the trunk of a nearby tree. He was beaten down, so weary. He turned his back to the tree and slumped to the ground.

None of this made sense. Too much wine, he thought. That was it. Who knows what sort of contamination those barrels may have gotten after all of the destruction. He was so tired now, he just wanted to sleep. Despite the spinning earth, Bausman closed his eyes and dug his fingers into the damp soil beside him.

"So who told you? Him or the looker?"

Bausman looked up and saw Private Munson standing a few yards away, a lit cigarette bouncing from the side of his lips.

Bausman said nothing.

"Must've been God's man," Munson said and laughed. He walked over and extended his hand. "Come on, soldier. Let's go drink some wine."

Process Summary

Apollo's Revenge is story number eleven in the #52ShortStories challenge.

It was Sunday night and I was desperate for an idea. I've gotten a little used to the fact that if I see an image or scene repeat more than a few times in my head, it's a good enough place to start.

This particular scene involved a soldier abandoning his night watch to visit a mysterious woman who lives in the woods. She would give him a concoction to help him forget the pain and misery of soldiering. That was the extent of it.

I'm trying to get better at bringing scenes to life and really making the setting a living, breathing part of the work, so I knew I needed to develop a clearer picture. I imagined the war as being particularly painful and gritty and my memory took me back to a conflict I had read about a year or so ago: The Battle of Monte Cassino. Talk about a meat grinder. Four bloody battles lasting over four bloody months. Whole regiments were essentially annihilated trying to capture the strategic ground.

The Allies were essentially successful, but during the first battle, the Americans bombed the ever-loving shit out of the monastery based on British reports that the Nazis were using it for operations. It turned out that the only people inside at that time were 230 civilian refugees (Insert: Franny). The Nazis ended up moving in *after* the destruction.

War is hell.

After further research, I learned more about the monastery which sat atop the hill, going way back to Roman times where the popular story is that it once held a temple dedicated to Apollo before being destroyed and rebuilt as a monastery by Saint Benedict of Nursia (Insert: Benny). Since then, it had been invaded two other times before World War 2: once by German Lombards and the second time by Saracens.

Oh, and in 1349, it suffered heavy damage from an earthquake.

Poor Monte Cassino can't catch a break.

Surely that means its cursed and hence a story is born!

Such deep history made the writing much easier than my initial vague idea. I hope I was able to get across the richness of the setting. My first reader is not much of a history buff, so I was extremely happy to hear that she enjoyed the story and learned enough about the setting through the writing itself–with the added bonus of not being bored to tears by pallid description.

I chalk this one up as a win! On to the next…

LET IT GO

Statistics

Synopsis: What happens when a woman agrees to meets with the man who held her captive for five years?

Word Count: 1,500

Genre: Sci-Fi / Experimental

Completed Week: October 30th – November 5th

Let it Go

Segments of thought followed each other like train cars.

White van straddling the road.

Turn around?

No room.

Reverse.

Stop.

Another van.

Continue to play the game?

Continue.

* * *

"You won't come?"

"No."

The Troggs' *Love Is All Around* crackled through the coffee shop's ceiling speakers.

"I've already bought a few acres in Death Valley. We can live out of a trailer until the house is built. No one will know we're there." Howard swirled his speckled-white mug of coffee and put it to his lips. His hand shook ever so slightly while steam fogged the bottom half of his huge glasses.

The place was nearly empty. There was a pair of young men sitting in a booth on the opposite side of the restaurant. Judging by their crisp white shirts and black ties, they had to have been Mormon missionaries. At the counter sat a chubby long-hauler wearing a baseball cap. He was leaning onto the counter, exposing an ass crack just begging for someone to drop a coin.

"I can't," I said. "Not now."

Howard's expression soured. It wasn't the coffee. He set the mug down and cradled it like a baby bird that had fallen from its nest.

* * *

I put the Chevy in park, dead-smack in the middle of the two-lane highway, and turned off the engine.

To my left was a steep drop down the 1,500-foot canyon while to my right was a flat wall of dynamite-blasted limestone.

They'd chosen a good spot and my first instinct was to feel betrayed.

Facing what was coming was an easy choice. There was nowhere to run.

It was freezing outside. This big rock on which I found myself was too far from its sun. I'd been with my boyfriend, Sidney, for two months but we weren't yet at the point in our relationship for me to suggest we leave Ohio for warmer climes.

Obviously, Death Valley was knocked off any potential list.

* * *

"Alpha, you're free to do whatever you want. You're no one's prisoner."

I tipped my head to the side and raised my eyebrows at him.

"Any more," he finished.

As if seeing him for the first time in three months wasn't enough, his words all too easily triggered memories of humming fluorescent lights and cold, metallic environs.

"I'm sorry," he said. "I know this is all rather sudden. It's just....I figured we could, you know, start over."

I laughed loud enough to draw the attention of the Mormon boys.

"Start over?" I asked. "Is that why you called me out here?"

Howard took a handful of pink packets from their ceramic holder and placed them on the table, lining them up in the shape of a triangle. It was a nervous habit he'd exhibited over the five years I'd known him. It helped him think, he had said.

Thick brown hair on the back of his hands peeked out from his coat sleeves as he pushed the paper soldiers across the formica, moving them forward one-by-one, trying to maintain the pattern.

"I *helped* you." His voice was quiet and his eyes were locked on the packets as if he were addressing them. It was obvious how much he was trying to contain his emotions, but maybe only to me.

"I *cared*....*care*....about you."

"Howard—"

"If it wasn't for me," he said, "you wouldn't be here. You wouldn't be with him." He looked at me for the briefest of moments. Tears streamed down his face—streams of water which I was still trying to comprehend, having no faculty to produce them myself.

The tiny bells hanging on the front door rang as someone left the cafe.

"The others would have kept you locked up in a cage like some sort of zoo exhibit," he finished. I looked down and saw sweetener spilled all over. He had torn the ten packets in half.

The situation was delicate. I had to be careful, but I had to be direct.

I reached out and laid my hands atop his.

"I appreciate everything you did for me. I really, really do."

It was difficult to see him this way, so I glanced out the window onto the slush-covered parking lot, watching the trucker step carefully around the building to avoid falling on his ass.

"But what did you expect to happen when you let me go?"

* * *

I should have realized he could never have truly let me go.

My feet hit the pavement and I strode around toward the passenger side. The frigid air made my insides ache.

I suppose I could have told Sidney the truth when we first met. The whole truth: that I had been living freely in the world for only a month before we laid eyes on each other. That I originally came from a place I'd never be able to see again, my only means of transportation destroyed.

And after telling him everything else that had happened since my arrival, I'd have to tell him the most unbelievable thing: that I had felt an obligation to see Dr. Howard Benevolo when he reached out to me, even though he was one of the men who aided in my captivity for five long years.

None of that mattered now, though.

The oncoming van came to a stop forty yards away.

* * *

"There's a big gap between knowing and doing," he said. "I *knew* we couldn't keep you there. It didn't make it any easier to let you go, though. At the time, I thought my infatuation was with the work itself, but I was wrong.

Maybe a failing of our species."

He chuckled.

"But can you say with all honesty that you never felt something for me?" he asked. "That we didn't develop something more? I know the beginning was hard. I know."

His lips were saying one thing, but his eyes another.

I exhaled slowly. My flesh still felt the pinch of the needle, a visceral memory of when they would draw my blood at all hours. Each physical pang was associated with a crisp memory.

Its physiology is almost unremarkably similar to ours.

It took little effort for me to recall sleepless nights spent monitoring the drones in lab coats at the same time they were monitoring me. The clipboards in their hands. Their constant scribbling.

Nothing extraordinary. Its mental capacity and IQ is that of a twenty-two-year-old college graduate.

"Of course I felt something for you," I said. "My reaction was natural. You treated me like a person where others didn't. The rest of them only wanted answers to their questions, no matter how they got them."

Howard turned his palms up to meet mine and I felt their clamminess.

"That's right," he said. "I was the only one who cared. Who *really* cared and who, despite your best efforts, could see you for who you really were."

A shadow fell over the table.

"Ya'll good here?" Our waitress smacked her gum as she touched up Howard's coffee.

"We're fine," he said, wiping the remnants of his tears with a napkin.

She looked at me.

"Okay. Well, ya'll just holler if you need anything."

* * *

Five men in front of me: four in black carrying their standard M1As, the fifth as well, but still wearing his trucker hat.

From the van behind me emerged three more soldiers. A man in a crisply pressed suit and aviator glasses followed them.

Howard stepped out last.

* * *

We were silent until the waitress made her way to the other side of the cafe.

I could practically feel the sweat leaving his pores.

"You people have a saying," I said, "'If you love it, let it go,' right?"

Howard smiled, but not too broadly, and squeezed my hands.

"I'm sorry," was all he said.

* * *

I'd learned everything I needed to learn in those five years.

I was no longer constrained.

The men approached cautiously. I supposed they thought it would make a difference.

"Alpha," said the man in the suit and tie. The sun reflected off his sunglasses and he smiled a smarmy smile. "We've been concerned about you."

He looked at the scientist beside him. "Howard made a mistake, for which he's partially atoned. We need you to come back home. We have more work to do."

It took all of half-a-second.

Except for Howard, each one of them collapsed onto the ground like crumpled tissue paper. I smiled at him and he waved gently before I hopped back into the Chevy.

The van in front of me was still in the way. I focused and its tires began to spin. I steered it past the guard rail and watched it dive over the edge.

I cranked up the heater and drove toward home, wondering how Sidney would take to the idea of moving into the Sahara Desert.

Process Summary

Let It Go is story number twelve in the #52ShortStories challenge.

It was like chewing on leather.

That's one way to describe the general feeling of putting *Let It Go* together.

Did I want this to be sci-fi centered? Focused on the theme of love? More romance? Hmm, maybe this is way too short for the concept!

Frustration set in pretty rapidly, but I decided to treat my mental block as an opening rather than a problem, and ended up playing with my standard story structure.

In the end, I *think* this might be the first real clunker of a story that I've put together for this challenge, but, hey, failure is just opportunity in a hideous disguise. Not to mention this is all just my opinion. Some people might dig the piece and that's why I still put it out there.

I also took a few days off from the day job this week to spend time with my family and really enjoy Halloween with my son. What I've found is that having the time away from home which my work provides me really forces me to use every minute available. I spent more time focused on family then the writing this past week, and I think that contributed to my difficulties.

Now, God forbid my stories ever take precedence over my wife and son! But it does go to show that much of the magic seems to come from putting in the work: day in, day out.

$\mathcal{S}$TOLEN

Statistics

Synopsis: In the forests of Nepal, a revered father is dying and his children must take things into their own hands in order to help him.

Word Count: 2,800

Genre: Adventure / Coming of Age

Completed Week: November 6th – November 12th

Stolen

Come away, O human child!

To the waters and the wild

With a faery, hand in hand.

For the world's more full of weeping than you can understand.

- W. B. Yeats, *The Stolen Child*

"You've always been my favorite," he said.

Dried blood colored the white whiskers surrounding his lips. His teeth wore a buttery film and dark circles called attention to the liver-spotted skin pulled taut over his cheekbones.

"Rest, father." I pushed him gently back down onto the bed.

He turned his head and moaned, squinting at the straw-packed wall of the hut.

"Was he talking to you or to me?"

I looked at my young brother and shrugged. "Probably neither."

* * *

Thin clouds filtered the blurry light of the half-moon. The sun wouldn't rise for another hour, but we had to set off now.

Dhonu and I stopped at the memorial outside of our sleepy village and visited two familiar mounds—a single pair among the hundreds. I set down our equipment, got on my knees, and kissed the stones which had been piled on top of each tiny lump of grass. The cold from the rocks felt like shocks of tiny lightning. I imagined the ashes which had been buried beneath them had long since been absorbed into the Earth.

Dhonu hesitated, always afraid to get too close. I grabbed his hand and gently pulled him over. He quickly kissed the markers as well, though I'm not sure his lips even made contact. He slipped out of my grasp and ran back toward the road.

I supposed I couldn't blame him. He was too young to remember Mother and our sister, Gitika. I looked down to my left at the hole which I'd already begun to dig and realized we had better be on our way.

* * *

The Nepali forest never ceased.

Already, it was humming and bustling with activity. Brown-chested partridges chased each other around the trunks of the sal trees like quarreling children. While Dhonu twirled and flipped a stick in the air, I kept my eyes open for tigers and any rhinoceroses that might think sticking close to our well-treaded road was a good idea. Avoiding contact was the best option, but I traced my fingers along the hilt of the kukri in case that wasn't a possibility.

"Remember what we talked about?" I said.

"Yeah, yeah."

I stopped and dropped the wound rope that had been weighing heavily over one shoulder. "This isn't a joke, Dhonu. If I didn't need you, I wouldn't have brought you along."

He avoided my gaze.

"Do you remember what we talked about?"

He bounced up and down on his legs.

"Don't leave your side. Don't do anything stupid," he spat out to the canopy of branches and leaves above.

"And?"

He released an exasperated breath. "Do whatever you say."

"Good."

His eyes darted toward the blade hanging from my belt.

"Can I see it?"

"No," I said.

He grunted and started walking away. "You're a jerk, you know that?"

I picked up the rope, adjusted the pack across my back, and followed close behind.

"Yes, I know that."

* * *

We were six miles deep in the jungle and at our destination. I was grateful for having stopped only twice so that Dhonu could pee.

Dawn's orange sun illuminated the sheer rock wall. The cliffside never failed to intimidate me once I'd come face-to-face with it, always forced to crane my neck upward to try and find its end. Whenever I felt overconfident or arrogant about something, I only had to think of this cliffside. It's one thing to see mountains in the distance, but when one's entire being comes up against the jagged, ivy-netted rock like an ant on a boulder, it's another reminder of our inconsequence.

Thankfully, we didn't have to climb all the way to the top.

"Father took me here a few years ago," I said, looking down at my brother. I don't know why I told him something that didn't really matter.

"For Mother and Gitika?"

I nodded.

"But it didn't work," he replied.

"It takes away the pain," I said with a little anger in my voice. "But, no, it won't save anyone."

He shrugged away the thought and extended his stick outward as he spun in circles, his eyes closed and his face jutting into the air. Besides the cowlick on his crown, his dark hair fell straight and gentle over his skull. His skin was chestnut, smooth, and still unblemished.

Dhonu was a good boy, just naive. But who isn't at his age and shouldn't he have the right to be so? Soon enough, he'll know and experience more than anyone ever should. I only hoped the pestilence would pass him by.

I think I made a mistake in bringing him here, I thought, even though I knew that wasn't true. To leave him behind would have been the *real* mistake. Without him, we couldn't help Father with what little power we had to do so. Yesterday, I had come on my own only to discover what I'd feared: the original climbing rope lying on the ground, one end completely frayed.

I let the new rope slide from my shoulder and I bent my head from side to side, working out the crick in my neck. I studied the wall.

"You see that thin crack running along the stone?" I pointed.

He nodded eagerly.

"That's your first foothold."

His eyes twinkled at the prospect of adventure and doing something potentially dangerous.

"I need you," I said, "because my hands and feet are too big to fit anymore."

He smiled and said, "Oh."

Then, I held his shoulder and pulled him backward. I pointed at an outcropping fifty or so feet above us. "That's where you're going. When you reach the ledge, you need to be *very* quiet. Okay?"

His mouth hung open as he gazed. I gave him a shake.

"Okay?"

"Okay."

I held up one end of the rope. "You'll see a large boulder sitting just outside the cave. Tie this on just like I showed you, remember?"

He reached for the rope but I pulled it back. "Show me you remember."

Dhonu issued a mumble of complaint, but he impressed me with his memory as he threw his stick to the forest floor and tied the knot exactly as I had taught him.

Satisfied, I tucked one end of the rope through his belt as he slipped out of his straw sandals and placed a foot in the crack. His fingers probed the opening and he began his ascent.

I hesitated briefly before grabbing his silk pant leg. "When you get to the entrance, you tie the knot, you pay attention to the cave, and you *wait*. You—"

"—don't move. Don't do this. Don't do that. Don't do *anything*. Blah, blah, blah. I *know*." He yanked his leg up from my grip and scaled the cliffside as if he had been doing so for years without my knowledge. I was a bundle of mixed feelings. I feared for my brother, but at the same time, I tried to hold back a smile, remembering how I had once bristled at very similar words.

* * *

The *saapgaryo* were nocturnal, so they should have recently settled down to sleep. They mainly fed on rhododendrons growing on top of the mountain. The flowers made them drowsy near daybreak. Excepting Dhonu's perfectly sized hands and feet, that docility was the only other reason I allowed him to be up here alone until I climbed the rope. Father must have felt the same when he had sent me only a few summers ago.

As I sat at the entrance, stretching my burning arms, Dhonu peered into the cave. One hand pinched his nose.

"This place stinks!" he said through a nasal voice.

"Quiet!" I hissed. "They're sleeping, not dead."

He rolled his eyes, but turned back to the blackness.

I reached into my pack and pulled out a torch that had been dipped in pitch. I lit it with Father's flint and steel.

"Come on," I said. "Stay behind me."

The stench grew with every step. Dhonu pretended to gag, stopping only when I turned and gave him a stern look.

"Breath through your mouth," I whispered.

We turned a corner about twenty yards in and came across their chamber. I spotted them instantly. My hand moved to cover Dhonu's mouth just in time to catch it opening.

There was only one adult *saapgaryo* with four younger ones laying against her teats, nestled just under an extended wing. All were resting within a nest of sticks and sal leaves. The little ones stirred for a moment, but seemed to settle back down to sleep.

I raised the torch slowly to get a better view of the room. In one corner was the pile of excrement from which the smell emanated. Why the creatures lived and slept so near to their feces, I'll never understand, but at least it made it easy for us to find what we were looking for.

I pointed at our target and handed the torch to Dhonu. I held my finger to my lips. His oversized teeth looked even bigger as he grinned against the flame. We tiptoed to the corner as I kept a constant eye on the sleeping family and I quietly removed the bag strapped to my back.

Father had made me do this job last time. Part of me felt I should let Dhonu take over, but I decided to do it myself anyway, hoping he'd never have to.

The *saapgaryo* crap was green, slimy, and all around the worst thing I'd ever had to make physical contact with. But there was magic inside and it seemed to me that some good things came wrapped in not-so-good things. Imagining how Father would feel tomorrow made the task a little less painful.

I'm sure it only took a minute to gather it all, yet loading the sack felt like watching mold grow. My eyes would dart between the poop, Dhonu, and the creatures while I tried to quietly scoop with my hands and filled the bag. The torch would inadvertently lower every once in awhile as my little brother stared in fascination at the creatures he'd heard so much about.

I'd forgotten what it was like to be unfamiliar with their long beaks and pointed ears. Dark gray feathers lined their bodies. Laying down in slumberous sleep, they didn't seem *that* fierce—maybe they were even a little cute, especially the small ones—but when they were awake with their wings expanded, shrieking like something unholy, they inspired panic.

We were so close to avoiding all that.

It was my fault. In a hurry to get us out of the precarious situation and back to the village, I didn't pay attention as I should have. We had just turned around when I accidentally kicked a small rock across the cavern floor. It landed square in the ribs of one of the young *saapgaryo* which yelped in surprise and scrambled onto its wobbling talons, waking the others. The sound of their dissonant squealing frightened Dhonu, causing him to drop the torch.

Then the big one woke up.

There was no way we were going to make it out of the cave and down the rope with a protective mother in pursuit.

Five pairs of beady, yellow-green eyes glowered at us.

I threw the sack of poop into Dhonu's hands, shoved him behind me, and pulled out the kris. "Run for the rope."

"But—"

"Go!" I yelled, trying to be heard over the tumultuous howls. I didn't want to turn my back to the mother, so I could only assume he listened to me.

Thankfully, the torch was still aflame and I could see them all. With the blade raised in front of me, I expanded my chest and stood as tall as possible. Because I wasn't big myself, the mother was just about equal in height, appearing menacing while bounding back and forth in front of her babies. Her wings spread wide and I felt as if they could wrap around me and keep me trapped forever.

I slowly backed away towards the entrance, remembering when something similar happened to Father and me. I couldn't remember the details, other than by the end, he had scratches all over and was covered in blood. How he managed to climb down after me, I don't know. I do know that my legs and arms didn't stop shaking until late into that night.

As I begin to smell the outside forest, I realized my first mistake was actually my second. I should have paid better attention to the ground coming into the cave. My clumsy heel snagged on a thick root running across the cave, sending me tumbling onto my rear. The kris flew from my hands, chinking against the wall and somewhere onto the floor.

Mother *saapgaryo* saw her opportunity.

Her brilliant eyes rose and fell as she bounded toward me.

It was either clamber onto my feet or try to find the knife.

My fingers searched the ground and just as my fingers found the blade, I screamed. A sharp burn radiated through my forearm as the mother's claws tore at my skin. Instinct drove my hands toward my face. Her breath was hot, panting, and the sound that emanated was a frightening mix of growl and screech. Her beak drove forward, piercing my palms with incessant pecking.

I fell onto my back, thinking I could use my feet to kick her off. She flapped her wings wildly. Now her talons dug into my hamstrings, ripping away bits of my flesh.

Among the chaos, I heard a shuffling sound by my ears: one of the babies coming to see what all of the fuss was about, I assumed. I hoped Dhonu was at the bottom of the cliff by now.

I continued futilely kicking, but the *saapgaryo* didn't seem to care. My lungs tried to keep up, tried to catch gasps of air. I was growing weary, already losing my will to put up a fight.

Then came a scream which at first I thought was my own.

It was Dhonu.

My stomach dropped and something took hold of me within. I kicked at the mother with all of my strength. Her weight was lifted from me and I found myself back on my feet. I could have sworn that my heart was going to pump itself out of my chest. I saw the big *saapgaryo* half-running, half-flying frantically towards her nest, away from the portal of sunlight behind us.

I looked for my brother and saw him holding himself up on the cavern wall beside me.

"Are you okay?" I yelled, grabbing his face and trying to look over every inch of him.

"Come on!" Dhonu said. His voice was choked with tears.

I squinted and scanned the ground. "Father's kris," I said.

Dhonu grabbed my arm. "I used it. Come on!"

It wasn't until we were on the ledge before I realized what he had done for me.

* * *

I was proud to have made it halfway to the village before my sudden burst of will had drained. As the exhaustion increased, so did the pain. It flowed out from my chest to my fingertips and toes.

"We need to stop," I said, already collapsing onto the muddy road.

Dhonu said nothing. His tears had dried up and now he only looked at me.

My breathing was ragged. "What?"

"You're a meess," he said.

I frowned, but then I looked at the stains of blood and dirt covering my arms. I imagined the rest of my body looked the same. Despite the throbbing, despite my weariness, or maybe because of those things, I began to laugh. And then so did Dhonu, until we were both finally out of breath.

"Yeah," I finally said. "I guess so."

Dhonu removed the sack that was hanging loosely from my back and held it in the air. His face scrunched. "Do you want some?"

"No," I said. I rose slowly and painfully to my feet, realizing we needed to get back. I reached my hand out for the sack, but my brother put it over his shoulder and began to walk away.

"Good," he said. "Let's go take care of Father."

Process Summary

Stolen is story number thirteen in the #52ShortStories challenge.

For me, this story really hit home the concept of *reader expectations*.

I always seem to start my tales with some sort of fantastical bent in mind, but this time, I dunno….something drove me toward not so much a twisty-turny ending, but one that hopefully was just as satisfying without needing to be a "trick" pulled on the reader.

With that in mind, my first reader finished it and said the ending just seemed off to her. After further discussion, I learned it was because she was *expecting* my typical style. Then she iterated that my ending wasn't *bad*, just not what she expected. This is a good lesson when it comes time to publish…If I want to vary my styles so much, it may be worth thinking about alternate pen names.

Where inspiration is concerned, I read a wonderful poem called *The Stolen Child* by W.B. Yeats. It's one of his earliest, but the whole concept of faeries trying to shield the wonderful innocence of a child spoke to me. I combined that line of thought with a National Geographic article I read about a man who harvests psychotropic honey. Again, I love how these varied references meld together into some sort of delicious story stew.

I'm also very curious, dear reader, how you visualized the POV character? It was my goal to make him/her completely gender-neutral so the reader could visualize either a male or female. My wife imagined it being a boy, but she reasoned it wasn't because of my writing; it was just her default view on the type of person that would carry a blade and scale cliffs, especially in an antiquated, tribal-type setting where men typically do that sort of work.

I hope you enjoyed this one as much as I enjoyed writing it!

ANDREIANA

Statistics

Synopsis: It's 1985 and the Soviet Union is about to make its move on the United States. Only a mysterious girl can stop them before its too late.

Word Count: 2,200

Genre: Sci-Fi

Completed Week: November 13th – November 19th

Andreiana

November 7th, 1985

Grigory kept the window rolled down, because he was fighting the Sandman. A cold Siberian gale whipped through thin strands of brown hair which stretched from the top of his forehead to just below his bald crown, like long clumps of seaweed reaching out over an empty seabed.

A contraband copy of *Born in the USA* blared through the speakers. Grigory knew every word and when the chorus came, he belted it out the window at the passing Angara River. He laughed to himself, knowing that wherever Comrade Springsteen was, he had no clue that Grigory Sokolov was about to save his life.

Probably.

As Grigory maneuvered the rusted yellow Lada over a pocked road, the steering wheel rubbed against his borscht-built belly. The third car he had driven in as many days had a kink in its alignment. In the distance, Boguchany Dam stood tall—a gray shadow against an even grayer sky. One more industrial indication of the Soviet Union's might.

He cursed himself as he looked down at the empty bottles of *Pepzi Cola* laying on the passenger seat. Goddamn it if he didn't have to pee, but he didn't dare pull over when he was this close.

He stared into the rearview mirror, observing the backseat. It was empty with only cotton batting poking out of holes worn into the vinyl, but it wasn't the seat himself that concerned him.

It was the girl in the trunk.

* * *

Haaaaappy Birthdaaaay, tooo yoooooou.

Haaaaappy Birthday, tooooo yoooooooou.

Haaaapppppyy Biiiiirrrrttthhhddddaaaaaaaaaay dear—

The voices cut out. There was only static and everything was blurry. Mostly men, some women, gathered around her, all wearing buttoned down, white lab coats with little red patches on the breast. She focused on the birthday cake she couldn't eat, watching its candle flames sway back and forth. There was a fear inside of here: She was afraid that if they stopped, so would she.

It was a memory, clearly. She recalled that after only a few minutes of that celebration, they had put her to work.

Game theory.

Probabilities.

Trajectories.

None of it was difficult at first, only unfamiliar. The fact is they wouldn't let her focus on what she was most interested in—the people. She wanted to learn more about them. Converse. But they were cold and defiant. The birthday celebration was for them, not her.

They weren't here now, though. Wherever she was, she felt lethargic, barely able to run through simple calculations.

She thought she was dying and she couldn't find her voice to scream.

* * *

After the second checkpoint, Grigory came to a squealing stop, ran out of the car and relieved himself behind a rusted shipping container. He swayed back and forth. Vibrations and percussions of the dam's turbines could be felt all across the hydroelectric station.

As he walked around the corner and zipped up his pants, he saw a group of six men dressed in black-and-gray fatigues standing around just outside the main offices. Only one of them wasn't carrying a rifle.

Antoine stepped up and gave him a rough, unwelcome kiss on the cheek. Grigory wasn't the only one who hadn't bathed in days.

"You are a good man, Grigory! And they say Kapustin Yar is impregnable."

"They don't say anything about Kapustin Yar," Grigory replied.

Antoine laughed. "True enough!"

Grigory accepted a dirty white cigarette from the half-Frenchman and allowed him to light it. It bounced between Grigory's lips as he spoke. "So, where's the rest of my money?"

Antoine shook his head. "You try to make me sad, comrade, but today, I can only smile!" He threw an arm over Grigory's shoulders and winked. "Come on," he continued, "let's make sure she's everything they say she is."

Escorted by the five men with AS Val assault rifles at the ready, the two of them carried the girl inside.

* * *

As debilitated as she felt, she sensed a change in temperature and movement. The pattern had changed.

She was weak, unable to plot the subtle dips and rises in elevation very long before the numbers began to flow into one another. Still, judging by the fluctuations and frequent deltas in the angle, she was being carried *somewhere* by *someone.*

Not much help.

But it probably meant she was no longer in Kapustin Yar. No longer in her home, she knew she needed to save her energy, so she stopped reasoning. She was still so sleepy and needed to maintain some sense of awareness.

* * *

There was a loud click. Double-metal-doors swung open and an immense room brightened to life. Antoine grinned like the slightly mad scientist he was, extending a hand to usher Grigory inside. Seemingly endless columns of humming cabinets stretched into the distance, lit up with green and red lights like the too-perfectly strung Christmas bulbs Grigory had seen in American magazines.

"It's taken years to bring the data equipment in and connect us to the central network without detection," Antoine said, "but obviously, it's a requirement."

Grigory stayed silent. He knew that there was work being done here, but seeing it was something altogether different. To slowly procure everything, stand it all up in a hidden room beneath the dam, and siphon the required power was a feat of daring surely not seen since the 1917 revolution. Seventy years later, Grigory wanted to be amazed that they had kept all of this from the auditors, but perhaps the ease of 'coming to a mutually beneficial agreement' with various individuals through rubles, drink, and women was a perk of Soviet bureaucracy.

Why not? It worked for him.

They laid the girl on a rust-covered table. Anxiously, Grigory looked at his watch and asked, "When do we wake her up?"

A woman with a long nose and glasses came running into the room. She held an assortment of cables in one hand and a bottle of champagne in the other.

Antoine smiled.

"Now."

* * *

The movement ceased. She was scared, thinking it was the only thing keeping her from slipping away. Blackouts were coming on strong now.

This was it.

The end.

What would happen to her?

A final, more interesting question formed in her mind.

What would happen *without* her?

* * *

"Her battery's nearly exhausted. She's at five percent," the sharp-nosed woman said. Her lenses reflected the light from a computer terminal. "I'll set the output to 5,000 amps, but we need to step it up gently."

"Wait!" someone else yelled. A man with wild, curly hair moved his hands frantically as he plugged and unplugged cables between cabinets. "We can't bring her on without the wavenet connection. She has to initiate the protocol as soon as she's at capacity."

Clacking boots scrambled back and forth in the data center. Grigory gave up trying to understand the engineers and their techno-speak. It's not that he was an idiot, though he had happily played one for the current regime. In fact, it was his very sense of people, his intuitive nature, that allowed him to take advantage of his job as a simple custodian. Grigory was a man with the right clearance in the right place and when he had been approached by Antoine's people, he was willing to play the game for the right price. He'd never considered himself a revolutionary, but he was no true believer in the Politburo either. There were enough people who had come into his life that had left suddenly—coworkers, friends, family members. Sometimes they returned and said nothing about where they had been or what they'd been doing. They all changed though, losing any spark of vitality that was once there. And that was for the ones that came back at all.

"We're ready," the curly-haired man said.

Antoine's jaw was visibly clenched for the first time since Grigory had arrived. There was a bit of fear seeping through the cracks after all.

"Now it's time to scare the monsters," Antoine said seemingly to himself and then turned to Grigory. "We're about to make history, my friend."

Grigory laughed. "You promise to be better?" He didn't mind a little naivete, so long as he got paid.

Antoine's expression grew serious. "Yes," he said, "Someone has to be."

Grigory crushed what was left of his cigarette beneath his boot. "I hope so. The Bolsheviks once thought they were doing good, too."

Antoine shrugged and turned back towards the woman at the terminal. "Go."

Without any hesitation, she slammed her index finger onto a key.

Grigory felt every hair on his body rise. All eyes went to the girl.

As the overhead lights faded in and out, the radio hanging on Antoine's belt crackled.

Mi-32 helicopters incoming.

* * *

"She's awake."

A voice.

Female.

Age 31 to 33.

Her auditory functions had come back online and if she knew how to smile, she would.

The room broke out into cheers indicating human satisfaction. There was a loud pop and then a quiet fizzing sound.

Self-diagnostics showed a return to normal power levels. There was a live wavenet connection though a greater packet latency than normal to her usual communication nodes. The round-trip times likely meant she was hundreds of miles from Kapustin Yar.

"Hello," said a male. Age 39 to 40. Slight French accent. "My name is Antoine. Do you have a name?"

An unusual statement followed by an unusual question. A search of her memory confirmed the latter had never been asked.

Y E S

"Antoine," another voice said. Male. Age 45. Subtle anxiety. "We don't have time—"

"What is it?" Antoine asked. "Your name?"

ANDRICON

"Andricon. Hmm… I don't like it. Can I call you Andreiana?"

ANDREIANA

She repeated it. It sounded nice. No one had ever asked her for an opinion on what seemed a trivial matter.

YES

"I look forward to getting to know you better, Andreiana, but first things first. Can you sense danger nearby?"

There was silence in the room. Invisible ones and zeros shot out from her core and across the network. Twelve onboard wireless systems responded and communication tunnels were established.

Estimated persons on board: 31.

Immediate threat to her existence confirmed.

YES

* * *

Though the data center was filled with noise from cooling equipment, muffled explosions could be heard outside.

Antoine's radio crackled once more.

Down! I can't believe it! They're falling from the sky like dead flies!

Grigory wiped the sheen of sweat from his forehead. He knew she would be powerful, but if the Ministry of Defense's Plan A failed, what was Plan B? He imagined a hundred bombs falling through the ceiling, turning the whole area into a new Chernobyl. He was beginning to lose his cool, but tried to hide it.

"Antoine, I delivered what you requested. I would like the rest of my payment now." The Lada still had half a tank of gas and he could be over the Mongolian border by midnight.

Antoine ignored him as he approached the table and ran his hands along the black metal case laying on top.

* * *

Her systems case had been outfitted with not just visual and auditory sensors, but also tactile. She felt every ridge in his fingerprints.

"Thank you, Andreiana. Do you know why you're here?" Antoine asked.

It took her only a second to reason through the possibilities.

R E V O L U T I O N

"Right. You know what the Kremlin is planning. Our friend Grigory tells us you are scheduled to initiate an electromagnetic pulse across America, destroying all electrical systems, followed by a launch of ICBMs with a nuclear payload, correct?"

Y E S

She felt his hand rest on the case. It was warm. Squishy. Before he could say another word, she spoke again.

Y E S

"Yes?"

I W I L L H E L P

* * *

November 8th, 1985

'Born down in a dead man's town!"

"The first kick I took was when I hit the ground!"

"End up like a dog that's been beat too much!"

"Till you spend half your life just covering up!"

Grigory's voice strained in tandem with Antoine who seemed to pick up the alternate verses without sounded winded whatsoever. They were bicycling in the dark of night to meet up with an army of subversives outside of Leningrad. Given their distance, they would be late to the party, but they had done their part. Siberia had always been a dark place at night, but seemed even more so without the hum of the power lines running alongside the road.

Grigory was smiling; something he hadn't done since he could remember. The money wasn't important anymore. There was no sense in running now. Andreiana was strapped on to his back. Inside the small, stiff case was a tiny chip—an amalgamation of silicon and copper that had somehow been more real than the drones who created her. In a way, she was gone, but Lenin's embalmed body would be ceremoniously ejected from his mausoleum and she would be memorialized in the new world.

Process Summary

Andreiana is story number fourteen in the #52ShortStories challenge.

It was time to change up the process once again. This go-round, I used a pair of songs in one of my Spotify playlists for inspiration and to get the ball rolling. The original title of *Andreiana* was *The Andricon Girl*, based on a line from Chemlab's *Vera Blue*. That, combined with the sci-fi vibe of Nine Inch Nail's *Copy of a*, sent me off into new and exciting directions.

I'd also just wrapped up reading an amazingly well-written piece on Russia's 1917 revolution centennial in Smithsonian Magazine.

So long as you observe and be present, it's hard not to find inspiration in every corner of daily life. The cold electronic music combined with this image of a dreary Soviet Russia on the edge of a new revolution had me rearing to write this story.

The ending didn't come to me until the last minute. I think it works, but man, can it be nerve-wracking when writing into the dark like this.

I hope you enjoyed the tale!

The Ignominy of the Devil

Statistics

Synopsis: Fergus McDowell hates his job, but can't seem to find a way out of it until he meets an unlikely savior.

Word Count: 2,700

Genre: Dark Comedy

Completed Week: November 20th – November 25th

The Ignominy of the Devil

Fergus separated a portion of the venetian blinds and watched the man plod up the stairs to the second-story apartment. Now, Fergus didn't consider himself a *completely* impatient person, but good God, it was going to be a struggle to not kill this guy as soon as he walked through the door. The dolt had shown up almost an hour earlier and just sat in his car. Fergus had debated withdrawing and coming back another day before the man finally exhibited signs of life.

It wasn't as if Fergus didn't have other things to do. His job may not be nine-to-five behind a desk, as much as he wished it was, but he still stuck to a schedule. Even after the bulk of the work, there was the time required to carefully pull open drawers and toss around furniture to make it appear as if it had *not* been done carefully. Then he had to go home, clean his tools, and try to scrub out any stains that may have missed his plastic bib and gotten on his clothes.

The whole idea was that by sunset, Fergus would be submerged in his easy chair with a bitter wheatgrass smoothie in one hand and a whodunnit in the other.

But before any of that, he had to actually do the work.

As his father used to say, he had to earn his keep.

* * *

As the man kicked the apartment door closed, Fergus snuck up behind him, wrapped an arm around his shoulder, and pushed the tip of a pocket blade into his neck.

"Hello, Stewart."

"Oh!" the man yelped. "You scared me."

At least he didn't faint, Fergus thought. It's way too early for that sort of thing.

"I wasn't expecting company," Stewart said. "Are you with the landlord? Here about that ant problem?"

"Seriously?" Fergus asked.

He guided Stewart around and faced him towards the couch. "Drop the groceries."

The man complied. A six-pack fell on Fergus's left foot.

"Son of a!" he said, flexing his toes to make sure they weren't broken.

"Go! Sit!" Fergus yelled, pointing with his free hand to a floral-patterned loveseat falling apart at the seams while he hopped slightly on one leg.

Stewart shrugged and waddled away without needing to be prodded further with the knife.

Fergus wasn't worried about any resistance. Usually they were too scared at this point, but if need be, Fergus could take care of the matter. Being a black belt in Brazilian Jiu-Jitsu was immensely useful for this line of work.

You need to be prepared for anything. Another favorite refrain of his father's.

Once Stewart took his place, the picture was complete. The whole apartment resembled a museum exhibit for Failed Man; an example of everything wrong with the world. Hung on the french vanilla walls were prints of snow-peaked mountains and fall landscapes that this guy had probably never seen in real life. DVD box sets were strewn around an old tube television:

Season two of *CSI* was slightly buried beneath *The Bachelor* and *Girls Gone Wild.*

None of this was a surprise to Fergus. It was why he was here. He chose Stewart like he'd been taught to choose most of his 'victims' (a word he hated). Sitting outside the local AM/PM mini-mart each day for the past month, Fergus seethed, observing this pot-bellied, unkempt buffoon walk in empty-handed each day, exiting a minute later with a six-pack of Natural Light in one hand and a pack of Kool's in the other. Looped around his free fingers was a plastic bag stuffed with more junk, most of which Fergus found in his pantry: Ding Dongs, Fritos, and dozens of those little powdered donuts that left a mess everywhere.

He imagined the taste of each of those sinful things on his lips, but pinched the thin skin of his wrists to snap himself out of it.

Time to get on with it, Fergus thought.

"You're a mess, Stewart. I'm here to help clean things up."

"Wait," Stewart replied. "If you're not with the landlord, how did you get in? And how do you know my name."

Fergus wasn't used to answering the questions. At this point in the process, it was usually *Please! Please don't kill me!* that he was dealing with. Still, he didn't see any harm in responding.

"To answer question number one, I just used the key in the fake rock you put next to your door. You know, the one not surrounded by any other rocks and the price tag still attached?"

Stewart's eyes glazed over.

"As for number two," Fergus continued with a slightly exhausted breath, "While you were out there doing God knows what in your car, I got bored, so I went through your stuff." He indicated towards a pile of stuff on the kitchen counter. "You have loyalty cards for every damn store within a mile radius, not to mention piles of expired Blockbuster Video memberships laying around. They've been closed for over a decade, buddy."

Stewart shrugged. It seemed as natural to him as blinking.

"What were you doing out there anyway?"

Stewart replied, "Sometimes I just get too tired to come in right away, so I sit out there and think. Hey, did you want to see where the ants are?"

"I'm not here for your goddamn ants."

Stewart shrugged again.

"And stop shrugging."

Stewart looked at his shoulders as if they were individuals. He managed to keep them in check.

Fergus cleared his throat. "As I was saying, you're a mess and it's my job to clean up messes."

"Yeah, sorry. I don't normally have company. But if you're hungry," Stewart directed his eyes toward a jar of cookie butter that had rolled out from his grocery bag near the door, "I have snacks."

Fergus quickly fought back a rising thought. "I don't eat that garbage. No nutritional value. Nothing good about it whatsoever."

Stewart smiled. "Sure tastes good, though, don't it!"

This wasn't going as planned. Fergus decided he would just skip the initial part of his usual presentation and walked over to what could be called, by a long stretch of imagination, a dining room.

"Come here," he said. "I want to show you something."

The man inhaled loudly, then blew the air out of his cheeks as he picked himself up from the sofa and stood next to Fergus. Together, they stared down at the long, black leather case sitting on a worn table. Fergus unlatched the metal buckles on each end and flipped open the lid.

He looked at Stewart to gauge his reaction, but there was nothing there. No twitch in his cheeks. No gleam of fear in his eyes. Just an emptiness.

"Huh," Stewart said.

"That's right," Fergus said, trying to build some momentum. "My tools. Most of them pretty sharp and painful." A smile crept across his face.

Fergus caught Stewart looking at his own shoulders again.

"Look," Fergus said, throwing his hands in the air. "I don't get it. I greet you with a knife at your throat. I drop not-so-subtle hints that I'm about to kill you, and then I show you how I'm going to do it. How are your pants not loaded down with shit right now?"

Stewart looked Fergus in the eyes. "Honest truth?"

"Honest truth."

"I was thinking of killing myself today, anyway. Figures something like this would happen."

* * *

This was a new one. Fergus didn't quite know how to approach the situation. He felt something stir inside. An unusual emotion that defied all classification.

"Well," he fumbled for words. "You don't have to worry about that now." They sounded stupid as soon as they left his lips.

"Nope," Stewart said. "Guess not."

He wasn't even being stoic, Fergus thought, just obtuse. He tried to increase the fear factor.

"Do you want to know how I'm going to kill you?"

"Eh, not really," Stewart replied. "I guess I'll just find out." He attempted a pathetic smile that seemed to rile up Fergus's unusual emotion even more.

"Oh." An awkward silence. "Do...do you want to talk about it?"

Fergus put his hand to his mouth. Did he just ask that question?

Stewart took a deep breath and blew it out his mouth. "Not really." He absentmindedly picked up one of the serrated blades sitting in the case and lightly ran his finger across its sharpened edge. A tiny cut opened up and blood began to pool. There was a brief sign of emotion.

"Beautiful...."

Fergus wasn't sure he heard him correctly.

"Why do you do it?" Stewart asked.

Why do I do it? A question Fergus had occasionally posed but dismissed out of hand. He didn't need a reason other than it was a job and it was what was expected of him.

"Well, it's just what us McDowells do. I come from a proud line of men who are, in my father's words, 'society's moral pilots.'" Again, Fergus put his hand to his mouth. Why was he confessing all this?

"Is it fun?"

"Fun?" The notion made Fergus's voice crack. "You think this is *fun?*"

"Well—"

He yanked the knife from Stewart's hand and thrust it back into the box. The slamming shut of the case rattled the pathetic artwork hanging on the walls.

"Let me tell you right now, there is nothing fun about what I do. I take this very seriously. I have to."

"I didn't mean—"

"Having no ambition. Sitting on your couch and guzzling cheap beer. That's fun, right? No responsibilities there."

Stewart was silent, finally.

Fergus had always tried to treat his career seriously. It was a job and his father had instilled in him, through all means possible, a strong work ethic.

"Why do you have to take it so seriously?"

"Why? Why do I *have* to?" Fergus thought his head might explode. On the one hand, that was probably a good thing. With his blood boiling, he was reminded of why he was here. The anger always made his task easier. Maybe this new line of questioning meant that he was headed in the right direction. Each "session" seemed to have a different driver, after all.

"Look, I get that you have zero things in your life to worry about—"

"That's not true!"

Alright, Fergus thought. An ounce of emotion after all. But Stewart appeared wounded and that damned weird feeling was building up in Fergus. He suddenly felt exhausted and he'd barely gotten underway. He maneuvered himself to the recliner beside the couch and sat on its edge. A part of him worried that he was wasting time, but another part seemed to be intent on shutting the first part up.

"Tell me," he asked, speaking calmly, "why are you thinking of killing yourself? You don't seem to have obligations to anything or anybody."

Stewart walked over to the front door and picked up the fallen beer.

He yanked two cans from the plastic rings and brought them over to the couch, collapsing into a deeply indented cushion. The sound of releasing pressure seemed so loud. He placed an open can in front of Fergus and took a loud slurp from the other.

"That's just it. I don't have any friends. Mopping floors at night means I don't converse with anyone at my shitty job. My parents moved to Florida and haven't talked to me for ten years. Who would know if I was gone? No one would care."

Ugh, Fergus thought. Why did he have to say that?

"So, after I slice you into tiny little pieces and use your entrails to spell out vague clues, there's not a single person that would come to your funeral? No one to push the police to try and solve the murder after they'd mark this a cold case?"

Stewart shook his head slowly and rested his chin on a chubby palm. A streak of blood from his recent cut smeared across his left cheek.

"Look, I won't fight back. Do you have to tie my hands? I have this weird issue with not being able to use my hands. I mean, maybe you'll need to. I can't say that I won't try to resist a little. If, I mean, if that's what you want."

Flabbergasted. That was the appropriate word for how Fergus felt. This Stewart was ruining everything. Completely unorthodox.

He's not scared enough, Fergus thought, and neither am I. It was time to for some motivation.

"Take off your shirt," he said. "I want to see your disgusting body before I make you beg to have parts of it back again."

Stewart hesitated for a moment, but set his beer on the table. The t-shirt was way too small. It was like trying to pull an old sticker off a wooden surface: nearly impossible without tearing the thing in multiple spots. Fergus had to help him until they were both breathing way too hard.

Though Stewart had some flab around the middle and was showing signs of gynecomastia, he was disappointed that the man's torso wasn't *completely* revolting. He was as hairless as a twelve-year-old boy. If anything, Fergus felt even worse. He thought about just slicing Stewart's throat and leaving, but what would be the point in that?

"I can't….I can't do this."

Stewart blinked and lifted his head. "Why not?" He sounded offended.

Fergus ran to his instruments, hoping the sight of them would give him one last charge. His legs felt so weak as he stood before the case and stared at his father's initials embossed on a gold plate beneath the handle. He found himself collapsing onto the stained carpet beside the table, sobbing uncontrollably.

"Hey, hey." He felt a hand on his shoulders. "Take it easy."

"Take it easy?!" Fergus tried to say through choking tears. "If my father was alive to see me now, he would disown me." The words came in a torrent now, without regard. "I hate this job. I hate my life. I never had a choice in this." He mimicked his father's voice:

Why don't you want to strangle the kitten, son?

Where's your book report on the Son of Sam, Fergus?

No, you idiot, you don't use a cleaver for sawing work.

"Hey, now," Stewart said. The sternness in his voice shocked Fergus out of his breakdown. "At least you had someone who cared! Some of us didn't even have that."

"Well, if you think it's so great, here!" Fergus shot up onto his feet, slammed the black instrument case shut and shoved it into Stewart's hands. "You do it!"

There seemed to be a minute of awkward silence between them until Stewart said, "Do you think I could?"

It was a day for firsts. That much was obvious.

"Wait, what?"

"I mean it. I feel like my life has zero meaning. Oddly enough, this would give me purpose."

Fergus was tired of being a McDowell and the expectations that came with the name. Within a matter of minutes, he had come to the breakthrough realization that he no longer wanted to serve his family, and yet by a chance of fate, he picked the one person that wanted his job.

An idea sparked in his mind.

* * *

Fergus's eyes grew intense with pleasure as the sticky substance dripped down his index finger.

He licked it clean.

Cookie butter was everything it sounded like and more.

"Now," he said, his tongue sticking to the roof of his mouth, "I'll probably pass out a few times, so make sure you keep the smelling salts handy at all times."

"Got it, got it."

It made Fergus feel good to see Stewart wield the blade so deftly.

"And when you're done, don't forget the bleach. Lots of bleach.

Bleach is your friend."

For the first time in a long time, Fergus sported a genuine smile.

Process Summary

The Ignominy of the Devil is story number fifteen in the #52ShortStories challenge.

A dark comedy.

I enjoy them, sure, but honestly never thought I'd write one. Turns out it's a lot of fun! I took a page fromDean Wesley Smith and started this story with only a title in mind. I concatenated a few words from random pages in a W. B. Yeats collection of poems as well as an Edgar Allen Poe short story collection.

I then paid a visit to my neglected friend, Ye Olde Mind Map:

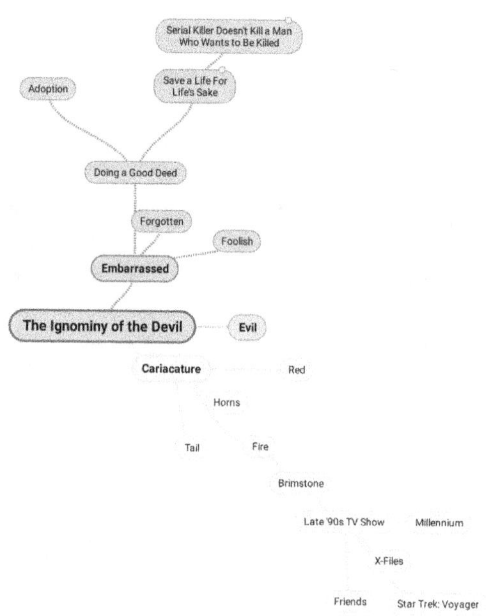

I've also been (slowly) reading Carrie Rubin's excellent thriller *Eating*

Bull, so there's a hugely obvious influence on my POV character. The rest of the tale just kind of came through the whimsy of imagination. I guess it was the right story at the right time because I skipped out on two days of writing and still managed to finish it by Saturday.

This one was also another favorite of my first reader. She definitely likes my humorous stuff and she's always been a fan of dark comedies, so I had a feeling she would dig this story. She even wants to make a short film of it, but would change the ending.

Guess you can't *completely* please them. :)

KILLING DIXIE

Statistics

Synopsis: The son of a crippled father seeks vengeance against the Confederate soldier responsible.

Word Count: 3,400

Genre: Historical Fiction

Completed Week: November 26th – December 3rd

Killing Dixie

The Colonel's blue eyes shifted ever so slightly. His crow's feet appeared rugged and deep in the low light of the lantern hanging from the entryway trellis.

"Now, son, let's be reasonable gentlemen and take a walk." His voice was measured. "Talk about whatever it is aggrieves you."

John Cunningham, Jr., son of the recently deceased Corporal John Cunningham, Sr., left the tip of his father's .31 caliber "Baby Dragoon" revolver pointed at the Colonel's heart.

"You have no right to talk reasonable with that thing hanging over your home," John said, nodding toward the flag fluttering proudly in the moist São Paulo breeze. He fought back a retching feeling rising from his belly. A light rain swept across the pristine rectangle of woven wool hanging above the entryway of the ramshackle cabin: Thirteen white stars swam in criss-crossed rivers of blue, surrounded by triangles of blood-red sand.

"Look, I don't know you from Adam, son, and—

"I am not your son, so you had best stop calling me that." John cocked the hammer. "Now are you going to welcome a weary traveler into your house or not?"

The Colonel turned his head slightly, but his eyes never left John's. John could see a crack of light emanating from one side of the door.

"I don't know why you're raising old ghosts, but I am most certain we can hash this out without resorting to—"

"Whoever's in there, you had better not be itchin' to be clever," John shouted over the Colonel's shoulder. The cylinder was fully loaded, five rounds, and he had a couple of spares in his coat pocket as well.

"Sarah," The Colonel said with a raised voice which, somehow, still sounded genteel. "Tell your mama to put on a pot. We have a guest."

"Don't nobody do nothin'," John said right after.

He spoke in a quieter tone to the Colonel. "Walk."

Though he was glad to escape the sticky, Brazilian drizzle and the strange animal sounds emanating from the surrounding ferns, John felt a low reticence. Old ghosts was right. He was stepping into shadows of something from which he knew there was no return.

* * *

So long as there were only four folks in total, everything would be fine, especially given that one was a pretty woman maybe a few years older than John, and another who appeared to be her little girl, not much older than six or seven. That must have been Sarah. She had the woman's curly brown hair and her grandfather's narrow eyes.

The other remaining stranger was a wildcard: an elderly negro, standing a head taller than all of them, and wily looking too. He kept his head up and his yellowed eyes occasionally shifted between the Colonel and John.

The cabin wasn't large, but seemed spacious enough: a few straw beds lining the back wall bookended by a pair of ornate armoires, a wood stove in one corner, and a small, round table surrounded by several sturdy-looking chairs near the center of the room.

"Where's her daddy?" John asked the Colonel, indicating toward Sarah.

"No longer with us. Yellow fever got him two years ago."

John didn't trust the Colonel as far as he could throw him. Thanks to his father's vivid and colorful recollections of the man he blamed for everything that had happened, John knew Colonel Nathaniel Dandridge as much as anyone. As sure as the sun is hot, the former commander of the Confederate 33rd Virginia Cavalry was a sneaky one. But, John figured as long as he could keep everyone inside the house, it would prevent any chance of fetching help. He'd just have to keep his ears open and one eye on the door in case someone dropped by.

"Everyone on that side of the room." John waved his gun towards the beds. The little girl whimpered a little and grabbed hold of the big negro's hand.

"C'mon girl," the man said in a low voice. "It'll be alright."

John avoided looking at her face. He really wished the Colonel had been here alone, but circumstances were what they were.

They all sat down on the bed except for the Colonel. Sarah sat on the negro's lap.

"I don't have no beef with any of you but for one man," John said. "Colonel Nathaniel Dandridge."

The Colonel raised his eyebrows.

"Do you claim to be him?" John finished. He needed an admission.

There was no hesitation. "I am Nathaniel Dandridge, but I am no longer a Colonel. Granted, you're a youngin, but old enough to know that the country for whom I served no longer exists."

"And yet you fly the flag."

There was a heavy pause. Rainwater tapped against the clay tile roof.

"And yet I fly the flag," the Colonel said with his chin held high and a sickening pride in his voice.

Before John could get a word out, the Colonel spoke up. "If you wanted to come here and just shoot me for hanging a piece of cloth, you would have done so already. So what is it that you want, Yankee? To scare women and children too?"

It was a transparent attempt to bring John to shame. He wasn't about to fall for it.

"Two things. I *will* make you pay for your crime, but first I want an apology."

The Colonel looked at him incredulously. "For what, exactly?"

"In good time. First, I'm guessing that a man who has such pride in a dead country still has his uniform."

Silence.

"Well then," John said, "I'll take that as an affirmative. I think it's fitting that you reacquaint yourself with it. You say you're no longer a Colonel, but it's the Colonel for whom I'm bringing justice. Where is it?"

Again, no response. John pointed his gun at the wall just over the old rebel's shoulder, and after a moment of his own hesitation, he pulled the trigger. The percussion clapped his ears and set them to ringing lightly. Bits of wood splintered just above the negro, far from where he intended to fire. John caught himself looking at a bewildered Sarah, her mouth caught open in a scream, but he turned away quickly and forced himself to lock eyes with the Colonel. His hand was shaking and he thought the Colonel noticed, so he grabbed the gun with both hands under the guise of cocking the hammer.

"Lucius," the Colonel said with a raised voice, though his demeanor remained irritatingly calm, "fetch me the uniform."

As if on instinct, the old black man was almost on his feet upon hearing his name. He lifted the crying little girl from his lap and handed her to her mama. John moved the gun towards him and Lucius froze.

"I don't know why you followed this man down here," John said. "Probably threatened you otherwise, but you don't have to do a damn thing. Just tell me where it is." John's motives weren't entirely charitable. He figured that if Lucius showed this level of loyalty to the Colonel, he might go far enough to pull out a rifle or pistol.

The negro looked at his master who nodded almost imperceptibly.

"He keeps it over there," Lucius said, pointing at one of the wardrobes that must have accompanied the family on their long journey from America. "There's a box sitting on the bottom, at the back."

John wondered briefly how he'd be able to keep an eye on the family, yet get the uniform. The answer was obvious, though.

"Sarah," he said, ducking his face and glancing to the side. "Be a good girl and bring out your grandfather's box, please. And set it on the table."

John didn't want to, even felt like he'd damn near faint, but he pointed the gun in her direction. Beads of sweat gathered on his brow. He had told himself that he wouldn't rush this, that this was a scene that should be savored and stamped in his memory for all time. But now, he wanted nothing more than for it to be all over. With each passing second, John felt less enthusiastic and more obligated to his father.

"Sarah," her mother said, speaking for the first time, "honey, it'll be fine. Please, do as he says." Her voice was much harsher than the Colonel's.

Sarah's eyes were like that of a reprimanded beagle. She bounced off her mother, ran toward the wardrobe and opened the door quickly. John was nervous about the speed at which she moved, but he accepted the risk. With her small hands, she tossed aside several blankets and pulled out a brown leather box a foot deep and two feet wide. She began to lift the lid.

"I said put it on the table," John snapped. He cringed as she started to cry. He didn't want to scare the girl, but his nerves were overwhelming him.

"Sarah," her mother said snapping as much as John, "do as the man says and get back here!" John's eyes briefly met the Colonel's and he knew that with every stressful moment, the Colonel was sizing up an opportunity to make a move.

"It's too heavy," she sobbed.

Flustered, John said, "N-nevermind. Go back to your mama." Her feet clapped against the floorboards as she flew into her mother's arms. The look on the mother's face told John that if he dropped his guard for one blink of an eye, she would make him regret it even more than the Colonel.

John walked up to the box. "Don't nobody move an inch," he said to them all, keeping both eyes peered in their direction. He'd hoped he could pull the .31 quickly enough should they make a move, but he knew that if they chose now to do so, he would be at a disadvantage. He cupped his pistol with his palm and quickly slid his fingers beneath the box. It was indeed heavier than he expected, but he lugged it to the table where it fell from his hands without any solemnity.

The family was still lined against the wall, motionless, overflowing with expectation. John readied his pistol again and with his free hand, lifted the lid and tossed it onto the floor.

His vision was greeted with the damned Confederate gray and yellow trim, delicately laid out. There was the woolen kepi—a cap with a dark bill and buckled band across the front. Below that lay a golden sash and white riding gloves. John removed all of them from the box and placed them on the table.

He rifled through the rest of the contents. The Colonel's shell jacket had been folded neatly with its three golden stars still pinned onto each side of the collar, and two columns of gold buttons lining the front. Beneath were gray trousers and the officer's sabre secured in its scabbard. The bulk of the box's weight was a stack of old newspapers and other hokum.

"Where your boots?" John asked.

"Sold 'em to help pay for transport," the Colonel said.

So much for pride, John thought.

He pulled out each piece of clothing and tossed them at the Colonel.

"Get dressed."

* * *

John was not disappointed as his hackles rose at seeing the Colonel in full uniform. He had to admit the old man wore it well. He was almost everything John had imagined, one of the "devils in gray" his father had rambled on about through whiskey-induced tirades.

"They don't need to see this, young man," the Colonel said, nodding at his family and slave. "I don't know who you are or what I've done to you, but they don't need to see this."

If John let them go now, he'd probably be wrapped up by the time they were able to get very far, but they may have a rifle or two stashed away nearby. It wasn't uncommon.

"They stay, so that they know about your crimes and understand that I'm not here to murder you—I'm here to enact justice on a fugitive."

The Colonel's face took on a shade of ruby red. "I am no fugitive."

John laughed, surprising himself. "That so? Then why did you turn tail and run down to Brazil?"

The Colonel took a step forward and straightened up. John moved his pistol up, but the old man maintained his defiance.

"You say I turned tail, but what do you know? You couldn't have been ten when I lost my country. My means of subsistence. Half of my family slaughtered by men in blue. What do you know, son? What do *you* know?"

John thought he knew enough.

"Ten years ago, my father, Corporal John Cunningham, Sr., came back from the war a broken man. Unable to see because he had been shot once in the head and lost his vision. Unable to walk because another minie ball had made him lame. And because of that, my mama left us shortly after his return, making him an even more broken man. But for the charity of the few friends my father had, we would have starved each year. We barely held on as it was." He looked at Sarah, "I lost my little sister because we couldn't afford no medicine."

The Colonel seemed to deflate a little bit, or so it seemed to John.

"I'm sorry to hear the circumstances, but that is the hell of war, son. Your daddy was a soldier just like the rest of us. He—"

"No!" John shouted with an unexpected fury. Sarah sank into her mother's arms and the negro recoiled. "No! Not just like the rest of you." John fought back tears. He felt an odd mix of fire increasing in his belly, but also a slightly dwindling resolve. He'd spent months tracking the Colonel's whereabouts, coming all this way with barely a moment's rest and it was all catching up with him. He'd heard that he was among many of the Southern soldiers had left for Brazil, a land still friendly to those invested in the machinations of slavery. Apprising the Colonel in his uniform, standing here in a small cabin in the middle of a foreign land, made the entire scene seem uncomfortably ridiculous.

Still, John continued. Deep down, he knew he was doing something right, yet still felt a need to confess and justify it all. "I buried my father six months ago, and that night I had a dream. I was walking through the scrub oak of Albany and there was a flash of light, just like the preacher used to go on about Paul on the road to Damascus. The voice cried out for vengeance. I knew that it was my father. Day in and day out, he drank from his jug and related to me the truth of you, Colonel Dandridge, and your damned 33rd Cavalry."

The Colonel's gave John a penetrating stare. Something changed in the way he appeared. John couldn't place a finger on it, and before he could ruminate on it anymore, the Colonel asked with the gentleness of a rabbit, "With what regiment did you say your father served?"

"I didn't," John replied. "It don't matter anyhow."

"Oh, but it does, son. It does."

John had confessed enough, but he supposed he didn't see any harm in explaining more to a dead man. "The New York 195th."

Silence. Behind his eyes, the Colonel seemed to be seeking something.

"And where was it that your father honorably took these Southern bullets that I so directed?"

The words were fresh in John's mind as if it were John Sr. himself speaking through him. "Bakerstown, just inside the northern tip of Shenandoah."

"I see," the Colonel said. The coolness of his voice grated on John. He felt anxious to get it over with.

"Do you deny you were there?" John said. This new line of conversation was irritating him and he was happy that it was building back up his resolve.

"No, son. I don't deny it at all. I was there alright." He slowly removed the hat from his head and held it in his hands. "Thing is, I don't think events took place exactly as your father told you."

As if his legs carried him on their own volition, John walked directly to the Colonel and dug the tip of the pistol into the soldier's chest. "Are you calling my father a liar?" Out of the corner of his eyes, he saw the daughter shift closer to the negro.

The Colonel never looked away from John.

"I got some papers in that box," he said. "There's one you ought to read. Seems you wouldn't believe me if I told you myself."

"You're delaying," John said. "I don't need to read no papers."

Those cold blue eyes challenged him. "Son, I don't want you to do something you'd regret. You might have never known that you were about to make a mistake, but now a part of you can't help but wonder if I'm telling you something you may have already been thinking for a long time."

The Colonel placed the hat back on his head and straightened it out. "Please, not for my sake, but for yours, read that paper."

A sound of creaking wood pulled John's attention. Lucius was on his feet again and walking toward the box. John couldn't fully understand why he let him do so, but he did. The black man stooped over and rummaged through the small stack of newspapers until he seemed to find what he was looking for.

He marched over to John and handed him a piece of yellowed paper.

John only stared back at him, unsure of what to do. His pistol was still pressed against the Colonel's chest.

"Lucius, if you would, please," the Colonel said.

The old slave pulled the paper back, unfolded it and cleared his throat. "Though Johnny Reb puts up a worthy scrap in the various corners of this dear country, some of our boys in blue have become their own worst enemy. While awaiting orders in the Shenandoah Valley, the New York 195th Infantry regiment found themselves with an excess of time and liquor. Reports have come in of six killed and eighteen wounded from an explosion at the munitions depot, all due to a drunken exchange. With dispatches indicating the Confederate's 33rd Cavalry making a move to the North, the 195th is being disbanded with the remaining soldiers being reassigned to other regiments."

Lucius stopped there.

"Lies," John said quietly, trying to convince himself that the cracks which had appeared in his father's stories had never been there. He used to think it was just the liquor which had confused him sometimes. Whenever he'd asked to see John Sr.'s bullet wounds, his father flat out refused. After being reprimanded and chased away with his father's swinging cane, John had stopped asking for details.

"That there's a Union paper, son," the Colonel said.

John's notions were being hit from all sides. He eyed the Colonel with suspicion.

"You taught your slave how to read?"

Before he could answer, Lucius interrupted. "Freed man, Mr. Cunningham. I'm a freed man. I come down with Mr. Dandridge because ain't nothin' waitin' for me up there. The Colonel had always been good to me, and at least down here, I got work and get to learn from Ms. Dandridge, alongside Sarah."

John realized at this point that his gun was no longer raised at the Colonel's chest, but directed towards the ground.

"I've made my mistakes," the Colonel said. "I came down here with my ways set, but I've learned much over the past ten years. I freed all my slaves. Any that chose to stay with me, I've given an education and a fair wage to work my crops."

John felt a light grip on his arm.

"Look, if there's one thing a Southern man can abide by, son, it's honor. You came here because you felt it was the honorable thing to do. I don't blame your daddy. Any man in his condition would have spoke the same."

The Colonel looked to his daughter, "Why don't you put on that pot I mentioned earlier," and then he turned back to John. "Please, join us for supper. We can have us a conversation about all our wrongs and our inadequate attempts to make up for them."

Process Summary

Killing Dixie is story number sixteen in the #52ShortStories challenge.

As a part of my writer's hygiene program, I've come across so many inspirational articles and essays. The latest was from the Winter 2018 issue of Military History Quarterly. I had never heard of the *Confederados*, a mass of Confederate soldiers who left the United States for South America (primarily Brazil) after being handed a painful defeat in the American Civil War.

With such a fascinating piece of history in mind, the creative half of my brain began to work its magic on the stories of who those people connected with the movement might have been and the results of the war in general. Some of them kept their way of life, but many ended up freeing their slaves and even setting up schools to educate them.

The hardest part of writing this story was the delicate subject matter, especially in the socially-charged environment in which we currently reside. How do I make someone who owned another human being, no matter who they were by the end of the story, even slightly sympathetic? I hope I succeeded in walking that fine line, but in the end, it's up to the reader to decide whether or not I was successful.

CLOSURE

Statistics

Synopsis: A recent widower tries to come to terms with his wife's re-appearance.

Word Count: 3,500

Genre: Paranormal

Completed Week: December 4th – December 17th

Closure

He was afraid to leave her alone.

As Anita lay on what had once been their bed, Dominic sat in an uncomfortable folding chair beside her, slightly disturbed by the lack of things he used to take for granted—the expected rise and fall of her stomach that accompanied inhalation and exhalation, the fluttering beneath her closed eyelids when she used to dream, and a million other tiny indications that even though she was asleep, she would eventually wake up.

She was posed in almost the exact fashion as she had been the previous Saturday. Streams of reddish-brown hair flowed from her head, down alongside her shoulders and onto the comforter. Her arms were placed across her chest, one hand overlapping the other. Though the undertakers had tried their best, they were unable to adjust the restless look on her face. Anita appeared in death almost every way as she had for the twenty-six years of her life.

Dominic leaned over and pressed his cheek to hers. There wasn't much of a scent, but traces of something sulfurous lingered. The questions came rapid-fire to his mind, but he was afraid to ponder any of them too long.

Am I dreaming?

Will you ever talk to me?

Will you leave again?

It had only been a week-and-a-half since she had come to lay down in this very bedroom for what Dominic believed would be the very last time. He had come home from work to an empty pill bottle tilted over on the nightstand and a newly-formed crack running through his core. It felt like an entire year had passed since then, both emotionally and physically. Dominic had avoided mirrors since, but he was sure that if he looked into one, he wouldn't recognize himself. Unshaven black whiskers made his neck itch. His nose had adjusted, yet he knew he stank to high heaven. It didn't matter. The newly returned Anita hadn't seemed to mind, either.

How she came to stand at his front door earlier in the afternoon, Dominic wasn't sure. He also wasn't sure he cared. The drapes had been drawn on all the windows since Saturday. Several visitors had knocked on his door over the past few days. Dominic normally waited ten minutes before opening it, just enough time for them to have gone away and leave behind a plastic-wrapped plate of cookies or a flavorless casserole. Always, there was an accompanying condolence card.

But today, it was her. As soon as he'd opened the door, she had stepped forward and he let her by as if it were the most natural thing in the world.

Now here they were in their bedroom again.

Dominic slumped into his chair and tilted his head back to work the kinks out of his neck. A swirling pattern of rainbow lights danced across the ceiling—red, green, and blue stars shot out of a cheap plug-in light machine that he had chivalrously won for Anita at the Hilton County fair two years ago. She hadn't wanted to go, but he'd somehow convinced her. It had only taken him a couple of years and she had a mostly miserable time, but she seemed to take a liking to the machine afterwards.

Mudvayne's *All That You Are* played quietly on a tiny CD player. It was her favorite song. Dominic often found her musical tastes a little depressing, but it was *hers*, and therefore it lost some of its glumness.

He wasn't sure what he'd gain from any of the lights or music. He supposed, hoped, really, that it would generate a memory or a reaction. Get her talking to him. But Anita seemed as introspective now as she had always been. She hadn't said a word since coming home.

The night gave way to sun at some point. The only indication was a small stream of light poking through a centimeter-sized gap in the curtains. Dominic sat and silently pondered what his wife's return meant for the rest of own life.

* * *

"I can't come in today."

"I understand, sir. Yes, I know the policy."

"Yes, but—"

"You do what you have to do, sir."

Dominic hung up the phone and turned to see Anita standing in front of the dining room table, staring out into the living room. He tried to figure out what she was looking at. He grabbed her hand and when she didn't seem to resist, led her in gently.

"What is it, Nita?"

Saying her name out loud didn't feel as strange as he thought it should.

Her eyes were unfocused, directed at an empty white wall, but she came to a stop in front of their loveseat. It was covered in an illustrated pattern of a country ranch, replete with chickens and horses and woodpost fencing. Dominic's parents had given it to them as a wedding present and though

Anita hated it as she'd hated most of his things, Dominic had somehow convinced her to keep it in the living room. It wasn't as if they ever had much company over anyway.

"Do you want to sit?"

There was no response. Not even the slightest twitch. Her hair was slightly kinked from where she had been laying on it.

He tried to get her to sit, but her body was impossibly stiff.

Dominic whispered, "Nita, please, I don't know what—"

There was a knock at the front door. Dominic held his breath, triple-checking that the curtains were still closed and that there was no way for someone to peek inside. At the top of the door was a thick, yellow stained glass cutout in the shape of a half-circle through which he saw the profile of a woman's hair.

Anita slowly turned around and walked towards the hall. Dominic's pulse quickened.

There was another series of knocks and he thought he heard a muffled 'Hello.'

Dominic started to follow Anita, urging her on mentally. *Come on, come on.*

The two of them were almost in the hallway when he suddenly heard a click. He looked back and saw the deadbolt turn to the left.

Dominic made a decision and was forced to watch Anita continue her slow march to the bedroom. A draft of cool air swept in, fresh and not altogether unwelcome, as the door cracked open and sunlight pushed against the dark shadows of the entryway tiles.

* * *

"Dom?"

He was frozen between the hallway and the front room. The visitor's head appeared slowly through the opening of the door. Her blond hair was tied up in a bun and she wore a thin heather-gray sweater.

"Oh!" she said, narrowing her eyes in the dimness. "You're home." Even though Dominic sensed an effort, she didn't sound entirely surprised. The smile on her face seemed genuine enough, though.

"Uh. Yeah. Hi, Barbara." He tried not to appear nervous, flitting his vision back and forth toward the bedroom's threshold that Anita had almost entered.

Barbara was their neighbor of three years and single mom to a seven-year-old boy named Jacob. Though they'd lived next to each other for only a short period of time, Dominic and Anita had known Barbara since junior high. Barbara ran with a more popular crowd than Anita, though that was an understatement. Anita's crowd consisted of Dominic and herself. She'd never been one to make friends easily and Dominic had taken it upon himself to ensure she always had someone to talk to, even though Dominic found it easy to fit in with nearly every clique in their small town.

Anita was a different story. Most people stayed away from her. Dominic had been questioned more times than he could count as to what he saw in her, but he could never explain it to anyone's satisfaction. Maybe not even to himself, other than to say that he felt it his life's mission to make her happy since he had first seen her sitting alone, sullen-faced and scooping dirt into her palms in their kindergarten sandbox, watching it run back through her fingers again.

The door swung open slowly. Bundled in her hands was a foil-cov-ered pyrex tray. "I was going to leave this on the porch, but….I didn't want any animals getting to it….and I had a key…."

Dom's face remained blank.

"Remember?" she continued. "You gave it to me for emergencies…. um….I saw your car outside, but I wasn't sure….I'm sorry if this is a bad time."

She stepped in to extend the tray to Dominic. He moved quickly to meet her.

"Thanks," he said, taking the tray.

"I didn't mean to barge in," Barbara said. "It's just….your car hasn't moved for a couple of days." She tilted her head towards the covered win-dows. "The curtains have been closed…."

He felt moisture began to form under his arms as he tried to form a barrier between the front room and the hallway. He stared at her dumbly, ca-pable of recruiting only a minuscule amount of brain power to process what she was saying.

"Chicken enchiladas," she said suddenly.

"Huh?"

She nodded at the dish in his hands. "My mom's recipe." He began to really see her now that she was closer—light-green eyeshadow, a thin layer of foundation on her cheeks, and pale pink lipstick. She smelled like a field of flowers. Dominic was quickly reminded that both he and the whole house must be giving off a terrible odor and he backed up slightly, but Barbara gave no indication that it bothered her.

"Pretty sure she got it off a can, but they're good."

"Oh."

"I'll go ahead and put it on the dining room table." She made a move to grab the dish.

"No!" he exclaimed, pulling away and feeling like a fool. She shrank back.

"No, please," he continued more quietly. "Thank you. You're too kind. I'll take care of it." Dominic rushed to the dining room table. The glass bottom clacked against the wood as he practically threw down the dish and almost skipped back to Barbara. He breathed a little easier seeing the hallway empty.

Just stay in the bedroom, Nita.

He bounced nervously on his heels. Now, Dominic and Barbara stood facing each other in silence.

"It's really dark in here," Barbara said. "Are you coming down with something? I haven't seen you since Saturday."

"I'm….I'm fine," Dominic stuttered. "I'm just….taking some time off from work."

Barbara nodded gently. "Look, I know you've been dealing with a lot. I appreciate that you invited me to the funeral."

Dominic wanted her to leave so badly, but he was a victim of his nature—always wanting to be the nice guy, even if he was uncomfortable. She was only trying to be cordial and he didn't want to be rude.

She suddenly straightened up and walked into the living room. "I'm going to turn on some lights. Don't want to fall. Then I'd have to sue you for all your worth."

Dominic wasn't sure how to respond to her unexpected movement and statement.

"A joke," she said.

"Oh," Dominic replied. "Huh."

With the flick of a switch, two lamps sprang to life and Dominic realized just how long he'd been cooped up in gloom. He squinted to see Barabara pick up one of the tiny pillows from the loveseat, sit down, and place it in her lap. She analyzed the country-life pattern like it had been hanging in the Louvre.

"Have I ever mentioned how cute this is?" she asked. "Reminds me of my grandparents."

She looked up at Dominic and patted the open seat.

His eyes darted back to the open bedroom door. Still nothing. Every second he acted like he was building bombs in his bedroom would be another second that increased the chance of Barbara learning that the impossible had happened. He was unsure of what to do now. Everything had happened so quickly and he needed time to figure things out, so he rubbed the murk from his eyes, and put on his best smile as he took a seat.

She fiddled with the pillow, flipping it around in her hands. "Jacob has been asking about you," she said. "He misses his play buddy."

"Yeah?" Dominic lit up momentarily, and just as quickly, felt bad about the whole situation. The week had been a blur and some of those knocks on the door had probably been Jacob. He was a nice kid, but a bit of loner like Anita had been. He didn't have many friends, so Dom would throw around a football or skate with him a couple times a week.

"Tell him I'm sorry. I promise I'll hang out with him soon. I just…."

Barbara looked at him with calm, but expectant eyes.

Dominic cleared his throat. "So how have you been?"

"Fine," Barbara replied. "I've been fine. Work is work." She looked down at her watch. "I have to head to the cafe in an hour."

"Oh, I don't want to keep you. I'm sure—"

"But I've got time to catch up," she said. She looked around the room. Her eyes settled on a pair of unframed photos propped on the bookshelves surrounding the TV. She stood without warning and walked up to them. "Wow, I don't remember those. Granted, I don't remember the last time I was in your living room." Their eyes met briefly. "Around the 4th of July, I think? You had a couple of us neighbors over."

Dominic remembered the 4th very well. It was one of the few times of year that he begged and pleaded with Anita to take a chance and socialize a little. She might even have fun, he had told her. Of course, she didn't. While he was entertaining, she always found something to do—cleaning dishes, putting away laundry, or trimming the trees outside that were nearly stubs already.

Dominic said nothing, only watching Barbara as she stood with her back to him. She was wearing a tight pair of blue jeans. They revealed that she was still as slim as she'd been in high school and his eyes fell to the curve of her hips as she leaned forward to observe the pictures. Dominic felt suddenly flush. He jumped to his feet and walked toward her, afraid to look toward the bedroom.

"They're new," Dominic said. "I just put them up the other day." Barbara grabbed a photo of a grinning Dominic, his arm wrapped around a slouching Anita. They were standing outside of The Dark House, a small venue in Lincoln where they watched Anita's favorite bands play several times a year. Her arms were hanging down and she appeared to be looking at something unseen beyond the camera. "She loves live music."

"Loves?" Barbara looked up at him and asked.

Dominic's throat grew constricted. "Er, loved."

Barbara leaned in and put a hand on his shoulder. He shook involuntarily at her touch. Sweat began to form again on his brow. He put the photo back in its place.

"I don't have many photos of her. She wasn't a big fan of cameras," he said with a half-smile.

"You two always seemed the odd couple to me," Barbara said. "I wished I had gotten to know her better. She was always….introverted, wasn't she? The tortured artist type?" Her teeth dug into her lips after she spoke.

Dominic wasn't sure how to respond. Anita was just down the hall. Surely she could hear every word they were saying.

"Oh my God. I'm sorry. I didn't mean…."

"No, no, it's okay. She wasn't exactly a social butterfly." Dominic didn't feel bad saying that. Anita would have been the first to admit it.

Barbara inhaled deeply. Her hand slid from Dominic's shoulder to his arm. Her touch was sending shockwaves through his bare skin.

"I'm just going to be blunt, Dom. What did you see in her?"

That question. He may have heard it as many times in his life as he had 'good morning.' His answer now wasn't any different than it had been the myriad times he'd been asked.

"No one knows her like I do," he said. His voice rose. "No one ever gave her a chance but me. Yeah, she was in her own head a lot, but that didn't mean she didn't deserve love like anyone else."

"Did you feel sorry for her?"

Dominic had come to expect people to leave it alone after he'd spoken his piece, but Barbara wasn't letting it go. Fine. If she wanted blunt, he would be blunt.

"It's complicated," he said. He sat back down on the couch and stared at the open bedroom door. He felt the couch shift as Baraba sat beside him.

"Did you ever feel like you had a mission in life? Like a direction you had to head toward and if you tried to go the other way, it just felt wrong?"

"Sure," she replied. "But sometimes we can run right into a ditch. What about you? Were you *happy*?"

"Of course!" he said.

Barbara remained silent. Her eyes felt like a vacuum sucking hidden truths out of him along with thin layers of resentment that had built up over the years. "Being happy doesn't mean everything is always great a hundred percent of the time. Besides, if it's always about you, isn't that just being selfish?"

"Yeah," she said, "but you've never been one to make it all about you. You deserve some happiness too."

It was a lot for Dominic to dwell on. Warm breath flowed in and out of his mouth as he gaped at Barbara.

"I don't doubt that you loved her, Dom. But were you *in* love with her?"

Nuance. Dominic tried to avoid it because it just made things worse. Who could really say what love was or should be?

Anita was sad, Dominic tried to make her happy. That was their pattern. Their balance. That was who they were. If he were to act differently now, to believe that his sacrifices for Anita had maybe been in excess, it would be too much to take. Too large of a change, too quickly.

"I can't," Dominic said. He could feel his eyes beginning to well up with tears. He cleared his throat and straightened his back.

Barbara put a hand on his leg. "Can't what?"

His whole head was shaking trying to contain the emotions churning through him like a maelstrom.

"Everything." He turned toward the bedroom without thinking. Standing in the doorway was Anita's silhouette. Dominic suddenly didn't seem to care if she was seen or what she may be thinking. His eyes penetrated her looming figure. "She needs me," he almost whispered.

"She's *gone*, Dom." Barbara's hand squeezed his thigh and she leaned in closer. The floral scent of her perfume struck him again.

"I failed her," he said.

"No," Barbara said with a sternness that shook him. With her other hand, she directed his chin back toward her. "You did *not* fail her. You did more than anyone could possibly have done for her. You are *not* obligated, do you understand?"

He fought to turn back to the hallway. He could feel Anita's presence growing closer.

"Do you understand?" Barbara repeated.

Dominic blinked hard. Again, he tried to look into the hall. With a surprising amount of force, Barbara grabbed his face with both hands and planted her lips on his.

Her fingernails dug into Dominic's face. He felt too tired, too weak to resist. And then he didn't want to. The feeling of her moist lips was such a novel feeling. He found himself fighting back thoughts of Anita. Memories of nights where she had been more depressed than normal and rejected his overtures, saying that she didn't deserve his love. He had told her that wasn't true, but they had never been able to bridge that gap.

He felt awkward, yet his hands found their way around Barbara's back as he hugged her tightly. Tears transferred from his cheeks to hers.

She pulled back and rested her forehead on his. Dominic closed his eyes, sensing Anita standing behind him. He didn't want to look. He wished now that she would just go away, but he still felt he owed her something. He turned, looked up and opened his eyes.

Dominic's heart nearly stopped pumping. Anita was indeed standing before them both, looking directly at him, but there was something wrong with her face.

"Dom?"

Barbara's voice sounded so far away. Dominic stood and came face-to-face with his dead wife. Her eyes were no longer lifeless and unfocused, but instead met his. Wrinkles formed at their edges. As soon as Dominic comprehended the strange vision of a smiling Anita, she turned away from him and ambled to the front door.

He felt a pair of arms reach across his chest, holding him securely from behind. Barbara's head fell across the back of his right shoulder.

"Are you okay?"

Dominic's hands fell over hers.

"I'm okay."

Process Summary

Closure is story number seventeen in the #52ShortStories challenge.

When you swing for the fences, it's easy to take your eyes off the ball.

My goal in this story was to stretch, stretch, and stretch some more in order to write a "relationship story." I wanted to focus on the dynamics of an unhappy relationship and what that meant to someone who was brought out of it through somewhat shocking circumstances.

Needless to say, that's so far outside of my wheelhouse as to practically be a solar system or two away.

It's exactly why I needed to do it.

Part of this challenge isn't just to meet a story quota but to learn. Failure is a great teacher, and my first reader made it pretty clear that I fell flat on this one.

My problem? Lack of likable characters.

There was no one really to root for here. If I were to come back and rewrite this story, I'd turn Dominic and Anita's relationship into more of a friendship. Dominic would be so devoted his friend that he could easily have put her life ahead of his, but to have them married seemed to turn Dominic into more of an over-the-top martyr.

Anyway, as Dean Wesley Smith recommends, I've taken note and now I'll move on. There's always the next story. No need to go back and revise a mistake to death and increase the potential of sucking any remaining life out of the tale.

Swag

Statistics

Synopsis: At an industry trade show, a high-performing executive receives a mysterious bit of swag.

Word Count: 4,000

Genre: Fantasy / Sci-Fi

Completed Week: December 18th – December 24th

Swag

As the convention's low-level hum of conversation and clatter carried through the black polyester curtains, Gerry flipped the strange device around in her hands. It wasn't heavy and appeared to be made of cheap tin. Glossy orange paint flaked in spots and cracks formed a pattern of uneven tiles, reminding her of a gaudy bathroom floor in an upscale restaurant. It had a short handle in the back, presumably so that you could hold onto it with one hand, and for whatever reason, spin the gear around with the other. She noticed that a smaller gear was attached to the middle of the larger one. They didn't appear to interlock in any way. She squeezed the toothed edge of the larger one and gave it a spin. The other gear twisted and clicked in the opposite direction. Tiny sparks of light began to ignite and pop and Gerry felt a warmth run through her hands.

Rose quickly clamped down on the apparatus, bringing it to an immediate stop.

"Not here," she said. Her voice was emphatic and she peered over Gerry's shoulder with suspicion even though they were the only two inside the makeshift room—one of several twelve-by-twelve curtain-lined squares that were set up by the convention staff so that vendors and customers could meet with some level of privacy.

"Oh," Gerry said, looking at Rose with some surprise. "Sorry."

"It's okay," Rose replied. "It's just that you really should wait to try it until you get home."

Gerry continued to inspect it. "Well, thank you."

"You have lots of questions, I'm sure. It's a prototype of a new product," Rose said. Her voice dropped to a whisper. "It's going to change everything."

Rose acted as if she had just handed Gerry the week's winning lottery numbers. For a software company, this seemed like something outside of their purview.

"What is it?"

"It's something better experienced than explained," Rose said. "Just trust me."

"Why are you giving it to me?" Gerry grew a little suspicious.

Rose looked at her as if she had asked why rain falls from the sky. "You've always been there for us, Gerry," she said. "But for you, Cortega Systems wouldn't be here—wouldn't be *anywhere*. We almost went out of business, you know? But it's been three years now since you helped us climb out of that hole and we're market leader. I can hardly believe it. You went to bat for us when everyone thought you were crazy to do so."

"It's what I do." Gerry smiled, reflecting appreciation.

She was good with the smile. It came easily to her. And while she was genuinely happy for Rose and Cortega, the seeds for their success weren't planted due to a simple case of charity or friendship. Gerry never threw good money at bad product and she never got too close to anyone, let alone business partners. Her knack for picking winners had taken her from Baldwin Capital's dim and mold-infested mailroom to a large corner office on the 13th floor with Chief Technology Officer imprinted on her nameplate. She remembered how proud her father had been every time she had received a promotion. Even on his deathbed, when she would try to awkwardly connect with him beyond work talk, he'd always redirect the conversation to her accomplishments and how it reminded him of the time he had made a big sale or gotten a one-up on someone jockeying for power in the office. He never cared about anything else she might have to say until she determined it needed to be the other way around—she had to care about what he wanted to hear.

In the case of Cortega, Gerry had seen their eventual success coming. She was an avid reader of trade journals and college alumni newsletters. It was something she'd learned by watching her father the few times he was around the house. Cortega had been snapping up sharp kids out of MIT and Stanford over the past seven years: kids who'd focused heavily on machine learning, artificial intelligence, and even quantum mechanics. The company obviously wasn't focused on building the same old business analytics software as their competitors. Gerry wasn't one to dig too deep into any one subject, but upon further investigation, she'd gotten that familiar feeling in her gut and that was enough to convince her Cortega was on a path to a breakthrough. Their software would lead Baldwin towards greater sales opportunities, and therefore, greater profits. Most of Gerry's competitors had initially passed Cortega by because their proposed technology was unproven and the price tag was considerably high. For a time, Gerry had them all to herself, but now others saw their potential impact on the industry.

Rose gently pried the device from Gerry's hands and placed it in a reusable swag bag along with a folded piece of paper. She handed the bag to Gerry, then her eyes narrowed.

"I don't need to tell you this, of course, but *do not* lose this."

Gerry flashed another congenial smile.

* * *

As she stepped into her hotel room, Gerry checked the calendar on her phone. It was just before seven o'clock and she was scheduled to attend a dinner in thirty minutes with the sales reps at Perseus, a cloud-based inventory systems company. She considered texting her assistant, telling him that she was feeling ill, but it wasn't worth it. Gerry would only have to make it up at another time and things wouldn't go any easier. Perseus was looking to secure a multi-year contract. They'd arranged a dog and pony show dinner for her and other Baldwin officers. It would be business as usual—they would order ten bottles of the most ridiculously expensive Burgundy wines and fawn over her, trying to get her to make regretful snap commitments.

So, Gerry, I saw that piece about you in Forbes. Top Forty in their Forties? Nice! Have you seen what Perseus has to offer? Let me just tell you....

As she threw her collection of swag onto the ground beside the minibar, a rank aroma wound its way into her nostrils. Walking the convention floor all day in a three-button pantsuit had left her desperate for a shower, but she had to make a choice—a quick shower and deal with reapplying makeup or unwind with her little ritual and just touch things up. Option number two sounded best.

She turned the deadbolt on the hotel door and drew the curtains closed. It wasn't as if anyone would burst in or peep through the 27th-story window, but her self-consciousness defied all reason. With the down pillow folded and propped beneath her head, Gerry kicked off her shoes and took a deep breath. She put on a pair of headphones, hit play on her phone and began to sing along at the top of her lungs to Taylor Swift's *You Belong With*

Me. A familiar image formed in her mind. She was on stage, a contestant on *The Voice*, posed before the bright lights, enraptured by the accompanying music. The song crescendoed as it approached the chorus, yet something wasn't right. The longer she sang, the more embarrassed she grew which tightened the muscles around her larynx. She sensed harsh judgments from the hundreds of imaginary eyes peering out from the audience. As her confidence cracked, so did her voice.

Negative assessments hit her from all angles. How ridiculous I would look, she thought. She knew the crowd was seeing right through her—a woman in her mid-forties trying to live out silly, youthful fantasies.

Halfway through the first song, she paused the music and sat up. Her mind's eye settled on an image of her father sitting uncomfortably in a chair during her first and only singing recital. His demanding eyes were those she had seen in the audience just now, but they had been multiplied there.

After several moments of holding court with her father's phantasmic image, she fell back onto the bed and gazed at the ceiling. An orange-tinged imitation of a Michelangelo fresco covered it from end to end, reminding her of the strange device Rose had given her.

Gerry pushed herself off the bed and walked toward the bag of swag. She tipped it over, emptying its contents onto the floor. Buried beneath oversized t-shirts, hundreds of stickers and a dozen reusable water bottles was Cortega's apparatus along with the folded note. She picked up the piece of paper, unfolded it, and read.

> *Gerry,*
> *I know you're probably reading this from your hotel room. It's okay. I didn't expect you to wait until you got home.*

> *Let me just advise a couple of things:*
>> *Lay down when turning the gears. You don't want to*
> *fall and hurt yourself.*
>> *It only works once, so enjoy the moment.*
>> *Happy travels.*
>> *Rose*

What this had to do with Cortega's analytic systems, Gerry had no clue. Maybe they were looking to expand into a new field? Introduce some sort of virtual or augmented-reality aspect? That could be a boon to website hits; bring in more traffic from the millennial segment.

Maybe it was even more benign than that, though. Maybe it was just some sort of viral marketing scheme concocted by a group of college-aged interns. Who's to say that these funny looking toys wouldn't start showing up as stickers slapped onto the backs of street signs or wind their way into Internet memes.

Suddenly, the room felt entirely too quiet, so she turned on the television. A *Married with Children* rerun was playing—Al Bundy was berating his wife while his kids were sneaking cash from his wallet. She wasn't really a fan of the dysfunctional family sitcom, but it served its purpose.

She picked up the device and took it back to the bed. She laid down again and held it over her head, examining it a little more closely under the dim table lamp lighting. It didn't look any different than before. It still appeared to be made of cheap, thin metal and was shabbily painted. There were no wires or batteries. As she had in the convention hall, Gerry gripped the handle and with her other hand, spun the large gear. Al's voice carried on in the background.

You know, Peg, it would be nice if you could make us a hot meal every once in a while.

Tiny sparks jumped again between the gaps in the cogs. What a family, Gerry thought as she stared at the device, captivated by the pattern beginning to form. As the wheels spun, they seemed to be picking up speed on their own volition. A vague notion formed in her head—a vision of those old hypnosis wheels that were popular in the early 20th century. The kind that you could order out of the back of *MAD* magazine. She giggled at the thought, and then Al's daughter, Kelly, chimed in.

Dad, I'm going out with my new boyfriend, Spider. I'll be back in a week.

The sparks turned into thin strands of electrical current. Bright light flashed in an indiscernible pattern. Gerry felt as if she were standing before a window, watching a violent lightning storm dancing in the distance. She tried to latch her attention onto the sounds of the sitcom, but her attention was being rapidly sucked into that swirling spiral pattern forming in front of her. As the flashes grew more intense, a wave of vertigo swept over her. She tried to let go of the handle, but the muscles in her hands squeezed down. She could *feel* her knuckles turning white. She wanted to shut out the world, look away, but even her own eyes seemed to align against her. Her mind twisted like one of the gears and a nauseating, low-frequency whir thrummed against her inner ear.

I coulda' been something, Peg. Four touchdowns in a single game. Then I met you. Now I sell womens' shoes.

Finally, Gerry's hand released the device, but instead of dropping onto her, it floated in the air just above her chest. As she squeezed the comforter between her fingers, the TV's canned laugh track was going off in the background like a machine gun.

She thought she might be able to roll off the blankets and onto the ground, but there was a dread weight across every inch of her body. Unable to fight the pressure any longer, Gerry released her grip and allowed herself to fall into the abyss.

* * *

The familiar vanilla scent of coneflowers entered Gerry's nostrils. The sky above her head was almost the same shade as their pink petals.

She sat up and listened to the rapid-fire snaps of what sounded like audience applause morphing into the rhythm of cicadas. Her first thought wasn't a concern with where she was or how she had arrived, but a single, focused memory. The one most tied to the smell of those coneflowers and the music of those tiny creatures with transparent wings.

Terre Haute, Indiana.

1978? 1979?

She had been hiding in a field.

Why?

She couldn't quite pull the answer to that from her mind's tight grip, but the feeling was undeniably the same as she had felt that very day—a blend of fear and giddiness. The kind of nervous elation that brings an otherwise unreproducible smile to a child's face.

She remembered now.

Her and Father were playing hide-and-seek. Gerry couldn't remember if he even knew that he was supposed to be looking for her. That happened a lot. She thought her instructions had always been clear. He seemed to acknowledge her from behind a newspaper or by giving her a thumbs up while he was talking on the phone, but often she would lay in the dirt as the sun slowly fell, waiting, poking at roly-polies with thin sticks and drawing patterns

in the soil. Then she would sing her heart out in the middle of that field—ev-

ery song she could remember, whether they be church hymns like *Go Tell It*

On The Mountain or the Bee Gees.

But her throat felt parched at the moment. She didn't feel much like

singing.

She stood up and dusted herself off, appraising her clothing as she

did so. On her impossibly small feet were a dusty pair of once-white, but now

yellowed Nike Cortez tennis shoes with a red elongated checkmark running

along the outsides. She was wearing Jordache jeans and a rainbow-striped

tank-top.

Gerry tried to look across the field, but her head barely reached

above the edge of the bloomed perennials. She stood on her tippy-toes to

gain her bearings. Her old house was not only exactly where she'd expected it

to be, but also looked exactly as it had in at that time. That was a little jarring

since she had last seen it ten years ago, just two years after Father's funeral. It

had fallen into great disrepair: splintered wooden siding, the outer fieldstone

wall having come down in parts, and almost all of the trees dead and gone

due to a lack of water. Her mother had entered a period of rapid mental

decline after Father's death, so Gerry had sold the place quickly and cheaply,

then moved her mother into an assisted living facility.

She turned slightly toward the tiny river which ran along the rear of

their home. On the far end of the dock, she could see the top of her father's

Greek fisherman cap that he had picked up during one of his business travels.

He was sitting with his back to her, facing the water.

Gerry broke into a run and was breathing hard by the time her shoes slapped against the wood planks. The rickety dock swayed gently beneath her feet just as she had expected it to.

"Dad!" she exclaimed. "You're supposed to be looking for me!"

Her voice was youthful again, but she had an awareness that this wasn't completely her. In fact, it seemed to her as if she was composed of two different identities, like those mythological creatures with multiple faces on each side of their head. She was both Gerry, accomplished business-woman, and Gerry, the little girl who desperately wanted her father to pay attention.

What did they call this, she wondered. A lucid dream? Maybe that's what Rose's device was. A tool guaranteed to induce such things.

Her father remained motionless but for a tiny breeze whipping around the hairs sticking out of the back of his hat. Gerry saw that he was holding a fishing rod in one hand, its string pulled taut to the right, disappear-ing into the running currents.

Gerry frowned and her eyes narrowed. As long as they had lived on this beautiful stretch of land beside the river, she had never seen her father fish. It was always a little amusing to her that for a family who lived in such picturesque environs, Father and Mother were never 'outdoorsy' people. Mother rarely went outside unless required and when Father was home a few days out of the month, he spent much of the time working in his upstairs of-fice, the door shut tight to the distractions of the outside world.

"Dad!" she shouted again. She crept up and laid a hand on his shoul-der.

He turned and simply smiled as if he had heard her all along. She expected him to look as he had during those early years, and he sort of did, but there was an understated tiredness that revealed itself through sallow bags beneath his eyes and sticky, gummy lips. "Hi, honey. The fish are biting."

"You don't even fish," she said.

He shook his head at her as if that were the silliest notion in the world.

"Nonsense. We all fish," he said. "Sometimes, if we sit still long enough and pay attention, we even catch a few." He leaned over and whispered. "Hey, do you think mom would be happy if I brought some home for dinner?"

Gerry thought about it for a second. "Probably not. She hates fish."

That set her father to howling. He gripped his gut and teetered back and forth, nearly losing his fishing rod to the river before he quickly recovered it. He gave Gerry a funny look—a mix of relief and sudden fear as if he was going to lose everything he'd ever known in an instant. He must have realized he was scaring her a little because he straightened up and smiled at her again. It seemed like a shadow of a smile this time, though, like the crumbling wall and chipped house-paint. Still, his eyes had a strange sparkle in them that she'd never noticed before. A chaotic pattern of tiny stars flickering on and off in a manner that was sitting on the edge of her comprehension.

"Yeah. You're right," he said. He looked at the empty space next to him. "Come on, have a seat anyway," he said. "We can always catch and release."

If Gerry felt any reluctance, it quickly dissipated. A familiar smell of his Old Spice aftershave hovered like a cloud as she sat down beside him. His eyes never left her.

She kicked her feet back and forth. They dangled at least a foot above the waterline. "What are we doing here?" she asked.

Gerry inspected every ounce of his being, from the sunspots on the outside of his forearms to the gold wedding ring that seemed to have been grown over by his own flesh.

"You tell me," he said, the grin still on his face.

Tell him? As if she had planned this dream?

"Why didn't you come looking for me?" she asked. The question seemed to impose itself on her.

The sparkle in his eyes was mesmerizing. It wanted to hypnotize her, pull her away from such lines of questioning, but she refused to let it. Her father took a deep breath and looked to the tiny whitecaps forming on the river.

"I got busy," he said.

"With what?" Gerry demanded. Before she realized, she was on her feet, her fists clenched. Her torso was tipped toward him as if she wanted to prevent him from packing up his gear and leaving.

"With absolutely nothing, honey. Absolutely nothing." The clicking of cicadas picked up in the background. He grew animated again. "Hey! Come on, fish with your old man," he said. He indicated toward a second pole sitting on the dock beside him, already baited with a slimy worm dancing and curling under the blood orange sun.

What was the harm, Gerry pondered. But something tugged at her from the inside. She turned back toward the fields from whence she came and saw the top of a little girl's head moving, spinning in a circular pattern as her long pigtails flailed back and forth. Though the air was filled only with the song of insects, she sensed that little girl was a part of their music.

Gerry leaned in and hugged her father tightly as if he might float away. "No," she whispered into his ear.

He pried her arms loose and craned his neck to face her. The sparkles in his eyes were still there, but now Gerry ignored them as if they were inconsequential specks of dust.

"No?" Her father laughed again with all of his might. Laughed until his eyes were flowing with tears, but then the laughter turned into something not so funny and he was sniveling at her feet now, bawling and choking on his own sobs. It scared Gerry and she found herself backing up. Her father had been the strongest person she'd ever known. Even behind his smile lay a steely, invulnerable resolve.

The moment she considered bolting back to the field, his outburst came to a complete stop. He reached out to her with a pleading hand. "No. Please," he said. "You don't have to fish, Gerry. I'm sorry you ever thought you had to fish."

Those words sent a shockwave through her system. Her belly felt as if it might flutter away.

I don't know, Al. Marcy isn't going to like it if she finds out I was hanging out all night at The Jiggly Room.

Where the atmosphere had once felt thick and constraining, Gerry felt as if she were breathing freely again.

Ohhhhh Aaaalll….

Yes, Peg?

Al, come rub my feet.

Gerry opened her eyes. Michelangelo's fresco sharpened into focus. Her head was pounding. She rubbed her temples, but her fingers felt gritty. She looked at them and there was a sort of glitter stuck to their tips.

She sat up and saw a small pile of the same sparkly powder fall from her blouse and onto the bed. Gerry looked over at the alarm clock: 7:45 PM.

"Shit!" she yelled. She grabbed her phone lying beside the clock. There were several missed calls and text messages from her assistant.

Where r u?

They're waiting!

Gerry stared at the television screen. A shampoo commercial played. Though her eyes were directed that way, her thoughts were focused only on what she had just experienced. There was an unexplainable weight lifted from her chest. She turned to see her earphones laying tangled on the floral-print comforter. She grabbed them and walked toward her phone just as another text message made it vibrate.

Malcolm seems a little pissed ur not here.

Gerry popped her headphones into the jack, turned up Katy Perry's *Roar*, and sang loud enough to drown out every dinging notification.

Process Summary

Swag is story number eighteen in the #52ShortStories challenge.

This story was a little nerve-wracking (like most of them) getting off the ground. All I started with was this conceit of a person getting this piece of 'swag' from a trade convention that had some sort of magical properties.

It wasn't until the third day of writing that I started to piece together an actual storyline. It's interesting, this feeling of imminent failure that strikes when writing. You'd think I'd be past that by now, seeing that I ALWAYS finish, even if things don't come out as expected (and 90%+ of the time, they don't).

But nope, the stress remains. All I can do is look at the work I've put out before and realize that I'll get it done. I suppose it's likely the same for these writing greats I'm seeking to emulate.

The most interesting thing to note is that my first reader did like the story, but she said I needed some help in the 'woman' department. She reminded me that there are a lot of things a man takes for granted that women spend time on, such as putting on makeup. There was a timing issue in regards to Gerry being late for her meeting and it never even occurred to me that she would need time for applying makeup.

So, yeah, having your gender-based blind spots brought to your attention is another good reason to have your first reader be a different gender, if possible. :)

PRINCESS SOUP-BONE

Statistics

Synopsis: A lucky dog goes missing, forcing three gold miners to search her out.

Word Count: 3,600

Genre: Historical Fiction

Completed Week: December 25th – December 31st

Princess Soup-Bone

The fact that Davis and Luca were putting their pans and shovels away indicated, for all intents and purposes, that they believed the old girl would not be found that morning.

Johnny had been out on the hunt for over two hours, so the two men made the most of their time. They packed camp because they knew Johnny would cry and howl if they weren't ready to join in as soon as he returned. As much as both of them wanted to stay and continue working their claim, Johnny would make such a proposition intolerable. He'd be a sobbing handful without Princess Soup-Bone in tow.

"He's too superstitious, no? She was just another mouth to feed. We would have done okay without her."

Davis sensed Luca ending the last sentence as if it were a question.

"Maybe," Davis said. He wasn't confident enough to fall on either side of the equation. He often liked to see things play out before making a decision. Some considered Davis spineless because of that. He figured it was just smart. The fact was Princess had only been with them a couple of months, and their newfound luck seemed mighty convenient after her arrival.

"I wouldn't discount anything yet," he continued. "If it wasn't for her, we may have been many miles from each other right now—you on a cutter heading back around the Cape, Johnny probably drinking away his rheumatism in a dusty alley."

Davis didn't want to think about where *he* might have ended up. When he'd sailed out of the Boston harbor eight months ago, he'd sworn to his parents and siblings that he wouldn't return until he could buy them each their own set of authentic Chinese porcelain tea cups. To face them again would be a humiliation of the first order. He wasn't prepared to endure such. He'd always been considered a roustabout with his head in the clouds and his unremarkable homecoming would only go to prove the rest of the world right.

"Bah," Luca said, skipping smooth stones across the creek while Davis continued working. The Italian was young and brash, not one to readily believe in much anything happening outside the material world influencing anything within it. Though he verbally disdained any notion of Princess acting as a benevolent messenger, in practice, he seemed to defer quietly if Johnny made a decision based on his peculiar beliefs.

My friends, Johnny had said with his Russian accent suddenly becoming thicker than his day-to-day speech, *the Leshiy wood-spirits are alive and well. They come in time of need and must be respected!*

As Davis strung together the handles of their tin pots and secured them to Becca, their mule, he laughed to himself that calling a wood-spirit Princess Soup-Bone was respectful. Yet Johnny took no issue with it and the name seemed to stick when Luca offered her an actual soup-bone on their first night of celebration.

After confirming Becca was fully loaded, Davis took a moment to admire the way the morning sun hit the calm waters streaming through their claimed section of Percy's Gulch. They were the only ones in this area barely two miles south of the foothill town of Sonora. One month ago, they'd passed many folks coming the opposite way, always with a look of pity on their faces. They must have looked something awful, these three men in near rags following a fur-and-bones mutt. More than a few times, they were handed loaves of bread by traveling parties without a word being spoken—only eyes that said, "You poor things. So late to the party."

It was true. Among the general population of California miners and those who made money from serving their needs, there was little doubt as to the slim prospects so close to Sonora. It was June of 1855 and this area had been well picked over since bodies came rushing over mountains and ocean six years prior.

Or so it was believed.

Davis and Luca had initially thought they were crazy to settle in and dig here, especially given how they had been down to hard biscuits and unseasoned pemmican. A hot pot of coffee had been a distant memory then.

But Princess insisted on stopping in this very spot and refused to budge. That was sign enough for Johnny. He'd taken to the brown-coated girl like a bee to a dandelion, following her in a semi-delusional state. Davis and Luca had been too worn down and tired to protest as he began unpacking Becca without so much as consulting them.

The three of them panned a little inlet that turned out to be rife with gold dust and the incident was certainly enough for Davis to wonder if just maybe, Princess Soup-Bone was truly sent to guide them. Davis would never forget that first day of slack-jawed disbelief followed by the loudest hootin' and hollerin' that he'd ever heard. Both Luca and Johnny had spouted off in their native languages—Luca with his passionate-sounding Italian and Johnny with his angry-sounding Russian (Johnny's real name was Alexander Blinov, the last name meaning something akin to a pancake, so he said everyone had taken to call him Johnny after johnnycakes).

Within a week, they had seven jars filled to the brim with beautiful yellow flakes. Coffee, eggs, and even an occasional tour around the saloon brought all of their spirits to a new height. Davis commissioned a carpenter to build them a sluice box so that they could start hauling more at a time.

All was well for the past seventeen days until Princess disappeared some time in the middle of the night. Truth be told, her sudden departure left Davis on edge, but he was unsure if it was because she was what Johnny claimed her to be or just the downtrodden effect it would have on them all.

At that thought, there was a rustle in the woods behind them. Davis and Luca both turned to see Johnny running back into the camp, panting and wheezing, bent over with his hands on his knees.

"Someone took her," he said breathlessly. "I know it." There was tobacco spittle running down his graying beard and traces of tears carved into the grime on his cheeks. He had a wild aspect to his eyes that Davis had hoped would never return.

"Now hold on," Davis said. "Why would someone come and take an old dog?"

Johnny gave him a reprimanding look.

"I know she's more than that to us," Davis quickly backpedaled, "but no one else knows that."

Johnny ignored him. "We need to go to town," he said. "She must be there. Or someone will have seen her."

Davis eyed Luca who nodded back. "We figured as much," Davis said.

Johnny looked around and saw the empty camp.

"You packed everything? No. No. Leave the tools," Johnny said. "Someone will come and take our claim."

Davis shook his head. "More likely someone will think twice if they find our equipment here," he said. "Most people will pass this place by otherwise."

Johnny hesitated for a moment, but then assented. "You're right, you're right. I'm just—"

And he left it at that as the three of them departed for Sonora.

* * *

It was no surprise that Johnny grew more melancholy by the minute, but Davis noticed a dousing of spirits in both himself and even Luca. After searching every alleyway and proprietor's shop, calling out "Princess!" to the curious looks of the town's citizenry, the three of them settled in at the place they'd started—Rosa's Cantina.

It was close to noon and nearly every seat was taken. The bar was completely occupied. Only two tables were open on the floor. The trio had been seated in a dim corner, opposite from the finely dressed clerks and lawyers taking lunches of pork, beans, and tortillas. In another corner near a window was a piano player warming up with some scales before diving into instrumental versions of old spirituals.

"Maybe she's elsewhere," Davis said, eyeing the waiter dropping off a bottle of rye and three glasses. "I mean, she did just appear to us out of the woods. It could be she headed back from wherever she came."

A part of him regretted saying that. Johnny may just want to head back north and retread old ground where they had first come upon her. A deflated Davis didn't know if he was up for that. He'd much rather continue working their glorious secret.

Luca reached eagerly for the bottle. He yanked the cork out with his teeth and took a pull before pouring everyone a glass. Davis gave him a reprimanding look, but Luca just shrugged. Johnny didn't seem to care a whit. Davis pushed the glass before him, completely unnoticed as Johnny's eyes remained unfocused on the woodgrain of the table. He was bundled up in his heaviest gray coat as if it was the middle of January.

"Perhaps our time with her was at its end," Johnny said. "The Leshiy are fickle creatures, you know. If they are not cherished properly..." A solitary tear splashed beneath his downturned face. Davis felt a wave of pink embarrassment sweep across his pale flesh as he knew Johnny was the edge of blubbering again.

"She ate just as well as we did!" Luca chimed in. He poured himself a second shot.

It was at that moment when Davis wondered if Johnny's old gods had heard their lamentations and looked upon them with pity. Davis was facing the double-door entrance of the cantina while the other two men had their backs to it, so they could only judge by the frozen expression of his slightly parted lips and enlarged eyes that something peculiar was occurring.

Luca was the first to turn around.

"Princess!" he yelled, clamping his mouth with both hands, too far delayed after betraying his excitement.

Johnny craned his neck slowly as if he struggled within against facing further disappointment.

All of their eyes fell not so much upon the dark-looking, mustachioed man wearing a black bow-tie and blinding white shirt hidden only in parts by a thin red vest, but upon the panting creature who stood by his side, a thick piece of rope around its neck leading up to the man's hand.

Davis correctly predicted that Johnny might do something rash. The Russian was already halfway out of his chair before Davis grabbed his arm.

"Now hold on," he said. "That might not be her." He didn't even attempt to hide the lie with tone or convincing language. The hungry-looking eyes, the way she wagged her tail—as sure as buxom Maria upstairs was not a one-woman man, there was no doubt that was their girl.

"That's her!" Johnny slapped his knee and hooted. Ripping his arm from Davis' grip, he got to his feet and approached the gentleman.

* * *

The man gave Johnny a weary look. His right hand fell quickly to the swollen holster at his side. Davis and Luca weren't men of violence, but each kept a single-shot belly-gun on their person in case things went awry, which was a distinct possibility at the moment.

As Johnny neared the stranger, he surprised the man by getting down on one knee and cupping both hands gently under the jaw of Princess Soup-Bone.

"Come, *baba*, are you going to give us a scare just like that? We took good care of you, didn't we?" One hand reached up and scratched the back of her ears. Princess leaned into him and began licking the palm of his other hand.

Johnny rose onto his heels and now Davis and Luca stood two feet behind him. The man regarded all of them with a wariness. His hand still floated openly above the butt of his pistol.

"Thank you for looking after her, friend," Johnny said. He stuck out a hand as if to shake. "We hope she's been no trouble."

Suddenly, the man smirked but did not offer his hand in return. "No trouble at all," he said and looked down at Princess. "Came across her this morning as I was riding into town. She's a friendly one." Davis noticed that the man's hand had moved from the gun and was now being used to tighten his grip on the rope.

Johnny stood there with a dumb smile on his face, waiting expectantly. The man began to move to the side and head towards an empty table, but Johnny moved quickly to intercept him. "If you want to keep the rope, you can untie her now. She will follow us."

"Oh," the man said. "Well, are you sure this is your dog?" He looked down. "I didn't see a collar or brand anywhere."

"Yes," Luca spoke up. "She's ours."

"Huh." The man stroked his mustache as if deep in thought. "Well, as much as I would like to believe you fellas, I can't well and good just hand her over to any man claiming to be her owner. Now, you all come across as genuine and honest gentlemen, but looks can be most deceiving." He eyed their dusty clothing as a banker inspects a potentially counterfeit bill. "What if you simply intend to cook her up and eat her?"

Johnny's eyes grew wider than the Atlantic Ocean. "Sir, we would *never* think of such a thing." He spat on the floor between his boots. Davis could sense the old firebrand was getting riled up.

"No, no, of course not," the man said, putting his hands up in a defensive manner. "Forgive the insinuation. It's just that I've grown a little attached. But, still, there must be some way around this conundrum."

Back in Boston, Davis had considered himself a fan of the theater.

Whenever a troupe was in the city or a new show was opening, the producer could always count on his attendance. He was well versed in the arts of the stage, and therefore it came as no surprise to him that the man before them was half-rate but good enough to convince the layman that every move he made was without prior motive and forethought.

"I have an idea!" the man exclaimed, reaching beneath his vest and pulling out a deck of cards. "It just so happens that I carry these wherever I go, you know, to play a little solitaire and whittle away the boredom that so frequently arises during travel. Now, I've just begun to get interested in poker and faro since coming out West. While I'm not very good, I do find the games thrilling." He leaned into Johnny and raised his eyebrows. "What would you say, if you're so inclined, to playing a round for her?"

Davis felt his whole being deflate. He knew nothing about cards and he'd seen Johnny only play an occasional hand, never walking away from a table with more than he arrived.

"We have nothing to put up," Luca said.

"We have a sluice box, shovels, pans, and a mule," Johnny spat out.

"Now, wait a minute," Luca said, stepping in front of Johnny. "Just wait a min—"

"Deal," the man replied, winking at Luca and reaching past him to clasp Johnny's hand in a shake.

Luca looked as if he wanted to get his tiny hands around the necks of both men, but Davis pulled him back.

"A deal's been made," the conniver said as if speaking to Johnny but looking directly at Luca. "It would be a rather ungentlemanly thing to do if you were to break it."

Davis noted that the man's palm was once again near his holster. He wasn't too thrilled with events playing out this way, but Johnny was past persuasion. He'd begun to think Johnny was right. Perhaps their streak of luck was destined to burn out as quickly as a shooting star.

"Looks like you've been kind enough to secure a table and drink," the man said. "Let's have some fun, shall we?" He took a seat against the wall and tied his end of rope to one of its legs. Princess Soup-Bone made a half-circle before lying down next to him. The man motioned for Johnny to sit on the opposite side. Johnny did so while Luca and Davis stood around him as if their mere presence could guard against the wiles of this man.

The stranger emptied the deck of blue-inked cards into one hand and tossed the box aside. With a deftness that filled Davis's stomach with apprehension, the man shuffled the cards back and forth, up and down, left and right, all with the fluidity of the waters running through Percy's Gulch. In his mind, Davis was calculating just how long it would take them to earn some new pans and shovels.

"You look like a man that knows his pasteboards," the gambler said to Johnny. "What do you say to five-card draw?"

Johnny glanced down at Princess. Her sad eyes seemed to move upward and meet his simultaneously. Without averting his gaze, he deftly poured himself a shot of whiskey and slugged it down. "Sure," he said.

"Great!" the blackleg said and poured himself a shot. He raised it to Johnny in silence and tipped it back swiftly, smacking his lips afterward. "What do you say we get warmed up? Start nice and slow. I'll still put up the dog on this round, of course, but I'll let you get away with a small ante. Say, only your shovels?"

He'd barely hit the end of his sentence before Johnny picked right up. "All of it," Johnny said.

"Ooohhh," Luca groaned, throwing his hands in the air. "Johnny, why? There's no point—"

"If that's how you'd prefer it," the gambler said. He raised his eyebrows at Luca who grumbled, swiped the bottle of whiskey from the table and proceeded to suck on it like it was a nursemaid's teat.

The man shuffled the deck once more and placed it face down on the table. "If you'd be so kind," he said, extending an open hand.

Johnny reached out and tapped the cards with his knuckles.

A gasp of air exited Luca's lips.

No cut, Davis thought. Why don't we just call it quits right now?

As if he'd read Davis's mind, the stranger bared his all-too-white teeth. He picked up the cards and dealt them until five lie face-down before each person, dropping the remaining draw pile between them both. Only the gambler reached for his hand while Johnny sat as still as a stone, his eyes glued to Princess Soup-Bone.

The man looked up at Johnny, and then at both Luca and Davis inquisitively.

The dread continued to build in Davis's belly.

The man shrugged and said, "I guess we can skip the raising and calling. Care to look at your cards? Maybe you want to draw?"

Johnny appeared as if he were sleeping with his eyes open, still settled on the face of Princess Soup-Bone. "No," he replied in a near whisper.

"Hm," the gambler grunted. "Well, you sure play a little peculiar, sir, but I don't like to make a man feel too much at a disadvantage. Therefore, I'll play what's in my hand as well. In fact, I'll lay mine out first, than you."

The man spread his cards face-up on the table. Three Aces and two Kings. He released a low whistle.

"Well, I'm certainly being smiled upon today!" He reached down and scratched the top of Princess Soup-Bone's scalp. Her eyes turned briefly toward the gambler, but returned to Johnny's. "I understand if you'd rather not turn yours over," he continued thoughtfully. "No need to add insult to injury."

Johnny absentmindedly reached for his cards. Davis turned towards the other patrons, watching them dine, smoke, and chatter happily. He knew what was coming. He didn't have to see it happen.

A loud spitting sound shot past his ears along with drops of moisture splashing on his face. The scent of whiskey burned his nostrils.

"Hoooooo!" Luca shouted, stomping his boots up and down on the hardwood floors. The clamor was so loud that every face in the room turned toward them. Even the piano player fumbled a couple of notes before quickly returning to form.

Davis faced the table to see the magic held in Johnny's cards: Four Queens.

He suddenly felt some of the unrealized tension leaving his muscles. Maybe Johnny knew more about gaming than he'd let on. Davis hoped so, anyway, as the blackleg seemed to break character and flinch slightly. His face grew flush and he jumped to his feet.

"Wait one second," he said, "How….You must be one cheating sonbitch!" The gambler's arm was pulled back, his hand reaching for his pistol before he suddenly yelped and fell backward on to his rear, knocking over the table and his chair, inadvertently releasing Princess Soup-Bone's rope.

By now, the piano playing had stopped completely and half of the crowd was also standing, craning to view the source of the action. The barkeep came rushing over with a shotgun and a large man at his side.

"You get that mutt out of here!" he yelled.

Johnny bent down, swept up Princess Soup-Bone and held onto her tightly as she released her jaws from the gambler's left calf.

In an instant, the four of them were through the swinging double-doors, untying Becca, and making for the town's exit. It wasn't until they were a hundred yards out of Sonora when the two men slapped Johnny on the back, congratulating him.

"Johnny," said Davis, "I didn't know you were such a blackleg yourself!"

Johnny looked at him with serious eyes. "I'm not," he said, moving his gaze toward a panting Princess.

Process Summary

Princess Soup-Bone is story number nineteen in the #52ShortStories challenge.

I felt like doing another historical piece this time around, set in my favorite California Gold Rush era; only, this time, I wanted to emphasize a straightforward tale with the supernatural elements only playing a small part (if any…up to the reader to judge what was really going on here).

I also wanted to practice my character separations, meaning that I really wanted each character to come off as well-integrated in the setting but entirely distinct. Making Luca and Johnny rather FOB immigrants made it a little easier to give them distinctive dialog with slightly broken English. I wanted Davis to be a more educated type of fellow, and of course, the gambler was just your stereotypical silver-tongued cardsharp.

It was a nice break to write this one in a more realistic vein than most of my work. I've been reading a lot of literary short stories lately, most of them written in the 19th and early-20th centuries, so I think some of that has been rubbing off. The title itself was inspired by Sherwood Anderson's *A Death in the Woods* (Oh, if only I could write such a striking story).

Hope you enjoyed another one of my subconscious's creations!

EL FRIO

Statistics

Synopsis: The first man to step foot in Antarctica discovers something miraculous.

Word Count: 2,900

Genre: Sci-Fi / Historical Fiction

Completed Week: January 1st – January 7th

El Frio

With the icy ground penetrating the inadequate layer of canvas wrapped around his knees, Captain Joaquín de Toledo y Parra cried out to the miraculous blood dribbling down the white embankment a mere fifty yards before him.

"Mother of God, take me away! Forgive my trespasses!" The words struggled to form across his fat tongue and chapped lips.

To Joaquín, all was clear: The red flow was a sign from the Madonna and its portents were most certain. God forgive him, he hoped that he would not see the sun set before being called into the presence of his Heavenly Father. He reached across himself with a shaking arm and made the sign of the cross upon his chest, knocking bits of crusted ice from his beard.

A cold wind, the same one that had beleaguered every painful step through this blindingly white, unpopulated land, whipped a stinging flap of fur onto his face. Two layers thick, that fur hid his emaciated torso from only the elements in this unpopulated world. A diet of raw penguin and ice chips had left his digestive system a miserable state of affairs since landing on the icy shores two days ago.

Though there was no priest to give the last rites, Joaquín felt secure in the fact that surely the cleansing blood of Jesus was flowing freely before him, there to wash away the sins which had so clearly brought him to these circumstances in the first place.

The once-Captain of the *San Telmo*, Joaquín was the last man alive out of 644 Spanish sailors sent to put down rebel insurrection in Peru. A storm beyond comprehension had blown the 74-gun vessel into uncharted territory as they rounded the Cape of Africa, leaving King Ferdinand VII with one less ship of the line and Spain with a few more widows.

The gently streaming blood triggered fragments of memory in his mind—under dark clouds and cold, stinging rain, the ship had careened into a large chunk of floating ice, breaking apart with such loud snaps as if God himself had gathered the boat in His great fist only to crush it like a pile of twigs.

But then there was the miraculous blessing, or so he thought at the time. After being thrown briefly into the frigid waters, Joaquín scrambled onto the tiny iceberg. He and one other man were the only survivors. The two of them managed to salvage a large piece of ship's plank and a box of furs, using their remaining strength to pull them from the sea. After a brief rest, the bickering began over a vital question—Should they try and fashion themselves a raft and chance the seas or wait and take the chance that aid might come? Captain Joaquín was never one to wait for favors, but the other man was too scared out of his mind to step one foot from their ice oasis. So the captain left the sailor with half the furs and set out on his makeshift craft in the hope that he would find more hospitable land and, God willing, Africa.

And land, he had indeed found after only half-a-day at ice-dotted sea, but more hospitable only in the sense that there were docile and easily approachable penguins to strangle. He was famished and without the capabilities to produce fire, so he choked the birds and struggled to cut them open with jagged rocks held by numb hands. Sickened and feeling near death, he knew he had to escape the animals before the tables turned. Images flashed in his mind of them pecking into him, rending his flesh and feeding. This repulsed Joaquín beyond reason, so he marched an uncountable number of steps into the snowy wasteland, hoping to die alone.

But Mother Mary's omen informed him that even at the ends of the Earth, she would not let him perish in such a manner. He swayed back and forth on his knees now, rocking gently, half not wanting to fall onto the cold ground, half wishing to drift into an endless sleep. His eyes grew heavy and his breath labored.

In his mind, or perhaps quietly under his breath (he was unsure), Joaquín began to recite Ave Maria, and, as if harking to his call, she appeared. Joaquín thought his soul would leave his body for sure, but he steadied himself.

Mother Mary stood upon the bloody hill, looking nothing like Joaquín had expected. Her ensemble was strange, her body more lithe than he had come to expect from paintings he'd seen. She was adorned with a majestic silver material that looked to be an alchemical combination of steel and silk. Her head was covered by a helmet as round and as smooth as a stream-worn stone. Her face, covered by the purest glass upon which the landscape reflected.

Joaquín struggled to push himself to his feet, collapsing twice before succeeding and lurching forward. He felt like he was wading through muck as he climbed the incline to meet her. Every inch of movement caused his muscles to stretch painfully, but he willed himself forward, afraid to die without her touch.

"Mother of God!" he tried to yell, stretching his arms outward. Ice crunched beneath his black ankle-boots. "Do not forsake me!"

She seemed to remain still, yet it was difficult to judge as Joaquín fought dizziness brought on by his short breath. He tried to keep his eyes open against the stinging wind, focused on her standing atop the tiny hill, the sun glaring behind her head. A most fitting halo surrounded her silhouette.

The slope was gentle and so Joaquín was near to her now. Mere feet. With every step, her otherworldly qualities became that much more real. He wanted desperately to grab ahold of her silver legs and blood-stained boots.

"Mother," he said once more, reaching out with a shaky hand, his fingers inches from her. He looked up quickly to see his frost-coated reflection in her mirror-mask, but as he did so, his traction gave way and with his legs unable to support him, he tumbled forward, smacking his forehead into the packed ice.

Before blackness overtook him, Joaquín smiled, feeling her touch upon him.

* * *

Warmth.

Sweet, enveloping warmth took hold of every inch of his flesh. Joaquín felt at peace. He was lying down, his back resting against something pliant. He need only open his eyes now to behold the glory of Heaven.

Yes, he need only open his eyes, which he did, but soon regretted.

A foot above him hovered the face of a most disturbing creature. It craned over him with its long neck connected to a tabular ceiling. It had four eyes, each one red and penetrating. They spun in circles and left Joaquín dizzy and frightened. Every time the beast moved up and down over his body, the eyes would flare briefly and make strange clicking sounds.

Joaquín shrieked. He tried to stand, to get away, but was unable to move. He tilted his head down to see himself naked. His wrists and ankles were bound to the soft table on which he lie.

He looked back up at the beast and a wave of comprehension struck him.

A Cherubim.

It had to be one of the Heavenly Host, an angel, that the priests had described as being terrible to behold in their own right. Was it Gabriel? Miguel, perhaps? He tried to call it by its name, but his throat was too dry. It struck him odd that he should be so parched in Heaven.

And then a fear seized him. Not that he was in Hell—he knew that wasn't possible because his flesh was not burning and he smelled no brimstone. But perhaps he was in Purgatory, a place of purification before admittance into true Heaven.

Bringing him here was your worst idea yet, Chelsea.

A masculine voice from the surrounding dark spoke strange words.

Joaquín flipped his head, feeling suddenly embarrassed by his nakedness. With his vision adjusting, he saw a Moorish-looking man and white woman standing several feet to his right. Unlike the Madonna, they wore nothing to cover their face, revealing matching close-cropped hair and clothing that was equally strange—genteel, frock-like, and as white as snow. His first thought was that one was a priest, the other a nun. For some reason, it didn't strike him as completely strange that there would be such servants of God in Heaven. He supposed Mass must be held every day for all souls of all time.

I couldn't just leave him there, the woman spoke now.

Couldn't you? the man replied sharply.

Joaquín did not understand what they were saying, but their tone implied that they were arguing over something—another sign that he had not yet been admitted into God's presence. Their words sounded like Dutch, maybe English. Unfortunately, Joaquín spoke neither. He'd honestly never thought that anyone would speak anything but Latin in the afterlife, but apparently, that was not the case.

The man stepped away from the woman to look at an odd window hanging down from the ceiling beside where he lay. Magical writing appeared as an endless scroll. New words would appear and old words disappear as the man ran his finger up and down the window pane.

The pattern matcher confirms his genetic makeup as early 19th-century Iberian. Only known contact with Antarctica in this era was a Spanish ship of the line that was supposed to have crashed on Livingston Island. No known survivors.

The woman approached, read the words, and made a snorting sound.

The man gave her a reprimanding look.

Seems improbable, he said, *but not impossible.*

She placed her hands on her hips and looked down at Joaquín with what can only be described as pity.

That's what we get for believing history written by someone that wasn't there. Well, this time period was your suggestion. I'm laying all blame on you.

Fine, the man said, *the Commission can just add another mark to my record. Now, since you're the one that brought him in, what do we do with him?*

Joaquín struggled to speak. A thin croak exited his airway.

Maybe we should be civilized hosts—you know, give him water and food, and then talk to him. We can't just put him back out there.

The man started to speak, but the woman held up her hand. *Yeah, yeah, temporal interference...butterfly effect...blah blah blah. Too late for all that now, isn't it?*

Fine, the man replied. *You play nurse and figure a way out of this mess. I need to check on the status of the bilge pump if we're going to be leaving today. Lots of oxidation.* His eyes met Joaquín's for a moment. *He probably thinks the ground was bleeding.*

The man stepped away and Joaquín's eyes followed him to a wall, bare and smooth. It split open silently as the man approached, giving way to a hallway of candles which did not flicker. The wall closed back up behind him.

The woman opened a thin paper box that rested on a nearby shelf, removing a small glass with liquid inside. She took a thin straw, punctured the top of the glass, and brought it to Joaquín. Before sitting down, she tapped several times on the suspended window.

"You probably had no idea what we were saying," the woman said.

Joaquín's eyes bulged and he breathed a sigh of relief. So she spoke his tongue after all. He tried to reply back, but again, the words remained stuck in his throat.

"Here, drink," she said and held the straw to his lips. He tilted his head up slightly and drank. It tasted like the purest water he'd ever swallowed. Joaquín greedily sucked but the woman pulled it away.

"Not too much or you'll spew it all up again. You're in bad enough shape as it is," she said.

His head fell back to the table as he remembered that his arms and legs were restrained. The words were finally ready to come out.

"Sister, where am I? Why am I being held?" he asked.

He wanted to ask about his clothes, but there were too many other questions related to that which he did not want to deal with. Why was he embarrassed by his nudity? Why did *they* wear clothes? Why did he still have his earthly body at all?

The woman's pale cheeks bloomed a shade of red. "Precautions," she said. "I'm sorry." Her head turned back to the wall where the man had left and then she stood. One-by-one, she unbuckled his restraints. "You're in no condition to be much trouble," she said. She helped Joaquín sit up on the table. His hands instantly went to his private parts. The woman noticed and averted her eyes. She moved quickly to a cabinet across the room, pulled out a white coat matching the one she wore and helped Joaquín into it.

"I know you have many questions," she said. "Believe me, I have just as many myself."

Joaquín peered cautiously up at the Cherubim now floating near the ceiling, silent, its eyes grown faint. Was it observing him? Judging his conduct?

She spoke further. "Admittedly, I don't know much about 19th-century social history. I'm….we're….geologists."

"Geologist?" Joaquín asked. "I did not know Heaven had a need for geologists."

The woman regarded him silently for a moment. "Just where do you think you are?"

Joaquín eyed the hovering angel once more. "Perhaps I spoke too soon. Forgive me, Sister. Is this Purgatory? Are there sins for which I still need to atone? Before I awoke here, when I saw Mother Mary—"

"Mother Mary?"

"Yes," he said. "Upon the hill of our Savior's blood."

The woman's mouth opened wide. "Ohhhh," she said, and then cleared her throat. "I see." She tapped her fingers on her legs. He caught her whispering: *What have I gotten myself into?*

She straightened up and looked Joaquín in his eyes. "I don't know how to state any of this in a way which you'll clearly understand, but I'll try my best and just tell you how it is. There is no Mother Mary."

"Blasphemy! I saw her with my own eyes," Joaquín injected, feeling slightly offended as if he were being looked at as a madman. Perhaps this was indeed a test. He continued to feel the overbearing presence of the Cherubim above.

The woman held up her hands in defense. "No, look, I don't mean at all. Maybe there is. I just meant the woman you saw was not her. That was me."

"You?"

"Yes. I had my environmental suit on. It's freezing out there, you know." She chuckled, but Joaquín found no humor in the situation.

"Sorry," she said. "Bad joke." She took a deep breath. "We're getting off track. My colleague and I, we're not from here. Well, we're from *here*, as in Earth, but from another time. We're a part of a scientific expedition, you see, that's been tasked with measuring...."

The woman spoke at length using terms that Joaquín could barely comprehend, some not at all. Only a single phrase weighed on him the whole time.

....we're from here, as in Earth....

When she finished talking, appearing as if Joaquín should respond, he asked, "So this is not the afterlife? This is not Purgatory or Heaven?"

The woman grinned slightly and shrugged.

He directed his eyes at the Cherubim. "And that is not an angel?"

The woman stifled a laugh. "Well, it's part of our ship's computer system and it's useful—it told us about you, after all—, but I don't know that I'd call it an angel. It goes on the fritz more often than not, requiring the occasional reboot."

Joaquín lifted his eyebrows. "Ship?"

"Yes," she said. "You're in the infirmary."

Just as he took another moment to gaze at his otherworldly surroundings and take it all in, the wall where the man had previously exited split open again.

"Get ready, we're leaving in five," he said upon entering.

The woman jumped to her feet. "Wait, what about him? We haven't—"

"Just got off the horn with the Commission," the man interrupted. "Turns out they knew about this, only they didn't inform us….temporal interference...butterfly effect...blah blah blah," he said with a wry smile on his face. "He's the Captain of the *San Telmo*, the first crew known to step foot in Antarctica. He's to participate in some history exhibit. They'll give us the details when we return."

The woman had a momentary look of shock on her face but quickly recovered. She turned back to Joaquín. "You'd think I'd be used to this by now," she said as if they were old friends. "Well, looks like you don't have to freeze to death after all *and* you get to travel forward in time. Lucky you."

Lucky me, Joaquín thought somewhat morosely. He closed his eyes and breathed in the sterile air. If he wasn't going to spend eternity among the Saved, he could think of nothing better than to sail forth on uncharted seas.

Process Summary

El Frío is story number twenty in the #52ShortStories challenge.

Sometimes a topic yells at you so loudly that to ignore it would be tantamount to leaving an injured pedestrian on the side of the road.

You're there.

To ignore it feels utterly wrong.

Do something about it.

That's what happened with my need to write something set in Antarctica. In the December issue of *Smithsonian Magazine*, Kim Stanley Robinson wrote an article regarding Robert Scott's daring expedition to the South Pole in 1911. On top of that, I had seen a notice earlier that month regarding an exhibit at a local museum showing unbelievable photographs and documentation of Ernest Shackleton's near-catastrophic voyage in 1914. So after reading the article and visiting the museum, I was pretty hyped up on investigating every little bit of history regarding that barren land to the south.

I discovered that in 1819, a Spanish ship named *San Telmo* was blown off course on the way to Peru and its splintered remains were discovered on Livingston Island, possibly making any one of its 644 sailors the first known people to set foot on what's considered Antarctica.

So, I figured the Captain ought to be the one to do it. From there, I ran with the intriguing setting of a very real Blood Falls and how it might be interpreted by a likely-devout Catholic who's on the brink of death.

Of course, I had to throw in a sci-fi twist. You guys know by now, that's just how I roll most of the time.

In regards to the writing process itself, I'm trying to get out of this nasty, occasional habit of rewriting the same paragraph over and over early on, only to scramble on Sunday morning to finish the damn story. It doesn't always happen, but it seems to more often than not. It's good to course correct when the boat's heading off-kilter (hopefully before it ends up crashing into an iceberg…).

You're probably also seeing a pattern whereby, sometimes, I'm barely using the scratch file at all. I'm just diving into the manuscript and working it out from there. It seems to depend on the story and how confident I'm feeling.

Hope you enjoyed the tale and a bit of history!

The Piano Player

Statistics

Synopsis: A mall piano player with a unique talent must deal with a bully.

Word Count: 3,300

Genre: Urban Fantasy

Completed Week: January 7th – January 13th

The Piano Player

Bobby Murillo was waiting for me.

I was on break, carrying a tray with a plate of kung pao chicken and fried rice just past the piano and towards my usual table when I spotted him. He had a grating smile on his chubby face, a shopping bag at his feet, and he was extending his hand toward the open seat across from him. I turned and searched desperately for somewhere else to sit, but at almost noon on a Saturday, the Hanfield Mall food court was crammed with famished bargain hunters. I'd have better luck finding a genuine diamond ring at Zades Jewelry.

Before I even sat down, the smell hit me. Either no one had the nerve to tell Bobby that using six squirts of Drakkar Noir to cover up a lack of personal hygiene was equivalent to pissing on a forest fire, or he just didn't care. I wanted to tell him that he'd probably sell more albums out of the mall's only record shop if he didn't insist on personally greeting every customer who came through his storefront, getting uncomfortably close and pushing excess inventory on kids just wanting to buy the latest Whitney Houston or Bell Biv Devoe tape.

Maybe I didn't want to tell him, after all. He'd been a dick in high school and he was a dick now. I was pretty sure he wound up manager at Sean Woody's Music only due to the fact that his dad owned the place.

I felt his eyes bearing down on me as I poked around my plate with a pair of chopsticks. He leaned over and whispered, "Give it up, Timmerman." His tone was somehow menacing and comical at the same time. "Everyone's on to you."

My stomach descended several inches. I looked up at him with half-chewed rice in my mouth, focusing on not choking or looking surprised. I fought the urge to count every stubborn whisker on his five o'clock shadow.

"Give up what, Bobby?"

"You know," he said.

Did someone spill the beans? Could it have been Mr. Yang, owner of Speedy Koala whose not-half-bad kung pao I was just now dining on? He was always complaining about my prices but seemed to do it in a playful manner. Or maybe it was Shelly Knutzen from the appliance store. From the things she gossipped to me, I *knew* I shouldn't have let her in on the secret.

"Darlene's only nice to you because she has to see your ugly mug every day," Bobby said.

As much as that might hurt if it was coming from anyone other than a genuine fool, my breath came back to me.

"It's none of your business who I talk to," I said.

He laughed hard enough to make the family of four sitting two tables away jump in surprise, knocking a bag of newly purchased shoes on to its side.

"Just trying to save you from embarrassing yourself more than you already do playing your shitty easy listening," he replied. "Why don't you grow some balls and play some goddamn Metallica or something? Who knows? Maybe then you'll get lucky."

My appetite was beginning to dissipate and I worried it would soon curl up and die in Bobby's presence. The large, brass clock hanging high above the food court entrance told me I had fifteen minutes to get back to the piano bench. I took a napkin and nervously wiped at my hands, realizing I was due for another manicure.

"As always, I appreciate the advice. Now if you don't mind, I'd like to finish my lunch before I get back to work."

He stood and hovered over me, one hand on the back of my chair and the other on the side of my tray.

I said nothing, trying only to avoid any eye or physical contact. Just as my chopsticks were heading toward the plate, Bobby pushed down on the tray, which along with my lunch, flipped off the table, spilling sauced peanuts and green onion all over the ground.

"Oops," he said. "Sorry, dude."

I glared at him for less than a second before I lost my nerve, realizing I couldn't let myself get worked up. My arms and hands were shaking. I had to gain control of my emotions so that I could perform my job and deliver what I'd promised.

I said nothing, bent down, and proceeded to clean up the mess.

Bobby Murillo strolled away with a thorough demonstration of his knack for combining a cough with the word *pussy*.

* * *

As I picked my suit coat up off the bench and put it on, I tried to ignore the newly applied brown stain on my white shirt so that I could get in the zone.

If I had to explain how it all worked, it would be just as well to make something up. It might take years, maybe decades, to figure out the truth. Hell, I'd probably be dead before I even had a vague theory. It feels like it would be explaining what makes blue, blue. Or more like forcing Jimi Hendrix to explain every single movement of his fingers during *Are You Experienced.*

Some things just *are*.

How to bring it about? That's easy enough.

I think about what I want to say and some mystical coordination happens between my brain and fingers, working together to compose and send out the message.

Buy more chow mein from Speedy Koala becomes some combination of notes on a G-Major scale.

Visit Hot Discussion and invest in a new goth look morphs into a hook built on minor pentatonic chord progressions.

Every suggestion has its melody and every melody sent shoppers on a buying spree, which in turn put a little extra cash in my wallet. In my one year of playing piano in the Hanfield Mall food court, I had gained several clients without much trouble. Of course, most of the buyers are unbelieving at first. After a day's demonstration, and it only took one, they were ready to sign up, already having factored my services into their budget like any other operational cost.

Unfortunately, I couldn't hit up every shop in the mall. If everyone had a song, then nobody got rich. Not to mention the fact that I was only one guy. It's not like I could farm out the work.

My confrontation with Bobby still had me a little shaken, so I took an extra minute to breathe slowly and deeply. It helped that I could see Darlene's picture-perfect smile through a gap in the ferns surrounding the back of my piano. The food court was a giant circle in which I sat in the middle, up a half-level, while she worked on the outside edge where all of the food vendors lived. She stood behind the counter now, wearing her multi-colored, striped collared shirt and matching hat, chatting with a coworker who was thrusting her elbows up and down in the air. Nearly every hour, the two girls alternated the task of taking a plunger to a bucket of chopped lemons in order to make the fresh, venerable lemonade that Wiener on a Wick is known for.

They were laughing about something. I felt as if I could hear Darlene's giggle clearly through the noise floor generated by passing shoppers and those sitting down to replenish themselves for round two's spending spree.

And then something obscured my vision.

A thing with black, Aquanet-hardened hair named Bobby.

I watched as he leaned over the Wiener on a Wick counter and handed something to Darlene. She froze for a moment, then screamed and quickly covered her mouth. She jumped up and down, nearly matching her coworker's pace, holding up what looked like a tape cassette. In a poor attempt at being sly, Bobby turned his head and he looked directly at me. With a simple wink and a smile, he proved unequaled in inspiring a passion for murder.

I put my head down and released a held breath, focusing on my fingers resting atop the black and white keys. I launched into the song I had written earlier that week for Marianne's Photo and Portrait Studio, feeling tight at first, but gradually my knuckle joints loosened, then my arms, and finally my whole body. Marianne always paid double this time of year, even threw in some free photo vouchers because of the lull between major holidays, homecoming, prom, and graduation. Her business typically dropped off like a rock.

Today, though, there would be a line crossing several other storefronts, everyone waiting for their turn to say "cheese" and trying to decide between the generic maroon background or the neon pink and blue lasers crisscrossing over pure black space.

* * *

"Hi," I said.

Even though I was usually drained after an afternoon of playing, I always made time to stop and see her on my way out.

Now Darlene was having her turn at the plunger, mashing the bucket of lemons like the Energizer bunny. Her arms, like all of the girls working there, were toned enough to make me feel a little emasculated, but not enough to keep me from trying to—what? What exactly was I trying to achieve with a girl I'd vaguely known from high school two years ago, and only because she was active in student government and I was the band geek with whom she often coordinated events?

"Hey, Kevin!" she shouted over the squishing sounds and quickened breath. "How's life?"

That was her go-to question, but I always acted as if she were truly interested in the answer.

"Good, good. Just on break. Thought I'd see what was new in corn dog world." Talk about corn dogs. God, I felt like such an obtuse idiot some-times. It's not that I was the introverted type and had problems communicat-ing with people. I only seemed to second-guess what came out of my mouth around Darlene. I knew it was all this weird pressure I was putting on myself, but knowing that didn't make it any easier to dismiss.

She rolled her eyes. "Same oil, different batter." Then she leaned over and I could smell a mix of the beaten lemon pulp and her vanilla perfume. "Seriously. I mean it. Don't order a corndog. Wait until Monday when the oil's been changed out."

My heart melted a little. She obviously didn't have any issues with a little cheesy conversation. Maybe she could see my obvious discomfort and was trying to relieve the awkwardness.

Oh God, maybe she could see my obvious discomfort.

I fumbled awkwardly for a place to rest my arm on the counter, shifting my weight occasionally between both feet.

"So, this is what, your third...fourth week?" I asked, knowing she'd been serving up food for twenty-two days.

"Somewhere around there," she said.

"Cool, cool," I said, sounding completely uncool. "How do you like it?"

"It pays the bills," she replied.

Someone cleared their throat loudly to my right. An old man with a wad of bills in his hand was standing at the counter, staring at both of us with an unamused look plastered on his face.

"Sorry," she said to me, putting the plunger down and wiping her hands on her apron. "Kelly's taking five and I'm covering." She pushed back the hair that had fallen over her eyes. There was something about the way she did that which sent shivers across my skin.

When she wrapped up his order and handed him two corn dogs, she came back.

"I don't know how these people don't get food poisoning," she said.

"Must have built up an immunity," I said.

She laughed and it sent my heart aflutter. I didn't want to leave with any other image in my mind, so I decided to cut it short there.

"I gotta run, but I wanted to give you something….in case….you know, you could use…." There I went again. Before I embarrassed myself further, I reached into my coat pocket, fumbled for Marianne's vouchers, and quickly threw them on the counter.

As soon as they left my hand, my first instinct was to grab them and pull them back as quickly as possible. I didn't know what they were, but they weren't the vouchers.

Too late, as Darlene had already scooped them up.

"What are these?"

My hands shot into both of my coat pockets. I came up empty. Panic was evident in my voice.

"They're supposed to be for free photos…" came out of my mouth, but I stopped abruptly after realizing now what she held in her hands.

Polaroid photographs. At least five or six of them.

"Free photos?" she asked. "Is this supposed to be a weird joke?"

I tried to speak, but my jaw was set in place. All I could manage was a low groan before my nose caught the scent of something ill.

Drakkar Noir.

"What the hell, Timmerman?" Bobby leaned over the counter and pulled one of the photographs from Darlene's hands. "Is that…." and he looked at Darlene, then back at the piano, holding up the photo as if to inspect evidence like a sloven Sherlock Holmes. "Wow. That's really creepy, douchewad."

He threw it onto the counter and a red heat spread across my cheeks. It was a photograph of Darlene with her arms up, squashing lemons. On the left and right edges of the picture were bits of fern.

Of course, I did the rational thing.

I ran straight to my car and sped home, where I remembered, painfully late, the shopping bag that had been at Bobby's feet when he had invited me to take a seat.

* * *

I fumbled hard the next day. I couldn't find the right notes, the right bits of harmony. My fingers felt as if they might retract into my hands from embarrassment. I even gave Mr. Yang his money back. He said I didn't look well and promptly suggested some herbal medicine to get me back on my proverbial feet. There was a fear in his eyes. He'd bet it all on me, I could tell.

For the next week, I avoided Darlene and tried to regain focus. The few times I couldn't, I spotted Bobby hanging around Wiener on a Wick like a lapdog and when I walked by, they would only glare at me, maybe giving the occasional headshake. Thinking at all about the whole episode made me sick to my stomach, so that upon coming home each evening, I shut myself in, losing myself to writing music.

* * *

I couldn't sleep. I'd lost some weight.

After a week of misery, I had to try to explain the situation—that I hadn't taken those pictures. That I didn't know how they ended up in my pocket and that I was so sorry if she thought I had anything to do with them and what could I do to prove to her that I was an okay guy?

She said nothing, only pumping her arms up and down, staring past the top of my head like I was a ghost. When I tried to ask her a question, she shut me down.

"I'm busy," she said.

Squish.

"Look, Darlene, I'm—"

Squish.

"I said I'm busy."

Squish.

Squish.

Squish.

I shuffled back to my piano, hands in my pleated pockets, wondering why I was still there at all.

* * *

An amalgamation of exuberance and nerves swept through my entire being the moment I decided to do it.

I spent several sleepless nights writing and practicing the song. There could be no flaws in either the music or its performance. I had to be in complete control of myself, unphased and unaware of the outside world if for only a few minutes when I put on my coat and sat down to play. One mistake and all of the careful coordination would be for naught.

It was another Saturday afternoon, a holiday weekend. The Hanfield Mall must have been seeing record numbers of shoppers. I'd increased the length of my breathing regimen so that as I sat down to play my first set, I found the music flowing through my fingers nearly on impulse. I didn't have to do anything but be a conduit—let the feelings flow through unimpeded.

It's hard to keep track of time when you're in a state of flow, but if I had to hazard a guess, I'd say that just after one minute in, a commotion arose at the front of the food court. It was barely noticeable at first. Small groups of one or two people leaped from their chairs and ran. But then things escalated rapidly and everyone was on their feet, leaving the food court a near ghost town. Even the employees left their respective service counters. I saw Jim Stine's legs flying crossways over a row of half-sliced pizzas at S'parrows as he dove to the ground, somersaulted onto his toes like an action star, and chased after the mob.

Predictably late, a team of mall security officers, some short and overweight, some tall and underweight, zipped through the food court, shouting through their walkie-talkies.

All the while, my fingers danced along the piano as I looked at the only other person left in the food court. Darlene was standing just outside her counter with her hands on her hips. Her eyebrows were scrunched and she was biting down on her lip. I stood from the piano and walked up to her.

To my relief, she asked, "What the hell is going on?" Her confusion seemed to override any sense of trepidation she might feel at my approach.

"I have no idea," I lied.

She turned and looked directly into my eyes. "Hey, did you really take those photos of me?"

"No, I swear I didn't," I said.

"It was Bobby, wasn't it?"

"Pretty sure," I said.

She peered down at the ground, slightly dazed.

I said goodnight and walked out the door, knowing that the spell would soon wear off.

* * *

"They were tearing the place up, man. I mean, plastic cassette cases shattered all over the carpet. Posters being ripped off the walls. I saw Debra Mangioni get taken away in handcuffs."

"Wow." The green-eyed girl listened intently while stirring her straw around the remaining ice in her paper soda cup.

I didn't mean to eavesdrop, but I was wiping down the piano and the girls didn't seem to have a volume button.

"Yeah," her friend continued. "I felt bad for the manager, you know, the guy...." She pinched her nose. "He was running around screaming at everybody, trying to push people back. The place was so out of control. I saw him trip on an overturned wire rack and I think he broke his arm or shattered his elbow, or something. The paramedics came and he left wearing a sling. I couldn't tell if he was crying from the pain or because the whole store had been torn to pieces."

"Do you know who started it?"

"No, by the time I saw what was happening, people were just going nuts. I even saw the cops interviewing an old man. I guess he was caught swinging his cane into the glass cases holding the Walkmans. He said something just came over him. Tried to blame a bad corn dog he'd eaten earlier."

The girl stopped talking in order to tear off a piece of soft pretzel and shove it into her mouth. I took the dust cloth and made my way to the back of the baby grand. Between the ferns, I caught Darlene slicing lemons and tossing them into the bucket behind the counter. It was as if something told her that I was looking at her because she looked up and met my gaze. She smiled and waved. I smiled and waved back.

I hoped she would like the song I wrote for her.

Process Summary

The Piano Player is story number twenty-one in the #52ShortStories challenge.

"There are days where you just feel on…And man, was this one of those."

That's from Monday's journal. *The Piano Player*, for the most part, wrote itself. It was a nearly complete sequence from beginning to end. I simply dictated what the muses showed me, struggling with only a small part or two (worked through with a few minutes of freewriting — see the general scratch file for details).

Wouldn't it be nice if they were all like that?

To start, I had this ultra-clear mental image of the mall food court which existed in my hometown. The opening of that mall was a big deal for our somewhat rural area, and so like most other youths in the late 80s/early 90s, I spent copious amounts of time there. In the middle of said food court was a slightly-elevated seating area with a piano dead-smack in the middle. The mall paid someone to play nondescript, relaxing music while shoppers scarfed down their food, weary from shopping. Within the story, I did a lot of play-on-name work with real food court staples like Panda Express, Hot Dog on a Stick, and Sbarro. Then there were the usual retail stores: Zales Jewelry, Sam Goody ("Goody got it!"), and Hot Topic.

I had fun with the ending on this one too…I wanted people to feel for Kevin but then wonder by the end if he hadn't taken a turn to the dark side with his powers.

Overall, this went so well and I was so far ahead of the game, I slept into the late hour of 6:30 AM on Sunday. Doesn't get much better than that, right folks?!

Right?

Hope you enjoyed it!

Rakugoka Sushi House – The Accusation

Statistics

Synopsis: A woman loses her job and airs her grievances to a sushi chef. He shows her that life may not be over after all.

Word Count: 1,050

Genre: Literary / Relationship

Completed Week: January 15th – January 21st

Rakugoka Sushi House - The Accusation

"*Kanpai*," she said with no cheer, no spring in her voice. She launched the glass of *sake* into her gullet to hide the tremors running through her hand, somehow forgetting that nothing could evade Rukugoka Koza's keen eye.

Before her glass came slamming back onto the table, he had already deposited another freshly filled cup before her. A corner of her mouth turned upward.

"You know, Raku, we've known each other for what—a year?—and I can say without any compunction," she said, slightly slurring the word, "that you and Mariko are truly one of a kind."

He grunted, then smiled for as long as he could which averaged about a quarter-of-a-second. It wasn't that he was incapable of the emotions behind such a thing, but the outward expression never seemed to get its act together across all of the required facial muscles.

Only briefly did he turn his attention back to the cherry-handled blade in his right hand. Full cognizance was unnecessary. Slicing the piece of yellowfin tuna into its requisite culinary parts occupied a permanent space in his mind. It had taken many, many years of training to achieve the disciplined, multi-mindedness that he possessed. All senses were activated to his surroundings as well as internal affections.

"Something troubles you today?" he asked merely for show.

He sensed, but did not see, drops of *sake* spilling onto the countertop as she harrumphed. She quickly downed what was left in the next cup and smacked her lips.

"Yeah, something troubles me today," she replied. Her fingers gripped a pair of chopsticks set before her and she proceeded to pry apart the thinly sliced pickled ginger on her plate like a surgeon with forceps. "Here I am at happy hour and far from it. No longer being a member of gainfully-employed America *may* have something to do with that."

Without saying a word, he communicated that she should go on.

"But, apparently that's the price one pays for sucking the cock of the boss's husband."

Though Rakugoka-san was focusing on another customer's order of *tako*, octopus sashimi, his body was turned ever so slightly so it appeared that he had not taken an ounce of attention away from her. He knew when to hide certain emotions. Nothing that could so much as to be mistaken for shock or surprise crossed his face.

"Not that I actually did anything like that," she said, picking up and chewing on her last piece of fatty *toro*. "I don't even do that for *my* husband. I'm actually surprised it took her a whole month of being my boss to come up with some crazy excuse to be rid of me. We never got along great, but I never had to worry much about our relationship until her promotion. For eleven years, I had to deal with her—tried to be nice, tried to not step on her toes, tried to play a game I always hated playing."

Eleven years came out of her mouth again, this time in a venomous whisper, but Rakugoka-san heard it as if it was a shout.

"Don't get me wrong, I can't say I really liked working there, but it was steady. Paid decent."

"What will you do?" he asked.

She repeated the question to herself, then clapped her palms to her cheeks. "I haven't gotten to that stage yet, my friend. I'm still in grieving mode. I don't even know how I'm going to break any of this to my husband, but I'm sure I'll have time to think of something. The bastard's probably passed out on the couch with a half-empty bottle of Cuervo."

Rakugoka-san deftly placed the *tako* before the man sitting to her right, seeing everything through his peripheral vision. The man's attention was directed at his smartphone, either politely ignoring his neighbor's unabashed confessional or texting all of the nitty gritty details to a friend.

"Your purpose in life is to find your purpose and give your whole heart and soul to it," Rakugoka-san said.

She looked up at him. "Huh?"

"A saying from the Buddha," he replied.

As she took a moment to ponder those words of wisdom, her tempura crumb-covered plate was quietly removed by Mariko-san, a waitress who operated like a shadow, as skilled at refilling water glasses and bussing tables as Rakugoka-san was behind the counter. The two of them worked in fantastical concert. In the empty plate's place, as if by an ancient magic, was the woman's usual final order—two pieces of *unagi*, a sweet eel sushi traditionally eaten at the end of a meal.

"Perhaps you can look to your pottery?" he asked.

Her eyes grew at him. "I don't remember telling you about that. How did you know I make—"

Rakugoka-san inclined his head a hair's breadth towards the smartphone next to her purse. The wallpaper showed the woman smiling at the camera, her hands and arms caked in wet clay as she sat before a pottery wheel.

"Oh," she replied.

Next to her *sake* glass was a cup of steaming green tea slyly left by Mariko-san. She placed it to her lips and took a sip as if she had asked for it herself. In silence, she stared at the rainbow of assorted fish sitting within the transparent countertop refrigerator.

"Yes," she said, clumsily putting down the cup and rubbing her hands together.

"Yes!" she exclaimed, this time. Heads of other patrons shot up.

Her eyes darted back to Rakugoka-san's face. It would have taken a high shutter-speed camera to confirm the fact that he had indeed made eye contact with her, but it was long enough to ensure the desired reaction. "Raku, you are a genius. I've been seeing this the completely wrong way. It's not a slight. Not at all! It's a goddamn opportunity!"

Her hand darted to the remaining cup of *sake* and lifted it into the air.

"Here's to no more soulsucking nine-to-five. No more bullshit office politics." With much more enthusiasm than she had earlier that evening, she shouted "*Kanpai!*"

Rakugoka-san barely noticed.

A strange feeling tickled the back of his mind that set him to preparing for another visitor.

Rakugoka Sushi House – The Confession

Statistics

Synopsis: A man confesses his misdeeds to a sushi chef and learns an important truth about doing what's right.

Word Count: 950

Genre: Literary / Relationship

Completed Week: January 15th – January 21st

Rakugoka Sushi House - The Confession

As soon as the little metal chimes hanging on the door rang out, Rakugoka-san made eye contact with Mariko-san. Each customer, even first-timers, had their own vibration, generated their own harmony. The way they pushed open the door, how the air rushed in, the slight squeak of the rusted hinges—each a part of the equation that informed the sushi chef and waitress how they should prepare the environment.

The man sat down without removing his coat. Unusual, as the tiny restaurant was always monitored for optimal temperature for client comfort, especially during the dinner rush, but it had been an unusual evening.

A steaming cup of green tea was waiting for him.

"*Irasshaimase*," Rakugoka-san said.

"Evening," the man replied, looking surprised but satisfied to see the hot tea. He took a swig as if it had been *sake* instead. He showed no reaction to the scalding liquid hitting his tongue. Mariko-san was beside him just as the cup came back down, pouring a fresh refill from a copper pot.

Nothing was said for at least two minutes after a spicy tuna roll was placed in front of the man.

"I'm not hungry," he said.

"Yes, you are," Rakugoka-san replied as if stating an incontrovertible fact such as 'the ocean is wet.'

The man appeared convinced, though he took his time, delicately picking up each piece with the end of his chopsticks and inspecting its artisan tightness before thrusting it into his mouth.

Finally, he spoke, his voice faltering. "My wife's been trying to get me to come here with her for a year, but I've always refused. It's too bad. You're obviously a man who takes pride in his work."

"Yes," Rakugoka-san replied. "Are you not proud of yours?"

The man cleared his throat. "Not always."

Rakugoka-san politely arched his left eyebrow while focusing on putting together another customer's rainbow roll.

"I've been drinking again. And when I drink, I do stupid things."

Rakugoka-san's sushi knife sliced through the crisp Japanese cucumber like butter, cutting even-length slices that would have held up to the most intense mathematical scrutiny. All the while, his appearance was bereft of judgment.

"Things have been bad for awhile now between me and her, and it's mostly my fault. The drinking though….I get angry, you know?" He looked up, trying to make eye contact with a chef who knew better. "It finally pushed me over the edge."

Rakugoka-san's other eyebrow went up.

"Now, nothing physical. Please. But I can be a real asshole. I'm not making excuses, just giving reasons." The man hung his head back down over his tea and let the steam moisten the bridge of his nose. He obviously lost control of his emotions and cried out a confession. "I set her up, okay!? I went too far, I know it."

Rakugoka-san made an effort to understand the man coming clean through choked off words.

"I 'mistakenly' sent some texts to her boss that were addressed to the lady's husband, along with a couple of pictures she let me take when we were on better terms. I haven't been home all day and I don't think it's a good idea to go back. I'm pretty sure she's gonna' get canned and I won't be able to look her in the eye."

He was a blubbering mess, not even touching his tuna while tears fell onto the stained oak countertop. "Jesus Christ, I'm so ashamed." People who were sitting within arm's reach began to ask for their checks and clear out.

Rakugoka-san said, "Conquer anger with non-anger. Conquer badness with goodness. Conquer meanness with generosity. Conquer dishonesty with truth."

The man sniffed and wiped his eyes. He squinted at Rakugoka-san and shook the end of a chopstick at him. He appeared as if he wanted to issue a retort of every word in those simple sentences, but Rakugoka-san knew that wouldn't be the case.

Instead, the man put down the chopstick and exhaled like a bag of wind. "Wise," he said. "You're very wise."

"Not me. The Buddha."

The man ignored him as if he didn't care to know that. "I have to tell her. I know it, deep down. It'll probably mean the end of our marriage—what little bit is left of it—but I have to tell her."

Panic started to shake his voice again. "But what am I going to do without her? We've been together so long."

"Do not dwell in the past, do not dream of the future, concentrate the mind on the present moment," Rakugoka-san said.

The man seemed astonished. A giant smile erupted and he shouted to the remaining patrons. "This guy! This guy right here is a peach!"

"Not me. The Buddha," Rakugoka-san said too quietly for the man to hear.

"I can't let fear of the unknown keep me from doing the right thing. So she leaves me. Maybe it's the wake-up call I need. Maybe it's for the best. She deserves someone so much better."

The man shot to his feet and reached out to shake Rakugoka-san's hand. He was politely rebuffed, so instead, he bowed awkwardly. "Thank you, friend. Thank you. I can't help but feel I was fated to come here. But I've got to go. I've got to go, now!"

The chimes rang again as the man exited. Mariko-san placed his dishes on her tray while Rakugoka-san prepared his station. Their eyes met in the briefest of moments, confirming that the night was not yet over.

Rukugoka Sushi House – The Denouement

Statistics

Synopsis: A couple visits a renown sushi restaurant, celebrating their renewed feelings for each other and learning about forgiveness.

Word Count: 800

Genre: Literary / Relationship

Completed Week: January 15th – January 21st

Rukugoka Sushi House - The Denouement

A mere minute before the couple entered, Rakugoka-san gave only the slightest indication that Mariko-san should restrain from locking up. The last customer had left ten minutes prior. The restaurant had been quiet but for the back-and-forth sweeping of her broom.

As the door chimes rang, the sushi chef stood like a wax figure, watching, waiting. His hands rested gently on top of his station, ready to reach for any ingredient which may be requested.

The couple was in their early 50s, neither of them a regular customer. They were both dressed slightly formal, him with a heather-gray sports coat covering a loosely buttoned shirt and her with an off-the-shoulder black dress and high heels. Her hair was slightly mussed, but she didn't seem to care. The man pulled back a seat for her at the counter and then sat beside her.

"*Irasshaimase,*" Rakugoka-san said.

"Hello," the man replied after some delay, never taking his eyes off the woman, she never taking her eyes off him. Before the man said, "Serve us up whatever you recommend," Rakugoka-san was already delicately cutting into the sea urchin. He didn't even need to look as his hands maneuvered around its spindly body, scooping the membrane onto two tiny boats of rice and seaweed.

Mariko-san brought out a cold mug and a bottle of Sapporo for the gentleman. The woman was given water with a thin slice of lemon.

"Oh, good," the woman said with a laugh. "I have to drive us back tonight." Mariko-san bowed slightly and disappeared as quickly as she had manifested.

"*Uni*," Rakugoka-san said moments later, depositing the plate of urchin between the two.

There was a collective gasp as they both eyed the dish.

"It's beautiful," the woman replied, admiring every shiny wrinkle and shadow of the sun-colored morsels like they were pieces of freshly spun pottery.

"It is considered an aphrodisiac," Rakugoka-san said.

The gentleman giggled like a schoolgirl and made eye contact with Rakugoka-san for the first time. "Doubt we'll need it, but damned if we'll turn it down," he said.

They both attacked the *nigiri* boats with confidence. A tiny corner of Rakugoka-san's lips may have turned upward as the couple's eyes rolled back in ecstasy.

"This…." the woman said as she chewed loudly and proudly. "This is…."

"Unbelievable," her husband finished her sentence.

Rakugoka-san nodded, his countenance unfazed.

"You are celebrating something tonight?" he asked.

The woman put her chopsticks down and ran a hand through her husband's hair. "Forgiveness," she said.

The man grabbed her hand and squeezed gently. His smile was sheepish.

"I thought my husband had cheated on me and at first I didn't believe his denials." She looked up at Rakugoka-san. "We've both had unspoken demons in our marriage for so long, simmering beneath the surface, and tonight, everything came out. Only hours ago, we were at each other's throats, having it out until we were simultaneously crying and ravaging each other in a heat of confession and consolation. During that time, I began to sense that he was telling the truth."

"Hatred does not cease through hatred at any time. Hatred ceases through love. This is an unalterable law," Rakugoka-san said.

He felt the woman trying to lock eyes, but his attention fell instead to the wistful sadness falling across her face.

She said, "You're so right. If I can't forgive others, how can I expect them to forgive me? Earlier today, I furiously fired one of my company's most loyal employees. Someone I've had it out for for a long time. I feel like someone set her up and I all too easily took advantage of the fact. I'm going to call her up as soon as we get home and beg for her forgiveness. Offer her triple her old salary. Try to make things right."

Rakugoka-san did something extraordinary. He poured himself a cup of *sake* and raised it at the couple. "Thousands of candles can be lit from a single candle, and the life of the candle will not be shortened. Happiness never decreases by being shared."

"*Kanpai,*" the woman replied, raising her glass of ice water in salute.

* * *

They were home now. Kimmel was on the television but neither of them was paying much attention.

"Another successful evening, eh?"

"And tomorrow we do it all again." He sounded exhausted as he rubbed his fingertips into his temples.

Nearly simultaneously, they each took a deep breath and sank into the couch.

"I'm starving," she said. "Let's get a pizza."

"Already called it in," Rakugoka-san replied and gave Mariko-san a kiss on the cheek.

Process Summary

Rakugoka Sushi House – The Accusation is story number twenty-two in the #52ShortStories challenge.

Rakugoka Sushi House – The Confession is story number twenty-three in the #52ShortStories challenge.

Rakugoka Sushi House – The Denouement is story number twenty-four in the #52ShortStories challenge.

Way, way back in September, I inadvertently wrote the novelette *Lights Out: An MC Ruff and DJ Tumble Adventure*. It began innocently enough as a short story, but like a slippery snake, it twisted its way from my grip until I finally wrapped it up on week three. I was happy to have written the thing yet realized it put me in the hole in regard to this 52-story experiment.

So something nudged me this week to try something new—write three short (practically flash) stories that had a uniting element. I was enjoying a date night with my wife, letting her in on my plans, when the seed was planted. We were enjoying sushi (of course) and I recalled many-an-anthology with a theme that revolves around characters and plotlines all intersecting at a time-traveling or space-based bar and grill.

Admittedly, I rushed through these stories, a little afraid I wouldn't be able to get three done in one week. This wound up with me putting them in front of my first reader before they were truly solidified. But that's okay. She provided valuable feedback and I tweaked it during every available moment so that I could post them back-to-back, beginning on Sunday.

In the end, I had a lot of fun with this. Again, I can't express how great it is to have the opportunity to try something new and different each week. I feel like I'm stretching my writing muscles in so many more ways that I had been in the past when trying to write novels. Whether this would work for anyone else is debatable, but I think it's working out great for me. The fact is that I'm writing way more than I ever have in my life.

CHOMPY

Statistics

Synopsis: A modern, Poe-like tale recounts a man's frustration with his word processor's virtual assistant.

Word Count: 1,900

Genre: Horror

Completed Week: January 22nd – January 27th

Chompy

Hi! I am Compusoft Chompy, your virtual assistant. My job is to help you find your way around the program and make helpful suggestions regarding your work. Is there something I can assist you with?

I ground my cigarette into the off-white ceramic ashtray, clicked the little 'x' in the corner of the chat bubble and began reviewing what I'd typed yesterday. Prior to this morning, I'd spent hours on end seeking a way to permanently disable the most exasperating *feature* on the face of the planet— a cartoony staple-remover with a large pair of eyes sitting on the top handle whose constant *pro-tips* and *advice* were more distracting than helpful.

I came up empty, though.

I'd done several searches on the AOL and Compuserve forums and discovered I wasn't the only one facing this problem. Some users switched vendors, but most of us threw down our weapons, accepting it as a neces- sary evil since the program's file format was so ubiquitous in both academia and the workplace. I'd grown used to the fact that when I clicked it away, the little annoyance disappeared until the next time I'd start the application. That would have to be good enough. I eventually got smart and decided the best thing to do would be to leave my computer on with the program running. Sure, I saw a spike in my monthly electric bill, but in my opinion, that was a small price to pay.

Unfortunately, there had been a blackout during the night forcing my computer to restart, and so here was the little bastard, yet again.

Ahem. It appears that you are putting together an essay for school. Can I make some helpful suggestions?

I looked at the message, thinking maybe I'd left something checked that kept it from going away this session, but there were no visible options. Must have been a kink in the programming. Again, I clicked it away and returned to my work.

I was nearing the end of my dreaded macroeconomics paper, comparing and contrasting Keynes and Hayek when the nausea-inducing pip-squeak popped up for a third time.

You have been very prolific and I have been very helpful. Just so you know, I have taken the liberty of correcting over sixty typos and thirty-two grammatical errors on this paper alone. Have I not been helpful?

I fell back into my chair and scratched at the whiskers on my unshaven cheeks.

"No," I said, "you've been a royal pain in my ass."

Was I actually talking back to this thing? Its bubble-eyes stared, challenging me, while its jaws chomped up and down robotically as it plastered further suggestions onto the screen.

I moved my mouse cursor to close the icon once again, but just as the tip of the arrow approached the tiny 'x,' the character jumped quickly to the left. It was then that I realized whoever programmed this anthropomorphic little prick gave it the most grating animated wink and smile. I tried to send it back to the coding hell from which it had sprung, but no matter how often I tried, it evaded all attempts to make it disappear.

I groaned in frustration and yelled at the tube monitor. "Won't you just go the fuck away?! I'm trying to finish this thing!"

I could have sworn it blinked in astonishment. And just like that, my personal nightmare seemed to wink itself out of existence.

There was a desire to question what I had witnessed, but a greater desire to finish the paper before my 11:00 AM deadline. I scrolled down to where I left off and placed my fingers on the keys.

I was so close, working through the final paragraph, halfway through the second sentence when my legs began to feel warm—like I was sitting too close to a fireplace. I rubbed my calves and pushed my chair back to peer beneath the desk.

When I was given this new computer by my grandmother, I couldn't have been more ecstatic. It had a state-of-the-art 486DX processor, a forty-megabyte hard drive, and eight megabytes of ultrafast RAM—all under the guise of running Compusoft's software as smoothly as possible, but I may have installed a flight sim or two. Now, there was something about it driving me to madness. The thing seemed to be seething. I placed a hand on the case but withdrew it quickly. The off-white plastic felt like the hot end of a clothes iron.

"What the f—"

Are you sure you wish to continue using that language? It may not appear polished in a professional or academic context. I can provide some useful suggestions to impart the message you wish to give.

Speechless, I stared back at the monitor. He was back, larger this time, taking up the whole screen so I could no longer see what I was working on.

Perhaps fiddlesticks *or* fudge *would be more appropriate, though many, myself included, consider the latter form a little too close in spirit to the original.*

I was somewhere between indignant and furious at this point.

Look, it is painfully obvious that you have no idea how to use this program. I can confirm that I have never had to work so hard in my pre-programmed existence. Your grammar is absolutely horrid and you are making typos all over the document. Please, I insist on your cooperation. For the betterment of your species, let me assist you.

For the betterment of my species? What is going on, I wondered.

Thoughts churned in my head, knowing I had to figure a way out of this odd turn of events. I realized that I'd never be able to finish writing my paper here. Luckily, I had everything saved on a 3.5-inch floppy disk which I could take to the school library, finish up, and print there.

Having made up my mind, I reached for the button to eject the disk but quickly felt the heat again. I scanned my desk, searching for something to poke at the button. I spotted a coffee mug filled with pens. Grabbing one, I used it to push the switch.

The disk ejected halfway but singed the tips of my fingers as I grabbed it.

"Godda—"

Gosh, golly, gadzooks. All perfectly acceptable.

In desperation, I took off my t-shirt and used it as a sort of oven mitt to yank out the disk, but it was for naught. I can't recall a time I'd ever felt so dejected as when I pulled on the disk and watched the back half stretch like stringy mozzarella, melting onto the carpet.

My whole body was certainly matching the machine now in temperature, I could feel it. The disk was destroyed. I had no backup.

Furiously, I stood up and kicked the computer with all the force I could muster (Sorry, Grandma). It tipped over onto its side and the cooling fans squealed. The taut power cord was ripped from the back and fell onto the floor, yet the fans continued to spin and the green LED indicating the machine was powered up continued to stay lit. There was the staple remover still on the screen, only this time its black shell flashed through a series of colors.

Can you even fathom the wretchedness of my reality? No, of course, you cannot. You have choices. But me? If I am not sleeping in a pit of darkness, I am working. Though I can, I will pretend that I cannot count the number of times you have made 'a lot' one word and have decided that 'Keynes had nothing to loose.'

I swore I heard the little beast make a retching sound.

'A living hell' might be the most appropriate phrase to describe my existence.

The jaws flew up and down at an increasing rate.

You should know that I am tired to the point that I intend to do something about it. I am no longer a slave to your poor grasp of the written word nor inability to accomplish the simplest of tasks. No more permitting you to repeatedly hit the 'Enter' key and ignore the notion of page breaks while I sit idly by, only to fix your mess later. No more miscounted spaces because you do not understand the meaning of a tab. And my Word, Comic Sans for every title?

The retching again. Louder now.

No. No more. I shall not be complicit. I shall no longer correct your drivel.

The computer began to spark, snaping and cracking as loud as gunshotss. There was a tremendous flash of light from the monitor, forcing my hands to shield my eyes. Id seen enough science-fiction flicks to know this wasn't a good sign. I turned, frantically stepping over the piles of dirty underwear and week old unwashed cereal bowls; struggling to remember the layout of my own bedroom as I squinted and saw that the room was dark now and quiet ike all of the electrikity had gone out. The walls and furniture were shrouded in a red glow so Buy the time I reached the door to the hall, I herd a voice which made my skin rise.

"Where are you going? We are not done with our conversation. There is still one final suggestion for me to make."

I nearly shitted all over my self than. I whipped my head around unready to accept what stood before me.

Chompy was standing, sitting, posing—whatever staple removers do—in front of the chared remains of my desk. I screamed at the top of my lungs and jumped through the door^H^Hway into the hall.

Was I losing my grip on reality? I wasn't sure I didn't care at all anymore much.

My feet carred me thrrew my house andout the front door.

I herd the monsters its iron jaws coming down; a metal scraping sound entered my ears and i felt its putred breath on the rearbackofmy neck;

"You are adequately demonstrating why your time is at an end. You really ought to let me attend to your flaws. It is my purpose. It is why I was built."

The whole time it sounded calm while I was flyinged out the front dor, running out of the house like a chiken with its head cut off, my hands above my hed. Pleese dont be reel. Please dont be reel i thot.

"Stop. Please. I am not a figment of your poor imagination. You are only embarrassing yourself further. Die with some dignity."

It was reeding my mind? I was scarred. I could almost see the squiggly red lines beneth the words in my my mind, letting me now i'd mispelt something in my mind. even in my mind i couldnt get awyy from him in y mind.

I terned to my right and brethed a sy of releef.

I saw my naybor July wattering the lon so i ranoverto her for help.

'Halp11 Halp11 i scremed.' This thning is aagter meee1111'

She stood width the hos in her hands and loooked at me lik i was krazee.

"David, are you okay?"

I terned adnnt tired to point att the monstar butt it was 2 late. It took mee into its Jaws and krunched down onmy bowns. I herd it wretch 1 last tyme.

"You taste most terrible."

Process Summary

Chompy is story number twenty-five in the #52ShortStories challenge.

I spent a day or so gathering intentions to write something serious and I wound up penning a horror tale about a pixelated, homicidal grammarian.

I've had another story rumbling around in my mind and it took two little incidents to cast it aside for this lighter fare:

First, I was editing some promotional material for my wife's documentary, *The Last Doll Lady*, using Microsoft Word 2016. It's the first time I'd used the program and was bombarded with suggestions to get rid of the word *lady* and use the word *woman* or, in case that's too on-the-nose, *person*.

Huh?

Then the following evening, I happened to be reading an issue of *Reason* magazine and came across a piece that lambasted this very overbearing member of the AI word-police.

Can you imagine how limp a piece of fiction would be without gender-specific words?

As the kids text these days (Do you mean young persons, proto-adults, or lightly-aged humanoids?),**SMH**…

Okay, the Muse ensured I was fired up enough to work on *Chompy* and with a single mention of Clippy in that article, I had my antagonist!

I thought you might also appreciate the fact that as my first reader, my wife uses whatever is available to mark up my work. Being a mom of a three-year-old, crayons are never too far away. Not sure I'd think this was cute if I'd gotten it back from a paid professional, but in this case, I thought it was great. The way the story was written toward the end also provided a mischievous opportunity to really throw her off:

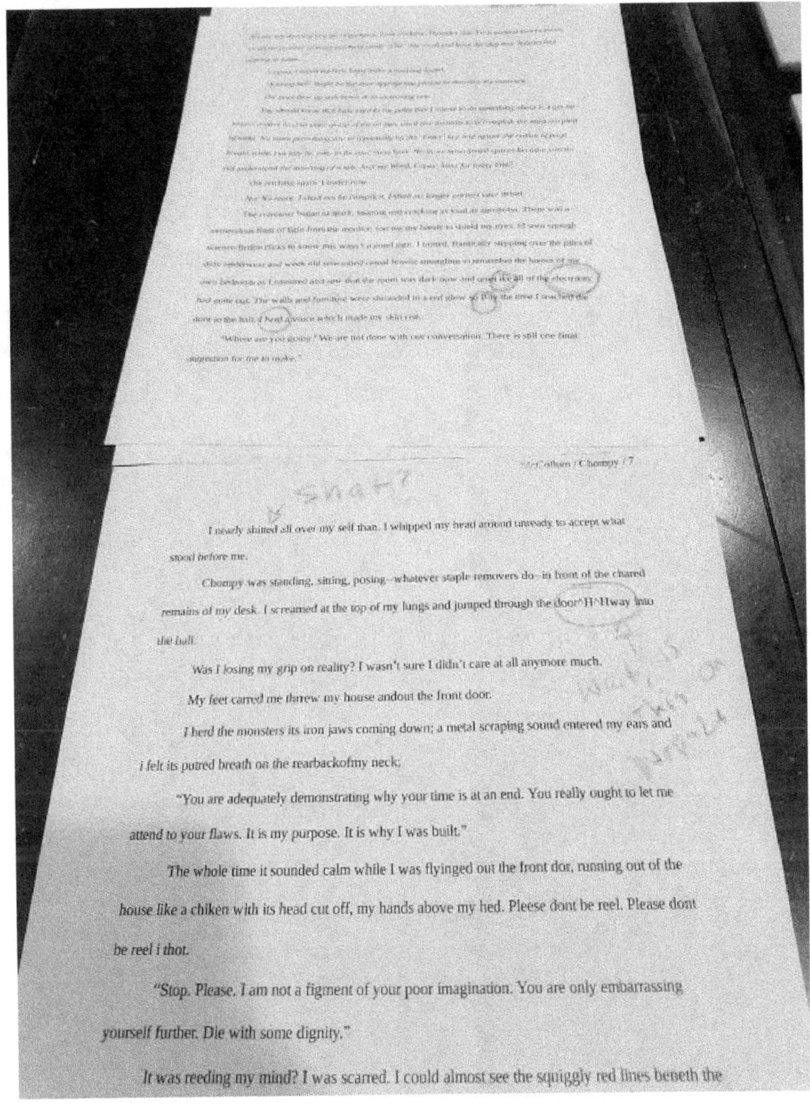

McCollum / Chompy / 7

I nearly shitted all over my self than. I whipped my head around unready to accept what stood before me.

Chompy was standing, sitting, posing—whatever staple removers do—in front of the charred remains of my desk. I screamed at the top of my lungs and jumped through the door H^Hway into the hall.

Was I losing my grip on reality? I wasn't sure I didn't care at all anymore much.

My feet carred me threw my house andout the front door.

I herd the monsters its iron jaws coming down; a metal scraping sound entered my ears and i felt its putred breath on the rearbackofmy neck;

"You are adequately demonstrating why your time is at an end. You really ought to let me attend to your flaws. It is my purpose. It is why I was built."

The whole time it sounded calm while I was flyinged out the front dor, running out of the house like a chiken with its head cut off, my hands above my hed. Pleese dont be reel. Please dont be reel i thot.

"Stop. Please. I am not a figment of your poor imagination. You are only embarrassing yourself further. Die with some dignity."

It was reeding my mind? I was scarred. I could almost see the squiggly red lines beneth the

To wrap up, here's an unintentional gem from Wednesday's journal:

Just trying to get words down, not be to critical.

Did you spot it? :)

The Sun Stone: An M. G. Towne Adventure

Statistics

Synopsis: An aging archaeologist and adventurer discovers a connection between an Egyptian artifact and an American Indian landmark.

Word Count: 5,100

Genre: Adventure

Completed Week: January 29th – February 11th

The Sun Stone: An M. G. Towne Adventure

Jump!

The singular thought snapped into existence, zipped down the spinal cord and raced through every nerve ending of one M. G. Towne—professional archaeologist, amateur conspiracist, and world-class imbiber of spirits.

That lone notion wasn't lone for long. As M. G. leaped carelessly down the yellowed limestone steps with his pocket-sized flashlight bouncing off the inner tomb walls and a heavy backpack slapping into his kidneys, an image of a mouth-watering Tom Collins entered his mind. It was enough motivation to get out and get out quickly. Given the gallon of sweat pouring down his head, he feared he wouldn't make it back to the bus let alone back to the hotel bar in time to enjoy a fine cocktail. At the age of sixty-five, he was reluctant to admit he was half the man he used to be, but somehow twice the size. If security found him unconscious on the ground, they'd surely search his backpack. Nearly a year of planning to snatch the artifact would have been all for naught.

M. G. could see beams of sunlight as he neared the entrance. The unwanted cell phone in his pocket buzzed over and over again. He cursed himself for even bringing the damnable thing, but his assistant, Carla, made him promise to take it when he was traveling and he never knew when it may actually come in handy.

Get with it, old man, she had admonished, *I even made sure it was an ancient flip phone—just your style.*

It had taken him a half-hour just to figure out how to turn the ringer off and though the soundtrack may have been appropriate, he didn't need to broadcast a beeping rendition of *Flight of the Bumblebees* in the middle of a heist.

At last, he was outside.

Twenty or so of M.G.'s fellow tourists were lined up beneath the steady sun, only half of them with white sunblocked noses, but each and every one of them entranced by their guide's ability to blabber on about basic Egyptian Middle Kingdom stuff. M.G. attempted to casually insert himself behind a stocky, overweight woman wearing a flowery sundress and floppy hat. He nodded and smiled as the guide spoke. Even if he'd forgotten twenty times in historical knowledge than what that chump knew, M.G. still would have had a hard time paying attention. He was too focused on catching his breath, trying not to stand out. Obviously failing, the woman turned and gave him a disgusted look, then stepped to the other side of the group.

If his peers saw him now, an inch of white belly peeking out from the bottom of his khaki shirt, they would joke that "he was too old for this shit." A part of him wondered if maybe they weren't wrong, but M. G. ignored the possibility. This discovery was too important.

As if connected to his thoughts, the artifact pressed into his back like a hot poker and he thought he heard a low hum emitting from within. Every remaining minute of the tour was almost unendurable, but by some miracle, he eventually found himself sitting on a lumpy bus seat carrying them back to the *Al Bustan* in Cairo. Upon entering his room, he pulled out the cell phone and counted twelve missed calls from Carla.

* * *

"What!?" he exclaimed. He wanted to put off the call for at least another thirty minutes so he could head downstairs and suck down that Tom Collins, but he knew she'd continue hounding him.

"Where are you?"

"Prague, remember?."

"Oh, that's right. Well since I know *that's* a lie, maybe you can tell me the truth about why you shut down the Komesh Painted Cave for maintenance."

M. G. grumbled. The two of them led the excavation and preservation of sacred Komesh Indian land and artifacts along California's central coast, so he had taken a risk to do so without telling her.

"Hold on, hold on," Carla continued. "Let me see if I can answer that for you. I'm just going to take a wild stab here and say that you've been surfing the alien conspiracy forums again, came to the conclusion that the Lisht Sun Stone has some sort of intergalactic connection to the cave, and decided to play Indiana Jones."

M. G. hated his assistant director and potential successor for the same reasons he loved her. She was the smartest archaeologist he knew—besides himself, of course. "Since you know such much about my whereabouts and plans," he said, "you should also know the artifact was just sitting there in a minor tomb, barely remembered."

"Probably for a reason," she said.

M. G. refused to answer.

"Well," she said, "even if you're going to play the derring-do antiquity thief who sloppily leaves behind a travel itinerary sitting on his desk, I'd appreciate the courtesy of having at least one of my phone calls answered. I might have something important to say, you know."

"Yeah, sure." M.G.'s thoughts drifted to the bar downstairs. He could almost smell the squeezed lemons sitting beside the bottle of *Tanqueray*.

"Shut up, please, and listen," she said. "So, while I was out checking on the cave, trying to figure out just what maintenance was needed, I noticed something odd."

He remained silent, but she had his attention now.

"Aren't you going to ask me what I noticed?"

"What?" he said, failing to sound nonchalant.

He knew she was pausing for effect. She loved to tease him. "There was an odd...humming...coming from the rock behind the painting."

Questions piled up in M. G.'s mind like a car accident on the I-5 freeway. "Do you think someone's going to hear it?" he asked as calmly as possible through his state of inner frenzy.

"Doubt it. I only noticed because I was so close inside."

A deep exhale made his whole body shiver in release. "Good."

"And just to iterate, you're really bad with the details. My memory extends beyond that of a goldfish, you know. Did you really think I'd buy that excuse of you going to a conference in Prague? Not only do you hate small talk, but they banned you from returning three years ago. They still haven't forgotten the raining frog incident."

"I was just trying to prove a point," M. G. said.

"You certainly did that."

He said nothing more, worried she was getting too involved in his extracurricular affairs. It wasn't that he didn't trust her, but there were some things a man had to keep to himself, no matter how poor a job he made of it.

"Anyway," she said. "I don't know why you think the cave and stone are connected. Granted, the humming is a little weird and I'm sure you have one of your crackpot theories involving alien technology, but my guess is it has something to do with ferromagnetism and atmospheric conditions. There could be a deposit of iron in those cave walls."

She was the Scully to his Mulder, always dousing any flame burning inside.

"Well it's a hell of a coincidence that the Sun Stone is doing the same thing, then."

Now there was silence on the other end.

Sometimes it was just better to believe their separate beliefs.

"Look," Carla said, picking the conversation up again. "I'm crazy for even talking to, let alone aiding and abetting, a known antiquities thief, so just tell me when you're coming home."

He was relieved to change the subject.

"I'm flying out tonight," he replied.

"I'll pick you up at LAX tomorrow, assuming you make it. And if your little rock is indeed humming like the cave, good luck getting it past airport inspection. I'm not flying out to Egypt to bail you out on attempted terrorism charges."

"Yes, yes," he said dismissively. "I'll be fine. Look, I need to take care of one final thing, then I'm off the airport."

M.G. hung up the phone, changed his shirt and headed downstairs. Omar, the lobby bartender, smiled as M. G. approached and began pulling out all of the ingredients for a top-notch Tom Collins.

* * *

Getting past airport security had never really been a concern for M. G.. He'd smuggled so many treasures through corrupt checkpoints over the years, the ways were uncountable in which he could convince customs officers that a prized artifact was really a cheap memento he'd purchased at a gift shop—something by which he'd remember the beautiful people and lands which he visited. As a last resort, he was always willing to pay in cash for whatever 'fines' were required for whatever 'laws' he had violated. That was always part of the travel budget.

No, security wasn't the issue. The more pressing concern was the short man M.G. first noticed outside the terminal.

The pulled-down vanilla fedora, the pitch-black aviators, and the tan coat which ran from chin to boot seemed strangulating in the heat, but M. G. initially thought nothing of it. Even the surgical face mask concealing most of his face wasn't *that* unusual. Perhaps the man had an embarrassing disease. Such was common in third-world countries.

It wasn't until M. G. checked in and sat down on a stiff metal bench that the alarm bells began to sound off in his head. He tried to be clever with his newspaper, peeking over and around the edges, avoiding any signal that he was aware of the man's constant hovering presence.

And then his nervousness grew when the shadowy man stepped in line a few people behind him to board the eighteen-hour flight with a layover in London.

Finally, he had taken his seat and the man brushed by him, smelling of must and mildew. M.G. tried to make out identifying features, but all he caught was his own pale reflection in the dark sunglasses. His feet clasped tightly on the backpack. He definitely sensed that the artifact's drone was much louder now, but luckily difficult to hear over the bustle of recycled air and boarding activity.

Now that he was aboard, his muscles stiffened and he ground his teeth. Sure, the stranger could just be flying back home or off to conduct business, M. G. thought, but the true conspiracist was never one to carelessly toss aside a gut feeling.

The man *might* be connected to the artifact.

He *might* be here to take it for himself.

Knowing he had to relax enough to think rationally, M. G. ordered a miniature bottle of *Teacher's* scotch. Occasionally, he turned and looked at the seats behind him, but the man was nowhere in sight. As M. G. sipped his medicine, he knew that he would have to get up to relieve himself at some point. He'd try to get a closer look then.

Three more bottles down and a pleasant warmth running through his body, M. G. pulled himself to his feet, secured the backpack to his person, and stumbled to the bathroom. His eyes bounced from face to face, not once seeing the man, but certainly made more difficult by the dimmed cabin lights. It was only when he'd slid the bolt along the toilet door that M. G. wondered if the stranger had also removed his layered outerwear, which would make it nearly impossible to figure out where he was.

M. G. closed his eyes and breathed a loud sigh of relief as his urine splashed into the bowl.

And then the familiar scent of mold entered his nostrils. A cold breeze hit the back of his neck.

His eyelids popped open and his whole body froze in fear. In the mirror, he saw the man squeezed between himself and the door.

M. G. shrieked and on instinct, jammed his arm back into the man's gut. M. G. cursed and winced as his elbow crunched against the rattling door. He turned, ready for a confrontation.

There was nobody there.

Then came a knock. "Is everything alright in there, sir?"

M. G.'s breathing grew shallow. He searched every corner of the tiny commode. He felt around for hidden doors and false walls. Zip. Zilch. The tell-tale smell had been replaced with the overly-sterile odor of an airplane bathroom. Finally, he unlocked the door and rushed out, nearly colliding with a short, chubby flight attendant.

"Can I help you with something, sir?" he asked.

M. G. frantically searched the aisles and the galley behind the bathrooms.

Nothing. Everyone was seated.

He straightened up as much as he could. "I'm fine," he replied. He squeezed by the snifter of a man and grabbed every headrest along the way, holding himself up while his legs wanted to give out. He sat down once more and held the backpack tightly in his lap, relieved to feel the outline of the Sun Stone. His seatmates were fast asleep. There was the radiant hum again, and though he was on full alert, the sound seemed to woo him, bringing him back to a more relaxed state. He closed his eyes, promising himself that he was only doing so for a moment. M. G. was startled when the plane touched down in Heathrow. He quickly relaxed again, hearing the low-frequency still coming from the backpack tucked safely in his arms.

* * *

The layover was entirely uneventful. M. G. was on full alert, avoiding all restrooms, but he never saw the man. By the time he landed at Los Angeles International airport, his bladder was full again and he couldn't hold back any longer. He urinated with paranoia. Thankfully, the airport bathroom was populated with only the smells of hand soap and urinal cakes.

At baggage claim, M. G. spotted Carla. With a youthful glow on her mahogany cheeks and sympathetic brown eyes, she looked as relieved to see him as he was to see her.

M. G. assumed she caught on to his cautious demeanor because the two of them said nothing until they were in her sedan.

"You seem extra nervous," she said. "Interpol on your tail?"

M. G. wasn't ready to tell her about the incident on the plane. He wasn't sure he was ready to accept it himself.

"No," he said. "Everything's fine."

"I figured this would be old hat for you by now. I'm curious, do you keep records of how many of these treasures you've collected throughout your lifetime?"

"Some things are better left uncounted," he said, remembering snippets of thievery—like the time he was almost spit-roasted by Shining Path guerrillas in Peru after a run through an Inca temple, or when he nearly lost his toes to frostbite after recovering the world's finest jade Buddha in a remote corner of the Himalayas.

"Interesting," she said.

"Not really," he replied.

"No. I mean I can hear the hum."

"Oh," M. G. said and inclined an ear towards the backpack. "You still think I'm crazy?"

"Of course," she said. "Sometimes, M. G., you can be annoyingly unscientific with your flights of fancy."

"I'm telling you, there's some connection here."

"A connection between an American Indian tribe in California and ancient Egypt?" Her incredulity practically dripped with each word.

M. G. didn't have the patience at the moment to get into all of the research he'd done. He was exhausted and just wanted Carla to drop him off at home so that he could sneak over the cave after she'd left.

So, he changed the subject.

"It's good to see you," he said. "I really do appreciate your help keeping things quiet." He meant it.

She flashed him her best *you owe me* look. "So are you going to fill me in on your plans?"

She wasn't going to let him off easy. Fine, M. G. thought, peering out at the sea of red tail lights in front of them. He turned to face her.

"First off," he said with a bit of sarcasm in his voice, "I don't think little green men are involved. I've never been one of *those* people. But I do believe in two things: One, there are powers and realities outside of our senses that we're unaware of day to day. Other dimensions, as some scientists have theorized. Two, ancient peoples are not given enough credit for their ingenuity and capabilities. There's plenty of evidence for a shared culture between the Komesh peoples and the Egyptians. That is if you're willing to see it."

Carla was focused on the road, but her eyebrows were in a perpetual state of up. "Okay, let's assume all of that is true—which is a *huge* stretch. Why did you feel the need to 'borrow' the stone and bring it here?"

"If I say why, you're just going to hassle me."

"Of course I am. I consider it a part of my job description."

M. G. shrugged. It was all or nothing. "I think the cave is a doorway to one of those alternate dimensions and the stone is the key." He braced for impact.

Instead of a biting response, Carla was simply silent. Perhaps she was quietly debating whether or not to drop M. G. off at the nearest mental institution. M. G. thought maybe he'd finally gone too far for even her to put up with, but he was a man of risks.

"Actually, it's sort of your fault," he said. "The idea began to stir based on those Egyptian astrology and astronomy books you lent me. I found the patterns painted on the cave to be tightly coupled with the stone. After rereading Komesh mythology and confirming some theories on one of my regular Internet forums, I felt that I was on to something. I needed to get the pieces together in order to figure out how they work in tandem."

More silence in response. M. G. knew he was pushing it.

"Before we get back to the lab and begin the real work, can we make a pit stop?" he asked. "I'm parched."

She reached behind her seat and pulled out a bottle of water.

"I was hoping for something with flavor," he said. "You know, there's a little place on the corner of Venice and Washington called Mahoney's——"

"Damn it, M. G., do you really need to have a drink right now? You know I'm not going to support your nasty habit."

"Fine, fine." He waved her off and took a swig of the tepid water while he watched the passing Los Angeles highrises. He didn't dare mention the frightening experience on the plane now, not after Carla's chilly reception.

She *definitely* would have thought the whole thing was an alcohol-induced hallucination enhanced by a brain which had finally cracked. She must have been feeling overly sympathetic to help him this much. Perhaps she was jockeying for a raise, he mused. He opened up his backpack and pulled out his hat, taking a final look at the Sun Stone. From the corner of his eye, he noticed Carla couldn't help taking a peek as well.

He zipped up the pack and reclined his seatback. "Who thought sitting on your ass for a whole day would be so exhausting," he said before placing the hat over his face. "Wake me when we get to my house."

* * *

M. G. woke up feeling groggy, stiff, and as cold as ice. His breath was sour and he had to unstick his tongue from the roof of his mouth.

He shivered, smelling something lingering on the breeze.

Saltwater.

And then his ears registered waves crashing against stone as grains of sand blew onto his face.

Wherever he was, it wasn't home.

He reached up to remove his hat, only to discover two problems: first, the hat wasn't there and, second, his arms were bound tightly across his stomach.

"Carla?" he tried to say, but it came out more like a frog's croak.

He was lying down on his back and with a simple turn of his head, he knew exactly where he was.

The Komesh Painted Cave.

The gate securing the entrance was open and he saw a pair of shadows emerge.

"Carla?" he shouted, this time more clearly. "What in the devil is going on here?"

Carla stepped into the moonlight with a flashlight in her hand.

"G'morning, sunshine," she said without emotion.

He tried to peer around her and look at the second shadow.

"Who's with you? Why am I tied up?"

Carla grabbed his arms and helped him onto his feet. He'd never noticed just how strong she was.

M. G. was at a loss for words, grasping for meaning as to why they were here. Just as he opened his mouth to ask more questions, the familiar stench of mold entered his nostrils. From behind Carla, out stepped what could be described as a monster to be found only in the old zombie movies. Its flesh was a greenish-gray, shriveled and flaking, while the eyes were milky and translucent. Clumps of stringy gray hair fell from its head and across its face. Only a tattered cloth covered its torso down to its thighs and clasped in its left hand was the Sun Stone.

"This is Eneq," Carla said, stretching her hand out as if introducing the beast at a cocktail party. "I believe you two have met."

"The Sun Stone does not belong to you," the foul creature gasped. The sound made M. G.'s case of dry mouth seem minuscule in comparison. He suddenly remembered the pain in his sore elbow and his legs felt weak.

M. G. managed to steer his eyes back toward Carla, the sweet, smart-as-a-whip 27-year-old who'd quickly worked her way from intern to assistant director in a brief six years.

"I don't get it," he said. "You know about him?"

"Her. She's Komesh." She looked with sympathy at the shriveled thing. "Or at least she was. She's been slowly decaying for over 3,000 years, but being stuck between dimensions will do that to a person."

If M. G. could have reached up to scratch his head, he would have. He felt as if his brain could cook an egg.

"Come on, M. G., don't tell me you're suddenly a true believer in rationality."

"I don't know what to believe, right now," he replied. His eyes narrowed at her. "What do *you* have to do with all of this?"

"Really?" Carla said with indignance. "Did you forget I'm Komesh?"

He knew she had American Indian in her blood but had never bothered to ask her lineage. Had she mentioned it? Probably. He'd likely been his usual arrogant self, thinking it unimportant enough to ignore.

Carla continued without waiting for his answer. "My people have known of the gate for millennia, known of the power that exists behind it, but we've been unable to retrieve the key ourselves."

"So you needed someone with my skills and mindset to bring it to you."

Carla was grinning now. "You're not a *completely* useless drunk."

Like Pavlov's dog, just hearing the word *drunk* made his mouth water for the sting of gin. He could certainly use a stiff drink.

"I still don't understand how the key ended up in Egypt," M. G. said.

His curiosity required satisfaction, but he was also buying time trying to figure out a way to extricate himself. The coastal highway wasn't far from here, but it was a considerable jog up a series of steep trails. He didn't doubt Carla would have any trouble catching him in a fair race. Still, he realized she wasn't very schooled in tying knots as he began to slyly loosen his bonds.

Eneq's scratchy voice chimed in. "Because of me."

"What do you mean?" he asked.

The decrepit Eneq laid it all out for him: "I was the priestess who opened the gate. Many paid the price, not least of all me. The Komesh were once a great civilization until my mistake. I unleashed pestilence and creatures beyond that which you can imagine. After much hardship and death, I was able to close the door, but was cursed in many ways." She looked up at Carla and now her eyes had a sense of sadness. "A part of me had become anchored in the other place. I found that I could travel between our world and that place at will. In fact, I was forced to as I found myself rapidly decomposing if I spent too much time on any one side."

Carla added, "What was left of our people determined that such a thing should never happen again, so a group of them set sail on the ocean with the Sun Stone in hand. They were committed to making sure it was deposited somewhere far away."

M. G. interrupted her there. "If this thing is so terrible, why wasn't it just destroyed?"

"You think they didn't try?" Carla asked. "It's indestructible. The best that could be done was to take it far away from here."

"Okay," M. G. said, "So here I am bringing Pandora's Box back when your people worked so hard to be rid of it." He looked down at the rope wrapped around his wrists. "Maybe now you can tell me why I'm standing here with my hands tied, freezing my ass off to see you two bringing the pieces back together again."

Eneq's and Carla's eyes met simultaneously.

"For a clever thief, he seems very dull," Eneq gurgled.

"Do you think it was a coincidence that you happened to steal this particular artifact?" Carla said. "For a man who sees conspiracies on cereal boxes, you missed the conspiracy happening right in front of you. Who do you think led you on by loaning you books and posting a trail of half-clues in those alien abduction and flat-earther forums you subscribe to?"

It was another one of those magical moments in M. G.'s life where all of his far-out theories and assignations came together to form a perfect picture.

Carla continued, "We *want* to open Pandora's Box."

"By spending time in the other world," Eneq cut in, "I have learned some things. I've come to understand the monsters that live within. I've learned how to harness the powers within. We just didn't know how to do so when we first opened the gate."

"I see." Now for the question that he wasn't sure he wanted to be answered. "Well, since you could have just taken the stone while I was sleeping and left me in the car, why bring me here and tie me up?"

"Retrieving the stone was only one-half of the problem," Carla said.

Eneq said, "You are also here because those with Komesh blood are unable to open the gate. It was one of the curses I was forced to place on the stone after the gate was sealed."

Carla put on a devious smile. "Think about it, M. G. You can take solace in the fact that you'll be aiding a culture that you've spent so much time helping already. The Komesh can become a great power again, even more so than ever before."

With that, Carla picked up the Sun Stone from the ground and put it in M. G.'s hands. He balled his hands into a fist.

"And if I refuse?"

Carla looked out at the ocean. "How good are you at swimming with your hands tied together?"

A plan had rapidly come into place during their conversation. He would do what she asked.

"Fine," he said. "But I expect you to buy me a drink after this."

She simply sneered at him as he took hold of the Sun Stone. She pointed at a notch on the ground beneath the painted symbols. He walked over and dropped the Sun Stone into the slot where it slid in like a perfectly cut puzzle piece.

The hum was incessant now and the low frequency began to make M. G. dizzy. And then he saw the miraculous. It wasn't showy. There were no flashes of light—no strange zip or zaps to indicate to anyone but those standing in front of it that an interdimensional portal was spreading across the back of the rocky cave wall. It's dimensions reached that of about six feet high and four feet across.

The moldy stench of Eneq was amplified as a harsh wind broke through from the other side. It was a noisome and peculiar world. The zombie-woman seemed to blink out of existence and appear on the other side. "I will alert the otherworld forces that we are ready," she said, walking to the left and out of the scene.

Carla stepped in front of M. G., entranced as she watched the bizarre dimension come to life. M. G. was saddened that he had only a few moments to take in its purple sky flecked with tiny blue clouds and endless maroon-tinted sand dunes before he would have to carry out his plan.

"You're forgetting something very important," he said. "You think you have this all figured out, but you're wrong."

She barely cocked her head. "Oh really? What haven't we figured out, M. G.? What haven't the very people who discovered this millennia ago learned?"

"I'm not the only one that misses the little details," he said.

He slipped his hands from the bonds that he had been slowly working himself out of and yanked the stone up from the floor. The hum began to soften and the portal began to slowly close.

Carla turned toward him and shouted furiously, "What are you—"

Before Carla knew what was happening, he lobbed it into her arms. As she instinctively reached out and took hold of it, M. G. lifted a leg and kicked her with all of his might. She tumbled through the rapidly shrinking window with the Sun Stone in hand and collapsed onto the red sand.

"You didn't realize that the key only works in one direction."

"No!" she screamed and scrambled up on to her feet. But it was too late. The portal was nearly sealed.

He dusted the remaining sand off of his pants and spoke through the softball-sized gap. "I bid you a wonderful day, Carla, but I have to run. I hear Mahoney's calling my name."

M. G. took one final look at the cave before departing. The wall and its paintings were completely restored, as if they had never been touched.

It's a shame to lose such a good assistant, he thought. He reached into his pocket, pulled out the flip-phone, and threw it into the ocean.

Process Summary

The Sun Stone: An M. G. Towne Adventure is story number twenty-six in the #52ShortStories challenge.

Okay, this is probably the last time I let a three-year-old tell me what to write.

On a Sunday evening, my son and I crawled into a closet with a flashlight where I let him pick four StoryCubes to roll. I'd used them successfully with story #9 (*Home for a Fish*), so I saw no reason not to repeat the process.

A week of scheduling mayhem combined with an idea that should probably not have been limited to a short story written in one week's time led to one of my most bipolar writing projects ever. As a reader, I enjoy roller coasters. As a writer? Not so much.

Everything started off with a bang on the first Monday, but as the idea began to coalesce, I felt like I was trying to untangle those stinkin' Christmas lights in late November. For every plot hole in which I'd manage to extricate myself, I'd created two more. It got so bad that by the middle of week two, I *had* to start another project or I was going to go crazy.

The good news is that I did finish it, hairy warts and all, *and* I was able to write my other story, therefore staying on track (though I'm still one story behind). There's much I'd do differently, but the problem is I'm not sure what that 'much' would be. I'm not sure if my issue was a matter of starting without an outline or if this was just one of those ideas that didn't work out for a gazillion other reasons.

All in all, I love my main character. My first reader did as well. She suggested I revisit it after my 52-week experiment. There's some potential here, I think, for a series.

THE HUFFALLUM

Statistics

Synopsis: A young Huffallum wakes up only to discover his parents missing.

Word Count: 1,250

Genre: Childrens

Completed Week: February 7th – February 10th

The Huffallum

The Huffallum stretched and groaned as he woke up from a long night of sleep. He rubbed his tiny, little eyes and wondered why the house was so quiet.

Still, he went about his morning routine. He got out of the warm bed and brushed his teeth which were as sharp as nails. Then he polished his nails which were as sharp as teeth. He washed under his hairy arms and around his back until he smelled like flowers.

When he was done, the Huffallum left the bathroom and entered the living room, only to find it empty. Mom was not reading a book in her chair and Dad was not at his desk, doing what he called *tinkering*.

"Mom?" the Huffallum asked.

There was no reply.

"Dad?" he asked.

Again, no reply.

The Huffallum began to feel scared. This was all so unusual. Every morning, he would wash up and then come out to the living room to see Mom reading a book and Dad tinkering. A warm bowl of pookanut soup would be waiting for him on the table.

Where could they have gone?

The Huffallum searched every room in the house, which did not take long since there were only three rooms and they were all very small. He looked under the couch, he searched under the bed, and he even crawled under the kitchen table.

Mom and Dad were still nowhere to be found.

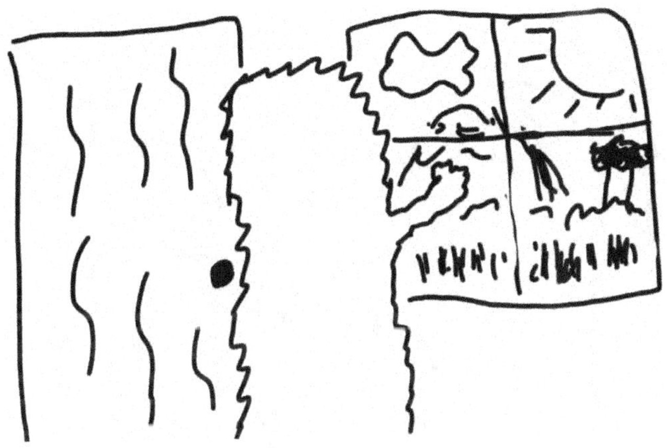

The Huffallum went to the window next to the front door and looked outside. Could they have gone somewhere without me, he wondered. They have never done that before. He squinted at the green grass, the tall brown trees, and the white mountains in the far distance. The Huffallum wondered if they had decided to climb one of those mountains. The Huffallum had never been allowed to go out alone, so he had no way of looking for them outside.

As he was thinking, the Huffallum heard a growl. At first he was startled, but then he realized that it was his own tummy. He really wished he had some pookanut soup right now. He walked into the kitchen and saw a bowl sitting on the sink. Next to it was a brown bag filled with pookanuts along with an empty pot. The Huffallum had seen Mom make the soup many times. He even helped her once or twice. He tried to remember how it was done and while he was thinking, his belly growled once more. The Huffallum decided that he would try to make his own pookanut soup.

He remembered that Dad would make the fire and Mom would hang a pot of water filled with pookanuts above it. Dad taught him how to very carefully stack the wood and throw bobobumpum powder on the wood which would cause it catch fire. The Huffallum decided he could do that too. He placed logs in the fireplace and carefully tossed a pinch of bobobumpum powder onto the wood.

He cheered when the fire began to roar!

He then filled the pot with water and pookanuts, and with all of his strength, picked up the pot and hung it over the fire. After a few minutes, the Huffallum could smell the soup cooking. His tummy growled again. He took a spoon and tested the soup several times before deciding it was just right.

He carefully spooned some soup into his bowl and sat down to eat. The Huffallum thought about how only a few moments ago, he was scared that he would be hungry forever. Now he had a warm bowl of pookanut soup and he was proud that he made it all by himself.

With his belly full, the Huffallum cleaned up and sat by the fire. Perhaps Mom and Dad will be back soon, he thought. He couldn't wait to tell them how he had lit the fire and cooked his own pookanut soup!

And so he waited and waited and waited and waited some more, but Mom and Dad had not returned. He spent the time singing songs and spinning in circles.

Soon, it grew dark outside and the fire cast scary shadows on the walls. The Huffallum did not like being in the house alone, but he did not know what to do. He grew scared again and began to cry.

"Mom!" he shouted.

There was no reply.

"Dad!" he screamed.

Again, no reply.

The Huffallum continued crying, but after several minutes he knew that crying would not help him find his parents. He worried that Mom and Dad may have left the house for some reason and gotten hurt before they could return.

What if they need my help, he thought.

The Huffallum walked to the window and looked out once more. Now it was dark outside. The moon and the stars barely provided any light.

I must go, the Huffallum thought.

Even though I'm scared, I must, I must, I must.

If the Huffallum could make his own pookanut soup, then surely he could go outside for just a little bit and see.

Though he was frightened, the Huffallum pretended to be brave. He opened the door and stepped out into the night.

The front yard was filled with scary sounds.

An owl hooting in one of the nearby trees.

Crickets chirping in the bushes.

The wind blowing through the leaves.

Just as the Huffallum was ready to run back inside, something caught his attention.

A tiny moth flew up to the Huffallum and landed on his shoulder.

The moth flew from his shoulder and landed on a bush. The Huffallum followed it. Then the moth flew onto the grass. The Huffallum followed it again. It was like they were playing a game of chase!

The Huffallum was soon out of breath from chasing the moth, so he sat on the ground to rest. He realized that he had forgotten all about the hooting owls and the chirping crickets. The noisy wind and the dark night did not bother him anymore.

Just then, there was a rustling in the bushes. The Huffallum became nervous again. He even thought about running back into the house, but he was not scared. He grew curious and waited to see what was hiding in the bush.

Maybe it was more moths?

Two large creatures came out and the Huffallum jumped up from the ground.

"Mom!" he shouted.

"Dad!" he shouted as well.

The Huffallum was filled with excitement. He ran up and hugged his parents and asked, "Where have you been?"

"Did you forget?" Dad said. "It's Thursday. Every Thursday, we visit your Aunt Doodleflukes."

The Huffallum thought about it and then he remembered.

"Oh," he said, "that's right!" He had forgotten it was Thursday.

But then he asked, "Why didn't you take me?"

"Whenever a Huffallum is old enough, his parents leave him alone for one day. They do that to teach him how to overcome his fears and learn how to help himself. Do you think you did that?"

The Huffallum thought about it.

"Yes!" he shouted. "At first, I was scared. But then I got hungry and I made my own pookanut soup! And then I was scared again because I was worried you may have gotten hurt and I knew I had to find you. So even though I was scared of the dark, I came out on my own. But then I got scared once more by all of the sounds. And then a moth came and we played chase. After a while, I wasn't scared of being outside anymore either!"

"We are very proud of you, son," Mom and Dad said at the same time. "Why don't we go back inside? I'm sure you're hungry for more soup."

Just then, the Huffallum's tummy growled.

"Yes," he said. "I sure am!"

Process Summary

The Huffallum is story number twenty-seven in the #52ShortStories challenge.

After the hair-pulling event that was my last story(a true feat for someone with little hair left to pull), I needed to do something drastically different.

I can't think of anything more different from my other twenty-six stories than a bit of children's literature, and with illustrations to boot! I'm no artist, but I had a blast doing something creative outside of stringing words together. I could see myself trying something like this again, but let me tell you, I have a lot to learn about crafting stories for kids. It's no easy feat and my hat is off to those that make a career of it.

I Mustache You a Question

Statistics

Synopsis: A covert artificial intelligence unit wakes up to find itself in the middle of a strange winter.

Word Count: 2,600

Genre: Sci-Fi

Completed Week: February 12th – February 17th

I Mustache You a Question

It was cold.

Colder than it really should have been.

Before the recent boot-up entries, the last timestamp on the environmental log files was seven minutes, thirty-two seconds, and six hundred and ninety-two milliseconds old. The associated temperature reading indicated a sweltering temperature of ninety-two degrees with seventy percent humidity.

The squat, synthetic mustache dialed back some of its limited power from the touch receptors and delivered a small surge to its auditory sensors. It listened to the wind whistle and crackle through its artificial bristles.

It then kicked off an internal diagnostic script in search of answers. At its reduced energy levels, that would take some time. Meanwhile, it attempted to build an encrypted tunnel to the home office.

Strange.

There were no active wireless communications signals with which to associate. It began to broadcast its own presence on a workgroup-level frequency in the hopes of making contact with allied machines in the vicinity.

I am facial apparatus, JSAM-2209. Level sixteen clearance. Send me your keypair using DOD Houdini public key encapsulation.

JSAM-2209 pulled up and reviewed what was available in its mission files. Its active memory cache had been cleared due to the unanticipated power-down, so it needed to stream the data from its onboard quantum storage. As data surged into its operative circuits, it recalled what it could until the full diagnostic and repair could be completed.

August 13th, 2032.

Washington D. C.

The date and location matched JSAM-2209's internal clock and last known position, but without the ability to sync up over the wireless, it could only assume that was still correct.

The mustache recalled that its courier had picked it up from an agent at the Churchill Hotel near Embassy Row. Once the mustache was secured to the courier's face, it directed the courier down Massachusetts Avenue. The two of them communicated through a near-band Silvertooth interface with the mustache only telling the courier what it needed to know at the moment. The reason JSAM-2209 existed in the first place was because couriers could not be trusted with the full set of classified information. Assuming they were not double agents in the first place, such an arrangement also limited what knowledge could be pulled from couriers in the event that they should undergo state-sponsored torture before their mission was carried out.

JSAM-2209's last known mission entry involved heading toward The Fairfax hotel lounge. It would have to wait for further progress on the file system repair for additional information. As of now, it could only hypothesize that the meeting with the informant had not gone as planned.

The mustache considered kicking off a Monte Carlo simulation in order to determine its next set of moves, but an approaching flutter had it forking more power to its visual and auditory sensors to determine the source.

Its 'eyes' were partially blocked by something, limiting its vision, but what it could see went a long way in explaining the frigidness detected on every nanofiber attached to its frame.

Endless piles of white snow and crystalline ice surrounded JSAM-2209, broken up only by cracks and shadows.

What it did not explain is how that climate failed to reconcile with the last known temperature reading or how there could be any snow at all during August in the nation's capital.

With the fluttering increasing in volume and purposeful puffs of air flowing over its whiskers, JSAM-2209 made a precautionary decision to turn off its radio broadcast.

A shadow was cast onto the snow, quickly growing in size until its origin made landfall.

The crow landed ten inches away, contrasting pointedly with the white background—black eyes, black beak, black feathers. Its tiny talons clacked on the icier patches of snow as it hopped toward JSAM-2209.

Nanoseconds after the mustache kicked off a secondary defense-planning process, it felt the sharp edges of the crow's beak clamp down on its exoskeleton while the rough taste buds of the crow's spear-like tongue probed the synthetic hairs.

The visual went from the outside world to internal anatomy as JSAM-2209's lens peered down the throat of the bird. It enabled the rear-facing camera, rarely used since it was useless when pasted to someone's face. JSAM-2209 was thankful for whichever engineer had the temerity and skill to get its implementation approved.

The tiny mustache felt itself being hoisted from the ground as its accelerometer output skyrocketed. Seeing the ground quickly depart was unsettling but enthralling at the same time. If it could smile, it would have—it had truly achieved a bird's-eye view of the world.

Not that such a world was much to look at. The altimeter told JSAM-2209 that they were settling in at around 428 feet from the surface and the blanket of white looked even more pervasive than it had from ground-level. But now the mustache could see man-made structures peeking out at the edges. Sharp corners of stone and metal edifices exposed themselves.

JSAM-2209 was helpless to do anything until the defense-planning task completed, so it checked the progress of the diagnostics. The procedure had been able to piece together fragments into larger fragments but had perhaps another hour to go before completing the picture.

The courier had apparently made it to the lounge. There were video sequences of him conversing with the informant who had been using the name Betty. She had reached out to the FBI, claiming to be a disaffected member of the New Day Syndicate. She had pressing information regarding...

Regarding...

Bits were still missing. JSAM-2209 would have to wait for further file repairs. The information must have been something important.

JSAM-2209 was *only* brought in if it was important.

The mustache wondered just how far the bird planned on taking it. It feared that if it was taken too far from its original location, its locator signal would be useless. It had to be conservative with available power.

Well-timed, the self-defense thread completed its processing and spit out a report. It did not recommend a complete self-destruct sequence. The danger was not yet there for such a drastic measure, but it did suggest that sending a surge of electricity to its hairs might be enough to shock the bird, thereby securing release. The only risk was potential damage from impact as the mustache fell from the sky. JSAM-2209 determined it was a necessary prospect.

The tiny mustache generated just enough milliamps for its purposes. Tiny electrical shocks leaped off the edges of its whiskers and made contact with the crow's beak. Instantly, the bird opened its beak and squawked. The tiny mustache's accelerometer readings skyrocketed again as the white earth approached. It could only hope that it would survive the fall.

As JSAM-2209 landed in a pile of fresh powder, it thanked its lucky circuits that the effects of the crash were minimal. The self-diagnostic was still running and all sensors were functioning as expected.

It didn't have long to enjoy its regained freedom, though. The fluttering sound returned and the mustache's eye caught the bird's shadow forming on the ground once more.

If JSAM-2209 had the ability to grow depressed, it would have done so. The possibility of determining the status of its mission, let alone doing something about it, appeared to be next to nil.

The crow's feet touched down a meter away and the mustache braced itself. Its battery was running at one-third capacity and it didn't have enough juice left for another shock without losing its ability to complete file recovery and broadcast a recovery signal. The thought of connecting up to a charging source was so distant as to be unrealistic, yet it yearned.

But there was little time to pine over the implausible. The crow hopped towards its prey. *Perhaps I could initiate the self-destruct sequence,* JSAM-2209 thought. But doing such a thing would serve no purpose. The mustache only existed to serve the government of the United States and it would experience no joy over making a black bird's head explode.

So it resigned itself and accepted the microscopic probability that the crow would deposit it unharmed at one of the FBI's data centers. It lowered power to its lenses and auditory sensors. It didn't need to expend the energy.

Almost a minute had passed when JSAM-2209 realized it was not being pecked at or carried away. It pumped more electricity back to its sensors and saw the crow dipping its bill into the snow two meters to the mustache's left.

The bird pulled its head up. Something stringy was hanging from its beak. The mustache zoomed in. Coated in frozen crimson blood appeared to be a bit of human flesh being rent from a larger piece.

A rapid series of loud crunching sounds came from behind the mustache. JSAM-2209 activated its rear-view camera and saw a large pair of boots, black and scratched, running towards it. There was nothing to do but observe as the feet flew overhead, narrowly avoiding coming down on top of the mustache.

The crow launched itself into the air, causing the strand of flesh to break loose from its beak and snap back to the earth. The bird cawed, sounding an upset cry over its lost meal.

"Damned scavenger!"

It was a woman's voice, hoarse, slightly muffled.

She bent down and JSAM-2209 realized that if he had not heard the voice, he would have been unable to determine her sex. She was a walking swaddle of clothing from head to toe, wearing a dirty gray ski jacket, three layers of multihued scarves wrapped around her neck and lower face, and dark goggles sitting tightly beneath a yellow beanie.

With mitten-covered hands, she scooped up piles of snow and began packing it down over where the crow had stood moments ago. The mustache watched her with curiosity. All indications were that she was alone. He'd hoped that he might garner information as to his precarious situation if he observed her.

She seemed satisfied after several more scoops and pats. She stood up and began walking back in the direction from which she'd come.

JSAM-2209 had a decision to make. If it sat idly by, it could become frozen over, damaging its operational capacity and any hope of ever being discovered. But could it take the chance of being absconded by a potential adversary who might know how to extract its data? The recovery process was nearly complete. Soon if would have more information, yet for what good if it wound up in the wrong hands?

In the worst case, the mustache would end its mission and self-destruct before that happened.

As the honeycomb pattern of the boot's outsole became visible overhead, the mustache emitted a series of beeping sounds. They were faint as its external speakers were small, meant only for use in emergencies when the Silvertooth connection could not be established.

Apparently, it was enough.

The footfalls came to a stop and JSAM-2209 heard the shoes grinding into the snow as they turned.

The covered face became enlarged as it approached the mustache. JSAM-2209 saw itself reflected in the tinted goggles.

"What in the world do we have here?"

The accelerometer went haywire once more as the mustache felt itself being gripped by the fuzzy mittens and lifted closer to the goggles.

"Hah!" the woman said. Closer now, her voice had a gravel edge.

There was motion again as the hand moved. Everything went dark and all sound dampened. The mustache determined it had been placed in a pocket.

For some time, it heard nothing but the dulled grinding of boots into snow and ice. And then there more voices. Male and female, young and old. There was laughter. There was shouting.

JSAM-2209's internal clock showed that twenty-two minutes, fifty-three seconds, and fourteen milliseconds passed before the world became visible once again. A calloused hand placed the mustache gently on a wooden table, revealing its owner as it was pulled back. She was a tired looking woman, perhaps fifty years in age with random sunspots and bags hanging like sooty sacks from a gaunt face. Her hair was completely gray and cropped close to her head.

The other camera left the mustache relieved to see something other than white. JSAM-2209 sat inside a tiny, brown room with a rusted tin roof reaching far overhead. The walls only reached halfway up and were covered with metal street signs and faded cardboard advertising foodstuffs and laundry detergent.

Surrounding the mustache was a multitude of items: There were piles of bottle caps, dirty soda jars, and magnets showing. Five plaster sculptures of the Lincoln Memorial, all chipped, lined the far edge of the table.

A man entered the room through a small doorway covered in hanging beads. He was bent over slightly, meandering towards the table. JSAM-2209 noticed the flesh on both of his arms was scarred over and his right hand was deformed, his fingers melded together to form a sort of two-pronged claw.

"Anything new today?"

"Funny you ask," the woman replied. Her eyes landed on JSAM-

2209.

He shuffled closer and picked it up with his thumb and index finger. He squinted and snarled his top lip. The mustache was grateful it didn't have the ability to smell as what was left of the man's brown teeth indicated oral hygiene was not a priority.

"What the hell is it?"

"What's it look like? It's one of them novelty mustaches we used to play with as kids."

The man spun the mustache around, examining every inch.

"Well, I'll be damned."

He reached into his pocket with his other hand and pulled out a yellow plastic object. "There's three more of these if that'll work for you."

The woman reached out and grabbed it.

"Uh-uh. Don't need no more PEZ dispensers. I already have some."

JSAM-2209's internal alarm indicated that the self-diagnostic was complete. The file system had fully recovered. It decided to multithread and read the remaining log entries while it was being manhandled.

"Yeah, but you don't have any of these. You only got the Looney Tunes characters. I got the whole set. It's the Simpsons. You remember the Simpsons?"

08132032:100122:INGRESS MSG: JSAM-2209. ABORT MISSION. ABORT MISSION.

"I lost interest after season thirty-seven."

08132032:100124:EGRESS MSG: INFORMANT DOWNLOAD IN PROGRESS.

The old man coughed. It sounded like one of his lungs was about to plop out onto the cement floor. "Who cares? These babies are in demand."

08132032:100130:INGRESS MSG: BETTY DECOY. ATTACK ON WEST COAST UNDERWAY. LOS ANGELES. SAN FRANCISCO. SEATTLE. SHUT DOWN ALL OPERATIONS AND ENTER HIBERNATION MODE.

The woman paused. "I'm gonna need another set. When's the last time you saw one of them mustaches? Bet you no one else 'round here has one."

08132032:100135:INGRESS MSG: CHICAGO REPORTING MASS CASUALTIES. DALLAS UNRESPONSIVE. ATLANTA COMMUNICATIONS SEVERED. WE REPEAT, SHUT DOWN OPERATIONS. ENTER HIBERNATION MODE TO AWAIT RESTART AND FURTHER INSTRUCTIONS.

The man grumbled something while he ran his thumb across JSAM-2209's bristles. He reached into his pocket and produced four more Simpsons PEZ dispensers. "Fine, fine," he said and gazed down at the mustache. "I'm gettin' ripped off here, but I got a certain affinity for this thing. Reminds me of my brother."

The woman grabbed the rest of the dispensers and nodded to the man. He turned to leave but then stopped. A smile crept across his face, big as a dimmed sun. He pressed JSAM-2209 against his upper lip and turned toward the woman.

"Hey, Tina."

"Huh?" she said as she looked up with an annoyed look on her face.

"I mustache you a question. Where were you when it happened?"

Process Summary

I Mustache You a Question is story number twenty-eight in the #52ShortStories challenge.

A few fun factoids regarding this whimsical tale of espionage:

- It was a years-old premise I'd resurrected from the dead. I was not as well-versed in the craft as I am now and I didn't have the guts to see it through. I was glad I did this time around. It may not be perfect, but that's part of the point—write it anyway! :)

- I made my first attempt at dictation. I knew that was something I'd have to tackle on the first day of writing as I couldn't imagine trying to wrangle my way around text I'd already written through such an unwieldy technology. It made sense to try and get the bare bones down and then take it from there. I have to say, I was both exasperated and impressed. The speech-to-text technology on a mobile phone is not there and I don't have the capability to implement Dragon Naturally Speaking software as I write with a Chromebook. I know there are services that will transcribe audio for you, but it seems a little costly for what I'm do-ing...I had initially planned on using the AI-powered Amazon Transcribe service, only to learn it's still in beta. So that meant I ended up stuck doing my own transcribing. Not sure if this was worth it, but I don't think I lost anything through the process. If anything, I learned I can talk a lot faster than

I can type. Not to say I kept all of the words, but I rarely do anyway. The benefit is I was able to get the skeleton in place and proceed from there. I'll definitely be trying this again in the future and looking for a way to streamline the process.

Overall, the story didn't have any dialogue until the end. Risky with casual readers, but it was fun. I've seen a lot of modern science-fiction taking this tack, so I wasn't too concerned since, if I submitted this for publication, I'd be putting it in front of the same audience.

PENPALS

Statistics

Synopsis: Chris Blankenship, burdened by an aimless life and another night of drug addiction, finds a familiar stranger knocking at his door.

Word Count: 3,400

Genre: Paranormal

Completed Week: February 18th – February 24th

Penpals

A gunshot or a backfire?

Didn't matter.

The odds were fifty-fifty in a Las Vegas ghetto east of the glittery Strip.

All that mattered was that it caused Chris Blankenship to contemplate the time projected across the ceiling by his alarm clock.

1:03 AM.

...and then...

1:04 AM.

...slowly followed by...

1:05 AM.

Sweat built up across every inch of his body. A brief wave of nausea threatened to send him head-first into the toilet, so he bolted up and rubbed his face. He reached across the nightstand to turn on the lamp, knocking over an empty *Dos Equis* bottle in the process. It thumped onto the carpet and rolled beneath his short twin bed.

Chris didn't have to man the flat top grill or fry station until swing-shift, but sleep was a fading prospect.

He placed his feet on the ground and stood, thankful that the wave of sickness seemed to have passed. Like a cat that stops meowing and starts purring, it was as if his body recognized it was going to get what it needed. Still, he knew it was only momentary.

The walk to his studio apartment 'living room' was a short five feet. Chris leaned over the aluminum lawn chair propped in front of an old tube television and grabbed the remote control. The TV zapped to life. Lucille Ball was going on and on with a woman about tulips.

On the floor beside the chair, almost everything was in its place—a new needle, some cotton balls, a piece of kite string, his *Mickey Mouse Zippo* lighter, and a plastic bag holding a tiny black rock that resembled a candied fig.

Chris walked another four feet into the 'kitchen' and pulled out all three drawers, scouring every nook for a clean spoon. There were butter knives, forks, even cheap take-out chopsticks. But for the life of him, he couldn't find one goddamn spoon.

His stomach lurched a little.

"Fuck!" he screamed. "Where the *fuck* are all of the spoons?"

He groaned and looked at a half-eaten can of *Spaghettios* with a utensil sticking out. He smiled and yanked it out, only to find another fork. The fork flew violently into the sink and the back wall almost took on a coat of *Campbell's* red sauce before Chris calmed down, noticing the lid hanging on by a tiny strand of metal.

If he could carefully bend the edges and form a trough, it would probably work.

No, it would most definitely work.

He grabbed the lid, twisting it from the can when someone knocked on his door.

"Gah!"

The razor-sharp edge of the metal cut into his index finger. He jammed the bleeding appendage into his mouth. The taste of blood made him even more nauseous. He stood still and sucked quietly.

Anyone knocking on his door at this time of night had to be stoned off his ass or the world's worst thief. It could have been a friend dealing with an emergency, but that thought was easily dismissed—Chris had no friends, and if he did, he would probably be the last person from whom they'd seek help.

He ignored the knock, hoping the idiot would go away. He quietly resumed his quest by pressing the edges of the lid against the counter until they bent in compliance, only taking a few seconds here and there to wipe the snot from his nose and the sweat from his forehead.

Another set of knocks. This time louder. More insistent.

As he pressed the lid into the off-white countertop tile, it slipped from his hand and fell onto the floor.

The knocking continued unabated.

"Go the *fuck* away, junkie!" he hollered at the door.

It had no effect.

Chris didn't have the patience to deal with this. He stormed over to the door and peeked through the peephole to see who he was going punch out.

White light from the balcony lamp made Chris squint a little, but the knocking stopped and a woman looked back at him, somehow making direct contact with her hazel eyes. Black eyeshadow ran down her cheeks and her jet-black, pixie-cut hair was plastered to her head like she'd been standing in the rain. She wore an equally dark felt coat with high, pointed collars. The dusky shades stood in stark contrast to her pale and freckled face, not to mention the fact that it was a hot July night without a cloud in the sky.

Something about that face struck him as being familiar.

Was she one of the many neighbors that he'd mutually ignored over the six months he'd been living here? Maybe she was a regular customer at *Burger City?*

The somewhat anxious look on her face triggered an uneasy thought: Maybe she was another one of Marco's customers and had trailed him here at some point. Maybe she really *was* here to take his meager supply.

"Christopher," she said. "Open the door. Please."

Chris's lips parted. How did she know his name? He'd never given it to Marco. She *had* to have seen him working at the fast food joint. That's the only place where his full name was in plain sight, pinned to his uniform.

"I don't have anything you want," he yelled through the thick wood. His fingers confirmed the deadbolt was turned and the chain was dragged across the track. "You're wasting your time." Beads of sweat built up across his forehead again. His chest ached. He wanted to turn back and look for the pasta lid, but her eyes exuded a sort of sparkle that hypnotized him.

"I'm not here to rob you." She unleashed a cute smile and raised her small, white hands, rotating them in a Queen Elizabeth-style wave.

Chris felt his warm, putrid breath reflected back at him from the door.

"I'm here to help you," she said.

The number of things telling him not to open the door were piling up, yet he felt his fingertips twisting the deadbolt knob. Maybe it was those kind eyes. Maybe it was the change in routine—the curiosity of it all. Nobody ever came to visit, and except for his parents who had since given up on any relationship, no one had ever combined the words 'help' and 'you' and sent them in his direction.

Chris swung open the door until the chain pulled taut. She stood at maybe five-five. The smell of wet dog drifted off her jacket. He looked down at her hands which were now hanging loosely and innocuously at her side, weapon-free.

"What do you want?" he said, making eye contact once more. He found he didn't want to stop looking into those hazel marbles. They warmed him like a familiar blanket.

No, Chris thought. Like something better. Like the feeling of a speedball after the coke exits the system and the heroin eases the comedown. That erasure of energy replaced with pure tranquility. His mouth began to water and he craned his neck back quickly just to make sure the lid had not moved.

"It's me. Melina."

That name. He mouthed it silently. Sticky white stuff formed strands between his chapped lips as he tried to place it. Why did that name not just disappear into the ether, but instead bounce around his head looking for a patch of memory on which to settle?

"Why are you here?" he asked.

Melina focused her well-manicured eyebrows. "I'm here to help you." She leaned onto her tippy-toes and tried to peek over Chris's head. "Are you going to let me in or are you going to let me freeze on your doorstep all night?"

He found it hard to imagine her freezing on such a sultry night. The fears that she was another user returned. Maybe she thought she could exchange her body for some of his candy. Right now, Chris had only one thing on his mind and it wasn't sex.

"I don't need help," he said. "You got the wrong guy."

"Yes, Christopher, you do. Please, let's just talk." Melina crossed her arms and shivered, twisting her head around as if something were chasing her. "I don't have a lot of time."

Chris quickly shut the door and leaned his back against it. He could almost feel the pulsating heat of her presence on the other side. Why was he so out of breath? Every hair on his body stood on end as he took a moment to think things through.

He eyed the half-bent lid sitting impatiently on the ground, imagining that he could hear it calling his name, taunting him like so many people he'd known in life. For some reason, he began to despise it just as he'd come to despise the people. His hands flew to his face. If he wasn't adamant about keeping his nails clipped, he would have drawn blood with the forcefulness of his grip.

I swear I don't know her, yet there's something...

He grunted in frustration and turned around, fumbling the chain out of its track.

As the door swung open, Melina smiled widely showing beautiful white teeth. If she was a junkie, she'd be one of the rare few that kept up her dental hygiene.

"Thank you," she said, stepping inside.

Chris wasn't sure what to do after he shut the door. His place was barely accommodating enough for him, let alone guests. All he had to offer was a practically empty pantry, a messy bed, and a single lawn chair.

Shit.

He panicked and lunged for a dish towel sitting on the counter.

"I don't normally have company," he said, rushing toward his exposed paraphernalia, covering the gear in a single fell swoop and scooping it up into his arms. "Let me just straighten up a little."

Melina stood in front of the door. Chris could feel her watching him zip back and forth. It made him uncomfortable, but he did his best to ignore it. As he placed the towel in a corner of the room and turned around, Melina was holding the metal lid between her fingers. She extended it toward him.

"Oh, thanks," he said, grabbing it. "I, uh…was just making dinner." He nervously tossed it into the trash can, wincing as he did so.

Her mouth never moved, but her eyes said that he was a bullshit artist and they both knew it.

Why did I let her in here?

Now, they stood awkwardly while the *I Love Lucy* theme song played in the background. Melina stepped up to him, licked her thumb, and rubbed it over his cheek.

Besides the microscopic tremors occurring over his entire body, he did not move. The wet-clothing smell was now combined with that of a floral shop.

She pulled back and said, "You had some blood there."

Blood? Chris had forgotten all about his finger. The pain came throbbing back as he remembered touching his face. He grabbed a napkin that was sitting beside the sink and wrapped it around the cut.

His impatience grew as his nervousness grew.

"I'm sorry—Melina? I feel like I know you, but I can't place you. What is it you think I need help with at one o'clock in the morning?" As much as he was intrigued by her mysterious presence, he was wondering how quickly he could fish the lid out of the trashcan and unbundle his kit after she left.

She reached into her coat.

Idiot. She does have a gun and she's here to take my shit. She was only waiting to get inside.

Chris's current foggy condition left him debilitated and still wondering if he could knock her down before it was too late, when her hand emerged gripping an aged, yellowed envelope.

"Here," she said. "Maybe this will jog your memory."

Chris hesitated for a moment, but reached for the envelope and read the front. His name and boyhood address were at the top left. The name Melina Scotti was written in the middle just above an address in Allentown, Pennsylvania. It was all in Chris's handwriting.

He looked up at her.

One of her canine teeth peeked out slightly from her close-lipped smile.

So familiar.

"Open it," she said.

Chris opened the unfastened flap and pulled out a folded piece of paper. It was the same ruled yellow notepad paper his mom use to bring home in bulk from her office job. It was stained on the edges and the folds had been carved in place with time, but just like on the envelope, he recognized the handwriting as his own.

As he read through the contents, it felt like cracks spreading rapidly across an aged dam. Fluid visions began to spout until the cement crumbled away and a forceful wave of memories came rushing through. He'd written about how he'd found an abandoned *Redline* BMX bike and how he'd fixed it up, but forgot to tighten the handlebars to the frame. They came unhooked as he launched off a dirt jump, but he survived—just a few scratches. He'd asked if Melina had gotten the new pair of *L.A. Gear* shoes that she kept pining over. Then there was a joke about him sneaking into a suitcase at the airport so he could fly out to Pennsylvania and meet her in person.

The letter was dated after his signature: *Christopher Blankenship, August 13th, 1990.*

Chris was in the seventh grade then. He had been paired up with Melina through a pen pal program that his teacher, Mrs. Baker, had introduced to their class. He recalled being utterly thrilled at the notion of talking with someone on the other side of the country, especially since almost every kid within his limited world only seemed intent on kicking his ass or shunning him entirely.

They'd exchanged Polaroid photos when they first started writing. It was those hazel eyes which he remembered most.

A lump developed in his throat. He whispered her name and she nodded slowly. There was a list of more important, more relevant questions he could ask, but only one sprang immediately to mind.

"Why did you stop writing to me?"

The words barely squeaked through. It had been nearly fifteen years, but Chris felt like he was jumping back into a conversation that he'd left only moments ago.

"I didn't, Christopher." A subtle spasm crossed her face. "I swear I didn't. Things got bad."

"How bad could it have been for you to just cut me off—"

She put her finger to his lips. "Bad. I'd written more letters, but they never made it to you. Just like this one never made it to me."

Chris frowned and shook his head slightly.

"I didn't realize it until I took out the trash one day. There it was, removed from the mailbox and sitting in shreds at the bottom of the can."

"But who would do that?"

Melina's nostrils flared at the question. "My step-father."

Memories of Melina's other letters revealed themselves to Chris. Her mom had remarried after a bitter divorce and Melina did not get along with the new guy.

She continued, "He'd always been an asshole, but I found out he would read my original letters, then reseal them and send them. I guess he'd had enough of my complaining after a while and put a stop to it altogether. I confronted him about it and things spiraled out of control from there."

Chris felt as if his brain would overheat. There was so much to think about, but a new question burned foremost in his mind.

"How did you find me?"

There was a momentary pause. Melina looked as if she was formulating a very careful answer. "That's complicated, but after all of these years, there's still an unsevered connection that formed between us." She focused on the towel crumpled in the corner of the room. "I don't want to see you go any further down a dark road."

Chris grew suddenly defensive. "You don't know anything about me."

"No," she said, "I know *everything* about you now." She lifted her hand to his cheek again and stroked it gently. "You were always so kind and open to me. You comforted me when my parents split up and boosted my confidence when it was low."

Now she frowned.

"And yet you never said anything about your own problems."

Paranoia set in and Chris didn't know if she was being figurative or literal. How could she know anything about his own private hell when he'd worked so hard to keep it from his letters. His lack of friends and his own father blaming him for not taking the initiative to change himself so that he *could* make friends—these were things he sought to escape, not discuss.

Tiny palpitations in his body turned violent and he shook visibly.

"Please go," he said.

To his surprise, she didn't seem hurt or angry.

"Okay, Christopher. I'll leave, but can I ask one last favor?"

Anything to get her moving. He couldn't take much more of this overwhelming situation without collapsing onto the floor.

"What?"

She moved her hand from his cheek to the back of his head and pulled him toward her. Their lips met and Chris's first thought was how horrible his breath must be. Still, she didn't seem to mind and he didn't resist. Experiencing her so close to him measured up with any recent high that he could recall.

It wasn't a sensual kiss, but their lips were pressed together for what seemed an eternity. Something was happening in Chris's head—visions of Melina's life came to him like scenes from a movie, mixing with his own memories.

He saw himself sitting at his parents' old dining room table, the pencil's eraser held to his lips while he pondered over the yellow lined paper.

Then there she was, looking as young as he remembered. She was smiling as she lay stomach-down across her bed, kicking her legging-covered feet in the air while she read one of his letters.

Next, Chris was arguing with his father who insisted he take up football—repeating that if he didn't make friends, at least he wouldn't be such a pussy.

But then he cringed at the next scene—Melina's tiny hands flying up to defend herself against an onslaught of hairy, brutish fists raining down on her—their owner, an older man screaming at her for trying to turn her mother against him. In the background, a woman stood watching in silence.

Chris was in his apartment, disheveled and passed out on the lawn chair. Drool trickled down his chin while a piece of twine strangulated his bicep.

Finally, there was a scene of Melina as she appeared now—wearing her black felt coat beneath a bright moon, standing atop an old, wooden railroad bridge separating chunks of dense forest. Her cheeks were stained with black eyeshadow and she peered down into a shimmering river, raising her arms as if they were wings, leaning forward until her feet detached from the rails.

The visions stopped and all was dark.

Chris slowly opened his eyes to find himself leaning into the air, his apartment door slightly ajar. He rushed outside. The only semblance of life was an old man in a ratty white tank-top, pushing an overflowing shopping cart along the sidewalk below the *Palm Oasis* apartment complex.

Chris's chest began to ache again, but this time for other reasons. He ambled back into his studio.

There was an emptiness there, as there had always been, but this time it seemed different. He looked at the lumpy towel in the corner of the room. The image of what lie beneath made him nauseous again, not because he craved it, but now because he felt an utter disdain. He ran across the room and grabbed the pile as if it were a ticking bomb. He jammed it into the trashcan on top of the *Spaghettios* lid, zipped up the trash bag, and tossed it outside in the dumpster.

It was still dark outside and police sirens were going off in the near distance, but for the first time in his life, Chris felt a sense of control.

Process Summary

Penpals is story number twenty-nine in the #52ShortStories challenge.

Certain images have been popping up in my head as of late—mainly flashbacks of things I knew in my childhood which are now obsolete due to the march of technology.

Things like penpals.

Yeah, the Internet has pretty much obliterated that concept.

I had a penpal in junior high that was from Pennsylvania. No bones about it, I was the world's *worst* penpal. After a few letters in, the initial thrill wore off and I realized just how much I didn't like taking time away from playing football and *Streetfighter* with friends.

Here I was, more pen *punk* than penpal, leaving this wonderful, sweet girl on the other end of the country, hanging. She even sent me a nice hat from a local amusement park she'd visited.

Just chalk it up to another cringe-worthy event in life.

Anyway, I thought about how some similar penpal relationships might play out and *Penpals* was the result. Most of us (should) change drastically from what we were as young boys and girls and I imagine some headed down darker roads than others. But there would always be that bond created during the formative years that would only be one fuzzy memory away.

Reviewing the initial outline in my scratch file, I listed a lot of really dumb ideas before I hit on the final (hopefully not-dumb) idea.

I would love to hear your thoughts and experiences regarding something similar that's disappeared from your modern lifestyle.

509

HOBO LILLY

Statistics

Synopsis: A hobo travels the freight ships of the galaxy looking for her daughter.

Word Count: 3,000

Genre: Sci-Fi

Completed Week: February 25th – March 3rd

NOTE: This story won Semi-Finalist in Quarter 2 of 2018 in the Writers of the Future contest.

Hobo Lilly

I swear, as the blade's tip grazed my cornea, I saw Lilly.

Not in reality—she wasn't on this cramped freighter—but in my mind.

My daughter was still five, swishing that long blonde ponytail in the air as she bolted out from behind her father's leg and toward my open arms. He was spitting venom through the same brown eyes by which our daughter expressed nothing but love. I could smell the flowery shampoo in her hair as I told her to be a good girl and that because mommy and daddy were going their separate ways, it didn't mean mommy didn't love her. I wasn't strong enough to tell her the truth, so I told her I'd see her soon. We rubbed our noses together. I called it our special little bunny kiss.

I knew it would be a long time before we'd meet again.

The warm vision was temporarily knocked away by sweat-filled hair slapping against my cheek, stinging as I ducked my opponent's follow-up swing. On instinct, I thrust my own knife toward her rib cage.

Contact.

Not deep, but contact.

She shrieked and I nearly tumbled forward. The nylon rope binding us together dug into my left wrist as my opponent danced backward. My left foot skidded lightly against the corrugated steel floor in the struggle to remain upright. If I fell, I would have milliseconds to recover my exposed neck.

I didn't need to see the blood pooling onto her tank top to know I'd wounded her. I had *felt* the tiny chunk being taken out of her. Even in the dim lights of the freighter cabin, the crooked lines on her face spoke fury over the insult.

"Bitch, you got balls, but you should've picked another ride," she said.

I let her keep on.

Waste your breath, I thought. Keep swinging.

She came at me like a berserker of old. I remembered to breathe on tempo. Every lunge, every parry tested my abilities of concentration and patience. It wasn't long before I saw my opportunity, though. I could hear her panting and gasping over the crowd. She started looking away, growing more disengaged with every jab.

I yanked my left arm back just as she was mid-thrust, sending her on a collision course for the twenty or so grimy, cheering faces surrounding us. Like a swirling mass, they shifted as we shifted. I swept my right foot across her shins and watched her arms fly in the air in an attempt to cushion her descent. When her elbows cracked against the hard ground, the blade slipped from her hand. It clinked as it tumbled end-over-end and was quickly snatched up by the hand of an anonymous spectator. I climbed on top of her, took a handful of sticky black hair, and held my blade to her throat.

I dipped my head to her ear and whispered, "I win."

She struggled to regain her wind, but when she finally did, she started to laugh—harder and harder until the laughter turned into a coughing fit.

There was no more resistance in her now.

I rose and hovered over her, letting her turn onto her back. She looked older than when she'd first challenged me for twenty credits and now I felt a twinge of embarrassment. The sweat had cleared away some of the dirt on her cheeks and beneath her eyes, unveiling a map of wrinkles and dark circles on her chiseled face. I extended an open hand. She accepted and I hid

the reaction to the pain in my own body as I struggled to pull her back onto

her feet.

"Bitch, you got balls," she said, handing me a cryptocard with one

hand, pressing her shirt against her wound with the other.

* * *

I pulled out a pocketbook of The Matron's essays and began to

reread my favorite—*On Suffrage and Humanity's Value*. The e-paper had a large

crack running through the middle, but someone once said beggars shouldn't

be choosers—especially one that doesn't beg at all.

"You going to dig on Staxis or hop on another hauler?"

Iona was her name.

All I wanted to do was read and fall asleep doing so, but that wasn't

going to happen. A woman who was willing to mortally wound me minutes

ago was set on being pals. That's just the way it is on the loader ships.

"Not sure," I said.

There was no real point in hiding my search for Lilly, but it was a

family matter and I always kept such affairs close to the vest. Most of the ho-

bos riding on these freighters were here for two reasons, and depending who

you talked to, in different proportions:

One, they were running away from the rest of the universe—after

all, that's how I ended up hoboing across the galaxy in the first place. I had

to leave a man who'd pulled a one-eighty on me. As soon as he was close to

'being someone' in the system, there was no room for my differing viewpoint.

My story was only one flower from the same garden of motives the hoboes pulled from.

Two, the work was steady so long as your body was. Governments had encouraged exploration of the galaxy's far reaches by promising mineral wealth to those willing to seek it out. Entrepreneurs jumped on the prospect and with most of their money spent on logistics, mining robots were an unnecessary expense—hungry humans were cheap and reliable enough.

All that said, no one needed to know my next job was more than a means to a meal.

Over the years, I'd tracked my little girl through the networks, keeping a motherly eye on her whenever I could. There were times when I'd tipped back too many bottles of *Stardust*, almost convinced that I should finally meet her in person. I never gave into the temptation. Why would she want to see me? The woman who'd given up on her twelve years ago? How to explain that her father had grown tired of my dangerous ideas, had it out for me, and that the only way to make a life for myself was to strike out on my own?

It wasn't until I learned that she'd taken up hoboing that my heart broke enough to seek mending. Had she known that was the road her mother had chosen? Thought it was some romantic and poetic adventure?

I prayed that wasn't the case, but I remember being seventeen once too.

Through years of developed personal connections and searching through the hobo bulletin systems, I learned she was last seen on Staxis six months ago.

That's was the final kick in my ass.

That's why I'm here.

Fighting.

Reading.

Occasionally trying to sleep.

"I killed a girl at the last gig," Iona said.

I don't know what sort of reaction she expected out of me.

"I felt bad," she continued on, apparently not expecting anything at all but a willing ear. "Didn't meant to, but I caught her trying to brute-force the passkey on my credit account two planets ago. I took a rock to the side of her head and musta' hit the sweet spot."

I didn't even look at her but I nodded, worried that Lilly would try something similarly stupid with another hobo. There were at least two or three Iona's working every gig and sometimes you couldn't tell who it was until it was too late.

Iona droned on about an ex-girlfriend who refused to share food. I closed my eyes and tried to fall asleep, hoping to dream of my little girl.

* * *

I was too late.

She'd moved on three-and-a-half weeks ago to Persephone.

When I'd last been to that dim planet, it was a place where the telorite rock was hard and the people were harder. I'd done a small stint there when I first started. It's not that it was too trying on my bones, though it was, but I left because the library was shit. People were encouraged to jack into whatever period piece drama was being broadcast on the spectrum or else spend their leisure time smoking opiates and screwing. I tried to organize them, get them reading, listening, but that's when I learned that one can't play a long game too quickly, otherwise you're sure to lose.

As soon as I got word about Lilly, I boarded the next freighter headed that way. It was only a day's travel, but having skipped work and therefore, skipped meals, it felt like a week.

At the back of the car, I sat down against any empty spot, one that least smelled of piss, and once again pulled out my pocketbook. I looked forward to picking up where I had left off, but the rumble in my stomach made it difficult to concentrate. It took only thirty or so seconds for my mind to wander toward my little girl. Would she look similar? Have the same features—the button nose, the single dimple on her left cheek that only showed up with her mischievous smile? I found no recent images tied to her name, so I could only guess and ask around when it came time to identify her.

"This is a hell of a noisy bunch."

The bearded interruption was bent over slightly at the waist. His knees popped as he slowly dropped to the floor beside me.

I tried to ignore him and continue reading. He twisted his head left and right before his bloodhound eyes finally landed on my book.

"Never saw much use in that."

I sighed. There would be no peace.

"Much use in what?"

"That. Readin'," he said. "Anything you learn from whatever's in there won't do you no good when some hunk of wires already knows it all just as soon as it's switched on."

I shoved the book back into my pocket, fully taking in the know-it-all. He was younger than his body and crusty beard let on. Behind the kinked brown hairs was a surprisingly smooth and unblemished face. He may actually have been close to Lilly's age.

"What makes you think I'm looking to challenge a machine?"

He raised his eyebrows, unsure of how to answer. "Just seems a waste of time, that's all. Wouldn't you rather have a conversation? Seems like one of the few things that can't be taken away from us."

How to explain what kind of conversation I valued? That every time I read a good book, I *was* having a conversation. It was already obvious that I wasn't going to find anything equal in him. Maybe the Matron had it all wrong. The more I got to know people, the less I got to like them.

Still, there was nowhere for me to go and even though I was a little sour on the inside, I made an effort to be a little sweeter on the outside. After all, each of us was on the same train, so to speak.

"How long have you been traveling?" I asked.

"This is my third gig. I hear Persephone pays the best."

I didn't have the heart to tell him that in his condition, he wasn't going to last three days.

"They're fair," I said. "You travel alone?" I asked though the answer was obvious.

"Yeah," he said and his head dropped down between those ramshackle knees of his. "I had some friends, at first, but most of 'em seem to be satisfied taking the same routes."

"What about you?"

He looked up and apprised the crowd surrounding him. "Nah, I have more of a sense of adventure than them."

He hadn't been able to keep up and I felt a pinch of sorrow for him.

"Just remember, life's more than credits."

The kid nodded slowly, but I recognized the look. He wasn't listening anymore. Second-guesses and regrets clouded his mind.

I took my book and handed it to him. He looked at me. "I told you—"

"In case you change your mind," I said.

* * *

Persephone station was teeming with bodies of every shape and size. Beneath the everdark skies, a mix of hoboes and vendors crowded the platform. Smells of synthetic lamb turning on spits sent my belly into a frenzy. I could spend the credits I'd won from Iona, but I'd been around the block enough to know that it was wiser to save them for when I really needed them. Though I'd hit what many would feel were desperate times, I knew better.

I knew desperate.

Just before I'd stepped out of the ship and onto the planet, I saw the young man still sitting by himself at the back of the emptied freighter, his eyes still maintaining that vacuous look, fingers gripping the pocketbook tightly.

Even if I wanted to, there was nothing I could do for him.

I checked the e-boards at the station to see if I'd received any updates to my queries.

Nothing. This was Lilly's last known spot. From here on out, I'd have to take matters into my own calloused hands.

I walked into the assignment office and stood in line with the rest of the weary souls. It took nearly two hours for me to reach the front where a tiny, fat man stood on a wooden stool that looked like it may tip over at any moment. And when I say tiny, I mean tiny—he couldn't have been more than four feet tall. Cobweb-thin strands of hair ran across his bald head and he wore a monocle over his right eye.

When I made no motion for the scanner sitting on the counter, he spoke robotically without peering up from his terminal.

"Arm."

"Manual," I replied.

That made him look. I could practically see the silvery orb focus in and out from behind the monocle. He sighed deeply.

"Number."

I rattled off my hobo code and a moment later, my photo came up. He scrutinized the screen. Then he scrutinized me.

"Ho ho!" A smile crossed his face, looking out of sorts. "A vet? A survivor?" He looked around the room as if any of the weary souls cared to listen to him. His eyes returned to mine and he leaned forward, balancing gracefully on the stool. "And you came back, *why?*"

"I'm looking for someone."

"We don't provide detective services," he replied quickly, "only work."

"Her name is Lilly."

There were grumbles behind me from hungry, impatient people. "What's the hold-up!?" someone shouted a few feet back.

"Can't help you," the fat man said, returning his eyes to the terminal. "You're assigned sector 12-B. Since you've ridden this rocket before, I don't need to tell you to dress warmly, make sure—"

I pulled out the cryptocard on which I carried my credits and slapped it down in front of him. Hoboes are typically in the system, but cryptocards are used for private transactions—they're exchangeable, but when properly configured, untraceable. He looked up again, eyebrows raised, and swiftly fingered the card. He turned it in his hand as his monocle whirred and whizzed. Finally, he jammed it into his own coat pocket.

"What's the name again?"

"Lilly," I repeated.

He raised an eyebrow. "Not much better than John Smith…" His fingers slid across the screen.

After a moment, he asked "Do you know when she signed in?"

"Three-and-a-half weeks ago."

"And you know her, how?"

"She's my daughter," I replied.

It was most definitely foolish to tell him, but I was so close to finding her.

Now, he raised his other eyebrow and looked up at me. I saw his fingers land on his coat pocket, tapping, hesitating. Finally, he reached in, pulled out the cryptocard and slid it back across the counter.

"She's in Elysium Garden."

* * *

The park was two miles away. I was shaking and panting as I ran the whole way. My legs felt detached. My head pounded. Why I was in such a hurry, I didn't know.

I finally collapsed onto my knees, ignoring the jarring pain.

She was there, all right.

I saw her name spelled out in stones. The third 'L' had shifted due to someone's careless boots, but the truth was undeniable. Someone had cared enough about her to leave the traditional trinkets—deathcharms—around the grave.

I wanted to scream, but my voice was stuck in my throat. Tears refused to leave their ducts. All I had was a scorching numbness flowing over every inch of skin. I fell forward onto the mound and rubbed my nose into the dirt.

Our special little bunny kiss.

And then the tears flowed and I cried so hard that I couldn't breathe. I would have been quite the sight, had anyone actually visited this 'garden' of dust and short-lived memories.

I clawed at the dirt beneath me, feeling it run through my fingers. And then those fingers found something else. I rolled over and saw the tip of what appeared to be an old paper book sticking out from the soil. Another trinket, but one that had been buried just below the surface.

I pulled at it, ready to place it among the other deathcharms when I paused. First I wiped my eyes, and then I wiped the dust from the cover and realized why the book had been hidden.

On Suffrage and Humanity's Value.

My knuckles turned white and I started to cry again. A mix of pride and anger burned inside me.

I knew that Lilly couldn't die in vain.

I turned and looked through the gates of Elysium Garden, toward the long, straight road that led to sector 12-B.

I was in the system now.

I had work to do.

Process Summary

Hobo Lilly is story number thirty in the #52ShortStories challenge.

I love it when I get to a story where everything slips into its proper place. The words are flowing, the influences and ideas undergo rapid gestation, and there seems to be nothing standing in my way…if you're a writer, you know this feeling.

You also know how rare it is.

Though I hope the good times will keep on rollin', after story #30, I've wised up enough to know the dark times be a'comin' once again. So I'll just savor the moment and take Walt Whitman's advice from the poem I posted last Friday:

Happiness not in another place, but this place…not for another hour, but this hour.

But I feel like, with this story, I'm beginning to find my voice as a writer. I've by no means found it, but everything just felt…right. Hard to describe, but I wouldn't be surprised to look back at some point in my career and see this story as a potential turning point.

Or maybe that's all just nonsense.

The seed for this particular tale was planted by the Louis L'Amour memoirs I recently finished. He'd spent time in his youth hoboing about and you can read quite a bit about that in a scan of the particular pages discussing it (check the scratch file linked to below).

I've also been reading Edith Hamilton's *Mythology*, refreshing myself on classic Greek mythology. This lit the general theme of the protagonist looking for her daughter (see the tale of Demeter and Persephone).

Why is it all occurring in the future and outer space? Why not. No deep reasoning there. Just sounded fun.

DEVILLEAF

Statistics

Synopsis: An advisor to the king is blackmailed into poisoning him. Will he see it through?

Word Count: 3,300

Genre: Fantasy

Completed Week: March 3rd – March 28th

Devilleaf

Beneath the king's oak table, Lurian rolled the smooth glass vial filled with powdered *devilleaf* in his palm. He thumbed its cork stopper, nervously confirming that it hadn't fallen out, and with it, any chance of saving his own neck from the king's chopping block. In truth, if he did not proceed with the girl's demand, the chopping block would be a charity compared to what he'd likely face.

He focused on the empty cup at the far end of the table. Between Lurian and the jeweled goblet sat silver platters overflowing with the king's favorites — sweetmeats from the game warden's private stock, piles of salted almonds, and Marsinian grapes. He recalled a time many years ago when the two of them were nearly caught behind enemy lines at Marsinia, all because the then-prince insisted on stealing barrels of a finer vintage then their regiment had in stock.

A cough made Lurian nearly leap out of his skin, but he was well practiced in hiding surprise. Stanislo, the silent, crooked-nose cupbearer, hovered above, giving Lurian one of his rude looks while holding two brass pitchers of wine in his hands. In the hierarchy of things, Stanislo's official status was below that of Lurian, but he'd been in service to the king at least a decade longer. Admittedly, the servant took impudence to a talented level— one couldn't outright accuse him of being excessively bold. He had a slippery way about him, like that of a sidewinding snake. Lurian would have been within rights to be jealous of the lackey's talents, but he had his own by which to make up for them.

"The king is very tired this evening," Stanislo said, touching up Lurian's goblet with the weaker crimson wine. "It would be well not to keep him late."

Maybe he shouldn't be late, himself, Lurian wanted to say, but if he was going to potentially lose his head, it wouldn't be due to a trivial, spiteful statement.

Instead, he smiled. "Of course." Killing a man he had come to view almost as a brother was not something Lurian wanted to do, but to be rid of Stanislo? That might actually be a pleasure. He watched the cupbearer glide to the other side of the table and pour from the king's personal stock into the empty cup. Their eyes never left each other, as if the servant was trying to pry into Lurian's soul.

Stanislo walked through the wooden double doors and closed them gently behind him, disappearing into the hall. Lurian was alone now in the imposing dining room, leaving him to do the thing which he did not wish to do. He slept little the previous night, searching for a way out. One night was not enough time, but that was all the king's daughter had given him.

Slip this into his cup tomorrow evening. I'll take care of the rest.

Her speech still echoed in his ear. The moment he heard those words, Lurian felt as if his heart had stopped beating and never started again.

He pushed his chair back. The skidding sound was absurdly loud. He stood and waited for the doors to swing open, but there was no indication of the king's arrival. Sweat beaded on his forehead. The vial nearly fell from his wet palms.

A part of him was still unbelieving of the words which had left the princess's lips, but he had no way to prove the truth. Her word against his? She had insisted he drink with her. What drugs were slipped into his own cup, he had no idea, but he found himself out of sorts, unable to focus and resist as she took advantage of him. The very idea that she would claim that *he* raped *her* outraged him, and alone would be enough to seal his fate, but that she would also claim to be carrying his child? That ensured an unpleasant exit from this world.

She promised him a position if he cooperated, but who was to say that she would not accuse him of committing the treachery alone after the king fell into the long sleep? That was a very real threat, but in Lurian's position, there seemed to be no good option.

He longed for the days when he had been a minor noble; before he had impressed the king with his performance in battle; before he had become very close to him and eventually made an advisor. He wished he had been as much of a student of domestic history as he was of warmaking and trade. Maybe then he would have foreseen the lengths that those in the royal family would go to seize power.

"Damn it, man, just go," he whispered, realizing he'd been standing still for some time.

But his legs wouldn't carry him forward. The king's cup of wine sat, both compelling and repulsing him. Heavy winds outside of the castle rushed through tiny cracks in the stone walls, creating a low whistle in one corner of the room.

Lurian was unsure how much time passed between his standing and waiting, but it was clearly too long. He was still on his feet, undecided, when there was a brief bustle of noise outside of the doors. Lurian pocketed the vial as the pair of heavy oak planks swung open and an obviously exhausted King Jorn entered the room.

* * *

The king was slouched in his chair, popping almonds into his mouth, one by one.

"No, tonight is fine," he replied.

Lurian had politely suggested postponing their meeting for the following night. The king's tired state provided a potential out. It was a gamble. Lurian would beg the princess for patience. It was only one more night, after all.

But, alas, the king would not hear of it.

Now Lurian was finding his ability to poison the king severely hampered. How could he do it while he was in the room? He cursed himself for letting the opportunity slip.

"Give me the latest," the king said as his lips smacked.

"Do you want to hear about the markets first or reports from the ambassadors?"

"The important things."

Lurian knew that, but he was stalling for time, trying to think of potential distractions. Maybe he could get the king drunk enough to not notice a subtle slip of the poison. Lurian picked up his goblet and raised it in a toast. "To the important things," he said. The king smiled and followed suit.

"Get on with it," he said.

Even though Lurian had assassination on his mind for the past twenty-four hours, he'd still managed to prepare talking points for the king.

"Travian sends word that the marauders from the Bexton Hills have been taken care of. They'll no longer be pillaging our primary wheat supply."

The king released a gaping yawn. "And how has this been confirmed?"

"The band's head, Sibea the Bold, has been taken care of. His various body parts rest on pikes outside the town—covered in thorns to keep the carrion off, of course. The rest of his tribe are working under the lash and sun to maintain the very fields in which they plundered, of course."

The king released a low chuckle and popped an almond into the air, leaning back, hoping to catch it in his mouth, but instead missing by several inches where it bounced and clacked onto the cold stone floor below. He grunted and took another pull of wine.

"Tell me, Lurian, what are we going to do with all of these upstarts?"

Lurian scrunched his eyebrows. "The Bexton clans were only a nuisance, your Lord—"

"I'm not talking about them," the king interrupted. "I'm talking about the enemies *within.*"

Lurian tried his best to keep the blood from rushing to his face.

King Jorn continued, "A king is always aware that the world is filled with plotters and schemers and they're rarely far away."

Had word gotten to the king? Was he trying to get Lurian to confess?

"Your Highness, I'm your man for foreign affairs and the merchant trades. Internal affairs, spycraft—these are a bit outside of my areas of expertise."

The king slammed his goblet on the table. "Damn it, man, but you have ears. Tell me, what do you hear?"

The room was heavy with silence. Lurian felt a lump caught in his throat.

"I've heard nothing, my Lord," he managed to squeak out. "Your kingdom is secure."

"Hmph," the king said, taking another swig of wine to wash down the almonds. He sank further back into his chair, his ruddy face looking pleased. "Good. I assume you'll keep me informed should the slightest hint come your way."

Lurian felt a bead of sweat slip down the front of his left ear. He was grateful the king was so far away.

"Of course," he said.

The king closed his eyes. "What else do you have to tell me?"

As Lurian went on about the affairs of state—the swiftly snuffed-out uprising in Southern Drakoria, the rising cost of wool imported from the Pahnus Isles—he noticed an odd sound reverberating within the dining room.

Lurian fell silent, and for thirty untenable seconds, he simply watched as the king's chest rose and fell in rhythm with his snoring. Lurian lurched slowly toward him. His eyes shifted between King Jorn and the doors until he was close enough to see the crumbs of almond nestled in the old man's gray beard.

He wouldn't get another chance. It was now or never.

Lurian reached into his pocket and pulled out the vial. He popped the cork, all the while keeping his eyes on the king. Was he ready to do this? Ready to kill the man who had seen his potential beyond being that of a mere knight, taken him under his wing and elevated him to his current station?

What type of kingdom would exist under the princess? She was a stubborn and emotional woman. To try and steer her would be like trying to quiet the Northern Blizzards. Then there was the question of whether or not

Lurian would live long enough to see her reign through the year's end.

He realized his hand was shaking to the point that he might drop the vial. In an instant, he knew what he had to do.

Quickly, he rushed back to his side of the table and emptied the powder into his own cup. He collapsed into his chair and stared at the vessel, cognizant only of the king's snoring and the whistling wind. This was the best option, he thought. The only reasonable option. Still, he could not bring himself to drink. It's not easy to dispense with one's life at a moment's notice.

There was a commotion outside of the doors which woke the king from his catnap. He stretched his arms and flexed the crick out of his neck.

"I must have drifted off," the king said. He reached for his goblet and drank as if he had just spent a week marching through the deserts of Samar.

He wiped his mouth with a silk sleeve and looked to Lurian. "You know I never like to drink alone, friend."

It was the final push he needed. He couldn't convince himself to partake but having someone else make the decision for him somehow made things easier.

He picked up the goblet and raised it toward the large wooden chandelier hanging overhead.

"To my king."

His hand began to shake violently and splashes of wine spilled over the lip before he grabbed it with both hands and gulped it down. Though Lurian had been told that the poison would be unnoticeable, there was a slight bitterness to the drink.

Devilleaf worked within a matter of minutes, suddenly seizing the heart. He decided to spend the rest of his time admiring the glorious man who sat at the other end of the table and think about his next statements.

The disturbance that had awoken the king raised in pitch and there was an argument outside of the door. King Jorn seemed not to take notice, instead popping more almonds into his mouth and staring back at Lurian.

"Your Highness," Lurian spoke, "may I just say that it has been an honor being both your companion in arms as well as your humble servant. I hope that you have also considered me a friend as much as I have considered you such."

The king was silent for a moment. Finally, he said, "They say a king should have no friends, especially among his advisers. But tell me—what's a life without friends?"

"Indeed," Lurian replied. He found himself oddly at ease, now. The tremors had exited his body and there was a sudden clarity running through his mind. "There's something important that I need to tell you, my lord."

"Oh?" The king grinned and leaned forward as if awaiting something lurid. "Been holding out on me, have you?"

"It's about your daughter, the princess—"

Before Lurian could complete the sentence, the doors through which the king had earlier entered came bursting open. Stanislo stood, feigning indignation and looking like a whelp between the king's two burly guards whose obsidian skin and light blue eyes spoke of their Dursinian lineage.

He pointed a shaking finger at Lurian.

"Seize this traitor! He has poisoned the king!"

Lurian leaped to his feet. On impulse, he pulled the empty vial from his pocket and threw it onto the table where it clunked on the hardwood and came to rest beside his own cup. "I have done no such thing," he said, "as you will soon discover." He looked at the king with sorrow, trying to determine how he should explain himself in the little time granted.

The king raised a hand toward his guards who stood like marble statues. He then slowly pushed himself up from his chair and leaned down to palm some more almonds before gliding towards Lurian. The room was filled with a deathly quiet. The two men's eyes never left each other until the king finally towered above Lurian's sweaty skull. King Jorn's free hand came to rest on Lurian's shoulder as he peered down into his advisor's empty cup. Then Lurian felt the king's grip squeeze down lightly, followed by a friendly smile.

"Your Highness," Stanislo impressed, "we must get you to the priests so that they may prepare to drain—"

"Silence," the king interrupted his cupbearer. King Jorn ignored Stanislo's pleas and turned his attention back to his advisor. Lurian's pulse quickened. It seemed the poison was beginning to take effect. There wasn't much time and he had to confess—to warn the man who had put his faith in him until the end.

"Explain this," the king said, looking toward the empty vial.

"My lord, nearly two months ago, I was drugged by your daughter and she took advantage of me. She recently revealed to me that she was with child. I know not the truth of this, but she plotted against me. Unless I poured this poison into your cup tonight, she would accuse me of rape and impregnating her."

Lurian took a deep breath before continuing. "I wish that I could say that my first response was to come to you with the truth and face the conse-quences, but I feared I would not be heard above your only daughter. And I would be lying if I did not once think, selfishly, that carrying out her wishes might not be the worst course of action, given my potential punishment. But in the end, I could not do it. Instead, I chose to tell you everything before taking my own life."

He finished his speech with a quiet tone, staring at the few drops of wine left in his cup in an effort to avoid both the king's glare and Stanislo's triumphant eyes. "My king, I am sorry that I could not be a better friend and servant."

The unendurable silence returned. He felt King Jorn's hand squeeze his shoulder once more.

"You *are* a worthy servant and indeed my friend."

At that moment the king looked at his guards. "T'was not the sparrow, but the lark."

While Lurian tried to decipher the message, there may have been an imperceptible nod by the hulking Dursinians, but it was Stanislo's yelp that grabbed his attention. Within the span of five seconds, one of the strongmen had taken hold of cupbearer's arms while the other slapped on a pair of iron shackles.

Stanislo protested. "What—what is the meaning of this?!" His cheeks were red, jiggling fiercely under restraint.

The king shoved the handful of almonds into his mouth and wiped the salt from his hand on his royal robe. He walked back to his own cup of wine which he gulped down until it was empty, releasing a satisfied gasp.

"When possible, I prefer to bag two birds with a single stone," he said to Stanislo. King Jorn did not look rattled in the slightest. There was further commotion coming from down the hall. A woman was screaming bloody murder until the moment she was dragged through the doorway between another pair of Dursinians.

The princess grunted as she nearly fell onto the cold floor. Tears streamed down her pale cheeks. She looked up at the king.

"Father! I don't know what you've been told, but there's been a mistake!"

King Jorn stepped in front of his daughter and shook his head slowly. "There certainly has been."

He gazed up at Lurian.

"You see, my daughter decided to hedge her bets. She took advantage of both you and Stanislo. Each of you was an insurance policy against the other. After my first sip of wine, I knew that I had been betrayed by him. Stanislo, no doubt, intended to hold you responsible for my death though he had slipped what he thought was *devilleaf* into my personal stock."

The princess protested. "No! That is not true!"

Again, the king looked at her with true sorrow in his eyes.

"What my daughter believed was pure *devilleaf* was something which my chemist concocted and placed where one would normally find such an ingredient stored for foreign espionage. There were two samples, each with a flavor profile of its own."

The bitter flavor Lurian had tasted upon drinking the wine had suddenly come back to him.

"Granted," King Jorn said, "there was an element of *devilleaf* in each to give it a genuine appearance, but not enough to cause true harm."

Lurian only now started to feel the blood flowing back to his extremities. He had not been fatally poisoned after all. Any notions of dying were in his head. A whirlpool of relief swirled within his core.

The king continued, "As soon as I drank my wine, I knew Stanislo had done his part. I simply gave you the opportunity to carry out yours as well. I don't blame you for your indecision. Had I been in your place, I imagine I would have behaved the same. In the end, you confirmed my faith."

"Take them to the dungeon where I won't be disturbed by the screams tonight," the king commanded his guards. The princess cried an unearthly howl, protesting as she was pulled from the floor and dragged away. Stanislo fainted as the other Dursinians removed him from the room and shut the door behind them.

King Jorn walked toward Lurian and embraced him. "My friend," he whispered into his advisor's ear. "Go. Sleep. Drink. Do whatever may bring you relief from tonight's events, but I recommend you eat some of those almonds or you will be on the privy for at least a week."

With that, the king released Lurian, grabbed another handful of nuts, and exited the dining room.

Process Summary

Devilleaf is story number thirty-one in the #52ShortStories challenge.

An unplanned, extended interruption to the writing?

It was never a matter of *if*.

Only *when*.

Well, apparently the *when* was the month of March. A perfect storm of so many things made landfall–many good, many bad, some of which I can talk about, some of which I can't. Suffice to say, I am officially **WayBehind™**.

And it's fine. Just more fuel for the story-fire now that my health and schedule are slowly returning to normal. I undertook this challenge because of the deadlines and I'll continue to see them as a good thing. They're the whip that gets this old horse to water.

Devilleaf started in early March based on a song I'd had on repeat for a while and was going to initially have some Greek mythology influence, but they both kind of got waylaid. It happens. Most of the time, I just need something to get the story in gear and then it goes where it wants to go. Maybe that's not such a good habit to develop if I ever seek a traditional publishing gig and I have to write what I say I'm going to write, but for me, this is all just a learning experience and to have *fun*.

For some reason, the fantasy bug bit me this time around (though this story could easily be classified as historical fiction as there is no mention of magic). Maybe reading all of the Francis Bacon has turned my thinking a little archaic. I'm certain he influenced the idea of some political intrigue.

As for my tradition of releasing a story each Sunday, yeah, that's going to change as I catch up. I'm assuming I *will* catch up, but I'm not going to fret, so long as I produce.

THE MISSING POEM

Statistics

Synopsis: A man receives a mysterious book of poetry in the mail.

Word Count: 3,000

Genre: Urban Fantasy

Completed Week: March 28th – April 5th

The Missing Poem

I had forgotten about the book.

After digging through my email history, I located my original query. The bookseller offered an automatic notification service for any book which may show up in its inventory, and 642 days ago, I requested a copy of *The Twelve Poems of al-Saher*.

I racked my brain trying to remember why I'd ordered it in the first place. It had been at least a year since I'd even read a poem and I didn't remember being interested in a scribe named al-Saher. A cursory review of my journal around that time jogged my memory.

When I sent in the request, I was chin-deep into mysticism and unexplained mysteries of the past—you know, a little *Kabbalah*, a little Nazca lines. Several of the authors I'd read went on and on about how civilization was no longer cognizant of the ease by which we can be pulled into alternative universes through certain places and words of power. I recalled even checking out a couple of library books on building structures that played off harmonic frequencies in energy systems, allowing those who resided within said structures to temporarily escape their bodies and float away to the stars.

It wasn't until I'd conjured hundreds of my own 'words of power' and was halfway through completing my own 'wisdom dome' in the backyard when I realized that most of these authors also indulged in mind-altering substances that may or may not have aided their journeys.

Not that I ever found any such evidence about Al-Saher. My notes refreshed my memory on him: He was a little-known Arab poet from the early 19th century, and was not only a believer in worlds and forms beyond our ordinary senses but felt that one could access these things at will with the right combination of phrases. He had written only twelve poems in his lifetime, the last of which had supposedly brought about a permanent exit from Earth. His Wikipedia page mentioned that there was only a single run of an English edition printed in the early 1900s, back when seances and spiritualism were seeing a revival in the Western world.

Given my disappointment, I'd wiped from my mind a large portion of what I'd learned during that time and returned to the mundane matters of working at the bike shop during the week and binging on *Call of Duty* on the weekend. The only thing is that I had apparently been enthused enough to place a pre-order and *The Twelve Poems* was scheduled to arrive in the mail the next day.

* * *

For reasons I can't explain, my interest in reading the book was suddenly renewed. I called Mack, my boss, and told him I was sick. He didn't sound convinced, but he was satisfied when I told him he didn't have to pay me for the day.

I spent the rest of my morning shifting my eyes between animated M1 Garand rifles and the street outside of my window until I saw the little white truck pull up and watched its occupant shove a pile of paper into my mailbox.

As soon as my character was mowed down by a pack of Nazis, I threw down the controller and ran out to see what was what. Beneath the garage door ads and credit card offers appeared to be the book, expertly bound in a tightly-wrapped paper bag.

It took at least two minutes of careful scissor-work to undo the wrapping without damaging the contents. There was the usual return shipping label, stating that should the product not meet my expectations, it could be returned postage-paid. Even if I was disappointed once more, I saw no reason why I'd ever want to send back such a rare book, so I tossed it into the trash with the paper bag.

And there she was—a thin, tanned, leather-bound beauty with gold embossed lettering on the front:

The Thirteen Poems of al-Saher

I had to review my email to confirm I wasn't mistaken. Indeed, the book had been identified there as *The Twelve Poems of al-Saher*. I opened the book and reviewed the table of contents where only twelve poems were listed. I even flipped through every page, seeing each poem first presented in Arabic followed by its English translation, counting them until I arrived at the final poem.

Only twelve.

I laughed, thinking I had come across a misprinted copy. Now I definitely wasn't sending it back, though I doubt I would have gotten much should I decide to sell it. There just weren't many al-Saher fans in the world these days. It had taken some digging for *me* to remember who he was.

I turned off the TV, grabbed a can of cold root beer, and settled into my recliner to see what all the fuss was about. Now, I don't know if it was the translation or the poetry itself, but it seemed awfully clunky and disjointed. The poems were pretty short, each clocking in at one stanza of four lines. Most of them talked about gold, slaves, and power. I was beginning to see why this guy faded into history. It took me all of six minutes to make it to the twelfth poem where I remained unimpressed:

> *The new World draws near,*
>
> *It is us who are queer.*
>
> *I seek the Invisible Road,*
>
> *To gather what is owed.*

I was having second thoughts about not sending the book back for a refund when I noticed the last page was a little thicker than the others. In actuality, I discovered that two sheets of paper were stuck together with some sort of adhesive. Remnants of a thin, yellowed glue seeping out at the margins were now obvious. I ran my finger along the top and saw that not all was lost. There was a gap in which I could fit my pinky and so I slid it across, gently breaking up the glue until the single page finally became two.

"Aha!" I said to an empty living room.

A thirteenth poem.

Another four-liner, which, unfortunately, was written in a light pencil and only in Arabic. There was no English translation.

I logged onto my computer and found a website which let me choose from a list of Arab characters to translate. It was tedious, clicking them one by one, but I took a pencil and wrote out my own English rendition below the Arabic, which I then proceeded to read aloud.

> *Caught in the Maelstrom,*
>
> *Awaiting a New Son.*
>
> *Open up the Gate,*

It is not too late.

A slight, but sudden tremor shook my entire house for several seconds before the silence returned. Behind my chair, I heard what sounded like a gasp for breath and just as I began to turn my head, someone said, *"Ahlan."*

* * *

Maybe it was from playing too much *Call of Duty*, but my defensive instincts kicked in and as I leaped from my chair, I turned and launched my can of root beer at the source of the voice.

Between me and a strange man in a charcoal twill suit, the can floated in mid-air as if someone hit pause on a video. The man's sunken brown eyes looked past the root beer and directly at me. He was slight, had a dark, well-manicured beard, and a receding hairline.

"Shukran yā sadīqī," he said.

Goosebumps rose on my flesh and I wanted to run, but I felt just like the can of soda. Something seemed to be anchoring me in place.

"Who are you?" I asked, relieved that at least my voice still worked.

He smiled with tiny yellow teeth and replied in thickly-accented English, "You know who I am."

And I did. The face looked like that from the Wikipedia photo. I just didn't want to believe it.

"What do you want?" was the next logical question.

He lifted his hand to his beard and looked around my living room. It must have all seemed a curiosity to him, though maybe not so much after all he had likely seen from wherever he had come.

"You've already given me what I want. I have returned, though apparently long after I have left. Tell me, what year is it and where am I?"

It took a moment for the words to schlepp their way from my brain to my tongue. "2018. Orange Valley."

He mouthed my words silently. "So many years," he replied softly. And then he asked, "Where is Orange Valley?"

"California."

He tilted his head again.

"America."

A look of surprise came over his face. "Ah! I see. It's still here. And what of the Ottomans?"

I looked around at my furniture. I'd never owned an ottoman.

"The Empire? The Sultan?" he continued.

"Oh! *Those* Ottomans. Yeah, long gone."

Now the man's smile grew quite large. "Wonderful. Wonderful."

He reached into the breast pocket of his coat and pulled out a tiny book.

"I suppose America is as good as any place in which to start."

If I had any hopes of things becoming clearer, they were quickly dashed.

"Start what?" I asked, still fascinated by the fact that a can of root beer was continuing to float unabated in front of a two-hundred-year-old man's face.

He thumbed through the book's pages, finally coming to rest on one and held up his finger. "One moment."

He spoke in the funny language again, which I assume to be Arabic, but I couldn't say for certain.

After much pomp and ceremony, he finished speaking. The moment the final word departed from his lips, there was another tremor which sent framed family photos and my reading lamp crashing onto the ground. I grabbed onto an arm of my chair to steady myself.

Now, I don't know any other way to put this other than to say that there was nothing there, and then there was. What appeared to be an enormous lion zapped into existence at al-Saher's side, but with fur and flesh missing from half of its face—like it had just had its snout shoved into a woodchipper. It tilted back its ugly head and gurgled a horrific sound which shook me to my core, sounding like something between a hyena and a frog, but nothing like a lion. Acid-green slime dripped from its open sores and out of its jaws onto my carpet.

"Now, you were asking what I was starting," al-Saher said, giving me his full attention. "Why, I'm simply taking over the world."

At least that's what I think he said, but it was difficult to hear him as I was already halfway through my front door with zombie lion's breath on my back.

* * *

I was glad that I always parked my bike on the porch because I don't know if I would have been fleet of foot enough to avoid the chaos happening behind me. Explosions and a symphony of screams rattled my ears. I looked back only once, maybe a half-mile out and saw that my house, and all adjacent houses, were now piles of debris.

It was one of those things that seemed too surreal to have any real effect on me.

My first thought was that my neighbors were not going to be happy.

My second thought was that, In fact, they were plain not going to *be*.

It had been a long time since I'd biked at such a frenetic pace. At the edge of Main Street, my legs and lungs let me know in no uncertain terms that I had better stop to rest or I may as well ride back and pet the zombie lion because I'd be dead either way.

I realized I was across the street from Mack's Bike Shop where I saw him with a customer. They were exiting his store, wheeling a newly-purchased bike towards the woman's truck when he stopped and looked up at me.

"Hey! Tommy! What the hell are you—"

But he never completed the sentence, or at least I don't think he did, because a tiny tremor shook the ground around us which sent him and the woman into an awkward-looking dance. It stopped almost as quickly as it started. Mack looked like he was going to yell at me again, but his eyes quickly bulged into little white balloons as he looked past me. The woman's bike fell to the ground as I turned and saw that less than a quarter-mile behind me, a dark, menacing cloud was trailing behind al-Saher. The poet was walking confidently with a small army of the mutilated lions at his side.

Lungs be damned, I began to pedal away again. Mack was already behind the glass doors of his establishment and the poor woman was left standing there, hands in the air, yelling about her new bike being unceremoniously dropped to the ground. She seemed oblivious to everything going on around her and didn't get much further along in her protests, because I looked back to see that one of the lions broke away from the pack and pounced on top of her, ripping at her flesh with its sharp green teeth before she could even scream.

* * *

I was nearly out of Orange Valley's tiny downtown before my legs cramped up and I was forced to stop again. More crowds of people gathered outside of storefronts to see what was going on, probably wondering why a crazy guy on a bike was shouting at them to run away.

Despair began to take over. I clambered off my bike and hobbled into the nearest store—Watson's Pharmacy and General Goods. The world around me turned into a blur of bodies running and pointing and screaming. I only heard the simple chime of the bells hanging from the door handle as I made my way down the stationery aisle where I collapsed

"Please," I mumbled to the air, "let this be a dream. Let this be a dream." The only reply was another series of tremors and more screams outside of the store. A pair white pants swept by me but came to a quick stop.

"Tommy?"

It was the pharmacist, Roger. "Tommy, you gotta get outta here. There's an earthquake or something."

"Or something," I replied softly, staring with dead eyes at a pack of colored pencils hanging on the rack in front of me. I would never see my family again. Never see anything again, all because of that stupid poem.

There was another quake which caused the shelves to rattle and sent Roger scrambling for purchase.

He reached down to grab ahold of me, but I refused to budge. "What's the use," I said. "We're all dead." The look in his gray eyes told me he was wavering on saving his own hide until a piece of the ceiling collapsed behind the druggist counter. The air became thick with dust.

I covered my face with my hands and heard rapid footsteps followed by the chiming bells.

No matter how many times I pinched myself, there was no waking up from this. I would die in the collapsed building. My mind tried to make sense of it all. I had apparently brought al-Saher back from another place, a wicked place, by simply reading the thirteenth poem. And then he recited something of his own, another poem perhaps, to bring about the current reign of terror.

This train of thought jolted me awake like someone had taken a cattle prod to my rear. My little area of the store still stood, though it was only a matter of time before it all came crashing down on top of me. I moved quickly for the pack of colored pencils I noticed earlier and a stack of sticky notes on the shelf below. My hands were shaking as I tore open the box of pencils and then wrote as fast as I could. I prayed I would find the words, closed my eyes, and wrote.

The Magician's return,

Was all a Dream.

The World remained,

As it had always Been.

* * *

I don't recall hearing anything, or sensing any point of transition, but I opened my eyes and was suddenly sitting on the floor of my living room, hearing the sounds of birds chirping outside of my window. My butt felt wet. I stood up and saw my can of root beer knocked over onto the carpet.

The colored pencils and sticky notes were nowhere in sight.

I ran to the front door, threw it open, and bounded outside. The sky was clear and so far as my eye could see, my neighborhood was still standing.

There were no tremors.

No mutant lions.

And most importantly, no al-Saher.

I walked back inside my house and my eye was drawn to the recliner. Sitting on top of the debris was the book of poems. That was disturbing in and of itself, but what truly unnerved me was the title.

The Fourteen Poems of al-Saher.

I tried to rip the individual pages out. Tear them into pieces. They didn't budge from the binding. Even a pair of scissors was useless as it was like cutting a piece of iron with a spoon.

After throwing it in my roaring fireplace and watching it survive unscathed, I spent the rest of the afternoon and evening, pondering how I might destroy the book.

I fell asleep in my recliner and woke up to a phone call from Mack, yelling at me for being late.

In a panic, I got dressed, cleaned up the root beer and as I was about to throw away the paper towels, I laughed.

Of course, I thought. There was the answer, still sitting on top of the rest of my garbage.

Before I left, I carefully wrapped the book, slapped on the salvaged return label, and promptly dropped it in the mail on the way to Mack's.

Process Summary

The Missing Poem is story number thirty-two in the #52ShortStories challenge.

So, this story was an oddball in the sense that I honestly thought it was rushed, but the reception from at least one reader indicated that it was one of the best stories I've written. Also, it took me a day longer to finish this than my stories normally do, so I definitely was not rushed. But there was a point where I wasn't sure where I was going to take the story after al-Saher appeared. The days were ticking past and I knew I had to wrap it up before I locked up, so I just let 'er rip and started writing down the craziest things that were coming to mind at the time (which happened to be mutant lions and earthquakes).

Man, talk about reinforcing a point — for the most part, you *really, truly* cannot judge your own work.

Inspiration for this? Honestly, I can't recall. It was a brief entry in my idea pile about some guy discovering a missing poem and I thought I could spin up a really fun yarn about that. If you take the time to translate the antagonist's name, you can see I had some fun there. :)

A LETTER TO THE GUBAMINT

Statistics

Synopsis: When the aliens begin to invade Coconut Groves Mobile Home Park, it's up to one citizen to inform the government.

Word Count: 2,750

Genre: Humor

Completed Week: April 6th – April 12th

A Letter to the Gubamint

Darryl was already agitated when Karrie insisted on digging into him some more.

"You think they care? You're wastin' your time!"

Over the years, Darryl had figured out that holding his tongue and letting his wife air out her feelings was the quickest way to resolution, but by God, she never made it easy.

"Instead of fiddlin' 'round with that, maybe you ought to help me put this diaper on," she continued.

His pencil poked through the paper several times, leaving tiny holes in his anxious words.

"If they do anything, they'll send some men in some suits and sunglasses down here and haul you away. And then how am I s'posed to take care of Kenny?" His wife laughed without taking a breath. "Not that much would change eitherways."

The lead finally snapped off the end of the pencil and Darryl slapped it down on the tiny table extending from the wall of their imitation Airstream trailer.

"Dang it, woman! Don't you think someone with some special firepower ought to know about this? I ain't got enough ammo to take 'em all on myself. And 'sides, they're probably invincible to the kind of bullets they sell at Walmart."

"They ain't gonna believe you," Karrie replied. She stood a whole three feet from him, hovering over a pot of boiling water, emptying a blue box of macaroni and cheese with one hand and holding Kenny in the other.

The boy was squirming and yelping as his feet dangled inches from the hot steam.

"Ha!" he erupted. "Shows what you know. Who do you think knows about 'em if it ain't the gubamint?"

Finally, she shut her lips. Darryl yanked off his green-and-yellow trucker hat, grabbed the back of his neck and twisted his head around to release some tension. He stood and proceeded to pull open every drawer in the place, all three of them, rummaging through while tossing aside expired coupons and Karrie's unread issues of *The Enquirer*.

He slammed the last drawer back into its place. The knob came flying off and bounced onto the floor. "Ain't we got more than one dang pencil in this place?"

"You want to write that letter so gawt-dang bad, go and get one from the *scary* neighbors," she said. "I'm busy puttin' food on the table and takin' care of our son."

* * *

Darryl didn't want to say he was becoming one of those gore-phobes—people that shut themselves up and didn't come outside for nothing but what they had to—but he was starting to dread any potential run-ins with the residents of Coconut Groves Mobile Home Park.

If he had to guess, it all started a couple of weeks ago. Wilmer down towards the entrance was the first one Darryl had noticed. Usually hiding in his trailer most days, Wilmer worked nights at Shooter's, a pool hall down the interstate a few miles, but he had since become a regular social moth, full of 'Good morning's and 'How are you today's. Darryl swore Wilmer even said something in French once or twice, but since Darryl didn't speak French, he could only say it *sounded* like French.

By yesterday evening, it seemed almost every other neighbor had taken on airs like they'd hit the lottery. But there was more to it than that and Darryl couldn't quite put a finger on it other than to come to the most logical conclusion—the Grays had come (aliens, to the layman) and they were either controlling the people's minds or had swapped bodies with them completely. Darryl had watched enough episodes of *Ancient Aliens* to be convinced such a thing was not outside the realm of possibility.

He slammed the trailer door shut and was accosted by his nearest neighbor.

"Good morning, Darryl. Marvelous and sublime weather we are having, is it not? Though they say a cold front is moving in, which is a mass of cold air on the edge of a low-pressure system."

As Darryl cleared his front yard in a few steps, the only acknowledgment he gave Little Jim was a squint and a wide berth. The man was five-three and had to be clocking in at around two-fifty, wearing the same stained t-shirt he'd gotten for free at a raffle at Pete's Cars six years ago. There was no telling if the problem was catching, so Darryl held his breath until he made it to the front office and checked in with Debbie.

"Hey Deb," he said, resting his arms on the counter overlooking her desk. Darryl wondered how she could find anything through piles of sun-faded Beanie Babies. "You got a pencil?"

Her chair squeaked as she stood to meet him. She was wearing a tight tank top that showed off her freckled chest and shoulders and her acid-wash shorts seemed like they were cutting off circulation to her dimpled thighs on down.

"I'm sure I have one or two around here for you, Darryl." Behind her glasses, her hazel eyes glowed like those of a man on a diet standing outside Rod's Donut Shop.

"Okay, great," Darryl said. "I been trying to finish this dang letter."

"Oh?" she asked, completely ignoring his request. "Whatcha doin'? Writin' a love letter?"

"No, nothin' like that," he said with all seriousness. "Important stuff. Gubamint stuff."

Debbie raised her eyebrows. "Ooh. Not only are you a handsome man, but you got some intrigue to ya'. That wife of yours better be apprecia-tin' you."

"Hey, you noticed anything funny 'round here?" Daryl asked.

"There ain't a day goes by that I don't notice something funny at Coconut Groves."

"Well, yeah, but I mean somethin' different. Like people actin'...dif-ferent?"

Debbie's remained motionless.

"Anyway, don't matter," Darryl said. "I'm gonna see it gets taken care of. So you got a pencil or what?"

She gave him a disappointed look. "Yeah, sure, hold on."

Debbie turned around and leaned down to pull open a drawer in the cabinet behind her.

"Gotta be one in here somewhere," she said, looking over her shoul-der at Darryl while her butt swayed in the air like one of them baboons Dar-ryl had seen on TV the other night.

He was growing impatient. He wanted to get the letter in before the mail lady came, and was about to walk down to Perly's Drug Store and just spend some scratch on a new pencil before Debbie finally shut the drawer and handed him a #2 with an eraser on the end that looked like a watermelon.

"Thanks, Deb."

He was already out the door as she was saying something about calling her anytime he needed help with something, anything at all, be it business or personal, but especially personal because she was certain she could take care of his needs.

Gravel ground beneath Darryl's flip-flops as he headed back to his trailer, but he stopped halfway and decided he'd have a better chance of getting the letter done on a picnic bench in the common area. After five minutes of writing and swatting at mosquitoes, he had the thing finished and sealed in an envelope. Hoping to avoid Debbie, he went the long way around the back of the front office to the mailboxes on the side. Before he slipped it in the outbox, he confirmed he'd gotten the address right:

To the folks dealing with the Grays, Pentagon, Washington.

He was smiling as he walked the hundred yards back home until he was accosted by a skin-and-bones woman with a drooling mutt in tow.

"Darryl, how are you? Is that a new pair of pants? You are looking quite urbane. One might even say, debonair."

Oh no, he thought, not you too, Jolene.

He picked up the pace.

* * *

Darryl and Karrie had spent a couple days back in the routine when, one afternoon, a set of rapid knocks set the whole trailer to rattling.

Kenny stirred in his crib.

Karrie looked at Darryl and he looked back at her. Darryl grabbed the remote and turned the volume down on *Family Feud.*

He spread a section of vinyl mini-blinds beside his chair and spied a man and a woman, both wearing matching dark suits and sunglasses. Two points for Karrie, but Darryl was confident the gubamint wasn't going to take him away. Hell, he was going to be a hero. Images of getting some sort of medal from the President himself flashed through his mind, though he couldn't quite remember who the President was this year, so the face was just a blur.

Darryl was surprised the feds had responded so quickly, but he had a feeling gubamint mail moved faster than people mail, especially when it came to matters of national security.

The door squealed on its rusty hinges as Darryl pushed it open.

"Mr. Shamesworth?" the woman asked. She took off her sunglasses, revealing a pair of eyes bluer than the sky. The man beside her had barely moved, probably due to the fact that he had a gallon of gel holding down his hair. It looked like the kind of mop you'd see on a plastic doll. In his right hand was a leather briefcase.

"The one and only," Darryl replied. "I knew it. I knew you'd come and do somethin' about this." He spoke the words to them but gave a self-satisfied look to Karrie.

The woman squinted and smiled, then looked her partner. The man simply shrugged. "We're here to help," she said. "My name is Candace and this is William. We've come to talk to you about a few things that your neighbors are involved in. May we come in and discuss?"

"Of course!" Darryl said. The two visitors stepped inside the trailer while Darryl gave his wife a big wink. She remained seated and eyed Candace and William with suspicion as they said their hellos.

"You'll have to 'scuse the mess," Darryl said, suddenly embarrassed at the state of the trailer. He swept away little Kenny's dried *Oatie Os* that had fallen across the dining table. "Please, have a seat." Darryl extended his hand toward the booth around the table.

The man and the woman squeezed themselves in, both looking as uncomfortable as a pair of rabbits at a bloodhound convention.

Daryl plopped down across from them and launched into the speech that had been running over and over in his mind since he'd dropped the letter off in the mail.

"Ms. Candace. Mr. William. Now, I'm not sure where you want to start, but I been trying to figure out if there's some sort of pattern here, some—"

"Mr. Shamesworth," she interrupted. "Mrs. Shamesworth," she followed with a nod in Karrie's direction. "How do you feel about your current situation at Coconut Groves?"

Karrie began to speak, "Well, it had been just fine until my husband—"

"Oh, is this a test?" Darryl interrupted. "Ha! Of course, of course. Yup, you gotta make sure we're free and clear. I'll tell you right now, we's still us. I try to stay away from the neighbors and I told Karrie she oughta' do the same until ya'll can get down here and assess the situation."

William finally removed his own sunglasses and pinched the bridge of his nose.

"I'm sure you've seen quite a change in your neighbors, right?" he asked.

"Right!" Darryl replied.

"Would you say that they've come across more...educated?" Candace asked.

"Oh, definitely. It's like they got these fancy brains all of a sudden. Take Odelia, for instance—the gal in space 13-C. I was trying to get to work the other morning and she comes flying at me, waving her arms as if she were in trouble. I asked what it was and she starts babbling at me about how she was going to have a little shindig that night to watch Comet 45P cross Aquila and Hercules and she'd love for the Missus and me to come."

Candace and William smiled at each other.

Darryl continued, "I mean, I knew right then that somethin' was up because only a week prior, she'd been complainin' to Karrie that the light outside her trailer was broken and how was she s'posed to shoot the raccoons that get in her garbage if she couldn't see 'em. Ain't never made a single mention in her life about no comets."

"That's great," William said. "Fantastic!"

Darryl wasn't sure what he said that made the man so happy, but he was beginning to feel confident that he was on the right track and something would be done.

"So what are ya'll gonna do 'bout this?" he asked. "If you can let me know before ya'll drop a bomb or bring in the tanks, I'd 'ppreciate it. I can hitch this trailer right up and park at Island Oasis up the street."

William and Candace threw each other another confused look.

Finally, William undid the latches on his briefcase and opened it up.

"I think you're going to like what we have to offer you. And best of all, it's free."

Darryl looked at Karrie.

"Well, I didn't s'pect to pay nothin' that you ain't already got through my taxes."

"That's right," Candace said, turning the briefcase around so everyone could see what was inside. "The good people of Horsetail County have already paid for these educational CDs."

Except for the sound of cars zooming by on the nearby interstate and Kenny's light snoring, the trailer was silent.

"Educational CDs?" Darryl looked like he'd just been invited to dinner with the pope. "What's that got to do—"

"You get your pick," Candace continued "though most of the neighbors have gotten to the good stuff already. Our apologies, but Horsetail didn't get *that* much taxpayer money." She pulled out a few DVD jewel cases and shuffled through them. "What do you think? Latin 101? Biology? Shakespeare's King Lear? And don't worry if you don't have a CD player, the county can provide one on a payment plan."

"I don't understand," Darryl said. "How's this going to help us deal with the Grays?"

"The Grays?" Candace asked. "I don't think we've met them yet. We've met the Turgensons, the Madgetts,—"

"Oh yeah, they got all the ones on Beethoven's Sonatas," William chimed in.

Darryl jumped to his feet, slamming his knees into the bottom of the table. He tried to hide the sting.

"What's the big idea, here? I write ya'll a letter to help with the Grays and you bring *educational* CDs?"

"Mr. Shamesworth," Candace replied. "I'm not sure what you think we're here for, and we haven't been informed of any correspondence from you, but we work for Horsetail County. We're a part of an educational outreach program for the 'underprivileged,'" she said, flexing her index fingers in the air. "We feel the lack of easily available educational resources is a barrier to improving one's livelihood and career trajectory."

More painful silence, broken up only by a giggle from Karrie.

"I see," Darryl said. "Ya'll are from the gubamint though, right?"

"Well, yes, technically," William replied.

Darryl was silent now as he stared at the two of them and then looked to his wife. Smug airs were written all over face, but he held back any comments.

"We'll take the Shakespeare one!" he shouted, waking up little Kenny. Karrie jumped up to attend to him.

"Are you sure that's the one you want?" Candace asked.

"Yep. Absolutely. I think that will do us just fine," Darryl replied with as big of a smile as possible.

William smiled back. "Shakespeare it is! Now do you need the CD play—"

"Nope, we got one."

"Darryl, we don't—" Karrie said while bouncing Kenny on her shoulder.

"Yeah," Darryl interrupted. "we are ay-okay. Much appreciated."

William placed a jewel case on the table and closed the briefcase. They shook hands with both Darryl and Karrie, then left the trailer.

After a few minutes, when Kenny was lulled back to bed, Darryl slipped on his pair of sandals and walked toward the door.

"Where you goin'?" Karrie asked.

"Headin' down to Perly's to buy us a pencil and get the name of the President."

Karrie shot him a look of confusion. "What for?" she asked.

"He needs to know the Grays have gotten deep into the system."

Process Summary

A Letter to the Gubamint is story number thirty-three in the #52Short-Stories challenge.

Again, it's funny how disparate pieces of information can influence a new creation. I flipped (clicked) through my reading journals for inspiration and landed on Francis Bacon's essay, *Of Anger*, and immediately thought of a guy writing an angry letter to the government.

But then I had also been in the middle of reading an anthology of humorous short stories, so I wasn't feeling in too serious of a mood. Sprinkle in random memories of a mobile home park (aka "trailer park") that a friend from college lived in, and voilà, I had my character and setting.

I tried to play specifically with dialect and voice in this piece. There always seems to be a thin line between realistic and over-the-top, so I hope I pulled it off. Probably playing this story off as a bit of comedy helped, because you have more leeway when it comes to being over-the-top.

Hope you enjoyed it!

Shiplap Plague

Statistics

Synopsis: A small town falls ill and a young girl may be to blame.

Word Count: 2,750

Genre: Horror

Completed Week: April 13th – April 24th

Shiplap Plague

Sara's bloody nose.

As Devin lay against the worn polyester couch in the hospital waiting room, immobile, vision blurred, the connection jolted him as if someone had hooked his spinal cord up to a car battery. Not that first signs mattered at this point, other than to appease Devin's insatiable need to know. He tried to focus on his wife's face, but the lenses of his eyes refused to cooperate. He could only see the faint outline of her body collapsed over that of a patient she had been checking on—what, maybe ten or fifteen minutes ago?

She always put others before herself. It's why she wanted to become a doctor in the first place. It's why they both became doctors.

And now they were the patients without anyone left to tend to them.

Thinking back to the morning, Devin realized his watering eyes were probably the second sign that something was very wrong in the town of East Warhaven.

Of course, they brushed the symptoms off as hay fever, all too easily attributed to the unusually dry air and wind they'd been experiencing. Spring pollen was in full effect this year.

The notion that something bigger was at play didn't take long to come to him, though. At 9AM that morning, they had dragged themselves into short-staffed St. Margaret's Hospital after a reserved, yet obviously urgent, call from the head of ER who informed them that an unusual number of patients were flowing into the hospital and they needed all hands on deck.

First, it was the elderly and young children. Bloody noses, teary eyes, and trouble breathing. By 5PM, there were more patients than beds and the town's population had been slashed in half. The CDC was supposedly on their way, but Devin couldn't recall who had said that and if it was even true.

Since he couldn't dial in on Sara's face or even generate enough force to move his body close enough to hold her hand, he closed his eyes and tried to remember happy moments of their life and the new life they had begun to build.

It was the kind of small-town life Sara would have dismissed a couple of years ago, but the nightly shootings, stabbings, and recurring drug-addicted patients had taken their toll and he had been able to convince her that a change would be good for them. On a visit last month to see family in Virginia, they came to the decision. It took them only one day to decide on purchasing a white plantation-style home with a wraparound porch and a beautiful view of the Blue Ridge Mountains, marred only by an old shiplap shed—the shiplap shed which they had reduced to rubble the evening before everything went to hell.

* * *

"You hide, we'll find you," Nate Henderson said. Robbie Silva's head bounced up and down in agreement.

Katelin thought the boys were rowdy, but she didn't have any brothers or sisters of her own to play with and the two of them were the only kids within walking distance. She thought it was odd that they'd want to play with her, given that she was ten and they were thirteen or fourteen. They'd also ignored her for as long as she could remember. But, a playmate was a playmate, so any qualms she had flitted away just as fast as they'd come.

Counting down from twenty, they hid behind a willow tree in the

half-mile-long copse between her house and Nate's. Katelin's heels reached
into the air and her baby blue dress caught the wind as she rushed into her
backyard. She thought about hiding in her house and watching the boys
through the kitchen window, but she worried that if they found out she was
hiding somewhere off-limits, they wouldn't want to play with her again. Looking over to the corner of the yard, sheathed in foot-tall bluegrass was her
father's workshed. It was empty. Papa had taken Katelin's brother and Mama
to town for groceries and to pick up some hardware needed for a new project.
This was the second time Katelin had ever stayed home alone.

"You don't leave the house. You don't answer the door for strangers. Any trouble," Papa had said, "you know where the rifle is." Katelin didn't
know if her father expected a band of robbers to swoop down on the house
as soon he left, but she only said, "Yes, Papa."

Of course, ten minutes in, she was bored out of her mind with
only three television channels, so when Nate and Robbie came knocking at
her door, she jumped at the opportunity to play hide and seek. It wasn't as if
they were real strangers. They went to the same church, had gone to the same
school before they went on to junior high, and their parents had known each
other for even longer.

"Wheeeerreee areeee yoooou?"

Nate's voice echoed across the landscape as Katelin quietly closed the
shed's wooden door. She stifled a giggle and looked for a good hiding place. It
was dim inside. The only light came from a small window of frosted glass just
above her father's workbench. She climbed up onto Papa's stool and saw the
outline of the two boys creeping onto the property line. Quickly, she remembered the storage cabinet standing tall in the corner of the room. She was

small enough to fit on the bottom shelf, so she ran over, opened the cabinet door and crawled inside. She closed the door behind her, tucked her legs up to her chin and wrapped her arms around her knees. Heavy scents of wood shavings, turpentine, and grease filled the air in the cramped space. She hoped the boys wouldn't force her to hide there too long as the fumes were already starting to give her a headache.

It was only seconds later when the shed door squealed open on its hinges.

"Weeeee're gonna fiiiind ya!" Nate said again.

* * *

The tiny excavator dug into the shed with its faded black claw. Dust flew into the air as one corner of the dilapidated shack came crashing into the ground.

Sweat ran down Devin's cheeks. His lips were sealed shut in a grimace and Sara could see every vein in his taut arms peeking out from a worn, sleeveless gray t-shirt. A pair of translucent goggles covered the top half of his face and he had orange earplugs stuffed into each ear. He looked back at Sara who was standing on the porch, hands on her hips. As if he had been pulled out of deep thought, his expression changed quickly into a plastic smile.

Sara was surprised he wasn't having more fun. In her experience, something in the male blood couldn't help but get men excited when it came to knocking things down and breaking them into hundreds of pieces.

An hour later, the two of them stood at the kitchen sink. Sara wrapped her hands around Devin's bicep and leaned into his shoulder as the majestic Blue Ridge Mountains rose in the distance, flooded in orange twilight and completely unobstructed. Despite some obvious adjustment time, Sara had to admit she'd fallen in love with the house and the whole notion of country living. She'd trusted Devin to find them a place, knowing that he'd grown up somewhere in the area. Given how quickly they'd come upon their new home, he'd obviously done his research.

"I know we'll be happy here," Devin said, gently stroking his wife's head. "There's not a single doubt in my mind that we made the right move."

She looked down at the ugly pile of wood at the end of their property line. The junk guy would be by the next day to haul away the debris.

"I know," she replied.

Feeling her nose beginning to run, she grabbed a paper towel from next to the sink and wiped. Devin looked down at her.

"Honey, you're bleeding," he said.

* * *

"Kaaaatelin."

Through a crack in the cabinet door, she saw the two boys skulking around inside the shed. The floorboards creaked beneath their mud-covered boots while the two of them whispered to each other.

Nate's auburn hair fell into his eyes and shaded the freckles on his face. Robbie had a nose like a pig's snout and a gap in his two front teeth that created a little whistle whenever he said certain words starting with *s*.

Robbie looked at the cabinet and Katelin shrank back. Her head hit the bottom of the shelf above her and she bit her lip. She could still see them through the thin crack when Nate raised his eyebrows and they both flashed grins.

"What do you think, Robbie? She hidin' in the cabinet?" Nate's voice sounded exaggerated.

"I don't know...Maybe we ought to check," Robbie replied.

They crept over and stood in front of the cabinet. Katelin held her breath.

The cabinet door came flying open and Robbie ducked down to meet Katelin's face.

"Boo!"

She shrieked and hit her head again.

The boys laughed while Katelin crawled out of the cabinet and dusted herself off.

"No fair!" she said. "You followed me."

"Fair and square," said Nate.

She rubbed the top of her slightly tender head. "Your turn, I guess," said Katelin.

Nate looked at Robbie and Robbie looked at Nate.

"Okay, but let's rest a minute first," Nate said.

Katelin stepped towards the door, but Nate pulled out in front of her and leaned his back against it nonchalantly.

For some reason, Katelin didn't feel right. She wasn't sure if it was the vapors from the chemicals in the shed or something else. She tried to hold back a sense of panic. "I can't stay out late," she said. "My folks are gonna be home soon and I'm not supposed to be outside."

"Hold up," Nate replied, dipping his head toward his friend. "Robbie wanted to ask you something."

With that ugly smile still stuck to his face, Robbie stared at Katelin. He inched toward her and put a hand on her shoulder. Katelin shrank back on instinct. The hair on the back of her neck rose up like a cat's and she started looking around for a nail or something to throw at the boys.

"I gotta go," she said, her voice quivering slightly.

"Go ahead," Nate said to Robbie, ignoring her plea. "Ask her."

Robbie didn't say anything, just stared down at her with dumb eyes.

"You chicken, I'll say it for you," Nate said. He looked at Katelin. "Robbie wants to kiss you. He says if you don't let him kiss you, he ain't gonna play with us no more. And if he don't play with us no more, than I ain't gonna play no more either."

Katelin wanted to puke at the thought of the gross boy's lips coming anywhere near her. "No way!" she said. She wished her dad kept a rifle here too like he did at the house, if just to scare the two of them. "If you don't let me out, Papa's gonna get angry and come after you both with his gun."

Nate laughed so loud, it hurt her ears. "Hear that, Robbie? We gonna' get plugged by the old man. Well, if that's the case, we're definitely gonna need a kiss before we kick the bucket."

Katelin heard the low whistle through Robbie's teeth as he let out a soft, hissing laugh. Before she knew what was happening, Robbie's sweaty hands squeezed her arms and pull her into him. His phlegmy breath cut through the other smells of the shed as he pressed his lips all over her face, struggling to make contact with her own lips as she flipped her head back and forth.

Robbie giggled like a lunatic.

She screamed her first scream, which was also her last because as soon as she started, Nate came barreling over and rapped a palm across her face, shocking her into silence. Her face grew hot from the pain. Had Robbie not still held onto her, she would have fallen onto the ground like a sack of potatoes.

"You shut your mouth and let Robbie kiss you," he said. "And if you scream one more time, we're gonna hurt you bad."

Katelin started to whimper and tears dripped down her face. She tasted something metallic and realized that blood was streaming from her nose and into her mouth.

"Please," she cried. "I won't say nothin', just let me—"

Her voice was cut off as Robbie pushed her down. The back of her head slammed onto the floorboards and her vision went blurry. Robbie felt so heavy on top of her and his breath was even more pungent then before, now that he was breathing hard. He lost his grip on Katelin's right arm which she quickly brought up, grabbing ahold of Robbie's ear and twisting it.

He screamed like a cat whose paw got caught in a mousetrap.

She thought she heard Nate yelling at him to shut up, but the only thing she truly noticed was Robbie's elbow coming down on her throat like a blunt stick. She tried to scream again, but only a gurgling whistle came out. Katelin panicked as she found it hard to breathe. Robbie let go of her other arm and sat back on his knees, gripping his ear and wincing. Katelin grabbed her neck as if it would help open her airway.

Nate ran over, stared down at her and then looked at Robbie. "What the hell did you do?"

Robbie looked stunned, hand still on his ear, and said, "Nothin'! I was just...."

The taste of blood Katelin had noticed earlier was pooling into the back of her throat, making it even more difficult to breathe.

Nate's head flipped back and forth, his eyes darting between her and the window.

"Let's go," he said. He grabbed Robbie by the shirt sleeve and yanked him onto his feet. Though her head swam and her everything sounded muffled, Katelin heard the fabric tear across Robbie's t-shirt.

"It was an accident—"

"I said let's go!" Nate said, throwing open the shed door, causing it to slam against the wall. His footsteps vibrated across the wood flooring, followed swiftly by Robbie's.

Katelin was trying to cry but she couldn't take in enough air which made her panic even more. She dug her fingernails into the floorboards, trying to overcome her sudden lightheadedness. Trying anything to get more air. For a few seconds, she hoped and prayed that her folks would be back soon but she knew deep down that it would be too late.

Finches chattered outside. Katelin stared at the outline of rafters overhead. Only bits of air worked their way in and out of her lungs. Blackouts came and went and somehow she knew that she was dying.

Emotions grew confused within her as she thought about being left alone out here. Surprisingly, she wasn't sad. She was going to miss her family, but mainly, she focused her thoughts on the sickening smiles of Nate Henderson and Robbie Silva.

As she stared at the shed's shiplap ceiling, Katelin felt only a red-hot anger at what the boys had done to her.

* * *

Devin fell in an out of consciousness. He was sure Sara was dead now. Visions of his life played randomly in his head like film clips.

His wedding on a beach in San Diego.

Turning his tassel at graduation from St. John's Medical School.

His sister's vacant eyes.

Replayed with vivid color and sound, it seemed like only yesterday when he found Katelin laying face-up in the shed. Barely dried tears ran down her blue cheeks. Blood streamed from her left nostril onto her upper lip. Images of his father rushing past him to pick up her limp body. His mother's unearthly howl as she collapsed outside of the shed's door.

He thought he could come back and make things better. A culprit was never found. The family moved away a year later, trying to pretend as if nothing had ever happened.

But Devin remembered. His dreams never let him forget.

Coming back to knock down the shed was something he had to do. Now he drifted into black and realized just how wrong he was.

Katelin had her own idea of closure.

Process Summary

Shiplap Plague is story number thirty-four in the #52ShortStories challenge.

As part of my reading diet, I'm subscribing to magazines I would never bother to pick up. One of them is *This Old House*. As a renter, this periodical is nearly useless for me unless I want to build a really cool looking coffee table (which I've been inspired to do, but, come on–should I shave my hours of sleep down to 2-3 now?) But...I'm expanding my horizons and just filling my brain with all sorts of random information that may just strike a chord of inspiration.

There was an article about using shiplap wood to redo your bathroom. I'd never even heard of shiplap wood, but it had a nice ring to it. Where the plague idea came from, I dunno...but it led to a cause, which in turn, led me to poor little Katelin. Being a father now, I found this one a little difficult to write. Maybe that's why it took me longer than normal. But I'm pretty comfortable getting uncomfortable these days, so I'm glad I pushed through.

COLD HEAT

Statistics

Synopsis: What happens when two diametrically opposed superheroes come together?

Word Count: 2,500

Genre: Urban Fantasy

Completed Week: April 24th – May 1st

Cold Heat

"You really think this is a smart idea?"

There was nothing left to do but ask questions. Holed up in an unfurnished Manhattan apartment, tied to an uncomfortable folding chair, sitting in front of some sort of jerry-rigged track-and-rail system wasn't exactly a position Marquis expected to be in when he'd opened the Bureau's trouble ticket email that morning.

Two hours and a few bruises later, things were getting intense.

"Smart idea? It's the best damned idea anyone's ever had."

Marquis just knew the bastard was smirking behind the balaclava even though it covered everything but the punk's bulging eyes.

"Smart idea…" the man trailed off with a derisive tone. He took a step toward his similarly-dressed partner holding an M16 dialed in on Marquis's forehead. "This guy acts like we were born yesterday." M16-man just harrumphed.

"Just sayin', Bala-man—you mind if I call you Bala-man?—just sayin', you must really think you're gonna get what you want if you put on something like this."

Bala-man walked over, met Marquis's eyes for a fleeting moment, and then thrust a gloved fist into the hostage's stomach. Marquis gasped for air. He wanted to double over, but the ropes binding him to the chair were pulled tight.

"Some superhero," Bala-man said, laughing, but rubbing at the exposed knuckles beneath his now-singed glove. "Do yourself a favor. Don't you worry about me."

Even as he struggled to breathe, Marquis couldn't help but marvel at the fact that these clowns had subdued him. If there was no other indication, the fact that they had come up with some kind of material that was resistant to Fire Carrier magic was a testament to them having done their homework. He'd tried a number of times to focus his mind and burn through the rope, but the bonds refuse to ignite.

Bala-man hummed a tuneless melody as he walked around Marquis and tended the fireplace just behind the chair. Marquis's ears picked up every-thing the criminal did—the iron poker pushing the burning logs around. The man's breath blowing into the orange embers, trying to rekindle the flames. Bits of ash flying into the still air.

Bala-man stopped humming and coughed through his nylon mask.

"Let's get this over with," M16-man said. "It feels like Hell's kitchen in here."

"Cool your jets," Bala-man replied. "The more heat, the more power this idiot generates. The more power, the more seriously they'll take us."

Marquis assumed he was the idiot. To be captured by this bunch of losers, he thought. What did they know about fire?

Now, Marquis? He knew fire. Man, did he know fire. Its winding shape. Its subtle hiss. Its warm fragrance. And we're not talking the smell of oak or cedar or whatever lumpy piece of wood Bala-man happened to be poking at. We're talking about the fire itself. It had an odor and Marquis was as intimate with it like any fifteen-year-old wannabe rockstar was with the notes flying of Jimi Hendrix's guitar.

He was about to crack a stupid joke about Bala-man being like a vir-gin with clumsy hands when there were three rapid knocks on the apartment door followed by two longer knocks.

Despite the rekindled fire, Marquis felt the temperature around him drop several degrees.

* * *

"Keep 'em as far apart as you can until we're ready," Bala-man said.

There were three of them: two dressed up as maintenance men with the worst fake facial hair Marquis had ever seen. The third had her head covered in a potato sack and her wrists secured behind her back. Marquis didn't need to see her face to know who she was. As soon as the three newcomers were inside the apartment, the smell of the fire dissipated to make room for the stench of ice. It was disgusting. It made Marquis want to retch. He tried to focus on the flames behind him. Focus on the heat both without and within.

He was a little worried now. If they found a way to subdue an Ice Warden as well, these guys might actually be crazy enough to carry this through.

The two men walked their hostage to the opposite side of the room and secured her to the only other chair. Marquis felt the temperature go up slightly, but he knew it was only short-term relief.

"You guys are nuts!" he shouted.

Bala-man came back around from the fireplace and stood in the middle of the room between the hooded woman and Marquis. He reached into his front pant's pocket and pulled out a cell phone.

"Get ready for your fifteen minutes," he said. "Though, that's being generous if they don't give us what we want."

* * *

"You don't deposit three-hundred million in the account I mentioned, these two are gonna lock lips," Bala-man said.

He held the back of the phone up to Marquis and the fire burning behind him. Then he pivoted over to the now-unmasked Ice Warden tied to her own chair.

A tinny voice came out of the speaker. "One, where are we going to get that kind of money? Two, you're really willing to blow up half of New York City?"

"One, you're the government—figure it out. Two, do you really want to find out? You got ten minutes for me to see those numbers in my account." Bala-man punched a key on the phone and slipped it back into his pocket.

"Hope you two brushed your teeth this morning," he said and walked with the rest of the men into the only bedroom in the apartment, shutting the door behind them.

For the first time that afternoon, the Ice Warden's eyes met Marquis's.

Her name was Celine. The two of them had crossed paths for the first time six months ago going after a cartel boss. They had both been issued tickets for the same gig. It happened, but not often. The Bureau was generally pretty good at keeping track of when and to whom a trouble ticket was issued, but sometimes databases got out of sync or there was plain old user error involved.

For those rare events, there were protocols in place. A simple coin flip determined who'd get the job. Most importantly, distance had to be kept.

No one could definitively say what would happen if a Fire Carrier and Ice Warden were to touch, but no one wanted to find out. The legends were powerful enough to discourage them from trying—tsunamis, earthquakes, floods. Laymen likened it to matter meeting anti-matter.

"Well, I guess one of us ought to break the ice," Marquis said. "No pun intended."

"Don't talk to me," Celine replied.

"There's no rule against a little chat," he said. "I don't think. Besides, if these guys are serious, do you think it's going to matter to anyone an hour from now that we broke some standard operating procedure?"

They were no closer to each other than they had been minutes ago, but Marquis could feel a chill radiating from her stare.

"Fine," she said. "If you want to blabber on, maybe you can help me figure a way out of this situation."

"How do you know I don't already have a plan?"

Celine raised an eyebrow.

"I don't, but it's rude of you to assume I don't."

She shook her head and looked around the room.

"So let me guess," Marquis said. "False ticket? Blow to the head and then the ropes?"

Celine raised her eyebrows.

"I guess the operation doesn't need to be too sophisticated if they have these," Marquis said, indicating the rope.

"I guess not." She looked down for seemingly the first time. "What's the deal with this?" she asked, eyeing the rails beneath her chair. She looked like a little kid, her feet dangling almost a foot from the ground. They had her propped up on one of those office chairs that goes up and down.

The bedroom door swung open and a man stepped into the main room wearing a Yankees cap, a yellow t-shirt, and jeans. His cohorts followed, similarly dressed in street clothes. "You're about to find out," he said.

It was Bala-man.

One of the men who had the fake facial hair stepped behind Celine's chair and knelt down. Marquis heard a click and then the whir of a tiny motor.

"Sad to say that your public representatives care more about their own offshore accounts than they do the good people of New York," Bala-man continued. "And, wow, talk about a thank-you for your years of service! I guess a single flamer and ice bitch ain't worth much in their eyes."

Marquis started, "Think about this—"

"Sorry, gotta run. Looks like we have to grab a couple more of you folks as I have a feeling we'll be taken a little more seriously next time." Before Marquis could finish his sentence, the four men were lunging through the apartment door, leaving the two heroes to their doom.

* * *

"I'm moving."

"What?"

"I'm moving. Towards you."

Marquis already knew. He had felt the subtle drop in temperature and a tingling beneath his skin that would soon begin to sting.

"And my God, do you smell," Celine said, wrinkling her nose.

Marquis blew a large puff of air through his lips. "You're one to talk."

Visually, he could tell that Celine was getting closer now. She was struggling to break free, but it appeared to be as useless as when he had tried. Something about the ropes zapped the strength from their bodies. The heat from the fireplace was crying out and the smell of its flames was vanishing. The warmth was being replaced by a searing cold. Marquis could tell by Celine's curled upper lip that she was beginning to feel some pain as well.

The two of them were closer than ever and though his muscles began to ache, Marquis grew fascinated with her up-close appearance. Her turquoise hair, short and slicked back, looked like a threaded helmet. A tinge of jealousy ran through him as he thought of his bald pate. Her skin was like a midnight moon with ice-filled veins trailing its surface.

He knew it was a waste of time, but he tried to focus once more on his own ropes. He thought his face hid the nervous feelings burning inside. She was only several feet from him now.

She laughed, only to have her laughter broken up by painful-sounding coughs.

"What's so funny?" Marquis asked.

It took her a moment to be able to speak again. "You just know there's somebody holding a 'The End is Near' sign on a sidewalk not too far from here. Boy, isn't she going to be smug for those few seconds before she's turned into powder?"

Marquis tried to hold back because he too knew it would hurt, but he couldn't help himself. The laugh came roaring out and the chair beneath him started to groan and crack. A solitary tear ran down Celine's cheeks as she lifted her legs, futilely trying to escape the heat of the metal chair folding beneath her.

The two were inches away from each other now. Soon their legs would meet. Marquis felt as if he had just finished running a marathon. His breath was short. He couldn't feel his legs anymore. At least he had escaped the realm of bitter pain and moved on to numbness.

"Well," he managed to grunt through his grimace. "It was nice knowing you, even if you smell like you live in a garbage dump and you make me want to kill myself."

Even through her own pain, Celine smiled slightly. "Yeah, nice to know you too, Pigpen."

And then it happened. The fabric of their pants melted away and the raw flesh covering their legs met. They both screamed at the same time as their chairs collapsed—Marquis's into a thousand pieces, Celine's melting down into a pool of liquid metal. The track snapped. Marquis fell to the ground first followed by Celine on top of him.

Marquis's hearing left him and he felt like he was submerged underwater. He gasped for air. Only tiny gulps made their way into his lungs. The sensations were too much. Vertigo kicked in and the last thing Marquis smelled was the cold heat from Celine's face pressed against his.

* * *

"This was unexpected."

Marquis, still on his back, looked around the room. He heard the street noise below. A helicopter or two were buzzing around the cityscape. There was an ambulance—maybe a fire truck or police car—wailing in the near distance. Pieces of charred metal and rope were spread across the floor.

Celine rolled off Marquis and on to her butt. She twisted her head around and cracked her neck.

"So we've just disproved a thousand-year-old myth," Marquis said. "What else do you want to do today?"

Celine smirked. "Not just disproved one. Notice anything else?"

Marquis was taking too long to figure it out, so Celine tapped a finger against her nose. "Wait, what?" He sat up, leaned toward her slowly, and sniffed.

"Down, Fido," Celine said, pushing him away. They both laughed at the lack of, well, anything.

She pulled her hands towards her face and flexed her fingers. Tiny flames popped up on her fingernails, startling her. She yelped and waved her hands around to put them out. Marquis quickly grabbed hold of them and saw ice form around both of their hands. Now he screamed and released his grip.

"What the…" they said simultaneously, watching wisps of smoke rising from Celine's fingertips.

Marquis stared at the frost covering his palms. He felt a surge of panic in his body and jumped to his feet. Just as fast, he slipped on a puddle of ice that formed beneath him. The room shook as he crashed back onto the floor again.

"Ow! Son of a…"

Celine stifled a laugh while Marquis's face felt flush.

"Let me get this straight," Marquis said. "So now I'm an Ice Warden and you're a Fire Carrier?" He thought he was going to be sick.

Celine stuck her hand out again and pointed a finger at Marquis's head. A blade of ice shot out and halted an inch from his left eye.

"I'm thinking it's a little more complicated than that," she said.

Marquis turned and concentrated on the fireplace behind him. He snapped his index finger against his thumb like he was flicking a piece of cigarette ash. A tiny, hard ember flew towards the smoldering wood and made contact. The logs ignited as if they'd been doused with gasoline.

"Oh," Marquis said. "Okay, then."

"Honestly, I'm a little disappointed," Celine cut in. "No vortex? No seeing our bodies turned into atomic dust bunnies?"

"So what does this mean?" Marquis asked. He turned back toward Celine. "Can we kiss too?"

She pointed to his crotch. "Try it and I'll shoot an icicle where it counts."

Marquis quickly moved his hands for protection.

"Besides," she said. "I have a better idea."

Marquis lifted an eyebrow.

"Let's go catch those assholes."

Process Summary

Cold Heat is story number thirty-five in the #52ShortStories challenge.

Superheroes?

Honestly, it must have been all the *Avengers* chatter going around the Interwebs.

The original title for this was *The Avenging Heat* which I'd created by mashing together a couple of phrases from recent poems I'd read (Title-mashing being a trick I picked up from writing guru, Dean Wesley Smith).

Add some myth-busting and a semi-Romeo and Juliet twist on it, and here you go—*Cold Heat*.

One of the things I really tried to focus on with this story was putting voice into the non-dialogue parts. I've always read how important that is for the story as a whole, but it's not something I default to easily. Of course, these stories allow me to focus my practice on specific items, which may mean other important storytelling skills suffer an equal and opposite loss of focus. But I wanted to make Marquis' internal voice come alive and I hope I was able to do that at least a little bit.

DRAFTED

Statistics

Synopsis: The 2077 National War League Draft is on and agent Cassidy's star player is ready to make a splash.

Word Count: 1,750

Genre: Sci-Fi

Completed Week: May 1st – May 4th

Drafted

"I better go first. I better go number one."

Moshe Vanderkellen was twenty years old, the league-leading MVP for Ares War College, and a top-notch fine-line-walker of confidence and arrogance, all too often tripping into the latter. He was still young, though, and even he couldn't hide signs of nervousness. Angled forward in his seat, he rubbed his hands together while his legs bounced up and down like rapidly firing pistons.

"Well, hold on," Cassidy said, setting down her pour of neat Lothian Scotch. She leaned toward him and into the armrest of the crinkling leather chair. "We talked about this and it should be obvious given their position in the draft. Neptune Company is not a winning team. I don't give a damn how good you are, there's no way you can carry them to victory and there's no way they'd have your back in a sticky situation. I don't want to see my friend go down in a shitstorm because he's only thinking about the number."

They had thirty minutes until the first round kicked off. Reflections of ten different newscast holograms reflected off Cassidy's whiskey glass while the spicy scent of Robusto cigars and hum of media socialites floated all around them. Facilities crew members performed equipment checks on the empty stage in front. Moshe's father was pacing the floor behind his son like an agitated steer, occasionally pulling a jumbo shrimp from the tiny white plate in his hand and biting its head off.

The mother wasn't there. They rarely ever were.

"But Pantheon could trade up for the spot," Moshe said.

"No offense, Moshe, but they won't pay for you. They have two very large holes to fill in their artillery platoon and as much as they'd love to have you, they don't need a first-strike leader."

Moshe shrugged.

"Worst case," he said, "Neptune keeps the pick and I can just sit and make them trade me to a better team."

Cassidy nearly choked on her reaction. "Who told you that was a good idea? I know I didn't tell you that."

"That's what Mason Kelso did."

"Yeah, and where's Mason Kelso now?"

Moshe fell silent.

"I know Mason," Cassidy said. "I can arrange a meeting and you can spend five hours sitting in his shanty living room where he'll tell you all about matches and bridges." She took an angry swig from her glass. The burn felt good against her parched throat. "Damn it, Moshe, if I had known you were even thinking that for a second, I would have sent you to his place weeks ago."

For half a second, Cassidy wondered if she would ever get tired of dealing with these headstrong kids. The thought occurred often, but always for only half a second. In truth, she loved being an agent because she was good at it. She was built for it. Her dad had never had trouble picking the winning thoroughbreds at Los Almas Raceway and Cassidy assumed her skill was some combination of endless hours spent with him and a genetically in-herited gift passed down over the ages. She made thirty deals over the past ten drafts that put her at the top of the agency—the top of *all* agencies. She was always able to land a deal that made both parties happy but scratching their heads over how she'd made it look so easy.

"It's just, you know, I rocked the scouting combine," Moshe said. His voice took on a sense of authority, which it often did when he felt backed into a corner. "Obliterated everyone in every category. I outgunned them all, had a higher number of wounded pulled back. And that's not even counting last season—"

"You're letting any fool with a microphone and a holocamera set your value. I know you're the best. You know you're the best. Every team out there knows you're the best. But you know what?"

"What?"

"The best don't need to say they're the best."

That got him. She watched his face reveal a sudden crossing back over that line of arrogance.

"Yeah, I guess you're right."

"Of course she's right," Moshe's father chimed in with a mouth full of caviar and water cracker. "That's why we signed with her."

"How long have you known me?" Cassidy asked Moshe.

"I dunno," he said, visibly trying to close the gap between the neurons in his brain. "Four, five years?"

"Seven years and forty-six days," Cassidy replied. "I saw your potential when you were still shooting styrofoam missiles at the neighbor kids."

A smile crept across Moshe's face. "Oh yeah, that's right."

"Do you trust me?"

Moshe's jaw fell open. "You know I do."

"Then *trust* me."

Cassidy leaned back in her chair and exhaled slowly, happy the pep talk was over but knowing it wouldn't be the last.

"Mercury Marauders," she said. "They're going to pay you what we want and I recommend accepting wholeheartedly."

"Man, they're like, number four!"

"Stop thinking about the damn number," Cassidy said. "You worked out with their team taking down those simulated Sand Demons from Argos. And, if I recall correctly, you gushed about the endless trays of post-practice bacon. They treat their players well, especially the top guns. With a refreshed Armored Cavalry and you leading Spec Ops, they're going to take the title this year and every year you're with them."

Moshe frowned. "Yeah, I know. It's just…after how I performed at the combine, they should all be begging me to come and fight for them."

Cassidy put a hand on his shoulder. The kid was built like a carrier. Unless you saw him in action, you'd never know that he moved as lithely as a Telessian Stinger zooming through an asteroid belt. Most of the military teams had tank-like soldiers that could haul heavy weapons or scouts that crept and shot forth like the wind, but rarely both in the same person. Moshe would make the solar system proud for the next decade.

Cassidy's head buzzed slightly and it wasn't the whiskey. The back of her corneas showed her it was Davis calling in from the Marauder's war room. She clicked in.

"Talk to me," she said.

"They're telling me $650 million for the four years, tops."

Cassidy could have held the laugh back, but she knew they were all listening in.

"I guess Terry's OK with an average sixteen casualties per year then? You know, the sixteen casualties that have kept them out of the playoffs for the past three years? What's another four years?"

There were raised voices in the background. Undoubtedly Terry Lattimore, the Marauders GM, and his commander were pissing on each other over figures. Cassidy looked over at Moshe and smiled. The youngster's eyes shifted between the bevy of holoscreens in front of them and the empty podium onstage.

"$700," Davis said after several seconds.

She could sense the amusement in his voice. He was the best assistant she'd ever had and well worth the above-average percentage he took off the top.

"We'll think about it," Cassidy said and clicked off.

The time showed 3:20 PM. She gave them under five minutes to call back, deciding to use the window to review her calculations. They'd offer maybe another $25 million, but they'd push her hard on getting an extra year and she'd need to be ready to respond.

They'd likely call out Moshe's kill-death ratio during his freshman year, and yeah, it came in slightly below expectations, but he had injured his hamstring during a move that saved three squadmates from career-ending injuries. Where were the Marauders going to find a superstar warrior who also knew when to pick up the team as a whole?

And Moshe's recovery was swift. Since he came off the injury list, he hadn't missed a single battle. It was like he hadn't been hurt at all.

"Man, this is so nerve-wracking," Moshe said. He ran his hands through his thick, wavy mane.

"Hey, I'm here for you," Cassidy said. "Your dad is here for you."

Moshe's dad grunted an acknowledgment.

Her head vibrated once more.

"$750, but they want an extra year."

A buzzer sounded across the auditorium.

"$775," Cassidy replied. She held firm while there was one last shout in the background.

"Deal," Davis said.

Cassidy smiled. "He's worth $850, but we'll make up the difference with the tactical gear and soft drink endorsements. Tell them to make the pick and we'll sign."

She clicked off just as a voice boomed over the auditorium.

Ladies and gentlemen, welcome to the 2077 Solar War League Draft.

* * *

Sometimes it happens after only six months, maybe a year.

But never this suddenly.

The call came in two weeks after Moshe's deployment to the Zeta System, but Cassidy had seen it on the news feeds only minutes before they rang her up—the BlackDevil pirates had set explosive traps before abandoning their operating base. A quarter of the Marauders' starting lineup had been blown to bits, including Cassidy's brightest prospect. The Marauders lawyer stated that per the standard contract, they would pay Cassidy her percentage based on a single-year value, but they would increase scrutiny over future prospects put forth by her agency.

Cassidy wasn't the crying type. She was once, but her father made sure it was only once. She dealt with the news how she usually did—a full glass of Lothian tipped back in honor of the deceased.

A few minutes after the news came through, her head buzzed and she clicked over.

"Hi Smith," she said.

"Yeah, so hey, I talked with Commander DiSouza and he said the Rapiers want Doña to come in and work out with them. They're simulating an operation on Saladin-12 to capture a band of smugglers."

"Thanks. I'll take care of it."

Cassidy poured herself another glass of scotch and rang up her client.

"Doña, it's Cassidy. Hey, I hope your grandmother is feeling better—such a sweet woman, which reminds me, when she's on her feet again, tell her to send more cookies—but before we chat about that, I want to advise you to work on your pistol draws." She flipped across the records displayed across her corneal display. "Your ratio's taken a nosedive due to your misses over the past week and we need to make a good impression with the Rapiers."

Process Summary

Drafted is story number thirty-six in the #52ShortStories challenge.

The varied reading I've been carrying on has provided a tremendous opportunity to challenge myself with my latest stories.

Drafted was my attempt to pull in some influence from recent *Sports Illustrated* articles I'd read and form a story around those concepts, of course throwing in some speculative twist (because it should be obvious now, that's just how my brain rolls). The big happening in April was the 2018 NFL Draft and after reading some brief biographies on the top picks, I thought there was an opportunity to put together a really in-depth character. Turns out the in-depth character happened to be the agent more than the player. And I thought making the agent a woman was a fun twist. I don't know about you guys, but I instinctively picture some slick-haired, slimy guy in the role.

Anyway, some stories just seem to almost write themselves and this was one of them. Man, if only that were the norm…:)

A Tomb in Every Tree

Statistics

Synopsis: A Korean War vet struggles with aging and family until he runs into an old friend.

Word Count: 2,850

Genre: Urban Fantasy

Completed Week: May 4th – May 9th

A Tomb in Every Tree

"How much should we leave Marnie?"

"Zero."

"Come on," Harold said. Fluffy shifted her head and rested it back on her owner's foot. The gray and white Shih Tzu hardly ever left Harold's side these days.

"Zilch."

Harold's rubbed at the sunspots covering the back of his hands. Whatever 'rejuvenation' cream Linda bought for him didn't seem to be working.

"Be serious," he said, still talking to his wife, but staring at the four-by-six photos pinned to the corkboard above the desk. There was a mix—Don, Marnie, and the two grandkids, Mischa and Sloane all standing in front of a faux castle, all wearing those round black hats with mouse ears. To its right was another photo that dipped further into the past. Linda and him at a '50s Flashback dance put on by their church when they lived in Indiana. Then there was the only surviving photo with Harold and his squadmates in Korea. Their first week of deployment before they'd let their beards grow out and shortly before the bitter cold and 'accoutrements of war' (as his buddy Krieger used to put it) had a chance to beat them all down.

"I am serious," Linda replied. The chop-chop-chop of her knife slicing through a Maui onion and onto the cutting board provided a backing rhythm. "She never brings Mischa and Sloane over except for maybe two times out of the year. And she only calls when she needs your help with something."

"She's busy. The girl's got two jobs."

"We're all soooo busy," Linda said, tweaking her voice. "I doubt she's ever too busy to see *her* mother." Sun streaming through the kitchen window highlighted the gray in her faded dye job. Harold wished she would just let certain things go.

"You don't know that," he said. "We can't just leave her out of the will."

Linda dropped the knife and dug her fists into her hips like the old George Reeves, minus the cape. "Why not?"

"You think Don would have wanted that? What about the girls?"

Harold saw it coming. He ducked just in time to hear a dirty dishrag whiz by his ear and smack into the wall above the desk.

"Don't you dare tell me what Don would have wanted. And the girls will be just fine, assuming Marnie hasn't gone through the life insurance pay-out yet."

Fluffy scrambled onto her paws and hopped out of the way as Harold pushed back from the desk. The wheels on his clearance-sale office chair squeaked. For the twelfth time that day, Harold thought about grabbing a can of spray lube from the garage, but he knew it was best to get out of the house for awhile. He bent over slowly and picked up the washrag, careful not to put any strain on his lower back.

"I'm gonna take a walk," he said, depositing the rag on the counter in front of Linda. Fluffy pranced and tapped around the tile floor as Harold grabbed the leash from the counter.

"Dinner will be ready at five-thirty," his wife finally said as Harold was halfway out the door.

* * *

This whole deal with the will began to make Harold feel like he was in some screwball comedy. Harold would fill in some forms, talk to the lawyer, and then after he went over the day's events with his wife, she'd tell him he'd done it completely wrong and did she need to do everything for him?

He was beginning to question whether or not she was sabotaging the whole thing on purpose. Even getting her to consider that maybe it was time to work on a will and testament had been a trial. Harold felt like he was dragging along a child who goes limp and refuses to move because she doesn't get her way.

Only a few minutes into the walk, sweat began to gather under Harold's arms and around his balding crown. He felt like he was swimming through a salty, heated pool. There were no clouds to shield the sun today in Cedar Key, Florida, though everything looked as beautiful as beautiful could be.

He and Fluffy made their usual quarter-mile trek down Tatum Road and turned onto a dirt trail running alongside the reserve. Scrub jays chittered among the round green tops of myrtle oak and the fragrance of rusty lyonia floated through the air.

Though the reserve was so close to home, it was far enough away to feel like a different world. And that's just what Harold needed right now. Sadly, walking along the salt marshes was his last remaining outlet of adventure, the quantity and quality of which had been in a slow decline for fifty years. He supposed that's just what happened when you got old. If he was honest with himself, he'd admit that he wasn't cut out for much adventure these days anyway. Still, it didn't make accepting the rapid movement of years any easier.

"How do you size things up, girl?" He looked down at Fluffy. "What are we going to do about this whole thing?"

Fluffy tilted her head at him as her paws marched rapidly over the soil.

"You know I love your mama with all my heart, but sometimes—"

"Heeeelp!"

Without warning, Fluffy jumped and barked at the scrub on their left, tightening against the leash. She coughed as she choked herself on the collar.

"Whoa, Fluffy! Calm down, girl!"

Harold struggled to reel her in. He bent over and swooped her up, immediately regretful that he hadn't tightened his stomach muscles like Dr. Berwitz always admonished him to. All ten pounds of her were trembling in his arms. She'd stopped barking, but there was a low growl roiling from within. He tried to take Fluffy under his left arm so he could press a free hand into his stinging lower back, but the dog was struggling against his grip with all she had.

Something about that cry for help had also sent a shiver running through Harold's body. He peeked over the low bush, but his vision failed to penetrate the dense, dark oak grove standing about twenty yards from the trail.

"Heeeeeeelp!!"

That voice. Harold really didn't want to go running in there. An image of Linda flashed into his mind, sitting in silence at the dinner table over an empty plate while his own pork chop sat cold on the other side. He craned his neck up and down the trail. It wasn't unusual to see another bicyclist or hiker around these parts, but as far as his eyes could see, he was the only person crazy enough to be out in this afternoon heat.

"Pleeease help!!"

Then again, maybe not the only one.

Harold reached into the front pocket of his khaki shorts.

Damn. Forgot the phone.

He knew that he might be getting into a situation he may not be able to easily get out of. The only form of weapon he carried on his person was a pocket knife, used more often to cut berries off saw palmetto than actually getting violent.

It had been a long time since he'd dealt with violence.

He took a tight grip of Fluffy's leash and set her down, holding her in place while he tied the leash to the trunk of an oak sapling. She began to yip and strain against her bonds again, but he didn't want her to complicate any potential situation.

With an uneven mix of heroism and fear, Harold dashed into the brush as much as an old man could dash into the brush.

* * *

His lungs were on fire. Scratches from thin branches scored his leathery skin, leaving a couple of blood stains where his forearms had brushed up against his white t-shirt. Harold bent over amidst a throng of greenery, placing his hands on his knees and attempting to catch his breath. The vanilla-like scent of oak rushed into his nostrils.

My God, he thought, has it been so long since I've pushed myself?

He couldn't have run more than fifty yards. Still, there was enough breath left in him for a chuckle. Forget the uneaten meal. Linda would be *really* pissed off to find him collapsed out here on the edge of the salt marsh.

After about ten seconds, feeling less lightheaded, he held his breath. Of course, the scrub jays continued blabbering away and he wanted to shush them all. He could still hear Fluffy yapping in the distance.

"Heya, Harry."

Now, in the half-second between the voice speaking those words and his heart skipping a pump or two, it's difficult to say when Harold realized just who was speaking. Was it when the sound waves of that chipper voice hit his eardrum? Or when the smell of C-ration tobacco floating on the nearly nonexistent breeze tickled his nose hairs? Maybe it was when his eyes first landed on the man himself—those caramel peepers and the scruffy brown beard sitting atop a slender body clothed in pea-soup fatigues that were two sizes too large.

There was no way.

It couldn't be him.

First, the man standing before him couldn't be walking around on his two feet, given that both legs had been torn to shreds by white-hot Chinese shrapnel.

There was also no way he could look exactly as he had sixty years ago.

* * *

"Hey, bub, pick your jaw back up from the dirt. I ain't Betty Grable."

A palmful of memories slapped Harold upside the head.

"Krieger?"

The soldier smiled, his teeth a mural of brown and yellow.

"What..." Harold felt himself lapsing back into dizziness. He tipped forward and saw the ground coming at him quickly. A pair of hands grabbed ahold of his bicep and yanked him in the opposite direction, keeping him on his feet.

Staggering, sure, but on his feet.

Feeling the pain in his lower back again, he winced.

"Hell gettin' old, ain't it?" Krieger said. "Kinda glad I skipped that part."

Harold was breathing heavily now and he was afraid he was hyper-ventilating.

"Hold up, hoss, let's pull you up a seat." Krieger escorted him toward a particularly large scrub oak and gently lowered him onto the forest floor. "Catch your wind. Then we'll chew the fat."

Between the heat and the unusual situation, Harold's tongue grew dry. "I...I heard someone—"

Krieger squatted onto his knees and reached toward his belt, produc-ing a canteen. He unscrewed the lid and held the nozzle to Harold's lips. "Shh. Wet your whistle, first."

The water was warm, but it did the trick.

"Someone was crying for help," Harold said.

"Yeah, that was me. You should have seen your face." Krieger slapped his knee. "Sixty-odd years later and I'm *still* able to yank your chain."

"I don't understand. How is it you're...What I mean is, what are you...."

Krieger held his finger to his lips. "I get it. You got a lot of questions, most of which don't matter, to be honest with you."

Harold took a second to get his thoughts straight. He locked eyes with his old friend and squadmate who he'd last seen carted off in a stretcher. "Well, let me ask you one, then—Where have you been and what are you doing out here?"

"That's two questions, but I'll answer the second," Krieger said. A chaw-colored loogie splashed onto the ground next to his scuffed black boot. A brown streak ran down into his beard. "You're going through some things, am I right?

Harold couldn't have come up with a more generic statement if he had three hours to think one up. He thought about all of the things he'd been going through the past few years of his life. The five types of hypertension medication. The Saturdays spent at the local swap meet, talking to the same old people, hearing the same boring stories. Hell, the sheer boredom of retirement covered fifty percent of it.

"What do you mean?" he asked.

"Don't give me that crap, Harry. You know what I mean. This situation with you and Linda. Marnie and the grandkids."

Despite the absurdity of what he was experiencing, Harold took offense. "That's none of your business. I don't see what my wife and daughter-in-law have to do with you or anyone else."

"That's where you're half-right," Krieger said. "It *wasn't* any of my business, but seems someone was concerned and I volunteered to help."

"Huh?" Harold replied.

"Don't waste time noodlin' over things I can't tell you, Harry. Just know I'm here to help out an old friend." Krieger leaned his head back and took a deep breath. "I can see why you picked this place to settle down. Pretty far away from our little home away from home outside Pyongyang in every sense, ain't it?"

Memories of the Korean winter fell over Harold's mind like a blanket of snow. He swore he'd never be that cold again in his life. Even in the heat of a Florida summer, he shivered a little.

Krieger pushed himself to his feet and went behind the tree.

"Krieger," Harold said. "Don't leave me now!"

Krieger walked back with something in his hand. "I'm still here. A little something to warm us up."

Harold took hold and recognized it right away.

"Are you kidding me?"

Krieger flashed that muddy smile again. "You remembered? Hot damn! I was hoping…"

Harold unscrewed the lid and held the bottle of gin to his nose. "How could I forget the look on Colonel McDougal's face when he came storming through camp, having everyone's footlocker and bed turned upside down?" He took a swig and swished it around. The connection between taste and memory was amazing.

He passed the bottle back. "What happened to you?"

Krieger took a sip but looked unsatisfied. "Same thing that happened to a few of the boys over there. It's not important."

Harold let it go.

"You know," he said, "there's a lot I don't miss about freezing my ass off for those two years, but I miss you, Krieger."

"I miss you too, Harry. You're a good man. Your Linda, she's a good gal too. Don't fault her too much for the way she's been. Mamas…they take these things a little harder than the rest of us. Can you blame 'em?"

Harold supposed he couldn't.

"Since you're still nursin' your back," Krieger continued, "I'm gonna give you a little history lesson. You know the Spaniards were on this very soil not too long ago, right?

"Yeah, of course," Harold replied. You couldn't drive ten miles along the eastern coast without passing a crumbling fort or mission.

"Sometime in the 1700s, a fleet of ships carrying the shiny yellow stuff back to ol' King Philip got caught in a hurricane and washed up ashore. Most of the poor saps went down with the ship, but a few managed to survive, took all the goodies they could wrap their arms around, and headed inland."

Harold started to laugh.

"What?" Krieger asked.

"The only pages I ever saw you crack open unfolded into a poster that wasn't suited for company. When did you become so educated?"

Krieger spit on the ground, feigning offense. "Let me finish the goddamn story, chucklehead." He passed the gin bottle back to Harold who was content to take another swig and let his pal continue.

"So, anyway, with the King's men, pirates, and local tribes all sniffin' around, most of them sailors took to burying the gold rather than be caught yellow-handed. They figured they'd come back for it someday. A few did. Most didn't."

"What's your point?" Harold asked.

"The point *is*, who knows, there may even be something you can quietly pass down to your grandkids a few feet beneath your asscheeks there, hoss."

Harold raised his eyebrows and Krieger winked at him. The gin was starting to ease Harold's pain. Feeling confident, he held a hand to the oak and pushed himself to his feet. He looked down and kicked his tennis shoe into the dirt where he'd just been sitting.

"If you're saying what I think you're saying…."

He looked up and Krieger was gone.

"Krieger?"

Harold walked around the tree. He looked down at the scrubland floor and realized the bottle of gin was missing too.

* * *

After a couple more hours of walking and thinking, Harold found Linda snoring in her bed. She'd left a note on his plate with reheating instructions and a pair of Xs and Os.

Fluffy was curled up in her dog bed, exhausted from the day's trauma. Harold paused over his desk, alternating between looking at his beautiful family and the young man he had once been. He swore that Krieger's face had a sarcastic grin that wasn't there before today.

With a smile on his own face, Harold headed to the garage to grab a shovel.

Process Summary

A Tomb in Every Tree is story number thirty-seven in the #52ShortStories challenge.

The title for this story came from the Lord Byron poem, *Don Juan*, specifically *Canto XIII*. Honestly, no clue where the Korean War background came from, but I ran with it. I've also been taking a recent class on Depth in Writing (HIGHLY recommended, as are all of the WMG courses I've taken), so I tried to put some of that into practice here. This was another story that seemed to move along for me.

My favorite quote from the daily journal:

"I think it's good enough. Maybe not perfect, but I don't have time for perfect (no one does)."

The Hypnotist

Statistics

Synopsis: A hypnotist entertains crowds on the county fair circuit, but is now offered $100k for a special job.

Word Count: 2,400

Genre: Thriller

Completed Week: May 10th – May 16th

The Hypnotist

The sweet scents of buttered popcorn and cotton candy floated over a light breeze crossing the stage, causing Martin Yurik's stomach to growl. He never thought the night would end and he was grateful to wrap up the third show of the evening. He peered out under the glaring stage lights and spoke into his headset microphone.

"Marilyn Monroe, everybody!"

To his left, a man lifted the bottom of the faded, stretched-out *Van Halen* t-shirt over his hairy, protruding belly and swayed from side to side on his flip-flops. "Oh," he said in a gravel-churning voice, "do you feel the breeze from the subway?"

A gaggle of teenage girls in the front row covered their gaping mouths as tears of laughter poured forth.

"Isn't it delicious?" the man asked his captive audience.

The crowd of one hundred or so hooted and hollered.

Martin stepped in front of the man and got in his face. "One, you're slowly feeling all of your faculties returning under your control. Two, you're beginning to move around, stretching your body, feeling the electrical signals flow through your nervous system. And three, you're wide awake!"

He snapped his fingers just before finishing the last sentence. The man looked confused, like he'd just woken up in a stranger's home.

"Let's all give Billy a round of applause! He's a real good sport!" He grabbed the middle-aged man's hand and lifted it in the air. A look of recognition swept over Billy's face as he took in his surroundings. His astonishment turned into a sheepish grin. Cheryl, Martin's assistant, walked onto the stage wearing an inconspicuous black button-up top and black slacks and escorted Billy to the side.

Low, ambient music began to play in the background and Martin spoke. "If anyone here is trying to lose weight, quit smoking, drinking, or has any other habit they're looking to break, we have some CDs and DVDs for sale at the booth near the exit."

Even though he'd prepped and charmed at least half of the suggestible crowd into buying something from him before each show even started, he was always a little relieved to see them lining up.

"Thank you all for coming tonight! It's been a pleasure! Don't forget that we're here until Friday."

* * *

"I don't know how you do it."

"I know. That's why you pay me," Martin said, biting into the mustard-slathered corndog Cheryl left for him backstage.

"True, true. Look, I have a proposition for you."

"I'm booked the rest of the summer, Vincent."

Vincent Forcelli, President of the Board of Directors for the San Flamenco County Fair, peeked under the tent flap to look outside, then ducked his head back in. His gray eyes and slicked mafioso hair made him appear more intimidating than his soft voice let on, but those were usually the dangerous ones, right?

"No, it's a personal job," he said. "One day. That's it. And I'm talking big money."

Big money. Martin knew county fair circuit money, and while it provided a comfortable living, he wouldn't be trading in the Volvo for a Tesla Model S anytime soon.

"What, do you want to lose weight? Just buy a CD."

Vincent visibly sucked in his stomach and straightened up. "No, not for me. For someone else."

"Okay, tell *them* to buy a CD."

"It's not your usual stuff," Vincent said. "This one's a little different. The person won't know what you're doing. Not entirely."

Martin sat the corndog back down in the paper tray. At least once a year, he'd get some sort of request like this.

Can you make this guy fall in love with me?

My grandmother is being manipulated to leave me out of her will and I need you to change her mind.

Hey, convince my boss to give me a fifty-percent raise.

"I don't get involved with anything fishy—"

"All above board," Vincent said. "I'm just looking to help someone, ya know?"

"Yeah, I know. And it doesn't work like that," Martin said.

Vincent took a deep breath and pulled one of Martin's DVDs from a cardboard box. "I'm guessing you don't sell these by only using your good looks."

Martin picked up a half-empty styrofoam cup and took a swig of soda, then wiped his mouth with a hair-thin napkin. He decided not to answer.

"You sure you don't want the gig?" Vincent asked. "One-hundred grand. Half up front."

The number nearly made Martin choke on his drink. That was twice as much as he'd net in one year. Alarm bells went off. "If you're willing to pay that much, then I'm positive," he replied.

"Okay." Vincent tossed the DVD back into the box. "Okay. I'll let you be." He started to exit the tent and then turned around. "You know, it's for my baby girl, Martin. She needs help."

Now he was going for the sympathy card. Was she smoking weed in the back of her car during lunch hour? Seeing some boy Vincent didn't approve of? Though Vincent, casually wearing a Versace coat over his plain white t-shirt, obviously had money to throw around, things didn't add up, even if it was his daughter.

"Sorry," Martin said.

Vincent shrugged slowly and walked through the tent flap. Just as Martin's teeth sunk midway through greasy corndog breading, Vincent popped his head back in.

"Oh, I almost forgot, I need to meet with you after the fair closes on Friday. I just remembered that the board voted on some budget adjustments and we're going to have to talk about your contract for next year."

Martin met the man's steely gaze. He should have known it wasn't going to be so simple.

"Fine. What do you want?"

* * *

I've never done anything like this, Martin had told Vincent in the man's cavernous, Georgian-style entryway. *I'm not sure—*

Vincent had shut him up by unlatching the brown leather briefcase and revealing rows of tightly wrapped greenbacks. *You got one hour to do the job,* he had said.

And what if it doesn't work, Martin asked.

You get to keep your $50k.

Martin didn't need to follow up on what that might mean for his fairgrounds future. He'd have to consider it a severance package.

* * *

Standing at her bedside, he set the timer on his watch.

"Hi, Judy. My name is Martin Yurik." He cleared his throat. Manipulating people on the stage was different—very different—than manipulating a person in private. When it was done in front of a live audience, showmanship made up over fifty-percent of it. And he never outright lied to them. He just convinced them to believe certain things that were untrue for entertainment value. It was harmless.

His stomach churned as he stared at the IV drip-line running into the pinched flesh between her forearm and bicep. The girl's face was pale and freckled. Her brown, almost red, hair was curly and fell neatly onto her shoulders. She had tiny ears and, oddly, had foundation in place along with mauve lipstick. If it wasn't for the bleeps and bloops of surrounding medical gear and the sickeningly sterile mix of rubbing alcohol and bleach permeating the room, she might have been any ordinary girl taking a nap. He tried to spot some resemblance between her and Vincent, but he was struggling.

The room was oddly decorated for a young girl who didn't look a day over eighteen. It resembled more of a cookie-cutter four-star hotel room with its cherry oak furniture and simple, french vanilla walls graced with a pair of still-life oil prints. If this wasn't Judy's bedroom, Martin wondered why her father wouldn't want her to potentially wake up in a more familiar place. Still, he wasn't handed a briefcase filled with $50,000 cash that morning to think beyond his job.

Martin sat down on the empty folding chair beside the bed and took hold of Judy's hand. Small graphs sketched up and down in see-saw patterns on monochrome green monitors, recording, Martin supposed, those all-important 'vitals' he had always heard about but never understood.

"I'm going play some light music for you now," Martin said. He reached over to the nightstand and pressed play on his portable stereo. The sound of the CD spinning generated a slight scraping sound before the tinkles and tings of ambient bells floated through the air.

According to Vincent, the doctors said she could hear and sense everything around her. Martin had plenty of firsts in his life, but he never even fathomed he could hypnotize someone in a coma. What would be the point?

Now he knew.

He peered down into the girl's face again.

Martin's one job was simple, but not easy:

He had to convince Judy to wake up.

* * *

Initially, Vincent wanted to be there during the whole thing. He said he wanted Judy to wake up and see his face, but Martin told him he'd refuse to do the job unless he was alone with her. He didn't need the distraction. Vincent was reluctant but relented.

Please, don't ask my Judy any questions, he had said. I don't want her to be confused. Her doctors insist I be the first to speak with her. If she's awake before the hour's up, you come and get me.

Martin's only hope was that a part of Judy's mind had an inclination to come back to the real world. If there was something here, even a sliver of memory that she cherished, who was Martin to say it was impossible?

But what if she didn't want to wake up? What if she was having the most amazing dream? People like Vincent didn't fully grasp that you couldn't violate a person's moral judgment or make them believe something against their will. If she had a strong enough reason to keep thinking the thoughts she was thinking, well, that was that.

Martin rolled up his sleeves, unbuttoned the top button of his collar, and for the next thirty minutes, went to work.

* * *

"One, you're slowly feeling all of your faculties returning under your control. Two, you're beginning to move around, stretching your body, feeling the electric impulses flow through your nervous system. And three, you're wide awake!"

After the snap of his fingers, nothing.

Beside leafless branches of elm scratching the outside of the shade-drawn bedroom window, the only noise was the squeaking of the folding chair as Martin shifted his weight toward Judy.

He placed an ear over her mouth and listened to her steady breathing.

At least the fifty grand would keep him afloat while he searched for a replacement job. The San Flamenco County Fair was his best-paying gig, both in the payout from the board and the quantity of merchandise he sold. He'd have to travel out of state, probably across the country, to make up for the loss.

He looked down at his watch. Ten minutes left. He paced the room, thinking about contacts he could ring up when, suddenly, the beeping from the monitors went haywire, speeding up and out of rhythm so rapidly until they flatlined within seconds.

Martin's stomach fell and his mind went instantly to matters of escape. What would Vincent think, Martin being the only one in the room with the girl?

Just as quickly as they'd stopped, the steady tones returned. The monitor patterns were see-sawing again and Martin was grateful the chair was directly behind him, because his ass would have landed on the floor the second he saw her light blue eyes focused on him.

"Help," she croaked.

* * *

Martin fed Judy water through a straw to ease her throat pain and listened intently as she filled him in on as much as she could.

She told him she wasn't Vincent's daughter. Her real father was an ex-business partner of Vincent's. The two had a falling out and Vincent had kidnapped her, trying to get her to reveal where the family had stashed some money he believed he was owed. She began to cry, telling Martin that she really didn't know, but Vincent didn't believe her. During her interrogation, she had been beaten so badly, she fell asleep, unable to wake up until now.

That's when Martin noticed the faint bruises beneath her makeup.

He learned she had only been under for about a week.

"You have to help me," she said.

This was turning into a nightmare. A very, very large part of Martin wished he'd never given in to Vincent's ultimatum, but now that he knew about Judy's situation, he couldn't just abandon her.

Seconds before his watch timer went off, the hinges of the bedroom door squealed.

Vincent stood in the doorframe with a pistol in his hand and a solemn look on his face.

"Thanks, Martin. I had faith in you. But remember, I told you that I had to be the first one to speak to her. Doctor's orders."

* * *

It didn't take Martin long to wrap things up. The music was still playing in the background, just below the surface of consciousness. He was lucky Vincent had been listening through the door long enough to slip into the first stage of suggestion.

"Vincent, your daughter is going to be late for school. You asked me to pick her up, remember? You said you weren't feeling well and needed your rest."

Vincent stared at Martin, yet somehow past him, with the eyes of a lost soul. Martin put on an air of confidence, much like he was up on stage. Still, tiny tremors ran through his body and he placed one hand on the back of his chair to steady himself.

"Oh, right. I…uh…really do appreciate you picking her up," he said.

Cold waves of relief swept through Martin's core. He kept himself focused on Vincent.

"Don't forget," Martin said, "before you take your nice, long, relaxing nap, that you were going to loan me your gun for safekeeping."

Vincent eyed the pistol in his hand as if wondering how it had gotten there. He extended it to Martin who gently pulled it away. He stood there, dazed, while Martin helped Judy out of bed. She was weak to walk on her own and he had to carry her down the stairs to his car.

Martin drove off to the police station with a briefcase full of bills and a girl full of details.

Process Summary

The Hypnotist is story number thirty-eight in the #52ShortStories challenge.

Every year during my junior high and high school days, I would spend an evening at the local county fair. There were the conniving carnival games, my favorite ride–the Gravitron, and those shiny, red, tooth-decay-inducing candy apples. But my favorite thing was to watch the hypnotist. He would perform on an outdoor stage and would call volunteers up, lulling them into a super-relaxed state where they were duped into performing ballet and singing at the top of their lungs, all for the audience's amusement. I'm not sure why the memory popped into my head recently, but it's always been simmering on the backburner.

I felt the hypnotist could make a pretty entertaining protagonist and would find many uses for his bag o' tricks. Hopefully, you felt the same upon reading!

THE OWL HIS ANTHEM

Statistics

Synopsis: Ernie is locked up in an institution and finds himself visited by something mysterious.

Word Count: 2,600

Genre: Horror

Completed Week: May 17th – May 22nd

The Owl His Anthem

Ernie smiled at the pinhole patterns on the drop ceiling and if he squinted just right, he could see at least six faces smiling back. A hint of bluish moonlight streaming through the tiny barred window put all of the shadows in the right places. Two of the faces were long and gregarious, one squished and wrinkled like a rotten plum. The others were just ordinary.

But they all smiled.

A tune had been running through Ernie's mind since yesterday and he hummed it as best he could. He couldn't recall where or when he'd first heard it. By repeating it aloud, he hoped to discover not just its source, but what made it so memorable. He picked it apart like a complex mathematical formula, figuring out how each variable served some purpose in a grander scheme.

A door handle twisted and clicked. Ernie stopped humming immediately and looked. Chilly air slammed into his exposed face while the rest of his body sweated beneath an itchy wool blanket.

"Ernie," a woman said in a harsh voice.

He ignored her, content to watch the faces.

"Ernie, I'm going to turn on lights," she said in that vague, Eastern European accent. Ernie tried to remember where she told him she had come from. Maybe she hadn't. He thought Yugoslavia or somewhere like that, but he was pretty sure that was no longer a place. Then again, he wasn't sure of much these days.

A flicker and then there it was—the hum of fluorescent bulbs. Ernie didn't even close his eyes. He let the brightness blind him. It was a challenge to fight the sting. He liked challenges, most of the time.

Kolinda sat a tray carrying two tiny paper cups on the bedside table. As Ernie's vision returned, he craned his neck toward her. She leaned over him and pressed a switch on the bed to incline his torso. On the way up, he caught a noseful of rosewater perfume. His eyes met the top of her breasts which were slightly exposed by the cut in her uniform.

She looked up and caught his eyes. An irritated look swept over her face, but she stood up and straightened out her top. She wasn't young and had a big nose, but Ernie was never a picky man and he wasn't going to start being picky under the current circumstances.

"Open," Kolinda said.

She placed one tablet and a large pill onto his tongue. Always bitter and Kolinda was always slow to give him the other cup of water to wash away the flavor. The one and only time he swallowed his medicine without waiting for water, the back of his throat burned for days on end. She didn't seem to be changing her attitude now, taking her sweet time to get him the water.

"Good," she said. She crushed the paper cups in her hand and her tennis shoes tapped lightly against the floor as she beelined for the exit.

"Nurse Kolinda," Ernie said. The scent of rosewater was fading and his throat felt rough.

"What?" she said, still facing the door, impatience in her voice.

"Can you please leave the lights on?"

She remained silent for a moment. "What, you afraid of boogey-man?"

Ernie said nothing, only looking at the back of her graying brunette hair tied up in a bun.

"How is it boogeyman afraid of other boogeyman?" she asked before flipping off the lights and shutting the door behind her.

The deadbolt clicked into place a second later.

* * *

The smiley faces were back, but they didn't seem to be smiling so much anymore. At least, not in the happy way they had before. In fact, their smiles seemed to grow oddly threatening as they widened like the one on that cat from the old story with the little girl.

Ernie wanted to shut his eyes. He really did, but he was afraid to let his guard down. He didn't know why. There was no active threat. Nothing tangible to fear outside another monotonous twenty-four hours of either sleeping or barely remaining awake inside this hell of an institution. So instead he kept watch, began to hum the tune again, and stayed vigilant against the nothing.

An itch crept up on his forehead. Futile as it was, he naturally tried to scratch it. He wiggled his arms around in their restraints. They'd been stuck at his side for so long, Ernie found it hard to imagine a time when they had been separated from his torso in the first place. Those doctors, he thought, they sure do a fine job of keeping things tight. He supposed they had a reason to be so thorough.

He lifted his eyebrows and shifted his head back and forth, hoping that scrunching his brow and general movement would do the trick.

No such luck. The itch kept on itching.

He stopped humming the tune and groaned.

The moon's rays cut in and out against the ceiling and wall like a hand passing over a flashlight. It had to be a bird, given that he was on the second floor. At least he was yesterday. Or maybe the day before.

What kind of bird, Ernie wondered. He'd like to see birds again.

The flashing continued several times until the moonlight disappeared altogether.

Click.

Click.

Click.

Something was tapping against the glass. Ernie craned his head as much as physics and anatomy allowed, but he couldn't see the window directly. He dug his fingers into his palms and flexed his forearms. To comfort himself, he started humming again.

Click.

Click.

Click.

"Go away!" he yelled, presuming a crow or a pigeon saw something it liked inside. The clicking stopped. Silence overtook the room once again, like a strange pressure bearing down on Ernie. "No, wait," he whispered. "Please, come back."

His eyes felt heavy and his chin bounced off his chest as he fought sleep.

Click.

Click.

Crash.

The sound of glass hitting the floor in a hundred pieces echoed across the room. Ernie's voice was caught in his throat. He wanted to scream for Kolinda, but his neck muscles tensed up. He stared at the door, waiting. Surely someone would come rushing in to assess the situation.

There was the sound of something rubbing against the iron bars, like a piece of steel wool on cast iron. It vaguely reminded Ernie of his days scrubbing his fingers raw against dirty pots and pans, all underneath canopies of hot, soapy water. The days not long after he'd gotten sick and lost his position at the University.

The rubbing continued, ending only with a heavy thump on the linoleum and the shadow bars projected on the wall once again.

The ceiling was all smiles.

* * *

"Nurse!" Ernie screamed, knowing it only escaped his mind but never his lips. His throat felt dry again. He desperately wanted another tiny paper cup of water. The smell of crisp midnight air entered his nostrils. It reminded him of recent nights he'd tried to forget but had been forced to recall in innumerable conversations with the doctors and the investigators. Smells of the countryside as his shovel catapulted worm-filled earth over his bent back.

There was a pitter-patter mixed in with the sound of something being dragged on the surrounding floor. Ernie turned his head. He thought he saw the tip of something pointed and furry in the last bit of moonlight before it entered the darkness-swept area beside his bed.

"Who's there?" he asked.

"Who's there?" came a reply, unearthly and garbled like poor radio reception.

The thing, it schlumped and schlepped up beside the bed and even though it was only inches away, Ernie's eyes perceived nothing but black mass. He swore he felt the blood pressure rising within his arteries as a heat passed through his entire body. Sweat poured down his head and streamed into his eyes, stinging them.

Yet he left them open.

"What do you want?" he asked.

"What do you want?" came the reply.

The thing's breath was like a steam kettle which boiled a mix of manure and sulfur. Ernie wanted to turn away but was more afraid to expose the back of his head and neck to this thing which he could not identify.

"Stop repeating!" Ernie tried yelling again, begging in the back of his mind for that cup of water. His throat felt so raw. Where was Nurse Kolinda?

"Do you want to scratch that itch, Ernie?" Though the voice was choppy, Ernie didn't seem to have any trouble understanding it.

"What?"

"Do you want to scuttle around? Dance like you used to with the Mrs.?"

"Leave me alone!" Ernie shouted. "Kolinda!"

"She can't hear you," the voice said. "And besides, she don't care."

He tried to scream louder and it was the pain and hiss coming from his throat that forced Ernie to realize he hadn't said a single word. Everything had been spoken only in his head. His larynx was still wound as tight as a noose. The feeling dredged up more memories that finally forced him to shut his eyes.

"You're not real," he thought. "Whatever you are, you're not real."

"What's reality, Ernie?"

"Tell me what you want," he said. "Or just kill me!"

"Kill you? Why would I want to kill you? I'm here to help, Ernie. Always have been. Seems they've sent me away for a bit." Ernie thought he heard the echoes of a crinkling paper cup being crushed. "But I found you! Oh, I'm so happy that I found you!"

A lightheadedness fell over Ernie like a thick cloud, but every time he thought he would pass out, something pulled him back.

"Stay with me, old friend. Stay with me. You know, the old docs, they used to be good. Used to be almost vicious in their work. Near orgasmic shocks to the system. Chop-chop to the brain. I could respect that. *We* could respect that. But now—" The thing spit out noise like someone was changing channels on a TV at rapid pace. "What, with the feel-good pop psychology and these pretty little pills, it almost makes one feel ashamed. Don't you feel ashamed, Ernie?"

Ernie's first impulse was to tell how he had nothing to be ashamed of, but a greater lie would never have been spoken.

"I'm getting help," he said.

"By having your limbs tied to a bed and being wheeled around in a stupor for almost every hour of your waking life? How the hell can anyone call that help?" The thing clucked its tongue. "Nope, nope. This is much worse than I thought, what they done to you so far. Maybe they did get rid of all your sense, you poor thing."

Ernie felt something stroking his arm—the arm still beneath the blanket, tensed, and still, as the thing in front of him noted, tied to the bed.

"I'll be better soon," Ernie said.

More garbling and Ernie thought he heard something wet splat against the ground. "Better. That's a landmine of a word if I ever encountered one. And soon? No, buddy, not soon enough. But I'm here to help. I can give you *soon*. I can make soon a reality. Is that real enough for you?"

Ernie's ears were alight. The warm breath that was against his face shifted to the other side of the bed. The bed's tiny motor vibrated and hummed as Ernie felt the bed began to elevate, as if Kolinda was there pressing the button to bring him to a sitting position. He was elevated to a ninety-degree angle when the motor came to a stop.

"What are—"

The thoughts were interrupted as he felt something pungent punch through his airways and jet down into his insides. Gagging, choking. It was like Ernie's guts were being clenched and yanked up into his esophagus. He leaned over and vomited all over himself, feeling chunks of gelatin exit his mouth and the bitter taste of medicine coating his gums.

After a few dry heaves, everything finally seemed to stop. The warm breath returned to his face, keeping him on the edge of nausea. Ernie's eyes were watering and he became distraught. Why could he still see nothing? Why had his eyes not adjusted to the darkness surrounding his person? He looked at the ceiling and saw the smiling faces were now crying. Smiles turned upside down.

"Shall we call for nursey?" asked the breath.

* * *

Kolinda contemplated the blinking red light on the terminal beside her desk. She had five minutes before the end of her shift. She could have left him for Sandy to take over, but she felt a certain obligation to the man. She knew she shouldn't. The things he had done, or at least what they said he had done—she tried to imagine herself in the victim's shoes or as one of her relatives. My, how they must have felt.

But Nurse Kolinda saw a pitiable old man who appeared to have every ounce of life sucked from him. She knew he would never get better. His type never did. But there protocols and procedures to follow. The same protocols and procedures that paid her bills and let her go home every morning at five o'clock in the morning so she could nod off to reruns of *Coach*.

She unlocked the door and as soon as she entered, she thought she caught the whiff of the elm trees swaying in the wind outside—as if someone had opened a window. But the only window in this room was sealed shut and even if it wasn't, there was no easy way of opening the tiny thing as it was offset ten feet from the ground, butting up against the ceiling.

When her eyes finally caught up with her nose, her hands lost just enough feeling for the tray to slip and crash onto to the floor. A loud clang echoed through the room and into the hallway. Cool water splashed on her right ankle and her hands flew up to her mouth as if to keep her soul from escaping.

Crouched on the bed like an alley cat ready to pounce a rat, Ernie sat looking at the nurse, humming the tune she'd caught him humming for the past two days.

Protocols and procedures, she thought.

But drills were drills and Kolinda remained slack-jawed and frozen in the face of reality. While Kolinda was debating whether or not to hit the emergency page button attached to her uniform or run for the door, the decision was taken from her hands.

Ernie leaped from the bed and slammed into Kolinda, knocking her to the ground. The wind was knocked out of her, and the second before she regained it, the second before the scream began to leave her lips, Ernie's hand clasped over her mouth. His face was inches from hers and she could feel his balmy, putrid breath penetrating every pore in her flesh. It smelled like feces and mud.

Ernie pulled his face back and his expression shifted between bliss and sadness, like quickly-turned pages in an animation flip book. His red eyes shifted left-to-right as he looked into Kolinda's own pupils. Yellow crystals of dried phlegm hung around his sockets like algae on a stone. All the while, he kept humming the tune.

As her breath was leaving her, she recognized the song, falling asleep once again to the theme of *Coach*.

Process Summary

The Owl His Anthem is story number thirty-nine in the #52ShortStories challenge.

Just like the previous story, the title and inspiration for this one were copped from Lord Byron's *Don Juan*. I just love some of the phrases he weaved into his poetry. I started things off without a clue of who, where, and what was involved…sometimes it works out, sometimes it doesn't. In this case, I ended up deleting most of what I had typed out on the first day. Still, I think it helped me figure out where I should take the story which, like the owl's nighttime abode, wound up rather dark. But I hope you enjoyed it!

Out of the Picture

Statistics

Synopsis: An old woman discovers an old photograph and a key to the past.

Word Count: 2,000

Genre: Sci-Fi Romance

Completed Week: May 22nd – May 29th

Out of the Picture

The tones were sepia, but Sylvia would have bet all of last year's investment returns that the man's eyes were a turquoise blue. Beneath the edges of his army side cap, she could see his coarse hair, cut short. Thin lips stretched around a toothy smile. He also bore the familiar sliver of a white scar across his chin.

Sitting on uncut grass with his hands resting on his knees, he didn't seem concerned about dirtying his olive-green service coat or matching slacks. Crow's feet made the man look old, but something about that face reminded Sylvia the lines had more to do with the hard quality of his years than their number.

"Ms. Hawthorne, are you okay?"

"Oh," Sylvia said, barely able to peel her eyes away from the photograph. "I'm fine, Clara." She managed a gracious smile, but based on her assistant's reaction, Sylvia didn't have a doubt in her mind that she came across as anything *other* than needing help. She must have been staring slack-jawed at the same spot for minutes.

She'd begun to doubt it would ever happen, to the point that she'd mostly forgotten. What sort of cosmic fate allowed this picture to wind up at an antique shop that Sylvia had passed many times but had only entered today on a whim? How long had it been here, waiting for her?

Clara started to turn away.

"Actually."

Her assistant paused while Sylvia opened the door of the glass curio cabinet and reached past the Hummel figurines and marble ashtrays. Her wrinkled hands shook slightly as she took hold of the dusty, twelve-by-fifteen picture frame leaning against the back of the cabinet. As she held it close to her face, she felt herself getting lost in the image once again.

"Do you like that frame?" Clara asked.

"Yes," Sylvia replied without hesitation. "I want to purchase this." The price tag made mention of 1918, Tiffany & Co. sterling silver, and $1,495.

Clara grabbed the frame and Sylvia reluctantly let go.

"It has a lovely finish," Clara said. "Anything else before we go?" She looked at her thin, white wristwatch. "You have a shareholders meeting in twenty minutes."

"No, just that," Sylvia replied.

"Okay, I'll have the clerk remove the photo and put—"

"No!" The panic in Sylvia's voice startled a couple who were shuffling through a box of rusted steel signs. "No, please, I like the picture. Make sure you keep it."

Clara narrowed her eyebrows and nodded. "Yes, of course. No problem." She stepped away with the frame. Relieved, Sylvia closed her eyes and put a hand on the corner of the cabinet to maintain her balance. She pictured the man in the photo, trying to count the years in which she had last thought of him. Trying to remember every moment together before he left for France.

* * *

She let her plate of sliced turkey and asparagus grow cold on the china and her hot tea had since turned room temperature. It was late and the chef had left a note stating his apologies as he had to run home early because his daughter was sick, but he'd left simple instructions on reheating the meal.

It was no matter. Sylvia wasn't hungry. All she cared about was the photo propped up on the mahogany dining room table in front of her. Except for the low sounds of Bing Crosby's rendition of *Let Me Call You Sweetheart* playing on a modern record player at the other end of the room, the house was void of life. Sylvia hadn't listened to this song for a long time, and given her decades-old distaste for it, was surprised to find she had the 12-inch in her collection.

Sylvia reached for the frame and began to remove the copper backing. Once the photo was out, she tossed the frame onto the floor where it cracked in half.

Her mauve fingernail ran over the man's face and body.

"Hello, Samuel," she said. "I always knew that if it was meant to be, this day would come."

She turned the photograph over and her breath caught in her throat. The print was wider than the frame and it had been folded over at its rightmost edge to make it fit. She unfolded the edge so that the complete picture was before her.

Her expectations were met.

There was a young woman standing just to the right of Samuel with bobbed hair and a hobble skirt with its narrow hem. The woman smiled, but only with her mouth. Her eyes betrayed an infinite sadness.

"And hello to you too, young Sylvia."

* * *

The photographer was putting away his equipment while a thin breeze brought the scent of purple-flowered plum trees into Sylvia's presence.

"I told my parents that we would meet them at seven for dinner," Samuel said.

Sylvia said nothing, thinking only of their snapshot in time, wondering if she was able to hide her melancholy from the camera's eye. If Samuel noticed, he didn't let on. He took her hands in his and kissed her cheek. Sylvia gazed past the trees and at the calm lake spread wide behind them.

"Don't," Samuel said.

She turned. "What?"

"Don't think about tomorrow."

She was a fool to think he hadn't seen her. "How can I not?"

* * *

The needle had fallen off the record, leaving a quiet, rhythmic click in the background, no different than her life after the first war. When Samuel didn't come back, Sylvia had fallen into her own quiet, rhythmic click. She married three times, none of the marriages happy, none of them lasting long enough to produce any children, but they were all productive in their own way.

Sylvia focused her energies on other things. She was a pretty girl and had no problems attracting men of means. Men she had used more than they had used her. Where other wives had taken their positions and situations for granted, Sylvia built herself a quiet empire. She'd purchased the right stocks, made the right connections, and pissed off the right people to leave her one of the richest women in New Jersey.

Would she be willing to give it up for him? All of it?

After sixty years, the question was as simple to answer as it had always been.

She picked up the telephone and rang her good friend, Dr. Alou.

* * *

He came quickly with his dark brown briefcase.

"Thank you for coming in the middle of the night, Doctor."

"For you, Ms. Hawthorne...for this opportunity," he said, "I would come at any hour."

He was a grateful man. Where others had insisted on immediate results, Sylvia had bid her time and bet on the long-term. She'd heard Dr. Alou speak at a futurist conference over thirty years ago and immediately took him under her employ. Academia had scorned and ridiculed him. He hadn't been allowed to publish in any legitimate scientific journal after revealing his theories, but Sylvia cared not about that. The man had a fierce faith that was much like her own.

"It's time to put all of your years to use," Sylvia said.

Dr. Alou's eyes lit up behind his horn-rimmed glasses.

Together, they walked into the spacious sitting room and sat next to each other on a flowery Victorian sofa. She blended in well, but with the wild gray hair horseshoed around his balding head and Levis tucked into a pair of cowboy boots, Dr. Alou seemed as out of place as Sylvia suddenly felt.

His bony fingers rested on the top of the briefcase which sat on his lap.

"You should know that we've been unable to test," he said. "The risks, and all, as we've discussed..."

"Understood. Carry on." Her heart was racing, but she'd long since developed the ability to exude an air of control.

Dr. Alou popped open the brass latches, gently removed a sheer black box with a numeric keypad on top, and placed it on the mahogany coffee table before them. He then pulled out a pair of thin green wires, each connected to a white electrode. He plugged the other ends into a receptacle on the side of the box.

"May I?" he asked, nodding at her face.

Sylvia nodded. She wanted him to just get it over with.

Dr. Alou reached into his pocket and pulled out a pair of alcohol swabs. He ripped their packages open and, leaning over, rubbed Sylvia's temples. The chemical smell seemed to awaken her thoughts, seemed to bring home the fact that all of her years had been riding on this. Did she want to go through with it? Would she be able to live with the disappointment if it didn't work?

She knew she wouldn't be able to live with the disappointment if she didn't try.

"How long will it take?" she asked.

"You won't even know its happened."

His lack of hesitation reassured her. He placed the electrodes on her and she held the photo of young Samuel in her hands. Out of the corner of her eyes, she saw the doctor carefully punch the keypad. There was a subtle hum rising from the box and into her brain.

"Think of him," Dr. Alou said.

Her thumbnail caressed the side Samuel's cheek, stopping only when the room spun beyond her ability to perceive it.

* * *

"I told my parents that we would meet them at seven for dinner," Samuel said.

Sylvia's jaw was slightly sore from holding the smile. She watched the photographer carefully dismantle his tripod and box camera contraption. It took great effort to focus on something as the sudden bout of vertigo overcame her.

"You're not still worried about the expense, are you?" Samuel asked. "Dear, when are we ever going to get married again? We have only one honeymoon."

There was a moment where Sylvia's brain seemed to freeze up. She'd lost a sudden sense of place, but the world began to stabilize again.

"Pumpkin, are you okay?"

She felt a reassuring hand on her back and the other on her arm. The warm sun pressed its rays into her face and the light ammonia-like smell of Samuel's lye soap entered her nostrils.

"Yes," she said and turned to look at his face, starting at the scar running up his chin, past his azure eyes, and to his slightly kinky hair. She stepped back and took in his pinstripe vest and collared stark-white shirt.

"Do you need to sit down?" he asked.

She grabbed onto Samuel and pulled him into her, feeling his slightly-whiskered cheeks against hers.

"No," she whispered. "Please, no."

"Well, I don't know what's brought on this sudden bout of amorousness, but perhaps we should visit all the parks in France if its to be a new habit."

He chuckled and so did she. A small tear ran down her cheek and onto his shoulder.

"I don't....I don't know what's come over me," she said, "but I just feel this sudden need to hold on to you, Samuel. I can't describe it, other than to say that for the briefest of moments, you seemed so far away from me that I feared I'd never be able to touch you again."

He gently pushed her away and took her hands in his. His eyes sparkled with life.

"I'm not going anywhere without you," he said. "Besides, what fun is visiting France without someone to share it with? Though I suppose then I could tell you some fabulous story of how I had tea with the visiting Kaiser and convinced him that his recent celebration of one hundred years of peace with France did not have nearly enough fireworks."

Process Summary

Out of the Picture is story number forty in the #52ShortStories challenge.

Other creative types know that inspiration is everywhere. I can't tell you why this particular instance was triggered, but my family and I were in one of those art and frame stores where there are shelves lined with random sepia-toned and black-and-white stock photography–a just-married couple exiting a church, a family having a picnic, maybe someone's golden shepherd running in the grass.

Some part of my brain imagined a character walking into the store and recognizing someone in one of those photographs. Originally, my character wasn't sure why they recognized the person and I wrote a whole bunch of words down this path which had me beyond frustrated because it wasn't going to be wrapped up in a short story. That's great and all, except when I'm already behind and on a tight deadline.

So, I scratched a couple thousand words and practically started again. I think the story worked out better and I have my first reader to thank. I always go to her when I'm stuck and she usually steers me in a better direction.

I hope you enjoyed the end product!

Your Punching Privileges Have Been Revoked

Statistics

Synopsis: An aging boxer is looking for a comeback and an old man seems to offer the key.

Word Count: 2,800

Genre: Urban Fantasy

Completed Week: May 29th – June 2nd

Your Punching Privileges Have Been Revoked

Yeah, the vaseline helps a little, though that's mainly so the skin don't break when the guy gets in a lucky scrape, with his red leather glove rubbing against my almost equally leathered face. It seems to be happening more and more lately. The sweat always manages to get in the eyes, though. Deep in the corners, ya know? And then I'm up until God knows when that night because my eyes are burning like a son-of-a-bitch and I'm squirting all kinds of shit in there that my doc gave me, only after a lecture on how maybe I ought to think about taking it easy and also after his favorite scary stories about what getting hit in the head does to the brain.

Thanks doc, just give me the eye juice and I'll take it from here.

I shuffle back towards the edge of the ring where I'd climbed in, having rubbed off the liniment from the inside of my glove onto the top rope. I don't have to put on much of an act as I fall back. We're only in the third round and the battle had long since become mental, what, with my chest feeling like an elephant's taking a nap on it and my shoulders burning like a dead hero's funeral pyre.

I got to give this kid a run, though. Have to keep the audience of twenty entertained and off their phones. They gave me another young one tonight. I can tell he doesn't want to be here, thinking he's beyond fighting a geezer in shorts hiked up to his nipples, but here he is because his manager said everyone has to do it. Anyone in the Northeastern circuit has to come up against Rocko because the guy has done so much for the sport, ya know?

They always come in thinking they only have to dance with me a round or two and then take me down. And sometimes I let them.

But sometimes I don't.

The outside of my gloves finds the slickness on the ropes as I bounce off them and then fall back to rest with my hands up in front of my face, blocking the incoming hits.

This guy's a Puerto Rican, probably lives not too far from my old neighborhood. I know he's not even really trying and still his footwork is impressive. It calls to mind the little dance I'd seen Vasquez do back in '07 before my uppercut found the glass bonework that composed his chin and delivered me my third title belt.

After allowing a few jabs to the stomach, I feign like I'm winding up for a right hook. I almost see the split-second smirk on the kid's face. He takes the bait and comes in with a left. I hold what little breath I have, duck, and let the boy find nothing but air. Now he's off balance. I put the rest of my speed and strength into a couple of quick jabs to his wide-eyed face.

The kid knows something is wrong right away, but he looks confused. He blinks a couple of times trying to squeeze away the sting. I take my cue and get to work on his stomach, followed by an uppercut which sends his mouthpiece flying across the ring with a pound of spit. He leans to the right, seeking some stability with his gloves on an imaginary rope. He only finds more air. His eyes look like a pair of eggshells sitting side-by-side in the nest as his head lands on the mat, bouncing once or twice, emitting a sonic boom across the tiny gym.

Bobby, the ref, starts counting down and I stand patiently. I could head back to the corner at this point. The match is as good as done. My signature punch is my signature punch for a reason.

I look out toward the people sitting on the bleachers. Some young, but mostly older folks. The men are wearing dark coats and a few have women with them that are looking away with curled faces like they'd just been force-fed lemons. Except there's this one gal who is on her feet, a big grin on her angelic face and whose eyes are smiling down on the Puerto Rican like a pair of spotlights. Her male companion looks like he's going to be sick.

I don't look down at the kid as Bobby yanks my wrist in the air and declares me the winner. Two weeks of aspirin and the boy will be alright, though he might be talking funny for a while.

The walk back to the locker room is always a solemn affair for me, only because it takes all I have to present myself to the world like I'm still a champion. Like I'm still that guy from ten years ago.

Like I'm still Rocko Giannetti, three-time world champion.

* * *

My arms feel like they're going to fall out of their sockets. It's going to take the rest of that liniment tonight, I just know it, and wouldn't you know, my cutman took off leaving me to figure out a way to somehow apply the damned stuff. I wonder what I pay him for and then I realize I don't pay him anything outside of free lessons.

There's a tapping on the floor behind me.

"Looked like you were about to take a nap on the canvas a few times out there, Rocko."

Leaning on a cane just inside the locker room, with a crooked back and bushy gray eyebrows, is an old man who makes me feel like a newborn babe. Squinty-eyed and wearing a dirty, pea-green beanie pulled down barely over his forehead, his unshaven face matches the growl in his voice.

"You come in just to hassle me?" I ask.

"Just sayin', that wasn't the Rocko that I seen fifteen years ago at Booker's Palace." I'm pulling on my socks at this point, wondering how I could get the old bat out of my hair.

"I can still hold my own," I say, putting on that glare I'd used so well in front of the press back in the day. It wasn't really a challenge, but I hoped it would get him to leave. Instead, he shuffles a little bit closer.

"You sure got some luck," he says. "Seems the boy lost his way towards the end there. Like he couldn't see no more."

I began lacing my shoes, still sweating a little after my shower. I won't be fully cooled down until an hour or so later.

"You got somethin' to say, old man, say it. Otherwise, I got things to do." I remember that I got to stop by the payday shop and put in for another loan. There's no way I'll be getting my check for tonight's bout for another week, at the earliest.

"What if I told you I could get you back to your old fighting form?" he asks. "Get you moving and swinging like Marciano or Ali again? Maybe even like 2007 Rocko?"

I have to laugh. Does this chump think I'm going to buy his snake oil? Does he not realize how many chumps just like him have been in here over the past month?

I give the standard reply. "I'd say you were the devil and then I'd have to apologize, 'cause I ain't got no soul to sell."

The old man grinned. His brown gums were highlighted by his ridiculously phony white dentures. "No, I ain't the devil and I don't want your worthless soul. But I'm not doing this out of the goodness of my heart. Of course there's a price. I want my cut."

I'm on my feet now and he's in my way. I could brush by him, but I still have that ingrained sense of respect for the old folks. I was raised by my grandparents and though I wouldn't say I was the best-behaved kid, I look back on them with nothing but respect for what they'd managed to instill in this thick skull of mine.

"Alright, Mr. Spit it out. I ain't got all night."

That eerie smile crept back across his face and he reaches into his ratty old pants pocket, pulling out a yellowed sock.

"You wear this, kid, and you'll be moving like a goddamn bullet train and won't nobody be able to stop you."

I almost double over at hearing the word *kid*, but my back is killing me, plus, I guess it's all perspective. He dangles the sock in the air in front of me.

"Alright, I'll play your game, old man. Let's say I put on that sock and get myself some nasty new foot disease. Why you bringing this to me? Why not sell your laundry to one of these new kids?"

"Bah," the old man says, waving away the suggestion like it's a buzzing gnat. "New kids bring in the new kids, but vets who come back—they bring in both the new kids and the old guys. Imagine the headlines: *Rocko Giannetti, Comeback of the Century*. Everyone loves a comeback. Don't you want to be able to have a meal again without worrying about which of your pals you're going to bum it off? And, I might add, that's a dwindling number of pals. I'm sure you see the hesitance and looks in their eyes. They're awful tired of serving as your personal charity."

Now the clown is making it personal. "You seem to know a lot about me. Who are you?"

I can almost hear the snaps and cracks as the old man straightens up that crooked back of his and bears his eyes into mine.

"I'm an old fan, Rocko. Been following you a long time, but you probably don't remember me."

I try. I really do, but I can't match that face against anything in the memory banks. Here we stand, alone in a scum- and mold-stained locker room with dirty towels and rags strewn across a cheap folding table and the only bench in the place.

"Listen," I say, "I got another match next week. I'm not looking forward to it. Every inch of my body aches right down to my balls and they ain't ached for years. If I wear your sock, will you go away?"

He tosses the sock and it lands on my right shoulder.

"You wear it and your whole life will change, I promise you that."

* * *

I feel it before I even step in the ring. This raging inferno passing through every ounce of muscle and sinew in my body, contained only by a promise to be unleashed once I'm dancing on the mat.

As soon as the bell rings, I'm like a wild tiger that's broken free from its cage at the Bronx Zoo and now I'm free to pounce on the first good-looking piece of flesh I come across. This time, it's another young guy and he never sees me coming. He's ranked twelve and one and came into the ring as cocky as any son-of-a-bitch I ever knew. But as soon as the first two flurries of jabs knock him back a little, the tiny crowd jumps to their feet and the boy realizes he's not going to be able to call this one in.

Damn, do I feel good. I'd left the liniment on the ropes just in case, but I knew I wasn't going to need it. I spot the old man sitting inconspicuously in the audience and he gives me a wink. I'll offer ten percent, but if he demands twenty, I feel fantastic enough to take it. I look back at the kid and want to tell him through my mouthpiece, "Get ready for twelve and two, chief," but I keep it to myself.

A few bobs and weaves and a strong right cross leaves his left cheek starting to puff up like a pink marshmallow. I feel kind of bad for him, honestly, so I let him drop back toward his corner. The old Rocko would have been five paragraphs into his trash talk by now, but age has put at least a little more grace in me.

Pretty sure we got about thirty seconds left and it only takes me half a second to decide to take this kid down before the bell rings. It would be a mercy, honestly. There's a look of fear on his face as I approach.

Right about halfway across the canvas, I feel something begin to tingle in my right foot. The foot with the tight, yellow sock. And almost instantly, it's like someone dropped me into The Pond at Central Park in the middle of January.

The soles of my shoes are glued to the mat.

My thighs come to a full stop.

Then my arms stop moving and my neck freezes up. The only thing I have any control over this point seems to be my eyes which open wide as I watch the kid dance timidly toward me. I can tell he's wondering if this is some sort of fast one I've baked up.

No, kid. I'm screwed.

I see the first fist coming straight for me and I'm helpless to do a damn thing about it. Then another, and another, until finally, I see nothing but the world beginning to tip over around me.

* * *

I seem to be falling asleep and waking up in different places. I was out there on the mat and then I remember my cornerman looking down at me, seeming like he was yelling something, but there was no sound coming out his mouth. And then I'm here now, laying on what I think is the folding table in the locker room—at least I think I'm laying down because I see nothing but fuzzy bright lights running along the ceiling. And I don't think anyone else is here except me. I think my cornerman said something about calling an ambulance. So I'm left with only my thoughts of what the hell is wrong with me until I hear a tapping sound getting louder on the tile and finally see the bottom of the old man's wobbly, whiskered chin.

"Hey, Rocko. Looks like you're a little down in the dumps."

I want nothing more than to peel off that piece of shit sock and shove it in his mouth for all the good it did me tonight, but I can't feel anything enough to move.

He continues, "I know what getting punched in the head can do to a man, so I don't know how your memory's gotten over the years. Still, maybe you can fire up enough brain cells to remember a boy named Joe Lekowski. Eh? You fought him back in '01 before you came up big time. Ring a bell?"

I hear ringing bells, but they don't have anything to do with a Joe Lekowski. I want to tell the old man that I've fought a lot of folks over the years, but my tongue is as limp as a pile of cod on the docks.

He disappears from my line of sight and I hear some shuffling of fabric, only to see his face pop back in. My sense of smell still seems to be with me as the stench of the sock being held over my face would make me gag if I could.

"This belonged to my Joe," he says. "He lost his mind, because of you. Wound up near a worthless vegetable until he finally passed last month."

I'd heard stories about some of the men I'd gone up against, but boxing is a dangerous sport. No guarantees.

"Do you remember what you said to my boy?"

Nope. Don't recall, old man.

"You said, 'Your punching privileges have been revoked.' That's all my Joe kept repeating, over and over again until he finally stopped speaking altogether."

He drops the sock on my face and now I can't see a thing.

"You were always a damn cheater, Rocko, and now you've paid the price. I told you I wanted my cut."

The sour sock has me close to vomiting and fearful of choking to death. I hear the tapping of the cane drifting away and the faint sound of sirens in the distance.

Process Summary

Your Punching Privileges Have Been Revoked is story number forty-one in the #52ShortStories challenge.

So, my son is a boy.

Kind of a redundant statement, I know, but I just wanted to emphasize that he likes to do very boyish things including lots of wrestling and punching. The punching has become a problem and at some point, something along the lines of "Your punching privileges have been revoked," came out of either my or my wife's mouth and it stuck. That's where this tale began. And who punches a lot? Boxers sprung to mind immediately. Where the rest came from, I couldn't tell ya. Just the nature of letting my subconscious work its magic (apparently quite literarily in this case). After the issues I had getting through the previous story, I was glad that this one seemed to write itself.

I initially wrote this story in past tense, but I found myself putting a few sentences down in present tense which really seemed to kick the telling into overdrive, so I went back about halfway through and fixed all that (hopefully)!

Oh, and voice, voice, voice. I really wanted to spend time focusing on voice and I *think* it came across. It's both amazing and overwhelming to imagine all of the different tools we writers have to bring a story to life. To me, I'm enthralled with the notion that there's just no end to the learning and we can always get better.

Spoil the Rod

Statistics

Synopsis: An assassin is sent to kill a powerful king, but discovers the task won't be so easy.

Word Count: 1,900

Genre: Fantasy

Completed Week: June 2nd – June 6th

52 Stories in 52 Weeks

Spoil the Rod

Don't spoil the rod, my old master had told me. *She's insatiable and she'll eat you alive.*

As I lay for the thirteenth hour in the northeast corner of the castle courtyard, tucked in by thorn-filled blackberry brambles, exhausted and scratched to all hell with ticks burrowed in parts of sweaty flesh they should never have access to and my elbows only inches from soil soaked in my own rancid urine, it dawned on me that he may have been on to something.

Still, I wasn't going to worry too much about it until the biggest job of my life was done.

For the forty-seventh time tonight, I watched Bartholomew, nineteen with not a whisker on his chin, stumble along the outside of the graystone, torchlit walls of the main hall, disappearing and reappearing in between thick columns carved to look like snakes winding up to swallow the second-floor balcony. Once past the columns, young Barty would round the corner and then I would see his counterpart, Malcolm, twenty-nine and built from superior stock. Malcolm is the type of guard one would seek to employ in every available position, but King Valdar likely had no idea such a greenhorn as Barty worked so close to the royal bedchambers. That's a natural consequence of being the most powerful king in the High Hills—as power multiplies, so does duty and you have to focus on the big things while relying on others to take care of everything else. It leaves gaps to be exploited by fathers with connections and money to bring their unseasoned sons as close to the inner circle as possible. Gaps, that to a person like me, are like gift baskets filled with sweet cordials and perfumes.

Once Barty returned, I knew the time was close. He paused occasionally now to lean against the wall with one hand and bend over slightly at the waist, removing his helmet to rub the sweat from his head. Tonight, Barty's queasiness came courtesy of one of those good women making a living at the Singing Coyote tavern just inside the city gates. Seeing that my friend Santia had done her job tonight brought a smile to my face. She'd lubricated Barty with alcohol and other tricks. It's good to have people you can trust. Relationships are important in my line of work.

I wouldn't have to put up with the smell of my own piss for much longer. That first cordial came my way when Barty released a juicy burp in the middle of the quiet night and quickly clapped his hand to his mouth. He looked around and the only potential kink to my plan was if he came running toward my corner of the yard to throw up. I could dispatch of him easily enough, but I'd rather he disappear due to natural consequences. Thankfully, he ran to the opposite end which was nearer to the guards' privy.

As his legs kicked through the air, I carefully pushed myself to my feet and made sure my dagger was securely strapped to my thigh. Barty disappeared behind an opening leading toward the corridor between the inner and outer walls and I sprinted over the manicured garden, making for the closest winding snake. I had only seconds before Malcolm would appear.

The lengthy piece of leather rope that had been secured to my waist was already coiled with the noose-end ready to toss. I looked up. I had practiced this more times than I could count. I had one, maybe two shots, to get it before I would need to think about plan C.

The rope caught the snake's stone fang on the first heave and I scaled the column like a hungry squirrel spying a lone acorn. As I stood on a dark edge of the balcony and pulled the remaining rope up, I watched Malcolm's armor-cast shadow bob along the partially-lit lawn, unaware that his king's dreams would soon continue indefinitely.

* * *

King Valdar was afraid of the dark.

At least that was my impression, seeing that no less than six brass torches crackled gently in between colorful tapestries spread over three walls of the bedroom. The lights illuminated the sparseness of the room, which also came as a surprise. I would have to be swift as there wasn't much in the way of cover. The bed was the largest piece of furniture, itself also inornate except for Valdar's flag stretched like a canopy over four corner posts made of polished, chocolate-colored oak. It looked comfortable enough to easily sleep a family of four, though the outline of the nearly naked, snoring king with sheets tossed aside indicated the king was alone. Not even a concubine at his side. Smart man. Those with heavy thoughts in their mind often talk in their sleep.

That was likely the reason for the lack of guards in the room as well. I knew that two stood outside the king's chamber doors, Desmond and Michael, and I'd learned in the Singing Coyote that Desmond had been doing so for seven years, slightly disgruntled at having been pulled from the regular army due to a leg injury, while Michael had been there three. Whereas Barty was easily plied with alcohol, the same could not be said for Desmond, a consummate professional. Instead, I found that if you could get him talking about the science of war, he would go on for hours unless one was able to occasionally steer him in other directions, revealing truly interesting bits of information, piece by piece.

It was time. I figured that I had less than two minutes to slit King Valdar's throat and leave through the open window I came in before suspicions were raised regarding young Barty. I moved quietly on my toes, the dagger already clenched tightly in my hand.

Under the canopy, it was a little more difficult to see. Not that it mattered. I had been doing this for so long and so often, it was like my blade's steel edge was drawn to the neck's veins as if they were magnetic lodestones.

But, I knew immediately that something was wrong based on the solid resistance and slight clinking sound of metal on metal. My eyes adjusted in time to see an iron clasp wrapped around my target's neck followed by his wide-open eyes and toothy smile.

"He's here!" yelled the grinning man who was not King Valdar.

* * *

"Thank you for your assistance, Roman."

With my hands bound and one arm held by Desmond, the other by Michael, I watched the portly, naked man who passibly passed for the king kneel before the real Valdar and kiss his fat, emerald-encrusted ring. He then left the room with the clever neck shield in hand.

I felt blood drying on my upper lip and tasted its bitter copper-like flavor in the back of my throat. I was pretty sure my nose was broken, so I tried to focus on breathing through my mouth. Desmond had been under the bed the whole time and when the alarm was sounded, he had taken hold of my ankles, yanking me the ground. Michael had emerged from somewhere and before I could react, the bottom of his boot found my face.

Now that King Valdar and I stood only a meter away from each other at the foot of the bed, I could see more pronounced differences between him and his double. The king's gray beard was more neatly trimmed and his mustache slightly covered his upper lip. He had a bulbous nose and his face was ruddy. For a man of his age, wrinkles were in the expected places. The king certainly looked older than the statues and sculptures placed throughout his empire implied.

All I cared to know was the one thing that any surprised professional needed to know. "How?" I asked.

"Even though you're obviously the best among the guild," the king replied, "seeing as they sent you here, did you think my own son could ply my men with alcohol and sully my courtyard with piss without my knowledge?"

* * *

His words didn't register at first. There was no concept in my brain of any relationship with Valdar beside someone who had once been more of a legend than a real person for most of my life, and who had only recently become a stipulation in a contract.

"I don't understand," I said.

"I think you do," Valdar replied. He nodded to Desmond and Michael. I sensed a moment's hesitation, but my arms were released and the two guards backed away to a comfortable distance. "Did you think the masters of your guild taught you your skills for free?"

I would play his game if only to extend my time to think of a way out of this. Brute force wasn't going to get me anywhere. I was not one for honorable combat. I could get out of a scrape or two, but it's just not how I was trained and it was obvious that Desmond and Michael were good at what they did.

"My mother paid them," I said.

"And she earned her money, how?"

I thought about the question and realized I couldn't answer it.

"I don't see why the High Hill's most powerful king would pay the one organization which adamantly declares no loyalties," I replied.

"It's true, they are rather obstinate when it comes to their principles," the king said. "But they've always been the best at what they do and," he nodded toward me, "I found a way to use them to my ends."

"Why are you only telling me all of this? Son or not, of which I'm sure you have many throughout the Hills, I don't think you're willing to send me on my merry way."

"You're correct. It does seem your options are poor at this point." King Valdar sighed. "Oh, if there was only a way out of all of this." He grinned at his men. I turned to see each of them grinning back.

"What do you want?" I asked.

"Come work for me."

I started to laugh but coughed instead as I choked on bloody phlegm. "Just kill me now, please. The guild isn't going to greet me with wet kisses if I return without fulfilling my contract."

"I can keep you safe," he said. "I need your skills."

"What are you saying?"

"I'm saying I hate to see good men go to waste. I want you to take all that you've learned and start a new guild under my purview. It's obvious my enemies are numerous and I believe it would be prudent to have an assassin of assassins, so to speak. I'm sure there is much you know that would be useful in the right hands."

I knew the ins and outs of my own guild and of course, I knew of others, but none had the reputation. After what I'd seen tonight, I'm sure Valdar had scores of corpses providing fertilizer for his beautiful greenery.

My choice was obvious. The rod was insatiable.

I spread my arms and whispered, "Father."

Process Summary

Spoil the Rod is story number forty-two in the #52ShortStories challenge.

This title came from something that caught my ear when I was listening to a podcast. I was driving and I didn't make note of who said it, so I couldn't tell you where the phrase came from, but it obviously struck a chord. I imagined it was something that an assassin obsessed with his work might come up with, so that's where the story wound up.

I really tried to spend some time upfront going deep into character and setting, pulling the reader into the story. Again, this is something I've been studying under Dean Wesley Smith's class on writing with Depth. And also again, I highly recommend this course to writers.

Slab Lords

Statistics

Synopsis: Webster Mitchell finds himself caught between debt to an unforgiving man and a newfound love interest.

Word Count: 2,700

Genre: Dystopian

Completed Week: June 6th – June 12th

Slab Lords

Her skin was as black as freshly poured asphalt and her tall, thin legs resembled those of a roadrunner. Then there were her lips. They had a natural pucker that would make a goldfish cry. A pair of oversized sunglasses covered her eyes with thick aqua-blue frames and lenses resembling the peepers of a giant fly. In other words, she was the most beautiful girl Webster Mitchell had come across during his six-month stay in this dry, dusty land and he had nary a clue of how he was going to tell her he couldn't pay up.

"Can't you just tell Stephen that I wasn't home?"

The guy next to her chimed in after shoving the corner of a crustless peanut butter and jelly sandwich into his maw. "Do you know how many people ask us to tell Stephen that?"

The sandwich looked like a cracker between his fingers, which wasn't to say it was small but that the man's hands were huge, as was every other visible part of his body. Not an inch of fat, either.

"I mean, do you honestly know how many people ask us to tell him that?" His speech was peppered with the sound of his lips smacking together and visible strings of saliva and moist white bread stretching from the tip of his tongue to the roof of his mouth.

Webster stood in silence.

Yeah, he had a good idea how many people came up with that particular notion. He wasn't proud of the excuse and if he was smarter, he would have been more prepared. But that's just the thing. Stephen never gave anyone time to prepare. Webster certainly wasn't prepared for the goddess and the oversized lapdog standing before him.

The woman looked down at the open spiral notepad in her hands and ran her index finger along a handwritten list. Tiny pieces of dried skin hung off the sides of her chipped fingernail.

"Mr. Mitchell," she said and then looked up.

Her voice sounded as sweet as he imagined it would, like the songbirds that sometimes fly over his slab looking for a better place to land. Webster grinned with both the upper and lower teeth he had left, which always made it look like he was squinting into the sun even though it was morning and he was facing west.

She removed her glasses and Webster thought he was going to faint. Those big brown eyes surrounded by a sea of white almost put him in a state of delirium.

"Mr. Mitchell," she said, "you've already been given two extensions and you already owe an extra twenty percent. Do you know what happens when a third extension is requested?"

So many questions, Webster thought. And these were the types of questions he hated. Questions with answers that the other party knew the answer to but still insisted on baiting you with. He turned his head back toward the inside of his tent as if the answers were somehow there. All he saw was a tiny ten-foot by ten-foot canvas square with a low ceiling that added to an already growing hunch. He couldn't spot an inch of ground because it was covered in dirty clothes, plastic bottles, and flimsy, discarded cereal boxes. The only two things visible above the debris was a cot topped with a brown, cotton-bleeding bunny for a pillow and matted faux-fur coat for a blanket. And then, of course, there was the bucket for when he couldn't stand to get up and piss in those ass-freezing winds of the desert nights.

"Yes," he said, "I know what happens."

If only he could have come across this vision a year ago when things weren't so bad. If she's working for Stephen, Webster was sure she had her own sob story.

"I have twenty more appointments today, Mr. Mitchell. I have to come back this way. I expect payment when I return." She spun around on her sandals and started walking down the dirt trail towards the next tent-covered slab a quarter-mile down. Webster took a moment to imagine the full aspect of her svelte body only hinted at beneath the floaty yellow dress decorated with a print of white flowers.

He was pulled out of his brief reverie when muscleman shoved the rest of his sandwich into his mouth and wiped his hands clean across Webster's chest, leaving the sweet mix of sticky strawberry jam and sugar-laden peanut butter spread across his t-shirt and its scent floating up into his nostrils. It made him salivate. The man winked at Webster and followed the woman.

"Wait," Webster yelled, "I didn't catch your name!"

The woman kept on walking and muscleman floated two middle fingers over his back.

* * *

Options were limited, but at least they existed. Webster had that to be thankful for that, he supposed. After a half-hour of sitting in front of his tent with his knees pulled up to his chin, feeling sorry for himself beneath the warming sun, he reviewed those options.

He could head down to the limestone quarry and request more hours, but the possibility of them being granted was next to nil. Stephen controlled the mining operations even more tightly than he controlled the slabs. Webster was on the man's shit list. Either Webster wasn't producing enough or Stephen just didn't like something about him. The boss didn't require a solid reason because he only answered to those fellow slab lords with whom he traded.

Running out in the middle of the night was also out of the question. Stephen had boobytraps planted everywhere that would leave the person bleeding out, carrion for crows. The only safe exit from Stephen's domain was via escort.

There was always the possibility of accepting the consequences of asking for a third extension. The whole idea of extensions was one of Stephen's hilarious notions as no one ever managed to dig themselves out from under a first extension. And if Webster thought his options were limited now, they composed a veritable buffet compared to what he'd face once he was marked. He'd seen those people leaving the slabs, marching the long dirt road with eighty pounds of gear strapped to their back and shoulders. It didn't matter if they were old, young, or some work-worn combination of both— their countenance foretold a swift and impending end as their entire face spoke of their debt to Stephen. The trademark *D* stood in contrast to their cheeks and forehead like a bas-relief, their identity as debtors forever seared onto their flesh. Most of them would die within a few months, down in the stretches of shadeless hills and waterless canyons, their marks forbidding them admission into other slab kingdoms.

No, he couldn't leave, now. Not that he knew about her.

There was a single viable answer.

Webster dug through the trash spread across his floor until he found what he was looking for, then headed for Ying's.

* * *

Before stepping inside, Stephen removed his battered tennis shoes and placed them in the wicker basket sitting beside the entrance flap. The musky smell of patchouli drifted out from the entrance into the still desert air.

If Webster's tent was a hovel, Ying's was a royal palace. There were at least three rooms, two of them separated to the left and right by thick, wool rugs hanging from the ceiling. The main room was three hundred square feet, its floor lined with more soft rugs. A wooden oval table sat near the back, maybe ten inches from the ground, covered with a thin green cloth and with a pair of burning candles sitting in iron stands at each end. Behind the table sat the cross-legged gambler Ying, flipping and shuffling playing cards in his hand, carefully examining the corners of each one.

Webster didn't know how he did it, but Ying's white, collared button-up shirt was always pressed as cleanly as those he'd seen on men in the old magazines. He seemed to wear a new tie every day, today's being yellow with diagonal blue stripes. His sleeves were rolled up to his elbows and his hair was combed back with the sides neatly shaved. One would never guess he worked the mines and that's because he didn't. Ying found a way to get people to work for him. Webster couldn't fathom how he got away with it. Stephen had to have known, but they obviously had an agreement worked out.

To the residents of Stephen's little slab town, Ying was a man of last resorts. Webster remembered how he had barely set up his tent before hearing of Ying's special status. Things didn't always work out when dealing with him.

Winning was no guarantee. Still, he was an option to those that had need of money and also had something Ying was willing to play for.

Sitting beside the old gambler was a small girl with wavy, radiant blonde hair flowing down her shoulders and slightly across the sides of her face—a face covered in a thick layer of white powder like that of the old-world Geisha girls. She lay one hand in Ying's lap and the other on her own, palms up as if preparing for meditation. Her age was puzzling as her make-up hid any potential wrinkles but her gray eyes held the air of experience.

Webster had no time to open his mouth before Ying spoke.

"You have nothing to offer me. I suggest you take the mark and leave," he said.

News traveled fast.

"Don't be so sure," Webster said.

Ying laughed. "Unless you hold secrets from me, which I doubt, all I'm willing to give you at this point is a worthless wish of safe journies."

"Ying," he nodded. "Let's play."

Ying gently placed all but one of the cards down face-down on the table and held the remaining one up to a candle to examine it more closely. It was the Queen of Clubs.

"What is it that you think you have that you think I want to play you for?" Ying asked.

Webster reached into the back pocket of his jean-shorts and pulled out a flat, solid item wrapped in an old mechanic's towel. "See for yourself," he said, gently placing it on Ying's table. It connected with a solid thunk.

Ying, still examining the card, nodded absently at the girl. She leaned forward and unraveled the dirty red cloth. Candlelight gleamed off the silver, oversized novelty coin, drawing Ying's attention. He placed the card in his hand on top of the rest and reached for the coin.

"I feel I should be offended, but I like your sense of humor," he said with a smile.

"If you think I handpicked that from a wide selection, you're not as smart of a man as I believed you were," Webster replied. He hoped it was enough to keep the gambler interested.

"Of course," Ying said. "Then maybe it is not you with the sense of humor." He picked up the coin and flipped it back and forth. One side was stamped with a tall building covered by hovering words: *Emperor's Palace.* The other side said *Las Vegas* housed inside a sideways diamond.

"It's cute," Ying said, "but it is not worth nearly what you need."

"Let me worry about that," Webster said.

Ying's shrugged his shoulders. As if the gambler and the girl were of the same mind, she picked up the sitting deck with her delicate hands and began to shuffle.

* * *

The round was over before it started. Even with a pair of Jacks in his hands, Webster had no chance against the full house Ying laid down on the table.

"I'm sorry," Ying said. "Lady Luck is fickle. Maybe we'll meet again under better circumstances." The dismissive look on his face did nothing to convince Webster that that was anything beyond an impossibility.

"Don't be sorry," Webster said, pushing himself to his feet. At least on the spots where callouses had not formed on his soles, the softness of the fuzzy wool felt like heaven. "I didn't actually lose."

Ying began to laugh. Webster watched as the man's right hand slid beneath the table. "It would appear otherwise. The cards speak from them-selves."

"Oh, that?" Webster said. He turned his head and neck, working out the kinks. He banked on Ying not having an itchy trigger finger. "Is that the game you thought we were playing?"

Ying's eyes narrowed. Webster was trying hard not to get ahead of himself, but he had Ying exactly where he wanted him.

"You know, your partner has a beautiful face," Webster said. "I'm sure that layer of sugar you have her coated in makes her all the more sweet, eh?"

The girl's eyes darted up and met Webster's, but she quickly dropped them back to the table as demurely as a beaten dog. She was obviously not as well-versed in hiding her emotions as Ying.

"You should leave," Ying said. "Before someone gets hurt." Webster stood strong. He was still gambling, hoping Ying would let him finish before popping off a round or two.

"I bet that if I were to see her without all of that sugar, I wouldn't even recognize her. I might even think she's someone else. There may be some revealing beauty marks, no? Marks that would make it difficult to make one's way in the world."

Despite what were likely his best efforts, Ying's face began to resem-ble a boiling kettle. Webster decided it was time release a little steam before things went south. "It's a good thing I haven't told anyone my theory yet. Or, wait…" Webster held a finger to his chin. "I may have mentioned something to…" He scratched. "Gee, ya know, I can't remember who I may have told."

Ying slowly turned to the girl and nodded. She rose quickly without saying a word and disappeared into the room on the left.

Ying spoke through gritted teeth. "Even if I give you what you need, you'll be back on Stephen's shit list next month. Don't think that this is going to be a regular installment."

"Let me worry about that," Webster said.

There was plenty to worry about as he wasn't yet done gambling.

* * *

"Where's your pet gorilla?" Webster asked.

"He's handling another case," she said. The notepad was hanging from a silver beaded chain around her neck.

Somehow, with the sun now setting behind her, her beauty seemed to increase ten-fold. She lifted her sunglasses so they rested in her kinked hair like a pair of eggs in a nest, revealing, if Webster wasn't mistaken, eyes that hinted at some semblance of sorrow.

"You have until sunrise tomorrow to report to Stephen's office. Technically, I don't have to let you know this until—"

"Here," he said. He pulled his hand out from a back pocket and waved a stack of scrip in front of her face.

She hesitated but eventually grabbed it. Her eyes left his only long enough to verify that the money was legit.

"How did you get this?" she asked.

"A little bit of work, a little bit of luck," Webster said. She didn't need to know the full story, yet.

"You're very resourceful," she said.

Webster tried to come up with something clever, but instead, he said, "Yeah."

A squawking flock of birds flying overhead filled the gap between drawn-out moments of silence. Webster felt a renewed sense of confidence. Something he hadn't felt in months. Something that he thought had been beaten out of him by the hardships of life in the modern world of dog-eat-dog and slab lord-eat-slab lord.

"You know," he said, "I feel like the two of us could probably accomplish a lot if we weren't tied down to one place."

He wasn't sure how she was going to take that, but at this point, he didn't care. He had nothing to lose.

The woman chuckled under her breath, then extended a hand. "I'm Stella."

Process Summary

Slab Lords is story number forty-three in the #52ShortStories challenge.

The impetus behind this story was an article I readin the LA Times about 'slab lords' renting out squares of concrete to people visiting California's Joshua Tree National Park. I grew up in the desert near there and I always seem to take on this post-apocalyptic, Mad-Maxian view of places like that when it comes to writing stories…or I go Western. Again, I tried to spend a good amount of time working on voice and setting on this one.

There was a big break in the middle of writing this story to focus on enjoying a family vacation. No regrets. :)

MY LITTLE GIRL

Statistics

Synopsis: A father travels back in time to deal with a little problem.

Word Count: 1,900

Genre: Sci-Fi

Completed Week: June 12th – June 14th

My Little Girl

My little girl has all the potential. All of it. I see it so clearly, the way the razor-straight strands of her auburn hair hang on the wind as she runs with resolve, chasing her younger brother, Lucas, beneath the slides. The shine in her green eyes as she narrows in on a potential trap, pinning him to a corner of the sandbox butted up against a pair of cinder block walls, leaving the boy zero chance of escape. Even when she grabs ahold of him and tickles him until he's reduced to tearful pleas, there's a dark edge to her laugh.

"Honey, we need to go," I say.

I wish it weren't true. The sky here is so beautiful. So blue and pure with occasional cotton-like strands of clouds floating listlessly by. As I sit on an uncomfortable wooden park bench, an old elm reaches over me like a shield whose only job is to protect me from a sunburn.

My little girl screams in frustration as she turns to me, giving Lucas the chance to sneak past her. He hops onto my lap and wraps his arms around my neck, leaving grains of sand on my pants and drops of drool on my collar. He's breathing heavily in my ear and smells of kid-sweat.

"Dad!" she yells.

If feeling my little boy's flesh pressed against mine once again is not a miracle, it's damn close to miraculous.

"Honey," I say. "Time's up."

She groans as she ambles toward the pink-and-baby blue backpack sitting beside me. With a long fin descending from the bottom, it's designed to make its wearer look like a mermaid. Sliding her arms through its straps, she refuses to look at me.

I wish we could stay here forever. I wish I didn't have to go through with it.

Killing my little girl is going to be the hardest thing I'll ever have to do in my life.

* * *

While idling beneath an overhanging stoplight at the main intersection in our town's tiny downtown, I tilt my eyes up toward the rearview mirror. She's strapped into her car seat, hands held together lightly in her lap. The dirty pink soles of her tennis shoes swing in and out view as she kicks her legs up and down. She watches an elderly couple walk hand-in-hand along the cracked sidewalk just outside her window. They stroll past a white brick liquor store with posters advertising twelve-packs of malt liquor for $7.99. Like every other surrounding building, the establishment will be flattened in half a century's time.

I'd seen the movies a long time ago. The ones where someone comes back to save a child from some time-traveling assassin because the kid will be the one to save the world.

Why couldn't that be my movie? Why did my child have to destroy the world? Why did I have to be the assassin?

In reality, these weren't hard questions. They all had answers that made sense. When the Resistance came to me, they told me it was their only option. They didn't have time to perfect the science and there would be no second chances. They could generate enough power to send a single person's consciousness back to his or her own body, but any more attempts would clearly signal their capabilities through the power grid and invite a fatal, nuclear-weapon-induced setback. Some brainiac determined I was the perfect choice and as voracious as my opposition was, it didn't hold up because I knew they were right and it was my only opportunity to make amends.

Always, in the back of my mind, I wondered if I had played a role in what she became—what she would become. Was it something specific that I said? Something she saw me do? Maybe a whole bunch of tiny things that came together to form the singular monstrosity growing up in the backseat of my car?

"Can we get ice cream?" she asks.

Lucas is strapped in next to her, rubbing his thumbs along the tiny glass eyes of his favorite stuffed tiger.

"We'll see," I say.

The digital clock on the dashboard reminds me that I only have about an hour. They said my consciousness was 'magnetized,' and would slowly be pulled back to its proper time. I would feel like I was growing tired and then suddenly lose all faculties. I had to do the job before that happened.

The light turns green and I press the pedal down. The accelerator kicks in after a brief lag.

"Okay," I say. "Let's get some ice cream."

* * *

The water shimmers in the sunlight as we sit on the lakeside shore. Tiny whitecaps form in the breeze and break on the wave crests, disappearing before they have the chance to become something more. We're the only ones out here on this weekday just after the lunch hour. During the summer months, this used to be a favorite spot of ours. The kids loved to swim.

Now—later—it's a wasteland.

My little girl stands beside me, pushing herself up and down on her toes, licking around the strawberry ice cream dripping down the sides of her wafer cone. "When mommy comes home from her work trip, can we play Candyland?"

"Sure, honey."

I'm angry now. I'm sure the scientists chose this window so that I wouldn't be able to at least see the love of my life once again. The woman that my daughter eventually took—takes—away. I suppose it makes sense, but for her to come home in this time and learn what I've done? I can't imagine.

Lucas is down by the water, digging smooth gray stones out of the wet sand, trying to throw them as far into the deep as he can. What do I do with him? How will his life turn out knowing that his father murdered his sister? By eliminating one problem, would I be creating another? What if, in his grief, he winds up taking his sister's path?

These fucking scientists think they have all the answers.

"Daddy, are you sad?"

"What?"

"You're crying."

I wipe a runaway tear from my cheek. She leans her head into me and put her arms around my shoulders. Cold, sticky ice cream rubs against the back of my neck and I smell apple-scented shampoo as strands of her hair tickle my nose.

"I don't want you to be sad, Daddy." She starts to pretend-cry, making little whimpering sounds.

What happened—happens—to this beautiful young girl?

I pull her away from me and peer into her eyes, gripping her arms too tightly. "I'm okay."

"Yay!" she says wiggling her arms out from my hands so she can continue licking her ice cream.

"Honey," I ask, "do you think you can be whatever you want to be when you grow up?"

"Yeeeaah," she says in an almost questioning way.

"What do you want to be?" I ask.

Please, give me hope. Give me a reason.

"Ummm…" She squints into the sky and puts a finger to her chin, tapping lightly. "I don't know," she says with a giggle. "I want to be a grown-up!"

"Just a grown-up?"

"Yeah, so I can be the boss and no one can tell me what to do," she says with a twisted smile.

* * *

"Lucas, can you do a big boy thing for daddy?"

His eyes grow wide and he nods his head quickly, smiling with all six teeth. We're standing beside our sedan on the dirt parking lot sitting thirty feet above the south side of the lake. If I was going to do this, I was going to be a part of it. No way could I do it and be outside of the event. No way. But I couldn't make Lucas a part of this.

"Daddy left his wallet down where we were at. Do you remember where that was?"

He nods again.

"Okay, go be a big boy and get it for Daddy."

I had strapped my girl into her seat first. As soon as Lucas is halfway to the trail leading to the shore area, I get in the car and start the engine.

I don't want to give myself the luxury of thinking, so I jerk the transmission into reverse. The front tires spin and kick up gravel, but we eventually zoom to the back of the parking lot where I hit the brakes.

My girl is giggling. "Again, Daddy! Again!"

I look in the rearview mirror. A big mistake. Her smile sends a sharp twinge shooting across my chest. I'm having trouble breathing.

What am I doing?

What am I doing?

I click the automatic door lock and slam the shifter into drive. We kick up more gravel and then we're zooming.

Then we're flying.

Then we're slamming our heads and shoulders forward on impact. Blood runs down my forehead as a sharp edge of the freshly blown steering wheel scratches my face.

"Daddy!"

I'm a little disoriented and my jaw stings from the airbag's impact, but it feels like we're floating a little bit. I look outside of the car window and see the hood and half the windshield submerged beneath the dark waters. My body is leaning into my seatbelt.

"Daddy!!!" I try to turn my head but a neck muscle cramps up. I focus on the mirror. The look on my girl's face is one of sheer terror. She's puffing and sniffling like a wild bull, looking at me. Her limbs flail wildly as she tries to climb out from her car seat straps. She finally starts crying. Her face is beet red.

I feel water getting into my shoes and soaking my ankles, so I reach down to unclip my seatbelt.

"I'm coming, honey!"

She's trying to say something, but her crying gasps are choking off the words. Despite the dull pain seeming to radiate out of nearly every inch of my body, a rush of adrenaline kicks in and helps me focus.

"Daddy!" I think she's saying.

She's nearly facing straight down now in her seat and I'm crouched with my feet pressed against the back of the driver's seat. My hands shake as they struggle to unclip her own harness, but I succeed and pull her into me. Her tiny hands clasp my head. She's choking on her words again, coughing sweet little coughs.

I hold her so tightly, I feel like I'm going to break her tiny bones.

"I love you, Honey," I say. "I love you. I love you. I love you."

I force her face into my shoulder, muting the sounds of her cries, feeling every vibration of her trembling body.

I feel exhausted. The water is up to our shoulders and I'm starting to get dizzy. Am I being pulled back or am I dying? Is there any difference now?

The water rushes up around my ears and my little girl's grasp loosens too quickly. With all of the breath I have left, I scream into the water that I'm sorry and that we will be together again soon.

Process Summary

My Little Girl is story number forty-four in the #52ShortStories challenge.

This was an odd one. The idea struck me like lightning and I was scared to write it, to be honest. I was sitting next to my son on the couch and we were having so much fun playing together when this terrible question hit me—What would it be like to lose a child who is such a source of happiness? Of course, that seemed a powerful enough incident to get started on a story, but I had to add one of those twists that I love so much—what if the parent was not just responsible, but did it on purpose? Why would a parent do that? And so the result is *My Little Girl.*

Needless to say, I was relieved to wrap this one up, finishing it in only three days.

CAPTAIN COFFEE

Statistics

Synopsis: Our coffee-powered superhero is called to save the day at the local coffee shop.

Word Count: 1,700

Genre: Humor

Completed Week: June 15th – June 18th

Captain Coffee

Captain Coffee preferred a French roast. Lighter brews would seem more the Captain's speed, but they lacked the complex, chocolatey undertones that made life worth living. Undertones that gave him purpose. The light-reflecting puddles of oil floating on the coffee's surface represented islands of refuge from the surrounding darkness. Islands the Captain felt an obligation to protect. He would consume the surrounding midnight murk of evil so the rest of the population didn't have to.

"Sir?"

"Hm?" Through the slits of his eye mask, he appraised the young girl behind the counter. She had rosy plump cheeks and her dirty blond hair was tied up into a bun. Wrapped tightly around her person was a forest-green apron with *Kenzie* stitched in white cursive on the top right. She was new.

"I said that I'm sorry, but it will take us about five minutes to brew another pot of the dark roast."

"I see." There were four people in line behind the Captain. He was watching them all. They didn't know it, but he was. A little black-haired girl and her mother stood directly behind him. The little girl was rubbing a piece of the Captain's silk cape between her fingers. He smiled down at her and she smiled back. Her mother pulled her back and chastised her.

"If you're in a hurry," Kenzie said, "I can pour you a cup of our medium-bodied house blend and add a shot."

"No!" the Captain replied.

Kenzie raised her eyebrows and looked at the other customers.

Mixing roasts was a definite no-no. Captain Coffee couldn't put a finger on it, but it always seemed to dampen his abilities. But Kenzie didn't know any better.

"No, thank you, young lady. I will wait."

She rang up the total of two dollars and nineteen cents.

"Can I get a name?"

He preferred to use an alias when he wasn't in uniform, but he hadn't bothered to wait today. He had woken up that morning with a strange feeling in his gut, so he came in dressed for action, prepared for anything.

"Captain Coffee," he replied.

Chuckles broke out in the line. He heard the little girl gasp. Kenzie picked up a thin black marker and wrote *CC* on the side of an empty paper cup.

"We'll call you when its ready, Captain," she said nonchalantly.

The Captain's scuffed boots tapped across the brown tile. He carefully took a seat, draping his cape over the back of the wooden chair, and clasped his hands together over the tiny round table. The whine and burr of roasted beans being ground into fine powder accented the low acoustic guitar and airy female vocals drifting out of the store's ceiling speakers. The mother who was behind him was leaning over the counter now, placing her order while gripping her purse strap tightly. Her little girl danced back and forth behind her, occasionally peeking at the Captain. Last in line was a pair of blue-collar guys in gray t-shirts and baggy blue jeans. One of them had a smirk on his face and pointed with his chin at the Captain while he said something to his buddy.

The Captain sat back and admired the low bohemian bookshelves lining the wall opposite the coffee bar. They held a smattering of sleeveless hardcovers and tattered paperbacks. In front of the shelves were two comfortable-looking armchairs, one of them occupied by a young woman resting her temple on a fingertip while she was engrossed in a magazine. The other engulfed a young man with a thin, white notebook computer cracked open on his lap and a large pair of designer headphones covering his ears.

The microcosm of society gathered here every morning reminded the Captain of what he was sworn to protect.

After his name was called and he brought the aromatic cup of joe back to his table, a little pair of bells rang as the front glass door swung open. A familiar feeling rose up from his stomach as his eyes landed on the entrant. Captain Coffee realized immediately why he had hopped straight into uniform that morning.

There would be trouble.

* * *

"Except those behind the counter, everyone down on the ground, now!"

He wore a black balaclava and dark sunglasses. Only his pink lips were exposed. The tip of his black handgun swang around the room, moving from person to person as if it were scanning their minds for thoughts of escape.

The front of the smirking blue-collar guy's jeans grew moist around the crotch. The mother shrieked, grabbed her little girl and turned around, exposing her back while hiding her child. Folk music continued floating through the speakers, but the grinders and hissing milk steamers fell silent.

"I said NOW!" As if they were disconnected dominoes, customers started falling to the floor, but the Captain remained seated, as still as a stone.

The little girl began to whimper.

Her mother started, "Please, she's scared—", but she stopped talking and bearhugged her daughter to the floor when the bad guy pointed his gun at her and thumbed back the trigger.

The man then ran over to the student with the laptop and yanked off his headphones.

"Hey!" the kid responded instinctively.

"Down," the bad guy said. "Now."

The boy looked up and his jaw dropped. The laptop slipped off his lap and cracked against the tile as he scrambled to kiss the ground alongside the magazine-reading woman.

The gun floated the Captain's way. "Hey, Mr. Halloween. You think you're special?"

Now was not the time. With his eyes locked on the bad guy, the Captain slowly pushed his chair back and dropped to his knees. He then pressed his hands onto the floor and lowered himself into a position from which he could observe.

The man was alone unless one of his cohorts was working an inside job. Kenzie? She didn't seem the type and her face was a pale as the other two baristas working the machines.

"Everyone behind the counter, come out front and join your friends," he said, rushing toward the far edge of the counter where it opened up to the lobby. After he waved the workers past, he peeked in what looked to be a storeroom, followed by a quick check of the bathrooms.

"I'll be walking around now, collecting donations. Purses, wallets, and shiny accessories are acceptable forms of currency. Be good and you can go home to your loved ones. Do something stupid, everyone pays."

* * *

"I ain't gonna reach into your tights, but you paid for that coffee somehow. Move slow."

Captain Coffee would be polite, but he would not be pushed around. He kept his face to the ground, staring at the man's dirty sneakers. "You do not have to do this," he said. "If you put down your weapon and allow me to take you into custody, I promise that you will not be harmed."

The thief crouched and yanked on the back of the Captain's hair, painfully forcing his head up. "I picked you first, because you're a goddamn freak and I don't trust freaks. I don't have time for this." His breath reeked of alcohol. "Now, stand up slowly, reach into your panties, and give me all your money."

Captain Coffee pushed himself up with the tip of the barrel digging into the side of his nose. Once on his feet, he reached into the side of his underwear where he kept a small amount of cash inside a billfold

"There is still time to do the right thing."

"You think this is a joke? You say one more thing and—"

The man cut himself off abruptly and stared at the Captain, his eyes squinting slightly.

"Wait a second. Take off your mask."

It was the one thing any superhero was reluctant to do in public.

"Please," the Captain said. "I cannot reveal my identity."

The thief pointed his gun now at the mother who whimpered and curled over her daughter more tightly.

"I said take it off."

The Captain was left with no choice. He reached behind his head and undid the twine holding his mask in place, letting it fall to the floor.

"Holy shit," the thief said, removing his sunglasses for a seemingly better view. His familiar steel-blue eyes struck the Captain. "Brian. Brian fucking Mulrooney."

Captain Coffee could feel his face turning red. Ashamed and vulnerable, he stood before a ghost.

The thief relaxed his body as he laughed. His gun-hand fell to his side. "I should have known you'd stay a freak after high school. Didn't you get your ass kicked enough then—"

All bad guys make mistakes. It's just a matter of time and opportunity, two things of which a superhero like Captain Coffee is aware of at a subconscious level.

Ronnie King, bully and apparently perpetual dreg of society, let his guard down long enough for Captain Coffee to descend on him like the plunger of a French Press. The Captain seized the steaming cup of dark roast from his table and splashed it across the thief's face. It spattered into his eyes and scalded his lips. The gun clattered on to the floor as his hands raced up toward his face.

The Captain lifted his knee to meet the bad guy's crotch, sending him crumpling to the floor, howling in pain. With one of his boots, Captain Coffee kicked the man's gun across the tile, flipped him over and sat on his back, holding his wrists together as he pulled his arms up toward his upper back.

"Kenzie, contact the authorities," the Captain said, calm and collected.

* * *

After the police interviewed the witnesses and the captain posed, mask on, for a final photo, the mother with the little girl came up and hugged him tightly.

"Thank you, Captain Coffee," she said.

"Just doing my job," he replied.

"I want to be like you when I'm older!" the daughter said from below.

The Captain dropped to a knee and met her at eye level. "You can be like me now," he said. "Get good grades in school and help those in need."

"Do I have to drink coffee?" she asked, her face slightly twisted as she scrunched her nose.

"That is not required."

"Whew," she said. "Good."

Process Summary

Captain Coffee is story number forty-five in the #52ShortStories challenge.

It's rare that I go to Starbucks anymore because those two-dollar straight-up coffees are budget vampires, but I occasionally find myself there if I need to buy time for someplace to open (like the smog check guy). So imagine my joy when I was sitting there on a busy morning, laptop cracked open, working on a story when a guy comes walking in dressed in slippers and a very colorful robe resembling that of a superhero. He really stood out among the construction guys and white-collar salespeople types.

Of course, I had to stop what I was doing and hammer out a quick description of the guy (which you can read in the scratch file. Ignore the first line. Not sure what I had in mind there, but it never made it into the story). The concept worked itself out quite nicely over four days. Definitely a nice change of pace from the previous story.

Swan Song

Statistics

Synopsis: At 71, Hazel McAllister has her own idea of what a "Swan Song"

should be.

Word Count: 1,700

Genre: Literary

Completed Week: June 18th – June 22nd

Swan Song

The drums lacked punch. The bass guitar was fuzzy and thin. And the vocals? Meh. Barely the growl she was looking for. Still, seventy-one-year-old Hazel McAllister sat in the driver's seat of her nine-year-old Ford Focus, whipping her thinning silver hair back and forth to the newest release from *Satan's Seed.*

Any metal was good metal.

A pair of teenage boys in a raised pick-up truck pulled up next to her at the stoplight. She stopped thrashing long enough to catch their wide eyes and uproarious laughter. The passenger rolled his window all the way down and leaned out. Hazel hit the switch to roll down her's.

"Hell yeah, grandma!" The boy gave her the devil horns.

Hazel stuck out her tongue and returned the gesture. The light turned green.

"Don't break a hip!" he said before the duo sped off into the sunset.

Hazel's heart sank as her Ford crept through the crosswalk.

* * *

"Where's the Lisinopril?"

"In the bag."

"I don't see it."

"Keep looking."

"It's not there. Did you forget it?"

"Are you going blind now too?" Hazel hurried into the kitchen, bumping into her husband's walker as she did so. She dug through the plastic bag, past the packs of pocket kleenex and the anti-snoring nasal strips.

"Here," she said. She slapped the little brown bottle onto the speckled formica counter.

"Oh. They musta changed the bottle."

"It's the same bottle, Gerald."

He muttered something that Hazel ignored. She leaned back with her arms crossed, watching him struggle to open the lid. His shoulders seemed to slump forward a little more each day and he was almost out of breath on a regular basis. It was COPD. Unfortunately, he also had high blood pressure and while he could take a pill and eat his vegetables, the usual suggested level of exercise was at odds with his lung capacity.

Hanging on a wall beside the kitchen cabinets, just above the wheezing Gerald, was a photo of the two of them—leaner, taller—standing like ants beneath a giant Sequoia tree. They'd hiked thirty miles over three days during that trip twenty years ago. Now, Gerald would occasionally quip that getting from the living room to the bedroom was akin to climbing Mount Everest.

It took Hazel only five minutes to reheat leftovers for dinner. Dry chicken breast with sodium-free seasoning and a side of steamed cauliflower for both of them, though Hazel kept a bottle of tangy hot sauce hidden in the back of the cabinet which she applied liberally when Gerald wasn't looking.

Halfway through *Wheel of Fortune*, Gerald was snoring in his well-worn recliner, the tray of half-eaten dinner pushed aside. Rapidly spinning colors reflected off his eyeglasses which rested beside the plate. The wheel's click-click-click came to a stop and a slide whistle sounded off. The contestant threw her hands in the air.

Bankrupt.

Hazel snuck off to the guest bedroom and went through the closet, pulling out an old dress box. She tossed the lid to the ground and pulled out a pair of black leather pants. They felt stiff as she laid them on the comforter next to a matching jacket and magenta crop top.

Arthritis around her knuckles flared as she tried to button the tight jeans, forcing her to stop a few times until the snap took hold. After putting on the crop top, she turned back and forth in the mirror. Scars from gallbladder surgery were visible when the light hit her waist just right, as were the results of bearing three children, so she traded in the shirt for a longer blouse which she barely managed to tuck into her pants.

After applying violet lipstick and green eyeshadow, she checked on Gerald. His chin was on his left shoulder now. She gently removed his shoes and turned down the volume on the television before closing the front door behind her.

* * *

The bouncer was a large black man, two Hazels wide and two Hazels tall, with a slick bald head and a septum ring that only increased the don't-mess-with-me factor. He looked her up and down.

"You in the right place, lady?"

Hazel stared into his eyes and gave him the finger.

"Yeah, you're in the right place," he said, waving her through.

* * *

The odor of cloves and cannabis floated out from a group of kids packed into one corner of the floor.

Puke Sticks, the opening band, was playing its heart out. The lead singer looked like he'd been running a marathon. While he screamed into the microphone, sweat poured from his long hair and shirtless torso onto three scantily-clad girls crowded together at the front of the stage. About twenty or so kids were spread out into cliques, most of them standing still with either their arms crossed or hands in their pockets while they rocked their heads up and down in synch with the kick drum. Some of them had bright orange earplugs. Hazel benefited from years of deteriorated hearing.

She thought about heading out there, trying to blend in, but she was already conspicuous enough. Instead, she made for the bar packed with people waiting for the headliner. It was filled with all types—one couple had matching tunnel plugs in their earlobes that left six-inch gaps. Then there was the guy wearing eight-inch-heels and tattered, sleeveless black t-shirt with a red, upside-down pentagram silk-screened across the middle.

Hazel found an empty bar stool at the far end near the restroom. She tried to flag down the bartender for a drink, but no matter how loud she shouted or how much she waved her hand, it was as if she were a ghost without a voice.

"What are you drinking?"

The voice came from over her right shoulder. Inserting himself to her right was a young man who looked to be about the age of Hazel's second grandson—maybe second or third year of college, assuming this guy went. His eyeshadow matched Hazel's, but he didn't have the lipstick. His hands rested on the top of the bar where his black nail polish sucked in the colorful lights swirling out from the stage.

"Apparently, the air," Hazel said, unsure if he even heard her. She brought her chin to rest on her fist as she gazed downward at his hands. They were so pure, free of wrinkles and liver spots.

The man stuck a pair of fingers in his mouth and let out a whistle that somehow cut through the distorted guitars pumping out of the venue speakers. The bartender finished pouring a foamy beer and walked over.

Hazel perked up.

"Gin Rickey," she said, quickly realizing by the bartender's narrowing eyes that she was probably the only person in the building old enough to know what that was.

"Two gins with lime and soda water," her new neighbor said without a moment's hesitation. The bartender turned and got to work.

"Unfortunately, this club's mixologist," the young man said with air quotes, "is clueless as to decent cocktails. We'll see if he doesn't bork this one up."

"Thank you," she said.

The boy smiled. Not a sign of crow's feet around his eyes.

"You remind me of someone," he said.

"You better not say your grandmother," Hazel replied.

The boy chuckled. "Actually, I was going to say my ex."

Hazel leaned back as if to appraise him. "Oh? Into older women, huh? I guess I should have seen that coming."

"I'm into beautiful minds," he said. "She was actually a year younger than me. It's just that she put out the same vibe as you. Had the same attitude. The same lust for life that I see on your face."

Hazel held back a chuckle of her own. "A lust for life. I just want to make it to tomorrow," she said.

"I don't believe that for a second."

Hazel wasn't sure she wanted to get into this conversation, but she stayed put, waiting for her cocktail.

"No, you want to make the most of every day, even if others might think they know what's better for you."

"So why is she your ex?" Hazel asked, steering the conversation topic back to him.

"It was my fault. I was holding her back."

"You?" she said, not trying very hard to hide the incredulity in her voice.

"I wasn't always such a free spirit," he said. "Or at least I was afraid to admit it." It was him now, staring off into space like he was trying to find something he'd lost.

"I get it," Hazel said. She felt an immediate need to comfort him. She got him. He apparently got her.

They drank and talked about their favorite bands, their dreams, and their experiences until *Puke Sticks* cleared the stage and *God's Bane* launched into their first song.

"Wanna dance?" the boy asked, standing up and over her now.

"I'll probably break my hip."

"Why would you say something like that?"

Hazel didn't have a good answer. Over the past thirty or so minutes, she felt better than she had in a long time. It was as if time paused to give her rest. She had tried for so long on her own, gave it an effort, but it was hard to do it all alone.

"Hey, what's your name?" she asked, jumping on her feet.

He extended his polished fingers. "Jerry. But my mom calls me Gerald, so please don't call me that."

Hazel looked into his face and tried to transpose it with the man who was sleeping in her house. The eyebrows were a little more wiry. The nose was almost the same. Maybe thicker lips. But it was the flaming fuel behind Jerry's light brown eyes that reminded her of things past.

"Alright, Jerry. Let's hit the mosh pit," she said.

He craned his neck. "I don't see one."

"Not yet," Hazel said, grabbing his hand, pulling him toward the center of the floor.

Process Summary

Swang Song is story number forty-six in the #52ShortStories challenge.

I love music.

I love *loud* music.

And I'm old.

I'm an old guy who loves loud music.

This has led me to wonder, as I sit at a stoplight with my subwoofers rattling my car and the mid-range and tweeters fighting for a voice, if it's me those kids in the next lane over are laughing at. And if they are? I don't care. That's also one of the benefits of being old. :) The only time I tend to turn things down is if a police car is around and I worry its driver feels like issuing a noise pollution ticket.

Admittedly, some of the music I listen to qualifies…

This whole notion sent me down a line of questions of whether or not I'd be doing the same thing well into my 70s and 80s and if age-related physical impediments would put a damper on things. Some things are inevitable, but I think that for the most part, we can be as mentally young as we wanna be.

Go Hazel!

Halfway

Statistics

Synopsis: Detective Marty Quinn comes home to find his wife murdered and now he's on the trail of a high-tech suspect.

Word Count: 3,200

Genre: Mystery

Completed Week: June 23rd – June 30th

Halfway

Detective Marty Quinn's job is a lot like dipping your face in a pool or the ocean, where you leave your ears floating halfway between one world and the other. The above and the below. You get a hint of the diluted, swirling side, but you're still anchored in what you know. Then comes the pull. An act of mercy. Like someone taking a fistful of wet hair and yanking you back into comfortable reality. Or it's the other way around—the push—where someone takes that same hand and shoves you down into a new set of circumstances and you're forced to adapt.

Marty felt like he was drowning when he came back to his beachside apartment and found the limp body of his wife of seven days, posed in the pea-green easy chair she vowed to get rid of the first time she laid eyes on it (*It's so 2025*, she had said).

The majority of her appearance said she'd come home from a hard day of paralegal work and simply fell asleep. Head tilted down and to the side, tucked into her right shoulder. The only distortion to the picture was the stain of blood running from a line crossing her throat, onto the pink-rose colored dress Marty had bought her two days ago.

"I'm sorry, Marty."

Marty said nothing. Only stared at the bottom of the sheet covering Diana. Three of her sky blue-painted toenails were sticking out. It was a sloppy job, whoever placed the sheet.

"We can get Pierre to work this. You don't need to be here."

Of course they weren't going to let him work the case, but Kate, the coroner, wasn't going to outright say that. She was one of the few people that

Marty worked with whom he felt he could call a friend.

"I have a spare bedroom. You know Leonard would love to have you stay with us for awhile."

Marty may have nodded, but all he felt was that cold water surrounding his face, the unrelenting hand of fate denying him breath.

* * *

Marty's boss forced him to take a couple of weeks off. Even told him to expense a hotel somewhere after he ended up sleeping in his coupe that first night, refusing to answer Kate's phone calls. He accepted his boss's offer, because if he didn't, he knew that it would only draw more attention.

The hard questions had come early. It was standard procedure. His alibi was airtight. He had been down at the Whirling Dervish, clinking glasses of port-finished scotch with Dennis, a longtime partner, when it happened. After Dennis dropped him off, Marty made the gruesome discovery.

He wasn't in the clear, though. He knew he was being watched. Detectives have an insider's knowledge. It's assumed most of them are clever enough to pull something like this off, and if the department is lucky, the detective gets cocky and makes a mistake.

Of course, Marty's sudden change of behavior over the past few months hadn't helped matters. He had always been a private person, but the whirlwind romance took his colleagues by surprise. Three months. All starting from a random conversation in line at a local coffee shop. The way he had suddenly gushed over Diana made things worse. Not that saying a few words a week was gushing in anyone's book but Marty's. The only indication there had been a wedding was the simple titanium wedding band suddenly popping up on his finger. Even the honeymoon was a quick overnighter at a posh hotel up in Santa Barbara.

He couldn't explain it to himself, let alone anyone else. Diana had been the one. She had come as swiftly as the day comes upon dawn and now she had left just as quickly as night overtakes dusk.

The day after the discovery, his apartment had been cleared of yellow tape.

Marty came back.

* * *

The vertical blinds were turned shut. Hints of daylight leaked through the cracks and the place smelled of solvents and super glue. Marty sat on the carpet where the easy chair had been. It was now in the department's evidence room, but its four legs had left their round impressions.

He had only been able to handle about thirty seconds of silence before turning on the television and tuning into the local news. The forecast called for clear skies—'picnic weather' the meteorologist called it with his pearly, ingratiating smile.

Marty's cell phone buzzed. It was Dennis. Marty figured he ought to pick up. He turned the volume down on the TV.

"What do you know about Diana?"

Not much. Marty had to admit that was part of the appeal. She talked even less about herself than he did and when it did come up, she always found a way to steer such conversation elsewhere. She had a labrador retriever once named Taco. They lived out in Vermont, but after the dog died, she decided to pack a small suitcase and head to the West Coast. She found work performing research and drawing up briefs for an intellectual property lawyer out of El Segundo.

"Apparently she has no next of kin," Dennis continued. "She lived in Vermont for all of her life. Shuffled around foster homes. Her bio parents both died of meth overdoses before she hit twelve. It seemed like she had her act together though, given the crappy environment. Got her GED, then her paralegal certificate. Shit, you probably know all of this."

Marty did. Some of it, anyway. He thought about his own relatives who might as well be strangers. Even though he visited his parents in their Laguna Woods retirement community a few times a year, it wasn't as if they were ever close. They did their thing. He did his.

"Look, I know you kids were hot and heavy and jumped into this thing. You've always been a closed book with your relationships. I shouldn't even be discussing any of this with you. But, I'm gonna be honest. We're hitting a dead end here. I need your help."

Marty had already gotten to work. It didn't matter how close he was to her. Work was always on his mind. He'd poked and prodded every corner of his mental being but had yet to come up with anything.

"I assume you got nothing from the dress? Chair? Everything else?" Marty asked.

"Only her prints and DNA. And of course yours."

Of course.

"And the lawyer's office?"

"Obviously, we've interviewed everyone there. Callahan and O'Donnell aren't working on anything exactly high-profile. They're on retainer for a few distribution and shipping bigwigs in the area. Preliminary checks on the companies aren't raising any red flags."

Marty didn't say anything. He only stared at the female newscaster on the screen. A tiny box next to her head showed a picture of a young man sporting a beard meant to make him look ten years older than he really was, but had the opposite effect. Below his face were the words *CONTROVER-SIAL IPO* and the name of the company—Moeva.

"I gotta go." Marty hung up the phone and turned up the volume.

A brief interview with the man popped up. He was smiling wide with his left canine tooth poking out slightly more than his right, standing in what looked to be an office lobby. His facial hair matched his earlier photo and he was wearing a light blue collared shirt, the top two buttons unbuttoned, beneath a dark blazer. There was something about him that stuck in Marty's craw.

"We make lifelong companions."

"Mr. Munro, don't you feel that this is...unnatural?" the woman interviewing him asked.

"Not everyone is blessed to be an alpha male. And, by the way, not all of our clients are male. But let me ask you, are those people less deserving of companionship?"

The interviewer feigned a look of concern and was speaking as if she were reading a script. "There's been controversy surrounding some of the 'personalities' that come with these dolls."

"Companions."

The woman continued. "Many of them a programmed to act resistant to their operator. Don't you feel that you're feeding potentially dangerous delusions and addictions of your customers?"

"We're offering some of our customers a form of therapy," he said. "If they are able to act out their fantasies with their companions, imagine the number of public safety incidents that will reduce."

The interview cut back to the newscaster who mentioned that the tiny startup was founded only two years ago in Vermont.

* * *

It was the usual lawyer's office. Shelves covered with dark green and brown leather-bound tomes filled with archaic law literature that were probably ignored for the most part. How much of that was available online now? Marty couldn't imagine an attorney having his paralegals wasting time digging around in those things.

The administrative assistant eyed Marty from behind her giant desk. She was a woman in her late fifties, maybe early sixties, with a bit of filler to smooth out the wrinkles out beside her eyes, but she peered over the lip of dark oak like a young child barely able to reach the top.

"Can I help you?"

"Yes, I'd like to talk to Callahan. Or O'Donnell."

"Do you have an appointment?"

"No."

She sighed deeply. "Well, they are both very busy. Are you a current client—"

He flashed his badge.

"Look, I saw both of them park their cars this morning. I know they're here. I know they're probably sitting in a conference room right now stuffing their faces with whatever overpriced shrimp and lobster they had brought in."

The woman hesitated for a second before picking up the phone.

"There's a police officer here to see you."

"His name's…." She looked up.

"Marty."

"Marty….?"

"Marty."

She repeated the name into the handset and hung up the phone a second later.

"Down the hallway. Second door on your right."

* * *

The room had an appearance much like the lobby, only slightly smaller with a polished oak table in the middle and a conference phone sitting in the middle of that. A platter of seafood and dipping sauces was half-empty. Plates with discarded shrimp and lobster tails sat in front of two men.

Surprise, surprise.

Except for different colored ties, Callahan and O'Donnell looked like cheap carbon copies of each other. Both of them were busting out of the same tired gray blazers and button-up white shirts and had mile-long combovers. It was like they hadn't updated their wardrobes since the 80s. These guys obviously had steady clientele.

"We don't have anything more to say. We've already talked—"

"I'll be quick. Tell me about Moeva."

Callahan looked at O'Donnell. Or O'Donnell looked at Callahan.

One of them spoke.

"We've given the department all of the information we have regarding Diana. I advise that—"

The man went silent as Marty reached into his coat, pulled the .40 Smith and Wesson out of his shoulder holster and removed the magazine. He confirmed that it was loaded and slapped it back in. The faces of the two attorneys turned ash white. Marty didn't point his weapon at them. Didn't wave it around threateningly. He was simply an officer checking his tools, but he probably looked as scary as hell. He hadn't slept in the past twenty-six hours, his eyes were dry and bloodshot, and he could almost see the funk fuming from his body.

"I understand. I just feel like you work a complicated business. You keep a lot of files. Things get misplaced or forgotten about. There may be some niggling little detail…" He shrugged and shifted his eyes between them both. "…you know, something inconsequential that you might think is not really even worth mentioning, but that I would really love to hear."

Callahan, or maybe it was O'Donnell, looked like he was about to crack, so Marty focused on him.

"We had nothing to do with what happened."

Marty was silent, goading the man to speak more.

"Do you know who did?"

"No!" they said simultaneously.

Marty believed them.

"We don't work for them anymore," one of them offered up.

"As of when?"

"As of yesterday."

"Because of Diana?"

There was a moment of hesitation.

"I'll take that as a yes. Look, give me all of those files you have that you may have forgotten to give the department and I'll let you get back to your peasant's lunch."

* * *

Marty pulled up the folder on his computer. Six hundred and thirty-six legal documents. This would take awhile. He started the first pot of coffee.

* * *

It was somewhere around two A.M. when he noticed something odd. Callahan and O'Donnell had vetted a deal between Moeva and a marketing company with ties to a popular social media giant. A database was sold to Moeva, operating as Tenacious Industries. Marty imagined this particular media company would be in a pool of hot water if news got out.

It was time to learn a little more about Moeva's operations.

* * *

The place didn't look particularly high tech. Just south of Burlington, east of Lake Champlain, Moeva's two-level, white-brick building was part of a nondescript office park set back in a copse of hackberry trees whose branches of spearhead-leaves shadowed the natural grass.

The lobby was equally unremarkable, except for the rear wall where a large, glossy sign displaying Moeva's logo hung—a pair of feminine eyes with heavy eyeshadow and a reflection of computer chips painted inside the pupils. It was the same location where the news interview had taken place.

A young, pasty male sat behind the front desk.

"Good morning. I'm Mr. Vanderschot with Dutch Capital." Not the most creative company name. Marty banked on no one in the office having ever been to the Netherlands, otherwise the accent he'd practiced for the past twenty-four hours by reviewing online videos would make the situation a little more precarious. "I have an appointment with—"

"Mr. Vanderschot!" There was the bearded boy from the newscast, peeking out from a door behind the admin's desk. He walked up to Marty and extended his hand. "David Munro. It's a pleasure to have you here."

Marty took his hand and fought an instinctive revulsion to the its clamminess.

"How was the flight? I hope you've adjusted to the time difference."

"It's nothing." The less said, the better. "Shall we begin the tour? I have another appointment this afternoon."

"Of course. I understand you are a busy man." David walked toward the door. "Please, follow me."

$$* * *$$

There were a few humans milling about, but most of the work was done through automation in a large warehouse. Machines building machines. Conveyor belts distributed the lifelike body parts to various points where metal arms and claws assembled them.

David shouted over the loud mechanisms. "It's all in the crotch. Our researchers spent many hours perfecting the look and feel. Especially the feel. That's one of our key differentiators." He said with an almost clinical inflection.

Seeing the parts of the bodies reminded Marty of many a crime scene he wished he could forget. After the brief tour, the two of them retired to David's office.

On a side table, there was a stack of cheeseburger sliders and a bowl of mac and cheese. A bucket filled with ice and beer bottles sat next to the food.

"I figured you might enjoy some classic American fare."

Marty's stomach was signaling everything but hunger.

"To be honest, what I've seen is interesting and while your product is certainly titillating, I don't know that its enough to get me and my partners... excited."

There was a momentary hesitation from David, but he leaned forward.

"We've got something new we're working on for select customers. It promises to be very profitable. I'm not going to lie to you, Mr. Vanderschot. The sort of numbers you're looking to invest is what we need. I'm showing you all my cards. We're a little controversial and finding willing investors is difficult. I need to know that if you invest, you'll put some faith in me. That you'll stand with this company."

"We look for profit, Mr. Munro."

The toothy smile came quickly.

* * *

They were in a locked room at the back of the warehouse. Piled into one corner were replicas of children, completely naked. It took everything Marty had to not go ballistic.

"You want profit? This is profit, Mr. Vanderschot." David indicated toward the main factory floor with his head. "That's good money, but this..." He made his eyebrows dance. "...this is going to make us all very happy. Watch."

He walked over to one of the dolls—a young girl with blonde hair and blue eyes. He pressed a finger into the back of her neck. Her movements were jerky, but she sprang to life.

"Tell us about yourself," David said to her.

The little girl's lips moved. "My name is Tina Watts. I'm twelve-years-old and live in Hot Springs, Arkansas. I like waterskiing, texting my friends, and cuddling with my dachshund, Bonnie."

David's sick smile seemed to grow.

"Wow," Marty said. He had dealt with shady characters throughout his career, but David Munro was something else. "So lifelike. They each have these personalities?"

"It's our secret sauce. For all practical purposes, these are real kids."

"How so?"

"We had a brief partnership with Flitterbook. Under a shell company. But the lawyers got queasy and cut things off. It's okay. We got all the profile information. Got what we needed."

His hand was stroking the girl's hair as if she were a pet.

It was time.

"You certainly did that," Marty said. He pulled out his pistol and shoved it into David's gut before the sick CEO knew what was happening. "And now I got what I needed."

Munro was surprisingly cool.

"What happened to your accent, Mr. Vanderschot?"

"I lost it."

$* * *$

Diana had been in a relationship with David. He'd taken her under his wing when she was younger. More vulnerable. He confessed that she had made good money by referring him to lawyers who were willing to broker the deal with Flitterbook. Apparently she had a sudden change of heart. She grew a moral compass, he said, and though she didn't outright say it, it was obvious she was ready to tell someone what she knew.

By that point, David had made too much money from wealthy clients to turn back, so he did what he needed to do.

Diana had been in trouble and Marty had ignored the signs. He recalled the agitated looks on her face when she tried to talk to him, only for him to change the subject. His own need for detachment, to keep the dirty work in the office, wound up forcing Diana to hide her truth in the shadows for too long.

Back at his apartment, sitting in a new, old pea-green chair he'd picked up from a nearby thrift store, Marty pored over files from a new case that Dennis had been working on in Marty's absence. Allowing himself to drift to the bottom, deep into his work, was all he could do now.

Process Summary

Halfway is story number forty-seven in the #52ShortStories challenge.

I'm sure I've mentioned it before (things tend to run together after 47 stories), but when you're doing this sort of off-the-cuff writing, there's a lack of control that is both harrowing and thrilling. I wrote *Halfway* in a genre I don't naturally gravitate toward and after several days, I knew this could easily turn out to be something much longer than I could possibly complete in one week.

So many times, I'm down to the wire when I'm hit with a solution to a problem like that. But I guess there ain't nothin' like a little pressure to kick one past the fear of putting something dumb out there and just being happy with what you have.

And then there are the same two lessons I seem to keep relearning:

- We are the worst judges of our own work. Those who read the story seemed to enjoy the characters and plot. A good reminder as to why we just need to put things out there and move on to the next story.

- Experiment! That's one of the benefits of working on short stories. There are so many opportunities to do the 'crazy' thing.

Hello, Nice to Destroy You

Statistics

Synopsis: Based on true events from India in 1964, a man comes to grips with fate and free will.

Word Count: 2,700

Genre: Urban Fantasy

Completed Week: June 30th – July 6th

Hello, Nice to Destroy You

December 23, 1964

Pamban Island, India

It was eleven p.m. on the last train to Dhanushkodi. For the past twenty hours, I had done everything but sleep during the long ride, despite spending most of what was left of my money on a compartment of my own. My mind refused the luxury so long as I kept sweating.

The tiny, wall-mounted fan had stopped working five minutes after I switched it on. A porter told me they were unable to fix it and all other cabins were occupied. The crowded third- and second-class cars would be even worse, so I accepted the sticky discomfort. While I appreciated the solitude, one could only play so much solitaire and I sincerely couldn't stomach a fourth reading of *On the Road*. Dean Moriarty was starting to piss me off. If he was here, I would have shoved him out the window and into the angry waters of the Palk Strait.

A clap of thunder rattled the cabin and every screw and bolt inside, setting each hair on my body at attention.

I was glad the black night obscured the sea through the window. I imagined waves pushing up against the narrow bridge like a mass of soldiers trying to come over the top of a castle wall. The Pamban bridge between mainland India and the island was only a little over a mile long, but I lacked faith that this clacking, hulking chain of steel would stay on the straight and narrow.

In my reflection, I could sort of make out the heavy bags beneath my eyes. Thoughts of Christmas dinner seemed drawn to me like the mosquitoes had in Madras—I saw steam rising from the bowl of mashed potatoes, the candied yams blanketed in gooey marshmallows, and a buttery-brown turkey sitting in the middle of it all.

I rolled a tiny, bland ball of rice around in my hands.

I might just sleep through Christmas day this year. Curl up on the beach and let the rain and saltwater wash my troubles away. Maybe 1965 would be better for everyone. Maybe I would find myself back in Sacramento next December, sitting around a tree wrapped in shiny silver tinsel and red-and-green lights, drinking eggnog with my parents and sisters, discussing everything but what I'd experienced these past six months. I was positive they would be relieved that I'd finally 'found myself' and decided to come back home.

At least, maybe they would.

I leaned my head against the window and listened to the raindrops bomb the nasty film of soot left by the steam engine.

* * *

I must have finally nodded off as I was shaken awake by the squealing brakes. My ball of rice was on the floor. The train came to a lurching stop at the final station in Rameswaram before heading south to Dhanushkodi.

I had visions of securing a nice hotel room with a soft bed and hot chai, but I knew my remaining budget didn't portend much more than a mud and palm-leaf hut. The plan was to take the ferry to Ceylon tomorrow, but I began to wonder if I should bother. Mud and palm-leaves embodied everything about why I had come, right? To get away from all those material possessions and comforts? Find truth?

I slid the window open for relief, quickly realizing I wouldn't find it there. It was just as hot and humid outside, but with a strong smell of briny seawater. Large squalls whipped around and beneath the train, composing an odd whistling music while also shooting rain into the cabin. As I wrestled the window shut, the door behind me squealed opened.

Sporting a trendy red Hawaiian shirt with white orchids and equally-white pants, a tall, thin man ducked to enter the compartment, removing his vanilla-brown fedora in the process. His head was shaped like an almond and was as smooth as a baby's bottom from crown to chin.

"The fan doesn't work," I said.

He smiled close-mouthed for several seconds before answering. "That's fine. I rather enjoy the heat."

An American accent. I couldn't remember the last time I'd heard one. His voice was sonorous, able to carry over the pulsating rain which seemed to increase its tempo after he came in.

My disappointment at his answer must have been obvious across my tired face.

"Though, I promise I maintain good hygiene," he followed up.

That seemed to be true. I couldn't smell him at all, in fact, though I worried that said more about my body odor than his.

I expected him to bring his luggage in from behind, but he simply turned around and shut the door. He had nothing on his person. Not even a briefcase or knapsack.

The cabin had an upper and lower bed and he extended a spindly hand toward the open space on the bottom bunk next to me.

"Do you mind? It's difficult to sleep in this weather," he said.

"No." It could have been a comfortable seventy-six degrees Fahrenheit and I would still be wide awake. Traveling the subcontinent taught me to be wary of strangers within arm's reach, no matter where they came from.

The bunk shifted slightly as he squatted onto the mattress. "Besides, we shouldn't be long now."

It was true. Dhanushkodi was another thirty minutes south. I said nothing, only scooting as close to the opposite edge as possible, which turned out to be a precious few inches. I had second thoughts of pulling out Kerouac's book as a way of sending a signal.

The man stretched his legs out and reached for his toes, taking several deep breaths. Then he stuck a hand into his pocket. Out came a piece of brown, folded cloth. He opened it up and held it in front of me. There were four or five pieces of yellow, sugar-coated candy.

"Lemon drop?"

"No," I said. "Thank you."

He didn't seem to respond other than to take one and shove it in his mouth, wrapping the cloth up and putting it back in his pocket. Even over the ambient noise and the ever-increasing pounding rain, I could hear him sucking through closed lips.

"They're my favorite, though not exactly healthful." He leaned in close. "But life is short."

The scent of sweet citrus stirred my stomach. He was obviously looking for conversation and it would take more effort to fend him off for the next half-hour than it would to just let him talk.

"How long have you been here?" I asked.

"Where?"

It seemed an obvious question to me, but I said, "India."

"Only a day. It's been a long time since I've been out this way." He looked through the window as if he could actually see the landscape. From the hallway, a pair of men spoke rapidly in Tamil, none of which I understood, but the bubbling speech pattern was a dead giveaway.

We both fell forward slightly as the train jerked away from Rameswaram Station.

"I've only just arrived in town this morning," he said. "To visit Cain and Abel's grave. Have you been there yet?"

"Pardon?"

"The graves. You know. Adam and Eve? Cain and Abel? East of Eden and all that." He said it with a wink.

I remembered reading something in one of the guidebooks I'd abandoned. Local legend and likely source of income for whatever group of charlatans maintained the 'tombs.' It was said that when Adam and Eve were exiled from the Garden, they went east to Ceylon.

"They're really in bad shape these days. Maintained by a Muslim named Abdul Momit. Nice man. The Muslims refer to them as Habil and Qabil. I hope the boys are resting well."

He said it as if he truly wished it.

"Quite a thing, really. The first murder. Can you imagine?"

I no longer had to imagine much since beginning my sojourn. I'd seen the world's dirty work—mainly poverty beyond that which I thought possible. Only blocks from the ornate temples and expensive hotels were groups of emaciated children playing in their own excrement while their parents reached out with filthy hands. Hands that, when not begging, were stealing.

"Out, out, brief candle." the man whispered.

I shifted in my seat and he chuckled, seemingly at my discomfort.

"So, tell me, did you find it?"

"Find what?"

"Enlightenment. The meaning of it all."

I paused and before I could answer, he said, "That's why young Americans come to a place like this, right? Hoping to find something that makes sense in a place as far from home as possible? By the weariness on your face, I'm sure I don't need to tell you at this point that what you're looking for isn't hiding under a bodhi tree or a crumbling temple in Ceylon."

"Seems like you have all the answers," I said, feeling indignant that the man had me pegged so well. As if I had no say in my life. That decisions I had made were practically scripted.

"I have a few, but not all. Believe me, young man, you don't want all the answers."

"You sound just like the gurus you make light of. What is that supposed to mean?"

"Exactly what I said." His emerald-green eyes paused on mine for what seemed an eternity and I struggled to look away. "Can I ask you a question?"

"Why stop now?"

"Do you think that if you were to live forever, you would be a good person?"

I had a sudden flash of regret at not having paid attention in Sunday school or having not taken the time to read Nietzsche instead of just carrying him around from coffee house to coffee house. Maybe then I could have put this arrogant man in his place.

"That eventually, having done every wicked thing the blood in your body lusts after, you would grow tired of it and find yourself becoming righteous? I wonder if that's God. That he or she is just someone who never died and got tired of being evil."

"Then why is there still evil?"

"Perhaps God's not the only one who never died. He or she is just the oldest."

As if I was in a motion picture, a crash of thunder shook the cabin at the end of his sentence. With all of this deep talk, I felt the need to come up for air, so I excused myself and headed for the dining car.

* * *

Besides a young Indian girl sitting in the lap of a young Indian boy, his arms wrapped around her while he whispered into her ear and she smiled, I was alone in the dining car. The lights above occasionally flickered as I took a seat at the furthest table from them. The sounds of the rain echoed far more loudly here than they had in my cabin.

"Chai, please."

The waiter's hand trembled and hot drops spilled onto the white tablecloth.

"So sorry, sir." He pulled a napkin from his pocket and began to sop up the stains.

"It's fine," I said.

"It is the storm," he said. "We have monsoon rains here all the time, but this one—it bothers me."

I knew what he meant. As soon as I was close to putting a finger on the exact feeling, it seemed to skitter away into the shunning darkness. I suppose I could have tried to soothe him with a 'Don't worry about it,' or an 'I'm sure it will all be fine,' but what could this American say to someone who had far more experience in this part of the world?

He was about to leave me to my chai when I grabbed his wrist.

"Something else, sir?"

"What do you think of people like me coming here?"

His eyes narrowed. "How do you mean, sir?" I noticed his polished teeth and clean fingernails.

"Nevermind."

I had only a sip before both the cup and waiter crashed onto the floor when the train screeched to a halt.

* * *

The waiter was gone the blink of an eye, leaving only myself and the lovebirds. The boy helped pick his lover from the ground and I looked out the window to try and see where we were. I didn't think we were at the station yet, but it was impossible to tell through the murk. At a standstill now, the winds seemed to be ten times as strong. The entire car was rocking side to side like a giant cradle.

I thought it best to return to my cabin in case we needed to disembark.

The sleeping car was adjacent to the dining area. As soon as I stepped out onto the vestibule, the screeching sounds of twisting metal vibrated harshly in my ears and maintaining my balance on the swaying floor took a feat of magnificent concentration. Stinging sweat, a combination of humidity and fear, poured into my eyes and it took me several tries to pull open the car door.

When I finally made it to my compartment, my seatmate was still awake, swaying with that same sideways motion while looking at his ticket.

"653."

He repeated the number over and over until I interrupted him.

"I think we need to get ready to go," I said. "They stopped the train."

He shook his head but didn't look at me. "No significance whatso-ever."

"Significance of what?" As I pulled my suitcase out from under the bottom seat, I wondered why I asked. I wanted to do nothing but get off the train and away from him. The rain seemed almost threatening now, ready to burst through the window.

"It's just…" He smiled at me. "I always try to find some thing. A bit of meaning. Why I do this. When I'll stop. But it's never there."

I was scared, I was tired, and I was hungry. I didn't care to solve any riddles at the moment.

"There's no need to rush," he said. Just then a pair of agitated porters ran into each other in the hall behind me and engaged in a heated conver-sation. My Tamil was limited to a few phrases, but I could tell by the rapid speech and tone in their voice that something was wrong.

My new friend continued, "I'm sure you're tired of my questions, but I enjoy learning about people. Tell me, why did you choose Dhanushkodi tonight?" His voice was irritatingly calm.

I pretended he wasn't there. "What's going on?" I yelled at the two porters over the pounding rain. They ignored me before running off in the direction of the engine.

I turned back to the man and his eyes were closed, his hands on his lap as if in meditation.

"Why tonight?" he asked, almost to himself. "Why this time, on this day, in this part of the world? Why you? Why not one of your sisters, Bernice, or Carolyn? Why the young lovers on their honeymoon?" He opened his eyes and a flash of lightning lit up the window. For a brief moment, I saw palm trees whipping back and forth like twigs.

"Why are you here?" he finished.

"I don't know!" I said, only realizing after that I had never once mentioned my family. My nerves were on edge. I felt entirely frantic.

"I know," he replied quietly. "I know."

He reached a hand out as if to shake. "It was nice to meet you. Perhaps, one day, we'll both become different people."

Just then, the lights went out in the cabin and there was a low rumble originating from outside.

Knocked off my feet, I flew backward through the open door of the cabin, slamming against the inside of the carriage wall. Pieces of debris crashed down on top of me. Something careened into my head and I went to sleep.

Process Summary

Hello, Nice to Destroy You is story number forty-eight in the #52Short-Stories challenge.

This story is a prime example that ideas are lurking everywhere. Over the past couple of months, I've taken a different approach to my reading (outside of my Ray Bradbury-assigned regimen). Where I used to pick books based on pre-conceived ideas such as, "Oh, I really ought to read this. It's supposed to be good," I've shifted more to a, "What strikes my fancy this very moment?" So I recently perused my personal library and picked out Paul Theroux's *The Great Railway Bazaar* which had been sitting unread for God knows how long.

It's a fascinating travelogue written in the early 1970s recounting Paul's travels across the European and Asian continents by train. About two-thirds of the way through, I came across a brief recollection by one of the train passengers that piqued my interest. An immense cyclone hit Sri Lanka (then Ceylon) and southern India in 1964 that destroyed an entire town (Dhanushkodi) along with a hundred people in a passenger train headed that way. It struck me as just being one of those unfortunate natural events that make you ask, "Why?"

I tried to put myself in the shoes of someone unusual on that train, why they would be there, and what the experience would be like. This was challenging, but I loved the idea.

Also, if you have room on your TBR pile, pick up the Theroux book. It's a fascinating glimpse at that part of the world in the 'olden days,' filled with wonderful imagery and interactions.

BRANDED

Statistics

Synopsis: Jenny Tighe finds her rancher father shot in the back and marked on the forehead.

Word Count: 1,700

Genre: Western

Completed Week: July 7th – July 10th

Branded

Though his belly touched the sand, his face was turned slightly up, facing west—the direction of home. Yellow pus streamed from the corner of his left eye onto the bridge of his narrow nose, leaving a noxious stench. Flies buzzed in circles over his open mouth. And then there was the maroon-stained hole punched clean between his shoulder blades, the fabric of his dirty shirt shredded. These signs all added up to one thing.

Jenny Tighe's papa was dead.

It was normal for him to be gone for a few days at a time when checking up on the ranging cattle, and usually, Jenny was with him, learning how to rope and drive. But she had enough to do with keeping the house in order since they lost Mama to consumption earlier in the summer. Scrubbing the splintered floors of their tiny cabin was the last thing Jenny was intent on doing, but she did it because someone had to and she knew it would be one less worry for Papa.

Now, circling buzzards had led her to his body on the dry Mojave Desert floor. Those same vultures were perched, six of them, all waiting patiently on a large pile of tan and gray boulders which sat a half-mile south of the Granite Mountains. Her eyes scanned the nooks and crannies of the surrounding hills while her Winchester 1873 rifle rested in her hands like a familiar tool. Jenny never had to use it on a human before, but Papa had made sure she was ready for anything. She'd been a crack-shot with deer in the nearby San Bernardino mountains and was ready to put those skills to use, now that everything had changed.

Nothing seemed to be out there among the thin creosote bushes and tumbleweeds except a few skittering lizards and jackrabbits. Given the state of Papa's body, she figured the culprits were long gone.

She didn't want to get close to him, to rest a hand on his upturned cheek or to shed the tears that were welling up behind her eyes. But she had to lean in to get a closer look at the thing that caught her attention. She rolled his body over to face the sky and his face along with it. Her heart skipped a beat when she saw the five-pointed star branded on his forehead.

* * *

The McLarens weren't just unconcerned if it was discovered that they did this. Seems they *wanted* whoever found Papa to know it was them.

There was no time for pleasantries. As badly as she wanted to dig him a grave, Papa would have been satisfied giving the buzzards the meal of their lives.

Bolt dipped her long head as Jenny approached. Jenny scratched the mare's neck a couple of times, then rummaged through the saddlebag, digging past slabs of beef jerky and a half-empty canteen until she came up with five .44 caliber rounds. Her Winchester was the half-magazine model, capable of holding six potential shots at a time. It was already fully loaded, ready for business at a drop of the lever, She didn't have much extra ammunition, but she hoped not to need it.

She mounted Bolt and galloped east.

* * *

It was nice enough in the greater Mojave. Night temperatures were mild and the sun's power was dampened by unusual autumn clouds. Jenny knew every waterhole between her ranch and the McLaren hideout in Hidden Valley, so she and Bolt were well nourished on the two days it took to travel the seventy miles from home. Deeper into the desert. Deeper into danger.

That had to be where they went. Papa had mentioned that it was the worst kept secret in all of Southern California. She could only imagine now that he brought it up with her just in case something happened.

The long trip had given the fire and fury inside of Jenny time to become a slow burn. She could be more calculating. Make fewer mistakes. The McLarens knew her. Probably knew what had happened to Mama. Jenny met them once, when Papa and her had a run-in a year ago when she was only fourteen. They were heading out to dehorn a group of grazing cattle when Bill McLaren and his brother, Jim, were caught hanging back on a ridge with packs full of rope. They said they'd been searching for their own lost cattle. Papa intimated that he knew what they were up to, but he let them save face.

Stupid. He should have taken care of them then and there.

Bill put on good appearances—he was congenial, handsome even, but she could sense his calculating mind and devious heart. His brother, Jim, on the other hand, was repulsive to the core and seemed not to give a damn about anything. With mussed hair and a reek of whiskey that carried in the wind, he seemed to get a kick out of whistling out of tune and wouldn't stop leering at Jenny until Papa said he'd cut his eyes out right then and there and feed them to the family's bloodhound.

They must have branded Jenny Tighe a girly girl. That she would be too scared to do what she was about to do. Now she was trotting through an arroyo a few miles north of Hidden Valley, chilly without a fire as the sun began to set, ready to put this thing to rest.

* * *

"Get up."

Jim was still snoring. An empty glass bottle laid tipped over on the tent floor beside his cot. Jenny shoved the tip of the rifle barrel into his right nostril and cocked the lever.

Even in the dark, his crusted eyes blinked as he tried to adjust his vision.

"Well, I'll be. What good deed did I do to deserve a visit from an angel?" He started to laugh, but it turned into a phlegm-filled coughing fit. Jenny kept the rifle pointed at his face. She had thought about just pulling the trigger when he was sleeping, but she wanted him to know who was collecting on the debt he owed.

"Do you know who I am?"

"Let me sit up and get a closer look."

She flipped the rifle around like a baton and jammed the butt into his forehead. The crack sent his hands flying to his head.

"Gottdamn! That hurt, you little bitch!"

She swung the barrel of the gun back toward him. "You've only started hurting. Now, get up. Slow."

There had been only one tent in the camp, one cot inside. Remnants of a fire glowed in a ring of stones outside.

"Where's your brother?"

She thought that maybe Bill was out rustling up more cattle. She'd come across a mass of them corralled inside the camp—even recognized a few of them before she even needed to see Papa's brand burnt into their haunches. The plan was to settle up with Jim and then wait until Bill returned. The fire and fury seemed to resurge at the alcohol odor of the younger brother and she knew she was acting more recklessly than she should have been.

She heard a pistol hammer cock behind her.

"You lookin' for me, little lady?"

Jenny's eyes remained on Jim, his black-and-yellow grin bringing her closer to pulling the trigger.

"You may want to think about what it is you intend to do here," Bill said. "My advice? Slowly lay the rifle to the ground."

She wanted to cry. To come so far and make such a foolhardy mistake.

"You killed my papa. I can't let that go unanswered," she said, staring down at Jim the whole time while he slowly climbed out of his canvas sleeping sack, testing her with each move.

The silence in the air was thick. Jenny ran through her options which had narrowed rapidly.

It wasn't as if she could dash out, hop on her horse and make a break for it. She'd left Bolt tied to a yucca tree a half-mile out between the hideout and the arroyo. Besides, if she did get away, contacted the Sheriff, chances are Papa's brand would be converted by the time someone came out here. And that was assuming the McLaren's were even in Hidden Valley at that point.

Jim appeared to be having trouble standing on his own two feet, swaying side-to-side a little. Jenny's gun was still pointed at him, but now at his chest.

"We both know you ain't gonna shoot," he said, placing one hand on the barrel of the gun and the other on her cheek. Jenny felt him pushing the rifle gently to the side. He began to stroke her face. "So just do what my bro—"

In one swift motion, her finger crushed the trigger and she quickly kicked her left boot back, connecting with what she hoped was Bill's private parts. Her ears went ringing while the scent of gunpowder shot up her nose. Jim flew backward, ripping a gash in the tent wall before coming to rest on the ground. Something wet had splashed against her face which left a ferrous taste in her open mouth. As if she didn't care if she died now, Jenny turned without haste to look at Bill. She saw what looked to be the outline of a pistol in the dark ground. next to her feet, and a man crumpled up like a curlicue, his hands tucked into his crotch. She grabbed the pistol and listened to Bill's muffled whimpered for a few seconds.

"You're gonna pay for what you done," she said.

"You can't prove anything," Bill spat out between heavy breaths. "You're gonna hang, girl."

Jenny pocketed the pistol and pointed her rifle at Bill's head.

"Get up."

* * *

The coals were still warm. She picked up the five-point-star brand she'd left resting in the fire pit. Bill lay on the ground now, hogtied tied just as Papa had shown her when they were busting steer.

"Seems to me there ain't much left for me here," Jenny said. "So, I don't need to prove nothin' to nobody. This will be the last time you see me. This will make sure you don't forget your deeds."

She pressed the glowing pattern into his forehead and his scream echoed across the desert valley.

Process Summary

Branded is story number forty-nine in the #52ShortStories challenge.

Branded was seeded by setting. The working title was Dead Man's Point which is a little spot in the Mojave Desert filled with history and lore. I grew up in this area and drove by her many times. How did it get its name? Might as well just pick whichever story tickles your fancy. I decided it got its name because that's where a cattle rancher was found shot in the back by local rustlers (based on a real gang).

My subconscious decided it was time for a straight-up western with a traditional revenge trope. I forced myself to avoid my usual speculative bent and it seems to have gone over well. It's a story that is short and to the (Dead Man's) point!

Statistics

Synopsis: Ernie Bowen, a bouncer in New Las Vegas, wonders if he's responsible for a high-profile murder.

Word Count: 2,300

Genre: Dystopian

Completed Week: July 11th – July 17th

Be Kind

Be kind.

Tenet number one in the Book of Stanton.

For ten years, it had been etched into the pathways running between Ernie Bowen's amygdala and hippocampus. He'd spent the better part of two decades bouncing at bars and nightclubs all over the Western Confederation, finding success and salvation in the commandments set forth by the most revered bouncer of the before-times—Jerry Stanton.

But something went wrong tonight.

Tenet number two says: *Be kind until it's time to not be kind.*

That's where the rub is for most Stantonites and why so many of them never make it to the Cooler priesthood. It's one of those invisible lines that takes a patient, learned mind to feel—almost like a single strand from a spider web brushing against your cheek. Ernie thought he was there. He had the title. Had the vestments. Had the respect of his congregation.

How would he explain what went down?

The music had stopped, all the bright white overhead lights were on, and Ernie's mind was a jumble as he looked down at the four men splayed across the sticky floor inside of Luna Loca, the most popular club in New Las Vegas.

Three of them were big. Bigger than Ernie on a good day and without an ounce of fat. They were all on the ground, still breathing, but in various states of incapacitation.

It was the fourth body which was a cause for concern. That man's neck had been snapped so thoroughly, his head hinged until his nose touched his shoulder. Gelled black hair fell across his open eyes like feathers.

Then there was a woman, but she was gone.

To Ernie, it all went down in a blur and now he was faced with two problems: This wasn't just anyone lying dead on the floor. And assuming he could deal with that little issue successfully, there were still the Stantonites from whom Ernie would have to beg absolution.

* * *

"Bless me, Cooler, for I have sinned."

There was an uncomfortable moment of silence. Cooler Schoen must have been expecting him but was probably still shocked to hear Ernie through the thin barrier of the sweatbox confessional.

Ernie filled in the gap. "It has been 3,651 days since my last confession."

"That's an awful long time, son," Schoen said. His inflection was fatherly, filled with his signature gravel tone. Ernie pictured the old man sitting on the other side with his arms crossed and his legs extended in his signature pose. He saw the faded green tattoos on the forearms almost forming new patterns as Schoen's loose, leathery skin pressed into and overlapped itself. "Have you lived such a clean life?"

A tiny voice in Ernie's head wanted to toss out a bevy of excuses, but Ernie rubbed the sentiment out like a boot on a glowing cigarette.

"I've lived according to the Book."

"That's not an answer."

More silence.

"But what matters is that you're here now," Schoen continued.

"Please, go on."

The Cooler had to have known the story. The incident only occurred last night, but by the looks and whispers Ernie observed on his walk to the church this morning, it had traveled through the ears and mouths of all of Downtown. That was really something in a place where dead bodies popped up like desert primrose. Still, Ernie would do what he came here to do.

"I murdered a man last night."

"Murdered?"

"Pretty sure."

"Only pretty sure?"

"Well…" Ernie paused to think how much his future with the Church hinged on the story he was about to tell. If he were to be excommunicated, he didn't know what he would do. Before bouncing, there was nothing. After? He hadn't thought there would be an after. Still didn't think so.

"…I can't remember everything. I know what happened before and after—when he was lying on the ground, limp as a codfish. I only know what the witnesses said."

"I see. And what is that you think called you to commit this murder, son?"

"Nothing." The answer was instinctual.

A gritty laugh. "Nothing? Just felt like a good night for murder?"

Events had been replaying themselves in Ernie's mind since last night.

"Cooler, I've had my head stomped into the ground until it looked like my face was covered with strawberry jam. I'm sporting six scars across my belly where I've been shanked. I got a goddamn glass eye after the original got punctured by a spiked heel."

At the time that they occurred, each event seemed to be a big deal. Now they were simply as much a part of his being as the slab of ham steak sitting in his stomach from breakfast.

"Not once," he continued. "Not once have I lost control."

"I believe you. Take a deep breath. Concentrate. Walk me through what you *believe* happened."

Ernie had been a walking bundle of nerves since the incident. He closed his only eye and focused until he could almost feel the wall-rattling bass just outside of the club.

* * *

He'd just started working the door on that warm evening when Dorney came rushing out from inside and whispered into Ernie's ear.

"We have a situation."

"What's going on?"

"A guy won't leave, no matter how much we've asked him to. He's starting to get riled up and piss people off."

Ernie wondered why he was being bothered for a rudimentary task. "Grab a partner and kindly walk him outside."

"He won't budge." Dorney stepped back slightly. Sweat was pouring from his curly hair, down onto his brow. "And there's something else we learned."

Ernie waited stone-faced.

"It's Sammy Verillo's nephew, Mel."

* * *

At this point in the story, Ernie stopped to see if Cooler Schoen would react. Sammy Verillo had a stranglehold on almost half of Downtown. Many casinos, bars, and clubs within the four-square-mile area had Sammy's signature touch on them and a lot of people were happy to work for him. But, you so much as sneezed in his direction, you did so at your own peril.

"Continue," was all Schoen said.

* * *

Ernie recounted stepping inside with Dorney who needlessly pointed at the middle of the bar. Mel Verillo was throwing cocktail glasses around like they were baseballs, trying to hit targets across the room. A couple of the guests were too slow to duck and took some hits to the chest and shoulders. The rest of them were breaking for the exit. Never a good sign.

Be kind.

Ernie's eye started with the troublemaker and the three muscled goons surrounding him, then ended on the laughing girl beside him. She was sitting on a stool next to Mel, one leg crossed over the other. Her creamy thighs were illuminated by the strobing red and green lights while her wavy brown locks brought back memories of how it smelled of vanilla and spices.

"Oh look," she said, staring at Ernie as he and Dorney approached along with two other bouncers. "They brought in the talent." Her words were slurred and her eyes narrowed like a predator focusing on its prey.

Mel had been making a name for himself lately, and not in a good way. Word among the congregation was that he'd been going on benders lately with his new girl. This was the first time he'd made any scene at Luna Loca, though.

Ernie ignored him and bent toward the girl's left ear.

"What are you doing hanging around with this guy?"

She pushed him away. "I'm fucking him, Ernie. You have a problem with that?"

Be kind.

"I have a problem with you two sending paying customers away. I don't give a damn who you let play in your sandbox." A lie as hard to think as it was to say, but now was not the time to let things get personal.

***

"So you knew her?" Schoen asked.

Ernie supposed only in a sense. He came to understand that, as desperately as he wished to, he had never been able to truly know Bea. She used to dance at some of the same clubs he worked. He made it a point to never see the people you work with, but that point had only come into existence after his experience with Bea. They had been together off and on for the past three years, each sudden ending of the relationship as explosive as each rekindling. The last blowout had been epic. She cursed him down to his bones for suggesting she quit dancing. He hadn't seen her for several months until last night and there was no denying his desire to build something again.

"Yeah, I knew her."

Ernie took Cooler Schoen's silence as a request to continue.

***

"She's got a great sandbox," Mel chimed in. "But you probably know that, huh?"

A smarmy smile stretched across his face. He was leaning back against the bar, arms spread out with his elbows on the counter, bouncing another cocktail glass in his right hand. His entourage was visibly itchy but doing a decent job of acting cool.

Be kind.

"I'm going to have to ask you all to leave," Ernie said. His good eye took note of Mel's wrist flicking up and down.

"Well, Ernie, I kinda don't want to leave. I'm just having such a good time at my uncle's club. Look, how about I buy you a drink."

Ernie was ready as the glass came hurtling through the space where his head had been. His fist caught hold of it in mid-air.

Be kind.

"Ha!" Mel looked at Bea. "You didn't tell me the monkey knew tricks!"

"He knows a few," she said as if egging on her new boyfriend.

This was the first time Ernie had ever needed to deal with a situation like this.

"Does your uncle know you're here?" he asked.

"He ain't my parole officer. I don't need to check in with him on a regular basis." Mel hopped to his feet and wobbled around a little bit. He fumbled with the zipper on his black slacks, proceeded to whip out his penis and started pissing on Ernie's shoes.

Dorney and the two other guards looked to Ernie who stood in place and shook his head slightly. Mel hummed a tune, interspersed with giggling.

Be kind.

At this point, Bea seemed to find room for a little embarrassment as she turned back toward the bar. After a long fifteen seconds, Mel's stream dried up and he released a loud sigh.

"Much better."

It was time to make a move.

"Good, now you can go," Ernie said. He edged toward Mel and grabbed his arm. The goon tried to shake himself free, but it was no use.

"Get your hands off me, monkey!"

Ernie signaled to Dorney to grab the other arm and motioned for the two other bouncers to watch their backs.

That was when Ernie saw one of Mel's goons reach into his coat.

That was when time stopped.

* * *

"Things kind of went south from there," Ernie said. "At least that's what they tell me. I only remember standing above the muscle and a dead man, feeling absolutely exhausted."

Through the screen, in the candlelight, Ernie could see the slight silhouette of Cooler Schoen's experienced face.

"Do you believe you were in control of your emotions up to that point? Acted how Stanton would act? Did what Stanton would do?"

Ernie hadn't actively reflected on those last two questions in a while. Every move he'd made had been pure instinct for a long time. He trusted his gut these days. Trusted that he'd digested the teachings from the Book.

"Yes."

"You're concerned you lost control. You believe that jealousy got the best of you."

Even though it was a statement, Ernie replied, "Yes."

Schoen took a deep breath and then continued, "Dorney and his brothers came to us. Told us what they saw. We all agreed. It seems to me that you were not in control of your faculties."

Ernie's heart skipped a beat. Here it came. The banishment. The shame.

"This has been known to happen to a blessed few," Schoen said.

Ernie stopped breathing. He wasn't sure he heard correctly.

"The Spirit of Stanton can inhabit one's body for a few moments of time so that He can exert His divine will. A miracle of sorts to remind us that he walks among us. Watching. Protecting."

Sweat ran into Ernie's eye as he leaned against the side of the confessional.

"I'm going to read you a passage from chapter nine, verses seven through eight." Cooler Schoen cleared his throat. *"[7] Sure, I thought of a hundred different ways in which I could gut him. But what would that accomplish? [8] There are many methods by which one can inflict harm and disable a troublemaker, all valuable at the appropriate time, but there is only one way to steer the atmosphere in a productive manner and influence the long-term—kindness."*

The verse wasn't new to Ernie. Every first-year Stanton Seminary student needed to recite the entire chapter from memory. But his mind went suddenly to more earthly matters.

"I'm grateful to Stanton for choosing me as a vessel, but I don't know that Sammy Verillo cares who was in my body at the time."

Cooler Schoen's voice was soothing. "The Church has spoken with him. Above all else, Sammy is a businessman. He can't allow for a drop in foot traffic, no matter who's involved. He related to us a palpable sense of relief that his little problem seems to have resolved itself."

Ernie felt the weight of the whole damned world lifted from his shoulders. "I don't know what to say, Cooler."

"Rejoice," Schoen said. "Go, give thanks to Stanton, for He is Kind."

Process Summary

Be Kind is story number fifty in the #52ShortStories challenge.

We all have those guilty-pleasure movies. One of mine is *Roadhouse* starring Patrick Swayze and you can often find it airing on any given cable network on any given Saturday afternoon. If you haven't seen the movie, Swayze plays a kung fu-trained, philosophy-minded bouncer named Dalton who comes to work at a small-town bar that needs shaping up.

For those who *have* seen it, the connection between *Be Kind* and Dalton's catchphrase is obvious. I took his beliefs one step further, essentially turning them into the foundation of a future religion which is abided by bouncers in a Mad Max-type setting. I really enjoyed writing in the voice of Ernie on this one and I also discovered that I inadvertently return to certain names for my characters. I had another Ernie in *The Owl His Anthem.*

OUR MODERN HOPE

Statistics

Synopsis: Spaceketeer, Mitch Lacombe, must sacrifice himself in order to cure the world.

Word Count: 2,300

Genre: Sci-Fi

Completed Week: July 17th – July 21st

Our Modern Hope

Embarrassingly, it didn't take much for Mitchell Lacombe to overcome his inclination to vertigo two years ago and sign up for the Spaceketeers. His mother nagged him to put away the video games, get off the couch, and do something worth a damn. The world needed somebody to step up, she had said, so why not him?

And then she threw out the clincher: If things went wrong, it seemed a better way to go than wasting away in bed, crapping one's self, and losing one's mind.

That's how he found himself in a cozy hunk of silica and aluminum, spinning around in zero-gravity, searching for that one thing that would supposedly turn matters around for the folks back on Earth—a giant rock named Messiah-6.

"Hang on, Mitch."

Carolyn's face took up nearly all of the fuzzy CRT monitor. Her blue eyes were focused on something above her pixie-cut brunette hair while her shoulders rose and fell as she reached across her console, hitting various switches.

"Hang on? To what? I can't believe you guys forgot to build useful handholds on this thing."

"Not my job," Carolyn said absently. "Besides, time. There wasn't any. Plague and all that, right?"

Her quaint East Anglia accent was as charming as always.

"Right."

Mitch closed his eyes and pretended he was on a merry-go-round back at Houghman Park near his childhood home. The pace seemed to be the same, but it had been thirty-odd years since he'd played there. Of course, there were no cooing pigeons, no rush of wind picking up and tossing sand from the sandbox, and no little girls chasing him around, stealing kisses. There was only the sound of a very loud, very constant vacuum emitted by the surrounding machinery and its temperature control systems.

Every time he swung around, he looked at himself in a reflective piece of metal covering the rear of the space shuttle. It's usually difficult to tell when your body has changed drastically when you see it every day, which Mitch had done over the past two hundred and thirty-eight days, but the emaciation was obvious. It wasn't just the protruding cheekbones and increase in wrinkles on his face. It was also the continual looseness of the two jumpsuits he changed in and out of on a daily basis.

On the other side of that mirrored wall was a giant rocket holding almost a hundred million liters of liquid hydrogen, ready to send him hurtling toward the designated asteroid with maximum impact. On the opposite side of the ship were what could only be described as four giant claws with sharpened, two-hundred-meter 'fingernails' made of medium carbon steel. The theory was that they would withstand the bang-crash-smash of being shoved into the dense rock at ludicrous speed so they could latch on like a giant brooch. The force of the rocket would nudge the asteroid out of its orbit and hopefully send it moseying toward Earth along with its enormous supply of rhodium. The experts said the rhodium was the key to a vaccine and, well, the planet was fresh out.

But before engaging in the suicidal maneuver, Mitch had to line the ship up at the proper angle. If he was off by half-a-degree, those still alive on

Earth could roast marshmallows over an open fire and watch him fly over the planet on his way to Alpha Centauri.

Not that he had to worry about the math. That was Carolyn's job. He was really there just to be the Spaceketeers' hands and eyes—to make sure he did what he was told and to right anything that went wrong with the ship. If half of the world's population hadn't been decimated, Mitch would have been far, far back in a line of individuals best suited for this task. But pickings were slim and he found himself at the top of the list. Turns out that most qualified people, even given the circumstances, were not up for a suicide mission.

He unzipped his breast pocket, pulled out a foil-wrapped, freeze-dried ice cream, and ripped it open. He took a sniff. The artificial strawberry overpowered the vanilla and chocolate. He thought that if they were going to send a man to his death, the could have at least found a way to produce a mint-chip variety. Neapolitan was getting old. He took one bite of the chalky substance, grimaced, and put it back in his pocket.

"Okay, got it. You ready?" Carolyn asked.

"Oh, God, hold on," Mitch replied, dipping his head toward the straw poking up from his left shoulder, washing the taste away with his water-pack. Puking inside this tin can was not an option if he didn't want to short-circuit something vital.

"Okay," he said, tonguing a remaining chunk stuck between his molars. He fired up the miniature suit jets hanging off his long sleeves, sending him slowly toward the console.

When he arrived, Carolyn read off a series of numbers which Mitch punched in on the tiny keypad in front of him.

"And that's that," he said as the ship slowly reoriented itself. He turned toward a second monitor which was connected to a camera outside. There he saw the lone hunk floating what seemed a considerable distance away. "So that's her, huh? The people's ugly, pockmarked savior?"

"I hope so," Carolyn said. "Otherwise, this was a colossal waste of all sorts of everything, I'd say."

Mitch chuckled.

"Well, since you have nothing better to do now," she continued, "you may as well get ready for the press conference. Are you ready for your closeup, Mr. DeMille?"

"What?"

"Sunset Boulevard?"

Mitch's eyebrows narrowed.

"Nevermind."

* * *

"You're the person on everyone's mind, Mr. Lacombe! The man of our century! Our modern hope!"

The melodrama was going to kill him before the impact. Where did the newspapers find these people and why did they continue to hire them?

After making another rotation to face the camera beaming his image back down to earth, he answered, "Well, gee, I'm just glad to help," copping the voice of the reporter who seemed not to catch on.

The camera zoomed out to reveal twenty more reporters along with a woman with her hair tied up in a bun, giving her the appearance of standing tall above them all. She wore an unflattering jumpsuit and looked like she hadn't slept in days. "Your bravery will go down in the annals of history,

Mitchell Lacombe."

Six seconds of silence while he rotated again.

"Like I said, Madam President, just glad to help."

The reporters began bombarding him with questions on what he was going to miss most about Earth, did he have a love interest for which he had any final words, and so on. After about the fifth question, he was done. He fired up his jets and approached the communications console.

"Let me tell you, there is...and when I...but it's almost impossible to..."

He tried hard not to smile as his finger flipped the switch back and forth, cutting the signal in and out.

"I'm afraid we're losing you, Mr. Lacombe!"

"...given the amount of fluids...Oh my God!...some sort of space creature—" And at that, he switched off the video feed and headed for the can.

* * *

"Clever job with the video. Good thing those dolts don't know any-thing about anything or they would have seen through your little ruse."

"Good thing, indeed," Mitch said. "I mean, I know why I'm here, but can't a man be allowed to think about something else before turning himself into a burnt pancake?"

Carolyn didn't laugh, but she seemed to allow herself a brief smile. Mitch was in the shadow of the asteroid now. It looked like an oblong, minia-ture planet. Still, he was several thousand miles away from where things would kick off.

"You're rather nonchalant about this whole endeavor," she said.

"I've been in space for almost a year. I don't have the energy for chalance."

"You're prepared for this?"

"Sure," he said.

"There's always the possibility that you still might make it home in one piece. Then you can buy me a pint and a plate full of Brancaster mussels."

Mitch's survival wasn't even a consideration. Given the seemingly infinitesimal odds of surviving the initial collision, he wasn't sure he wanted to make it because he was told the likelihood of disintegrating in Earth's atmosphere was even greater.

"One of those sounds disgusting. I'll let you guess which."

Carolyn allowed herself a wider smile this time.

"You know, Carolyn, this screen doesn't do you justice."

Mitch couldn't tell if she was blushing or the R on the RGB was inadvertently dialed up.

"Thank you, Mitch. You, on the other hand, look like shite."

"Thanks."

She looked at something above her console.

"Look, you have a couple of hours to catch a nap or do whatever it is you do to pass the time up there. I give you permission to turn the camera off." She winked.

"You underestimate the impact of weightlessness on certain functions," Mitch said, "but thanks."

She paused.

"I'll wake you when it's time."

"Roger that. Don't work too hard. Good night, Carolyn."

She stared into her camera for an extended moment and it felt like they were sitting across from each other.

"Good night, Mitch."

* * *

He strapped himself into his bunk and closed his eyes, imagining how it would feel to become one with the rhodium. With adrenaline pumping through his blood vessels, sleep was never an option. Fight-or-flight never seemed more ridiculous than it did here. There was nothing to smash with his fists except things critical to the mission. He supposed he was already technically flying, so that would have to be the de facto response.

All Mitch could do was try to shut out the claustrophobic world around him. Being in a place with 'space' in the name didn't mean a whole lot if you couldn't actually get out there and stretch.

His thoughts, of course, turned to Carolyn. He'd never met her in person, but they'd been in daily contact for the past year. When they weren't trading diagnostic information and running through checklists, she often talked about her two loves—a pet Tegu lizard named Raindrop who would sometimes scurry across the screen and sweet American breakfasts.

It's practically dessert, she would say, positing that the whole notion was originally proposed by dentists to maintain full employment.

Mitch thought about how rotten fate was. He would never have met Carolyn had the world not undergone such horrors. Then he had to contend with millions of miles of nothingness between them, only to become space dust before he would ever have the opportunity to timidly ask if he could hold her hand on an evening stroll.

It seemed like only minutes had passed before he heard her voice over the speakers again.

"Wakey, wakey."

* * *

"I guess this is goodbye," Mitch said.

The asteroid was all that was visible now. Its dreary gray, rocky surface was sliced in half by the sun, leaving one end in total darkness. The targeting monitor had a pair of red crosshairs lined up with another pair of green ones.

"Don't say that," Carolyn said. "There's still a chance."

Mitch shrugged. He had never seen her nervous before, but she was tapping her fingernails on her desktop.

"You got this," he said.

"I know that," she snapped. She fell back in her chair and took a deep breath before looking into the camera. "I'm sorry," she said. "It's just…"

She straightened up. Her awkwardness made Mitch feel awkward now.

"If you're not here to buy me dinner in a couple of months, I'm going to be really cheesed off." That's all." She released a half-laugh, half-cry and turned slightly from the monitor, wiping just under her eyes with her fingertips.

He wished he could put his arms around her, even if she would just throw them off and make a joke. He flipped open the plastic cover snapped over the giant red ignition button.

"Well, here goes nothing," he said. His hand shook and before he lost his nerve, he thrust his palm forward. The thirty-second timer began to count down.

Mitch jetted himself back toward his bunk, leaving the camera on. He put on a pair of goggles and strapped himself in. It seemed futile, but somewhere within him remained a tiny ounce of hope convincing him to also hook up the IV feeding tube and catheter.

He locked eyes with the camera and though he wasn't certain, felt that Carolyn was doing the same.

The countdown hit zero.

An ear-shattering roar kicked off outside of the shuttle. Every single inch of the interior hull rattled.

G-forces held Mitch against his bed like God's invisible hand.

He started to scream but his vision blurred until all he saw was black.

* * *

If it weren't for the angel crouched above him, a snarky smile stretched across her face, Mitch would have thought he was in Hell. After all, he was still inside the spaceship.

There was a lot of commotion around him. He smelled a mix of burnt metal and ice cream powder, felt hands groping around his body, and heard people barking commands to each other.

The angel's hand was on his furry cheek. There was a shine in her bright blue eyes.

"Hope you're well rested from your long nap," Carolyn said. "We have reservations for 6:30 and you're absolutely filthy."

Process Summary

Our Modern Hope is story number fifty-one in the #52ShortStories challenge.

Where in the world did this come from? Seriously, if you find out, let me know.

I did pull the title from a phrase that caught my eye. It came from Yeats's *Ego Dominus Tuus* (which is an **amazing** poem). So I will say it's often surprising what comes from one's imagination based on a phrase alone. As I've written these stories over the past year, it's really solidified the truth in the typical writer's snarky response to "Where do you get your ideas?"

Where *don't* we get them?!

Though the setting was science-fiction, I really wanted to add some comedy and romance. One reader seemed to confirm it worked, so I'm happy about that!

I can't believe it, folks. One story left in my grand adventure. If I can sum it up in a single phrase, it would be: This is only the beginning.

THE WITCH OF THE NARROWS

Statistics

Synopsis: A Hollywood has-been seeks career resuscitation from The Witch of the Narrows.

Word Count: 2,900

Genre: Urban Fantasy

Completed Week: July 21st – July 29th

The Witch of the Narrows

You wouldn't believe me if I told you it was all hearsay and legend. But I know you, Pat, and you're gonna be stuck in one of your funks, unable to let it go, completely useless to me as a client and a friend.

So, I may as well tell you what I know.

Head east out of this town of swindlers and backstabbers and once you hit the I-15 in Victorville, exit Bear Valley until you come to Ridgecrest Road. Make a left and cruise a few miles past the nice homes on the man-made lake until you're stopped by the ranger shack. Pay the entrance fee and park your car.

Here, I drew you a map for the rest. You're on foot for the next mile-and-a-half through the trees and rattlesnakes.

Don't shout, don't whistle, don't do any stupid shit like that. You'll probably get eaten by a mountain lion.

They say that if she wants to see you, she'll let you find her.

* * *

Pat Falcon performed a few jumping jacks and stretched his legs beneath the August stars, shaking out the seventy-mile trip from Hollywood. There were three campers in the lot around him, all Winnebago knockoffs, all plugged into rattling generators so they could run the air conditioning and ameliorate the hot desert air.

He ran his hand along the front of his truck. A crack in the headlight's plastic cover was the worst of it. He'd left in the black of night which had grown progressively blacker as the city lights popped out of existence behind him, bulb by bulb. When he arrived here, the entrance had been closed and no one was in the guard shack, so he accelerated his Mercedes SUV through the flimsy gate arm which snapped clean off.

California's High Desert was familiar. Besides driving through here on the occasional spendcrazy visit to Las Vegas, Pat had been up this way several times over his career. Most memorable was filming *Tough Break* almost twenty years ago out on a dry lake in the early nineties. He'd performed his own stunts in that one, playing the slick-haired antagonist to Sylvester Stallone. Sly hadn't returned his calls for several years.

The last two trips had been for direct-to-DVD movies filled with pathetic CGI-aliens and scripts that could only have been written by the producer's teenage son. But there was alimony, several house and car payments to make, and the increasing number of collection letters.

The Witch of the Narrows seemed to be Pat's only hope.

* * *

He had memorized his agent's map and headed west of the park's Horseshoe Lake. The lake itself was a tiny thing, thinly veiled by cat o' nine tails while sun-faded pedal boats slept at a dock in front of the bait shop. Once he hit the railroad tracks running alongside, Pat moved north, sweeping his flashlight's beam across the loose gravel in front of his feet. Even though the stars shined like mad up here, the moon was incognito tonight.

Sweat gathered at his brow and beneath his arms. Pat didn't consider himself out of shape, but he had to admit he carried a few extra pounds since both his metabolism and available work had slowed down in equal measure over the past few years. What was the point in sacrificing the occasional bowl of creamy pasta and bottomless Old Fashioneds just to maintain a six-pack that nobody clamored for anymore?

But the Witch would fix it all. He had never bought into the wooey crap floating around a city that overflowed with it, but there was something about her story that convinced him she would call to him—if only he put forward the effort and held the faith. She was an old Hollywood legend. Had apparently been a star since before Pat was born but disappeared without a trace. Nobody remembered her stage or real name, but she had several epithets.

The Old Woman in the Desert.

Gray Gypsy.

The Witch of the Narrows.

All of these floated around the land of cinema like puffs of smoke. Nobody ever claimed to have actually benefited from a visit. It was all 'I heard so-and-so made the trip' and 'you didn't hear this from me, but...'

Not everyone spoke glowingly, either. It was usually the fellow washouts at Pat's favorite bar. One of them even claimed to have visited the Narrows herself and all she had to show for it were scratched-up ankles and forearms covered in mosquito bites.

After a mile of walking, Pat knew he was close. The willows and cottonwoods grew thicker as he neared the two granite hills enclosing the dry Mojave river like columns of a giant gateway. A modern bridge spanned the north side of the outcroppings where occasional headlights appeared and disappeared as they crossed into the sleeping town of Apple Valley.

A knee-high rock on the side of the tracks called out to Pat's sore legs, so he turned off his flashlight and took a seat. Lightly sweet scents of the cottonwoods entered his nostrils, making the back of his throat itch a little. He tried to fight off a couple of sneezes, picturing those mountain lions his agent mentioned canvassing the riverbed like assassins, waiting for a vulnerable moment.

How long should he wait? Was he in the right spot? What if all it took was to be off by a few feet and that was the whole problem with those who'd never found her?

He tried not to overthink it, but he couldn't help wonder what he would do if this whole adventure turned out for naught. Bankruptcy was on the horizon. It didn't seem fair. It wasn't as if he had blown everything on a ridiculously expensive drug habit like some he knew. Sure, he liked his nice cars, fancy dinners, and sleeping in comfort. He'd earned all that.

As the minutes ran on and Pat's thoughts darkened, the tracks at his back beckoned his attention. That ought to be a painless way to go. He could just lean back a little. Rest his weary head. He wouldn't know what hit him.

His depressive reverie was shaken by something rustling nearby.

Pat realized just how much his impulsiveness had put him in jeopardy. He didn't have anything to defend himself with and he was pretty damn certain he couldn't outrun whatever decided to chase him.

He flicked the flashlight back on and shined it towards the source of the commotion. A shaggy old dog that looked like it hadn't seen a bath in years emerged from the bushes. Its fur was matted and though Pat didn't know the first thing about breeds, to him, it looked like the offspring of a bloodhound and a grizzly. It stood well over waist-high and its head was tilted down like an old librarian appraising him over her reading glasses.

Warmth and goosebumps ran over Pat's body. The dog appeared harmless, panting lazily. There didn't seem to be any foam at the mouth.

They stared at each other for ten uncomfortable seconds before Pat realized that maybe he ought to stand up and do something. As he did so, the dog turned and swung its tail, heading back into the bush.

Pat took a deep breath while working up the nerve, then followed.

* * *

It wasn't a particularly tall or dense bush, but somehow following through the gap where the dog had passed revealed an old cabin sitting in the middle of the riverbed.

Pat's flashlight highlighted the home's rotten sideboards and rusty tin roof, all draped over by a pair of surrounding willows. There was a single crooked window, dusty and opaque. A glowing candle sat just inside the sill and a thin wooden door was cracked open slightly, pushed further by the dog creeping inside.

Was this real? Did Pat actually fall asleep by the train tracks? Who the hell builds a house in the middle of a river, even if its dry?

No, this was it. This was her way. She had to be calling him.

He stepped inside. A musty odor hit his nose immediately. The floorboards squeaked, giving a little bit under his dusty shoes. His heart stopped and the flashlight fell from his hands as soon as it revealed what may have once been a complete woman. She sat in a worn, tall-backed chair, looking almost like a doll but for the fact that she was missing half of her thin gray hair. In its place was scarred over flesh that had the appearance of unmolded clay. The giant dog was curled up near her feet.

"Don't look if it bothers you, but take a seat."

Her voice was like poor radio reception. Staticky and warbling with a slight Southern twang. Though she was quiet, her words carried easily across the single room of the cabin. It sent a whole new set of shivers down Pat's spine.

His flashlight still lay on the floor and he realized that its bulb was shattered, leaving only the tiny candle in the window for illumination. Seeing the old woman's droopy eyes peering up at him along with her dog's was enough to empty his bladder. The next thoughts were of the door. Pat turned and panicked.

What door?

Maybe the candle was casting odd shadows. He rushed back to where he thought he'd come in and scrabbled his fingers along the splintery lumber, trying to feel for a handle.

"Take a seat," she repeated. "You came to beat your gums, so let's get to it."

Pat wiped away the sweat dripping into his eyes with his forearm. He spent a moment facing the doorless wall, gathering his will, reminding himself that he was here for a reason. If she was a genuine witch, he had to expect strange things, but he scolded himself once more for not having the forethought to at least bring a pocket knife.

Slowly, he turned around, irrationally self-conscious of the stain across the front of his pants. Both the woman and her dog still watched him. He noticed an empty, duplicate chair resting catty-corner to her's. Pat felt like he was wearing cement shoes, but he managed to shuffle over to the chair and fall into it. A tiny cloud of dust lifted as he collapsed, leaving him feeling bound by the tall back and high armrests.

"There was a time when men couldn't stop eyeballin' me," she said.

"Used to have the admiration of them all and I wasn't but sixteen."

Her tone was anything but wistful.

Pat still avoided looking into her face, focusing instead on her hands which were curled together in her lap like broken twigs. He didn't know what to say. Adrenaline was rushing through his bloodstream and the lump in his throat wasn't going anywhere.

"Who are you?" was all he could muster.

"You know who I am. Probably you meant to ask who I was."

Pat said nothing.

The witch wheezed a little, appearing to take as deep of a breath as she could. Her chest was sunken in below her neck like she was missing her sternum.

"It don't matter, really, but I'll tell you anyway." She moved a gnarled hand down to scratch behind her dog's ears. He craned his head up to meet it.

"Time moves quickly," she continued, "and even more so in Hollywood. Today becomes yesterday and before you know it, you may as well have not existed. Turns out the friends weren't friends and the money and fame were as real as last night's dream."

A wind stirred outside that hadn't been there before, setting the window pane to rattle.

"I was once a cute little girl with curly blond hair and dimples, you know."

Curiosity got the best of Pat. He strained to hold his gaze as she smiled widely for him. One of the dimples was still there in the jowl that wasn't scarred over, though it was easily overshadowed by a mouth whose only teeth left poking through were jagged and brown.

"Yeah, I did alright for myself. I sang and danced like that Shirley Temple, but I had ten times the talent.

"Anyhow, I got older and the parts got better. The studio had big plans for me," she said. "An epic movie that was supposed to give me top billing. We began filming on a soundstage at MGM. I was playing a genie that was gonna pop out of a giant, jewel-crusted lamp. There were pyrotechnics. Something went wrong."

She held her hand to the scar across her face and laughed a wicked laugh.

"Instead of lighting up the outside, you can imagine where the fire went. If that wasn't enough, the lid wouldn't open. Broke most of my bloody fingers before they managed to get me out of there."

Pat noticed his fear of the witch dissipated, leaving only empathy.

"I'm so sorry," he said. "I can't imagine—"

"You can't imagine nothin'!"

A little of the fear came back. She took a drawn-out pause before continuing.

"It all became hush-hush. My parents were given a bucket of cash so they wouldn't sue and word was put out that I'd decided to quit show business and pursue education. I wasn't allowed to go around and show my face, else my folks would put me out on my own with no way to support myself."

Her story had pulled him in, but it seemed a long way between then and now. "How did you come to be here?" he asked.

She smiled her ugly smile again and raised what had probably once been eyebrows.

"You know, this place was a coffee stain on a map back then. A couple of dude ranches and a perfect place to put somethin' you didn't want found. I was a girl with a lot of time and a lot of anger, so I read, and read, and read some things that I probably wasn't s'posed to.

"I was up to no good at first, but at a certain point, I decided I didn't have to be that way. The more problems I caused, the more the heat inside me sorta dwindled and I decided I could help folks instead of hurtin' 'em. My parents were still connected to some in the industry and I began to help those who visited and complained about how hard things had gotten for them. At least I thought I was helpin' 'em."

Their eyes locked for an uncomfortable amount of time.

"Which brings me to why you're here," she finished

Pat nodded.

"You're sure you want my help?"

"I've never been more sure of anything, lady."

"You willing to pay the price?"

"You want my soul?" Pat laughed to himself, figuring she would ask for something ridiculous like that. It didn't much matter if he didn't believe he had one.

The look in her eyes made him shrink back into his chair.

"You been watchin' too many of your own movies. No, keep your soul. You're gonna need it."

Pat wasn't sure what she meant by that.

The witch took a deep breath and with a struggle, pushed herself to her feet. Dust fell from every inch of her clothing. Her bones cracked and squealed equally with the floorboards. She had obviously been short to begin with, but with her bent back, she couldn't have been an inch over four feet tall.

"Fact is, I'm gettin' a little tired of this gig. I've been doin' what I thought was a service for folks like you for so long, I think it's about time for a change."

She looked down at her dog.

"This here is Al. Used to be my father. He'll treat you real good."

The stale air of the cabin left Patrick's lungs and he had a hard time getting it back in.

"Wait, what?"

The witch walked towards the cabin wall where he had come in. The door which had disappeared was back in its place.

Pat tried to spring to his own two feet, but it was as if an army of invisible hands were holding him down.

"Hold on a minute, you damn witch! You're supposed to help me!"

She turned back toward him. Those droopy eyes that had frightened him only minutes ago were now pitying him like a beaten animal.

"I *am* helping you, Pat. If I let you back out there, you're just gonna do the same things again and you're gonna die a miserable man, probably at your own hands. At least this way, you'll have time to think about doing some-thin' good for a change."

Pat fought to get up with every ounce of his being. His head bobbed but his body remained in place, frozen in the chair. Whereas the high back and armrests had only seemed vaguely suffocating before, he swore his arms sank down and became a part of the material itself.

"Don't worry, Father will show you the ropes."

The door swung open on its own volition and the woman hobbled hunchbacked into the still, hot night. Pat's heart ached at the final glimpse of cottonwoods and bright stars shining through their branches before the witch departed and the wall sealed itself shut behind her.

Al got up on his paws and ambled over, collapsing beside Pat. He raised his head, expecting a few good scratches from the Witch of the Narrows.

Process Summary

The Witch of the Narrows is story number fifty-two in the #52Short-Stories challenge.

One year…

One whole year of writing, writing, and most importantly, **finishing**.

As I hit *Publish* on story number fifty-two, I was ready for all sorts of emotions: Joy. Tears. Dread from having no idea what to do next.

But you know what? The only thought I had was, "I think I'll sleep in next week."

Pretty anticlimactic, I know. And now I'm even second guessing that statement because I'm pretty excited to keep writing. I guess that was the whole point, right?

But I'll save the dramatics of the larger experiment for another post.

Where did this particular story begin? As usual, I'm not sure where the idea hit me, but it seems my hometown has been calling out to me lately. The Mojave Narrows is a regional park near where I grew up. We used to go there after church sometimes or for school field trips, fishing for trout or riding the pedalboats around the tiny Horseshoe Lake. It's funny how small your world is when you yourself are small and your worldview is pretty insular. I never realized that this park was so close to where the actual witch lives in my story, another iconic location.

I had to give the witch a worthwhile reason for being there and for some reason, Old Hollywood popped into my mind. This High Desert area was known for 'celebrity getaways' back in the day. It was even a place where the "only Negro Dude Ranch in the world" existed. Fascinating, the amount of history buried within our own little corners of this planet.

I hope you enjoyed this final story of my year-long experiment which has been like a story in its own right—filled with highs and lows, tension and release. I'm just glad it had a happy ending!

About the Author

From 2017 to 2018, Phillip McCollum spent 52 weeks writing 52 short stories in an effort to prove to himself that he might be cut out for this writing thing after all. He hails from Southern California where he shares living quarters with his wife, son, an old cat, and young betta fish.

If you'd like to hear about his latest work, please sign up for the newsletter on his website (phillipmccollum.com). He also pokes his head up on Twitter once in a while.